DoodLeViLLe
ART ATTACKS!

CHAD SELL

ALFRED A. KNOPF • NEW YORK

THIS IS A BORZOI BOOK PUBLISHED BY ALFRED A. KNOPF

This is a work of fiction. Names, characters, places, and incidents either are
the product of the author's imagination or are used fictitiously. Any resemblance
to actual persons, living or dead, events, or locales is entirely coincidental. Except
for the Art Institute of Chicago and Stan's Donuts. Those are real places.
They just don't (usually) have doodles causing mischief in them.

Copyright © 2022 by Chad Sell

All rights reserved. Published in the United States by Alfred A. Knopf, an imprint of
Random House Children's Books, a division of Penguin Random House LLC, New York.

Knopf, Borzoi Books, and the colophon are registered trademarks of Penguin Random House LLC.

Visit us on the Web! rhcbooks.com

Educators and librarians, for a variety of teaching tools, visit us at RHTeachersLibrarians.com

Library of Congress Cataloging-in-Publication Data is available upon request.
ISBN 978-1-9848-9473-1 (trade) — ISBN 978-0-593-56930-6 (lib. bdg.) —
ISBN 978-1-9848-9475-5 (ebook)

The text of this book is set in Creative Block BB.
The illustrations were created using Clip Studio Paint.
Interior design by Chad Sell

MANUFACTURED IN CHINA
10 9 8 7 6 5 4 3 2 1

First Edition

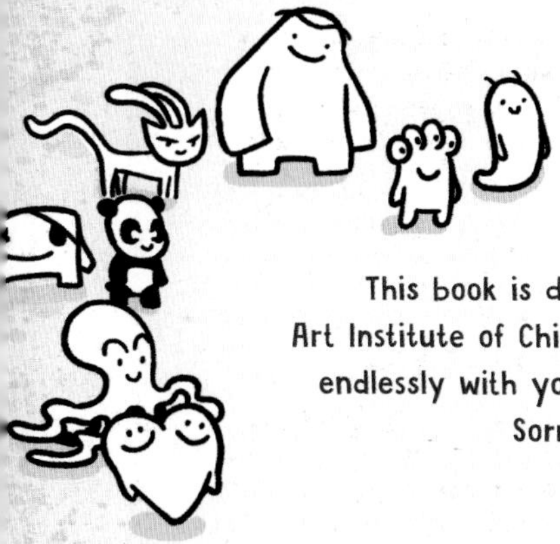

This book is dedicated to everyone at the
Art Institute of Chicago. Thank you for inspiring me
endlessly with your world-class collection of art.
Sorry for wrecking it.
—C.S.

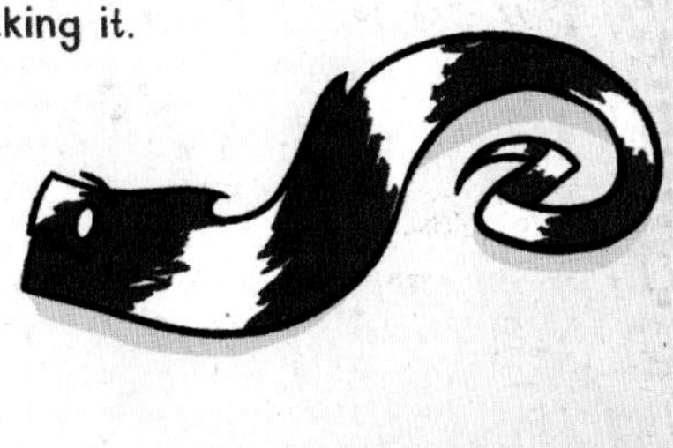

ART CLUB

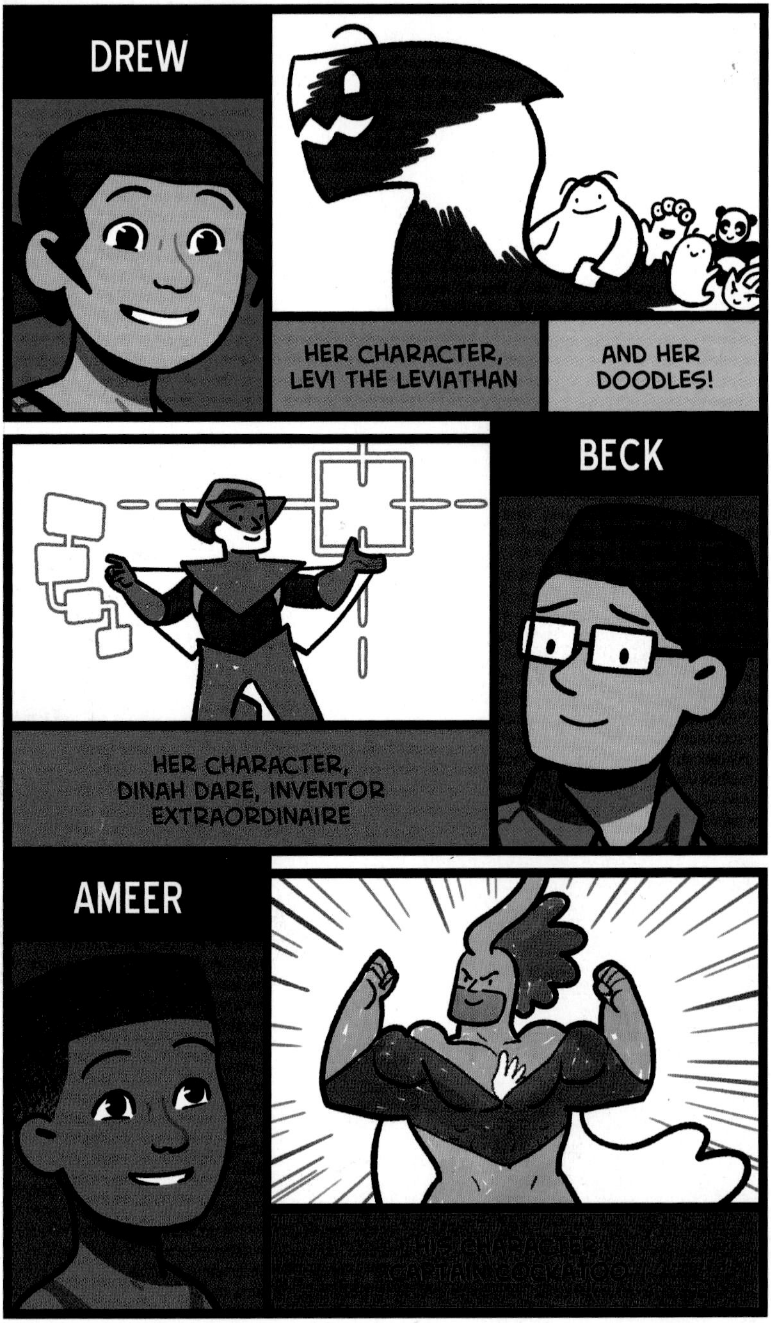
DREW
HER CHARACTER, LEVI THE LEVIATHAN
AND HER DOODLES!
BECK
HER CHARACTER, DINAH DARE, INVENTOR EXTRAORDINAIRE
AMEER
HIS CHARACTER, CAPTAIN COCKATOO

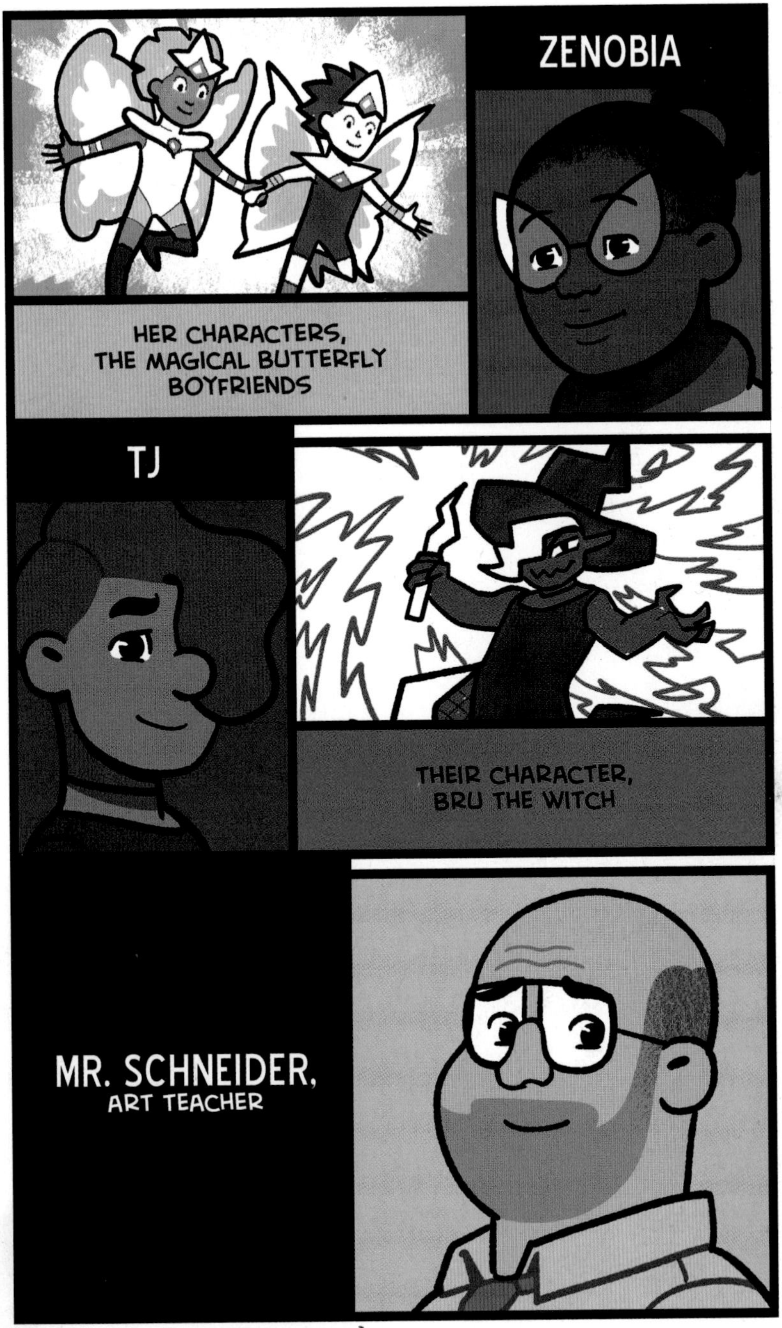
ZENOBIA
HER CHARACTERS,
THE MAGICAL BUTTERFLY
BOYFRIENDS
TJ
THEIR CHARACTER,
BRU THE WITCH
MR. SCHNEIDER,
ART TEACHER

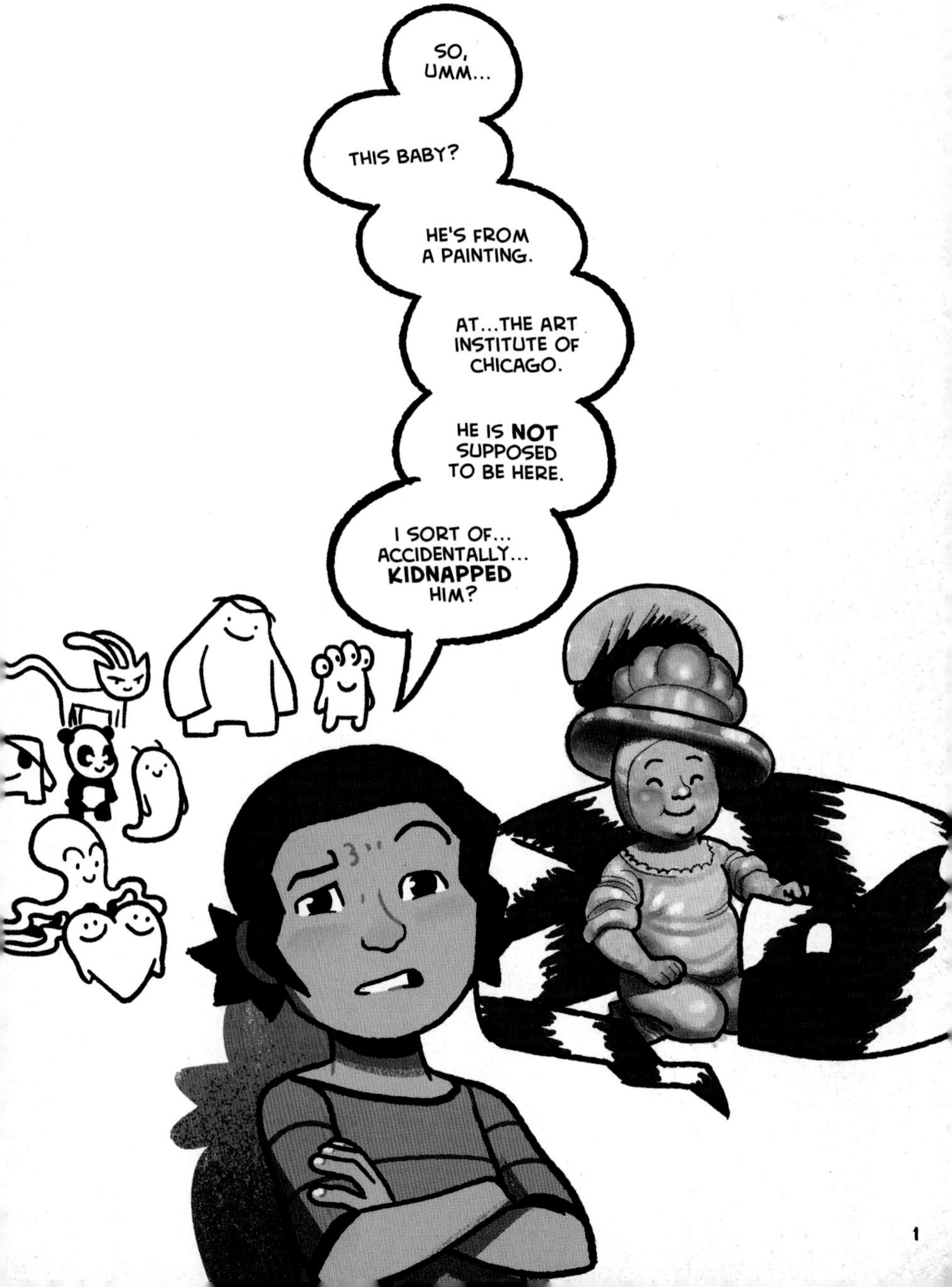
SO, UMM...
THIS BABY?
HE'S FROM A PAINTING.
AT...THE ART INSTITUTE OF CHICAGO.
HE IS **NOT** SUPPOSED TO BE HERE.
I SORT OF... ACCIDENTALLY... **KIDNAPPED** HIM?

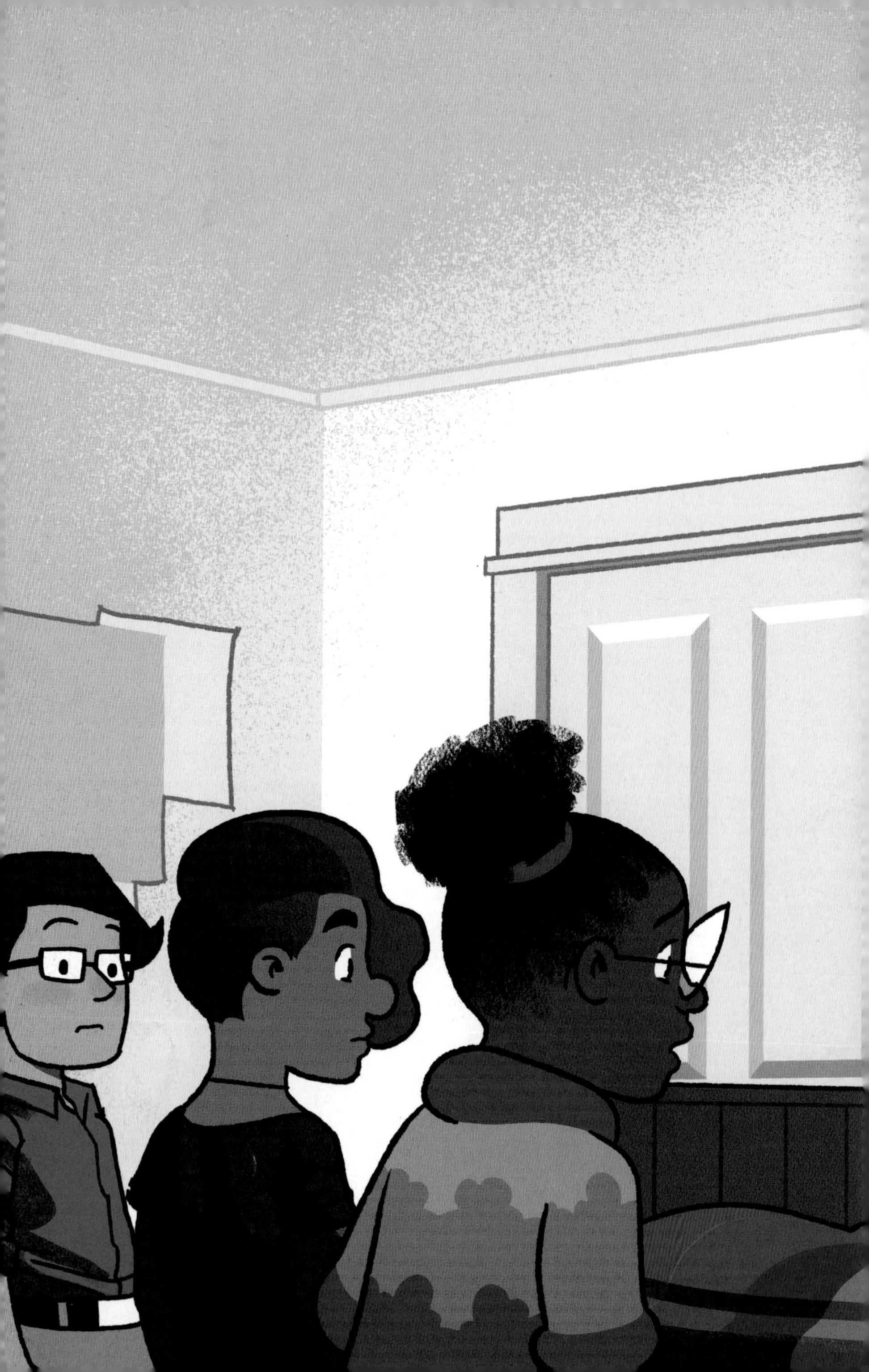

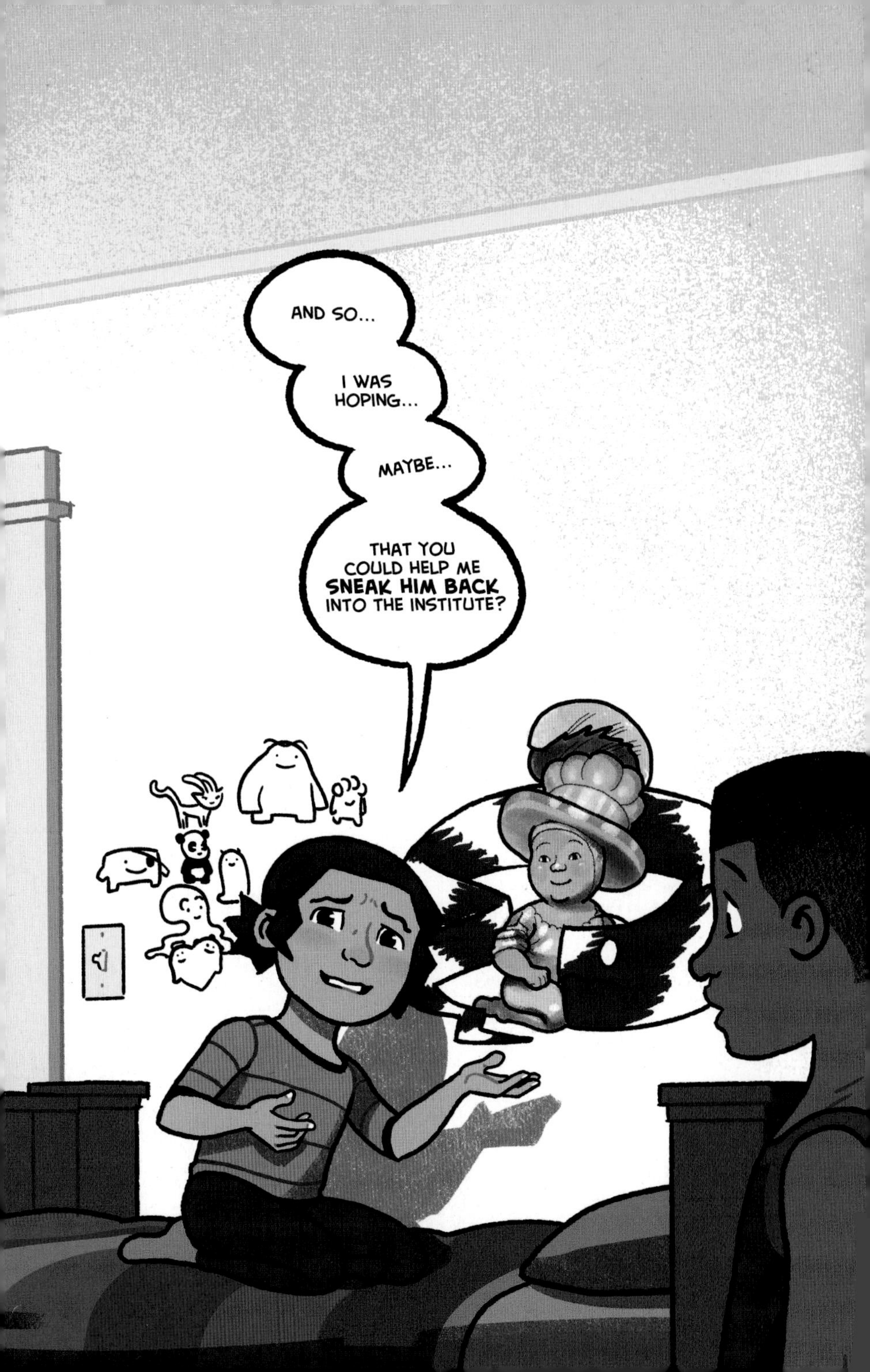
AND SO...
I WAS HOPING...
MAYBE...
THAT YOU COULD HELP ME SNEAK HIM BACK INTO THE INSTITUTE?

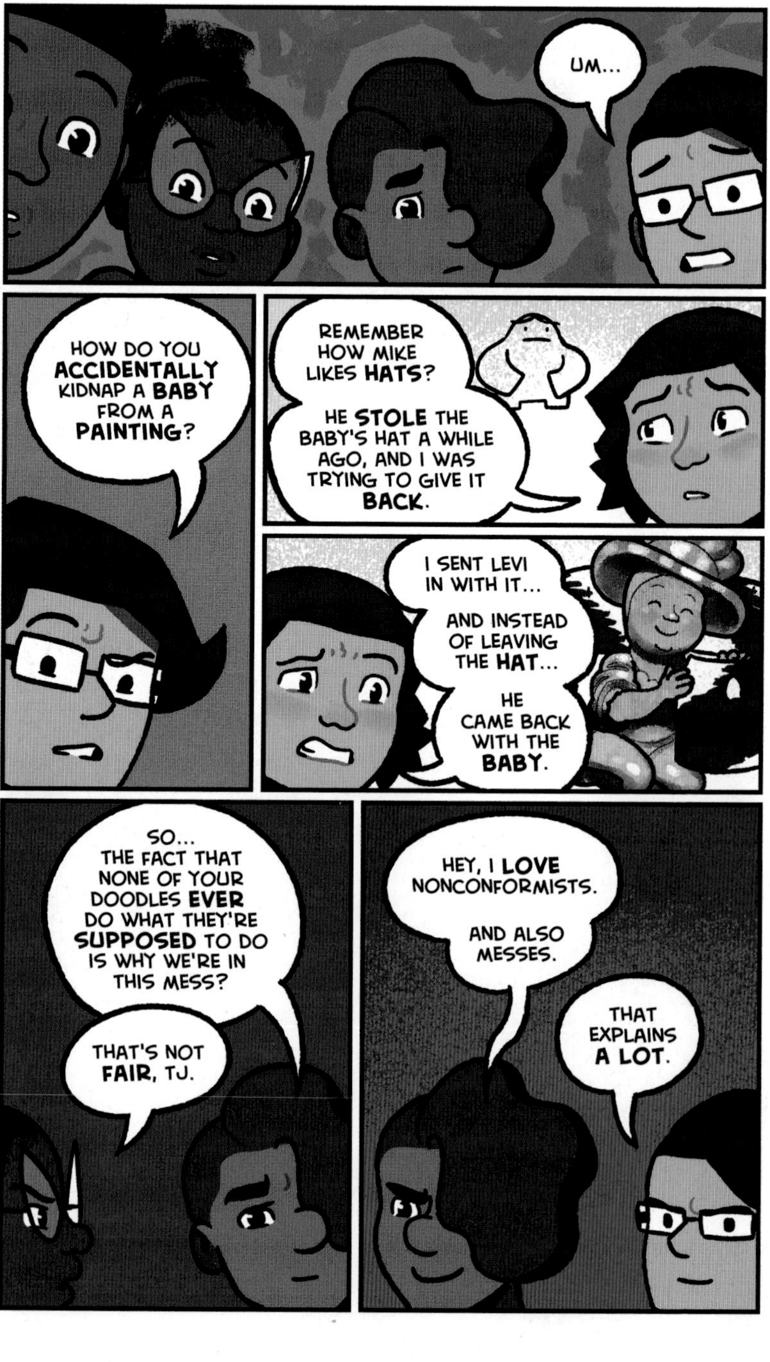
UM...
HOW DO YOU ACCIDENTALLY KIDNAP A BABY FROM A PAINTING?
REMEMBER HOW MIKE LIKES HATS?
HE STOLE THE BABY'S HAT A WHILE AGO, AND I WAS TRYING TO GIVE IT BACK.
I SENT LEVI IN WITH IT...
AND INSTEAD OF LEAVING THE HAT...
HE CAME BACK WITH THE BABY.
SO... THE FACT THAT NONE OF YOUR DOODLES EVER DO WHAT THEY'RE SUPPOSED TO DO IS WHY WE'RE IN THIS MESS?
THAT'S NOT FAIR, TJ.
HEY, I LOVE NONCONFORMISTS.
AND ALSO MESSES.
THAT EXPLAINS A LOT.

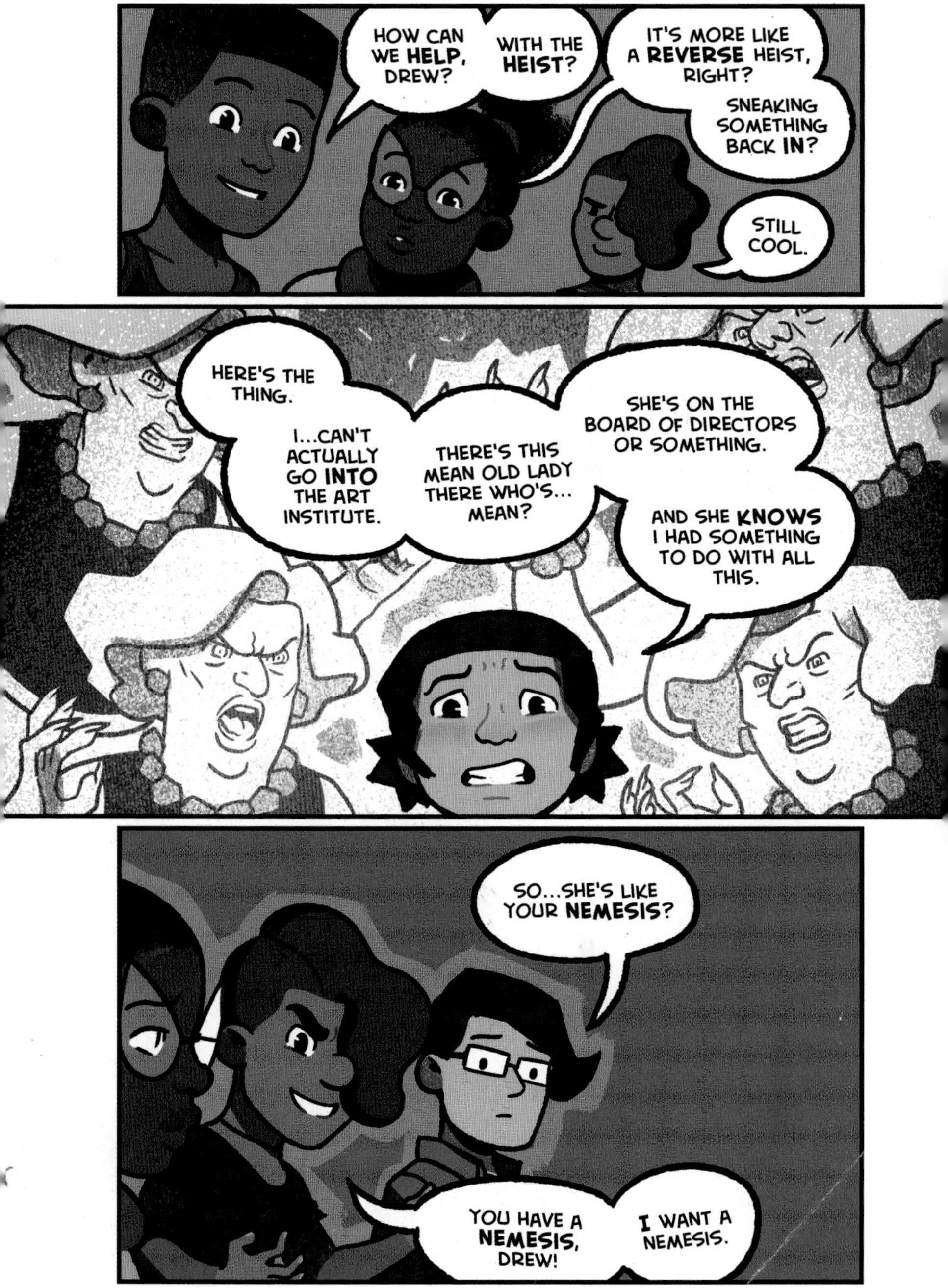
HOW CAN WE HELP, DREW?
WITH THE HEIST?
IT'S MORE LIKE A REVERSE HEIST, RIGHT?
SNEAKING SOMETHING BACK IN?
STILL COOL.
HERE'S THE THING.
I...CAN'T ACTUALLY GO INTO THE ART INSTITUTE.
THERE'S THIS MEAN OLD LADY THERE WHO'S... MEAN?
SHE'S ON THE BOARD OF DIRECTORS OR SOMETHING.
AND SHE KNOWS I HAD SOMETHING TO DO WITH ALL THIS.
SO...SHE'S LIKE YOUR NEMESIS?
YOU HAVE A NEMESIS, DREW!
I WANT A NEMESIS.

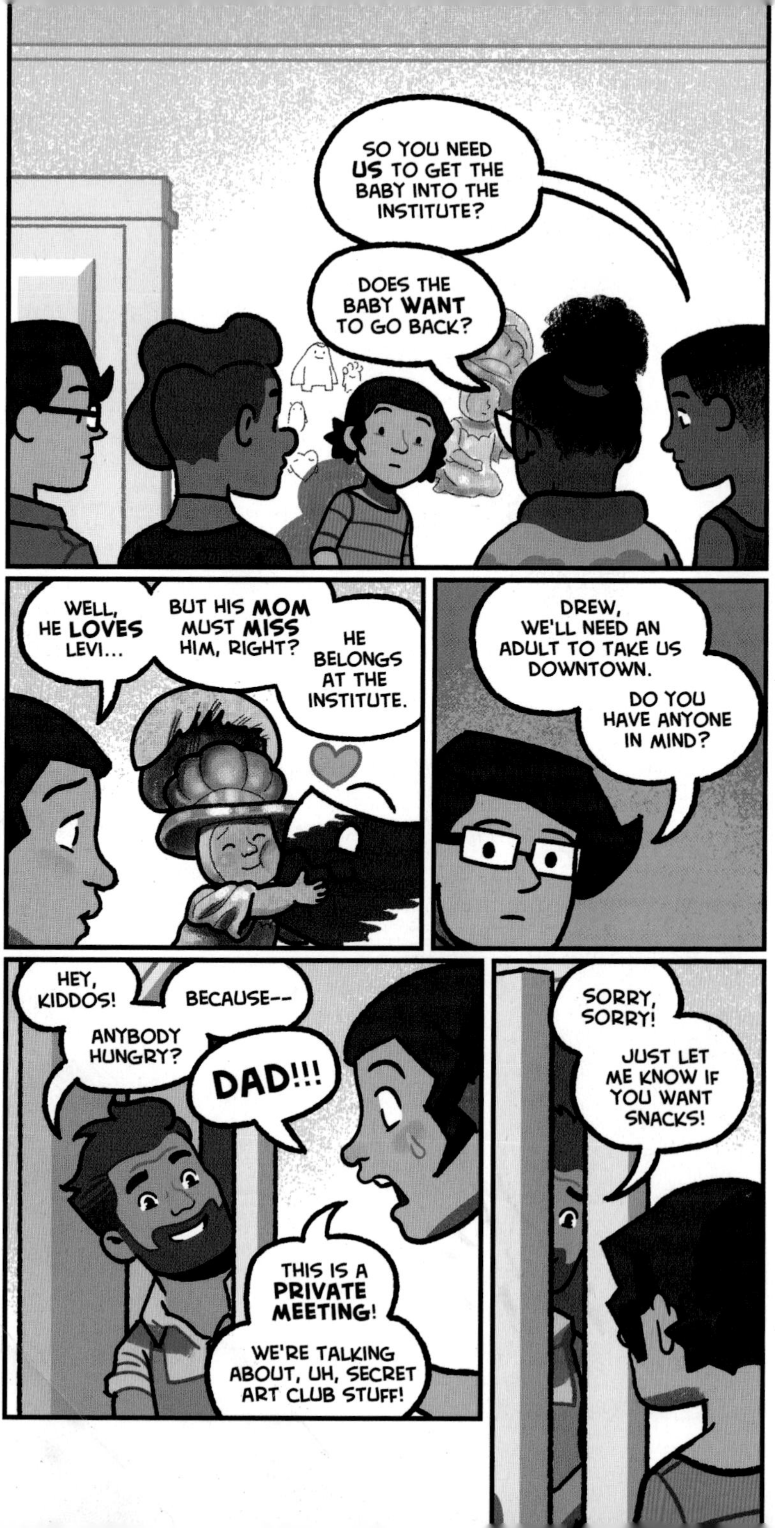

SO YOU NEED US TO GET THE BABY INTO THE INSTITUTE?
DOES THE BABY WANT TO GO BACK?
WELL, HE LOVES LEVI...
BUT HIS MOM MUST MISS HIM, RIGHT?
HE BELONGS AT THE INSTITUTE.
DREW, WE'LL NEED AN ADULT TO TAKE US DOWNTOWN.
DO YOU HAVE ANYONE IN MIND?
HEY, KIDDOS!
BECAUSE--
ANYBODY HUNGRY?
DAD!!!
THIS IS A PRIVATE MEETING!
WE'RE TALKING ABOUT, UH, SECRET ART CLUB STUFF!
SORRY, SORRY!
JUST LET ME KNOW IF YOU WANT SNACKS!

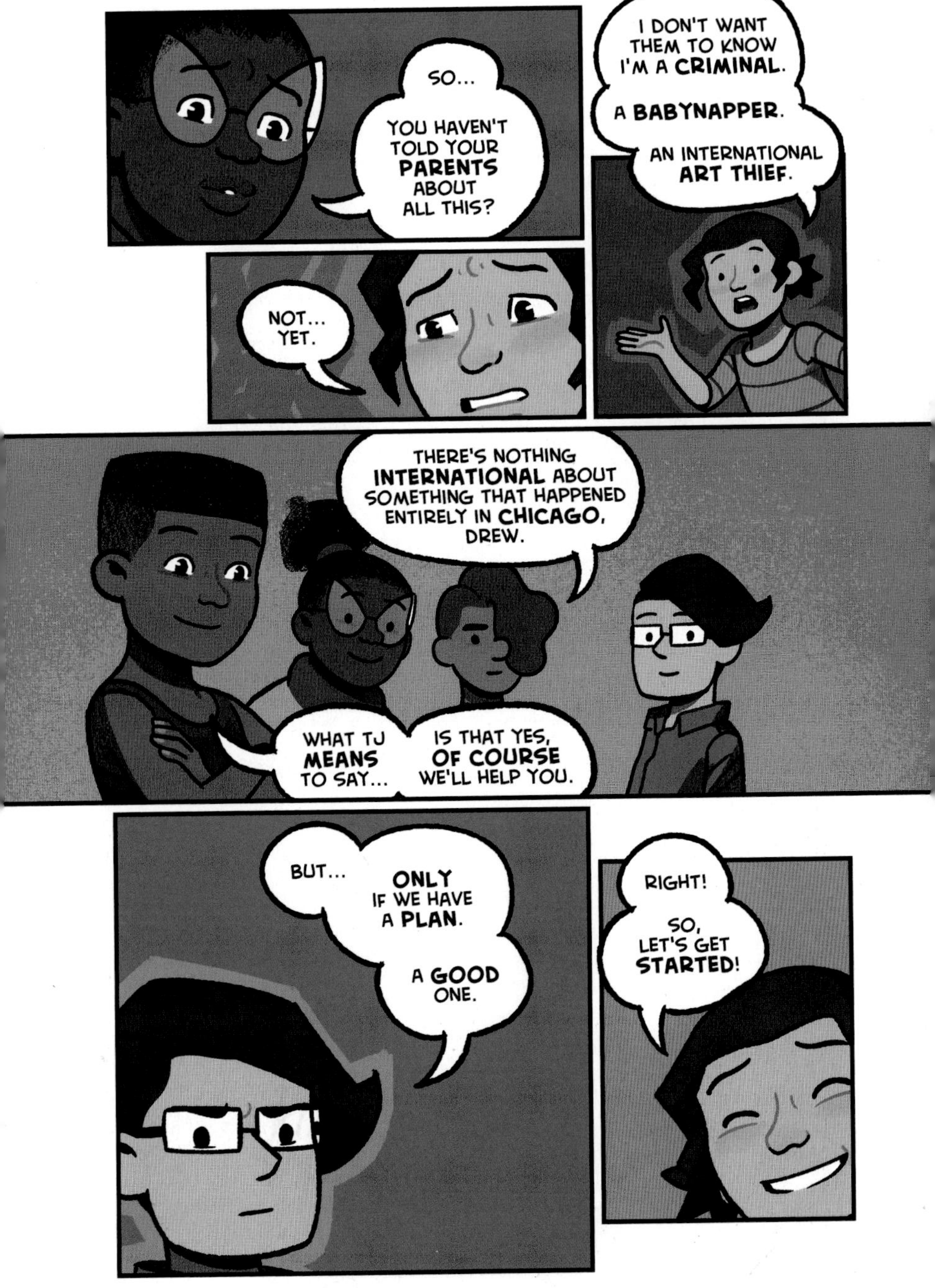
SO... YOU HAVEN'T TOLD YOUR PARENTS ABOUT ALL THIS?
NOT... YET.
I DON'T WANT THEM TO KNOW I'M A CRIMINAL.
A BABYNAPPER.
AN INTERNATIONAL ART THIEF.
THERE'S NOTHING INTERNATIONAL ABOUT SOMETHING THAT HAPPENED ENTIRELY IN CHICAGO, DREW.
WHAT TJ MEANS TO SAY...
IS THAT YES, OF COURSE WE'LL HELP YOU.
BUT... ONLY IF WE HAVE A PLAN.
A GOOD ONE.
RIGHT!
SO, LET'S GET STARTED!

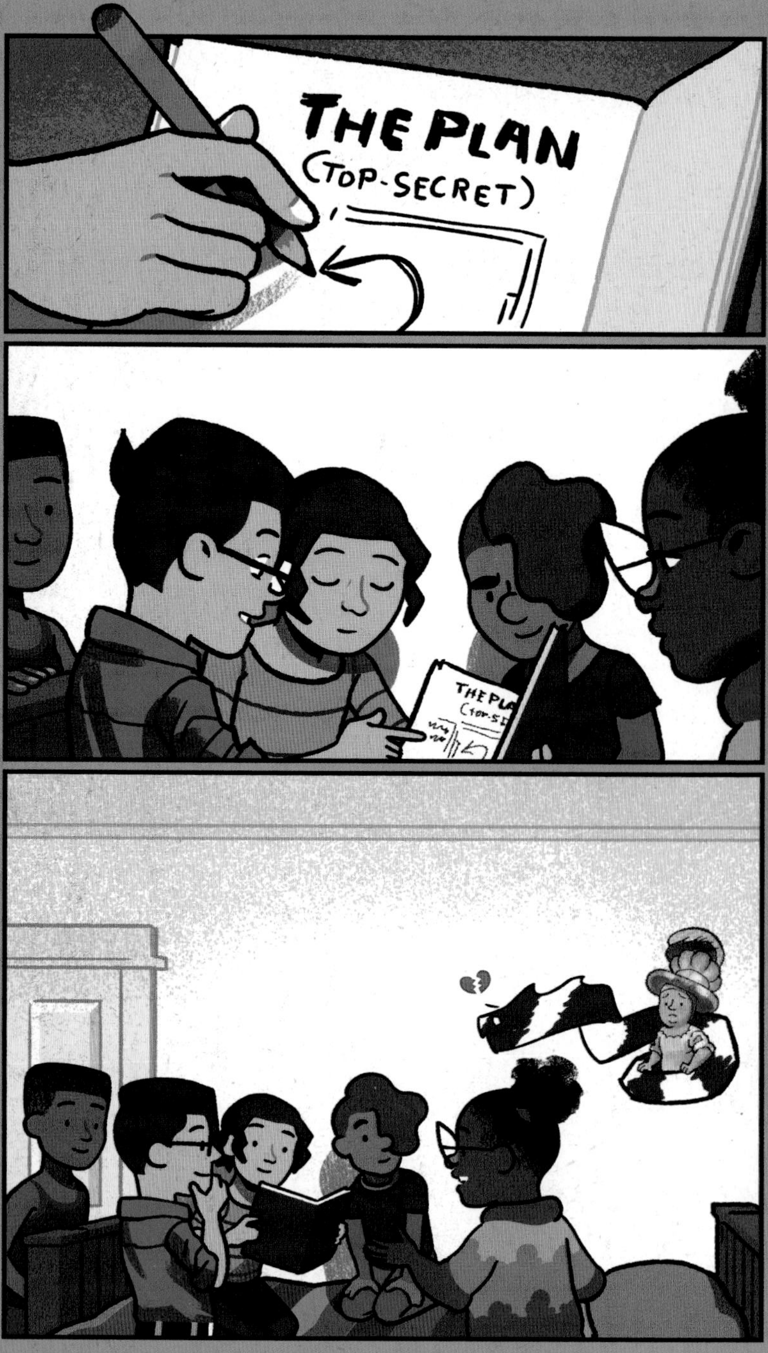
THE PLAN
(TOP-SECRET)

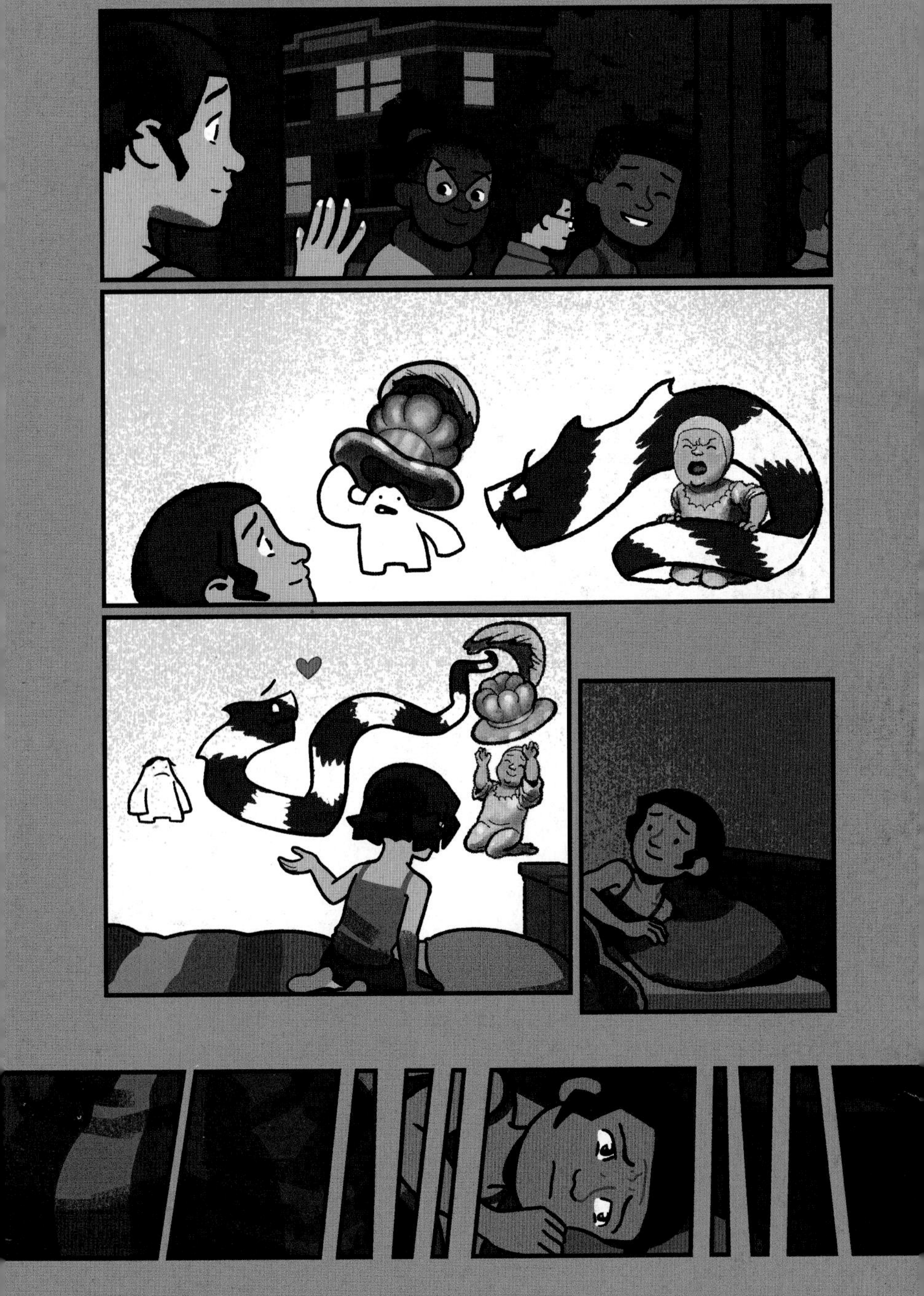

CHAPTER 1: SECRET ART CLUB STUFF

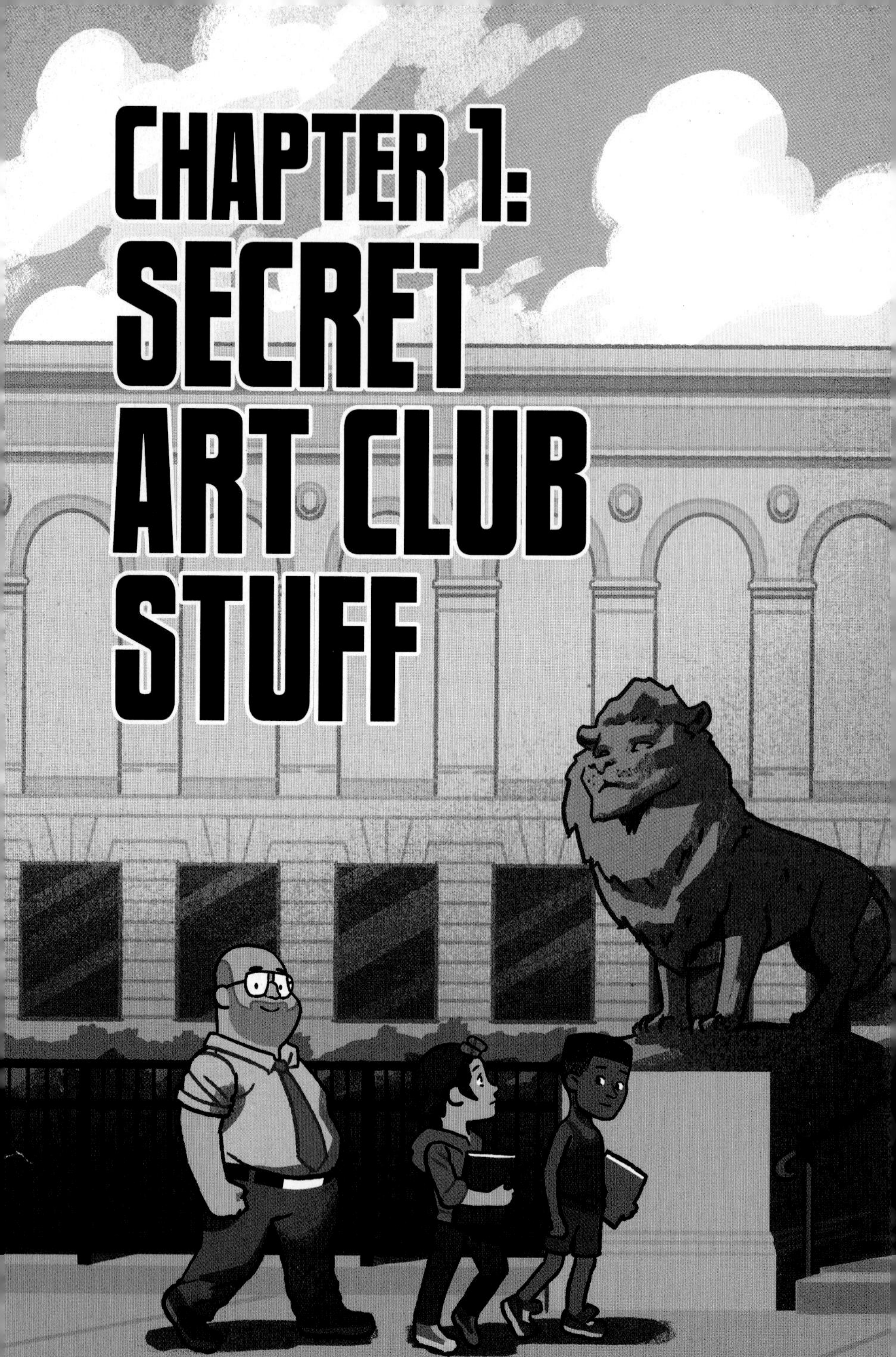

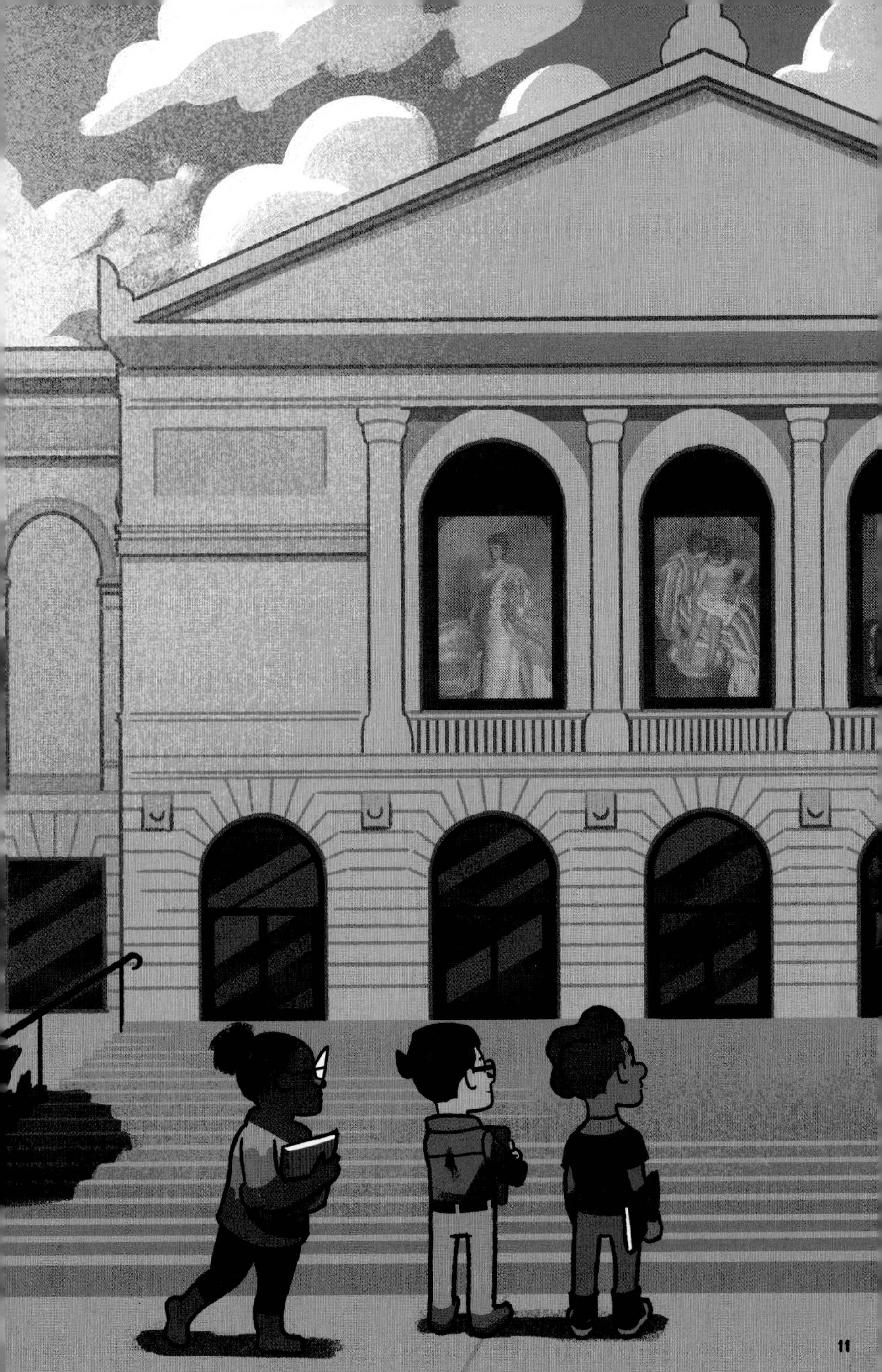

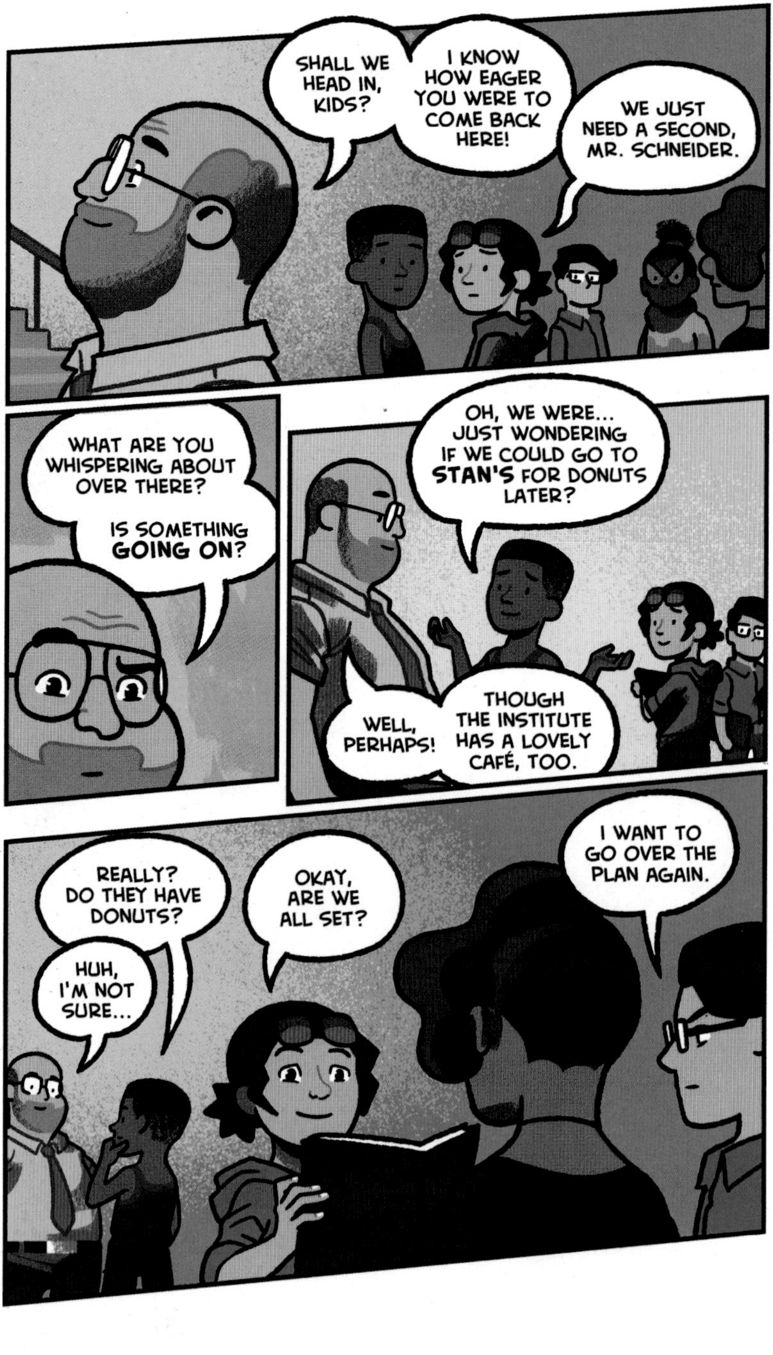
SHALL WE HEAD IN, KIDS?
I KNOW HOW EAGER YOU WERE TO COME BACK HERE!
WE JUST NEED A SECOND, MR. SCHNEIDER.
WHAT ARE YOU WHISPERING ABOUT OVER THERE?
IS SOMETHING GOING ON?
OH, WE WERE... JUST WONDERING IF WE COULD GO TO STAN'S FOR DONUTS LATER?
WELL, PERHAPS!
THOUGH THE INSTITUTE HAS A LOVELY CAFÉ, TOO.
REALLY? DO THEY HAVE DONUTS?
HUH, I'M NOT SURE...
OKAY, ARE WE ALL SET?
I WANT TO GO OVER THE PLAN AGAIN.

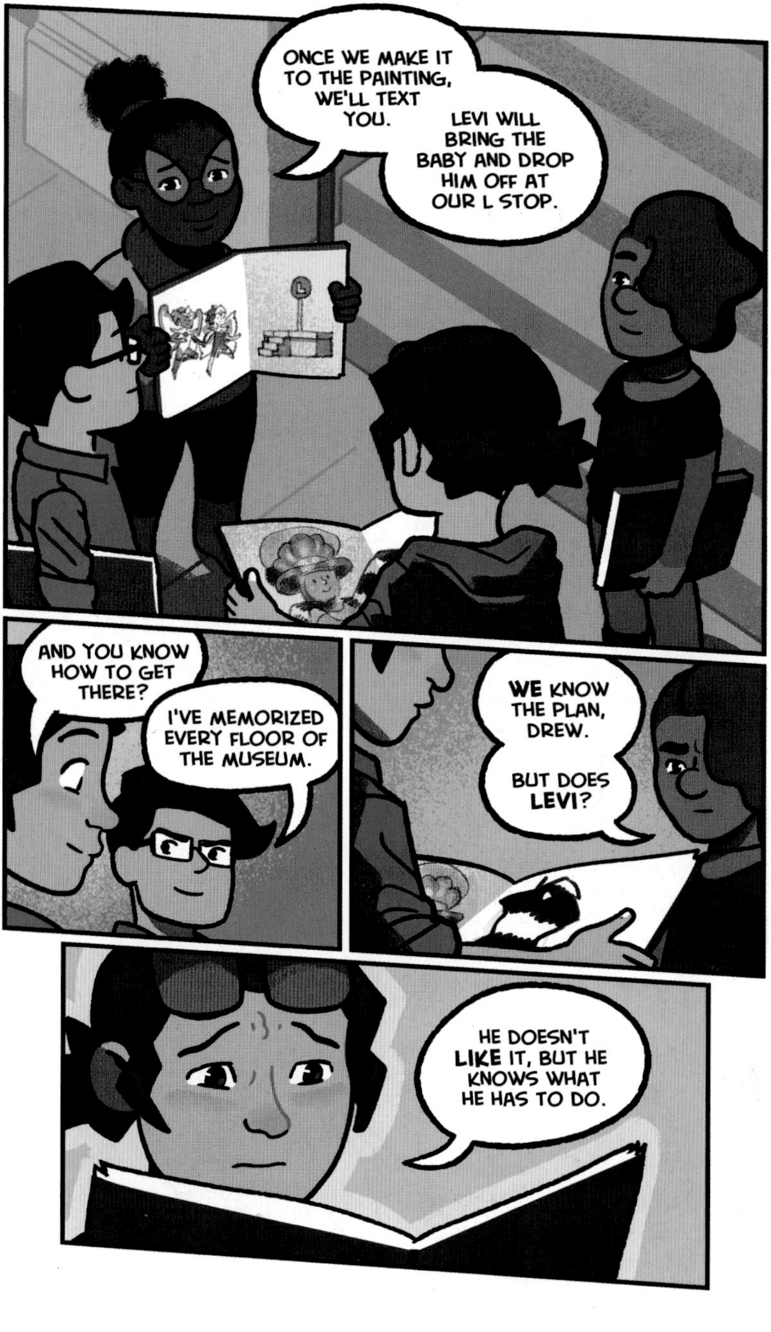

ONCE WE MAKE IT TO THE PAINTING, WE'LL TEXT YOU.
LEVI WILL BRING THE BABY AND DROP HIM OFF AT OUR L STOP.
AND YOU KNOW HOW TO GET THERE?
I'VE MEMORIZED EVERY FLOOR OF THE MUSEUM.
WE KNOW THE PLAN, DREW.
BUT DOES LEVI?
HE DOESN'T LIKE IT, BUT HE KNOWS WHAT HE HAS TO DO.

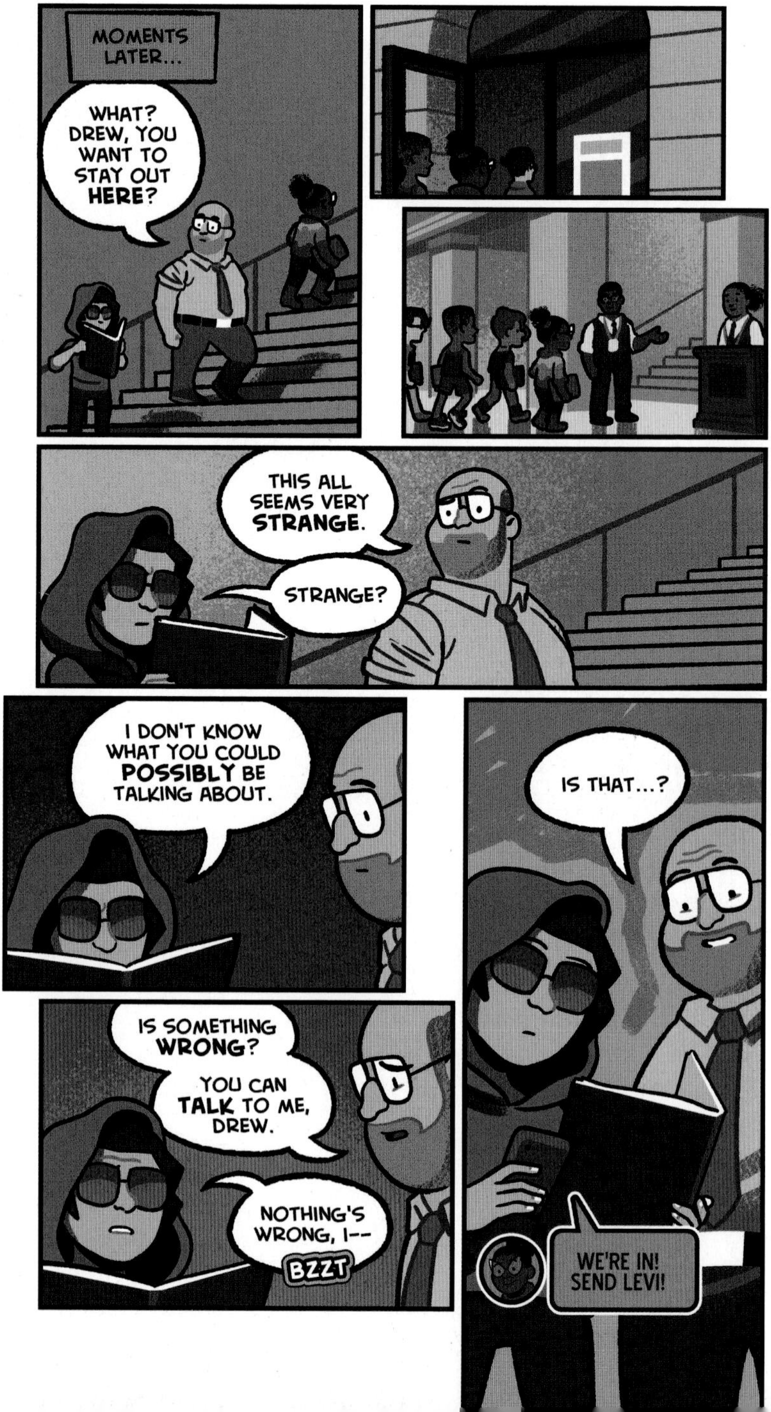
MOMENTS LATER...
WHAT? DREW, YOU WANT TO STAY OUT HERE?
THIS ALL SEEMS VERY STRANGE.
STRANGE?
I DON'T KNOW WHAT YOU COULD POSSIBLY BE TALKING ABOUT.
IS SOMETHING WRONG?
YOU CAN TALK TO ME, DREW.
NOTHING'S WRONG, I--
BZZT
IS THAT...?
WE'RE IN! SEND LEVI!

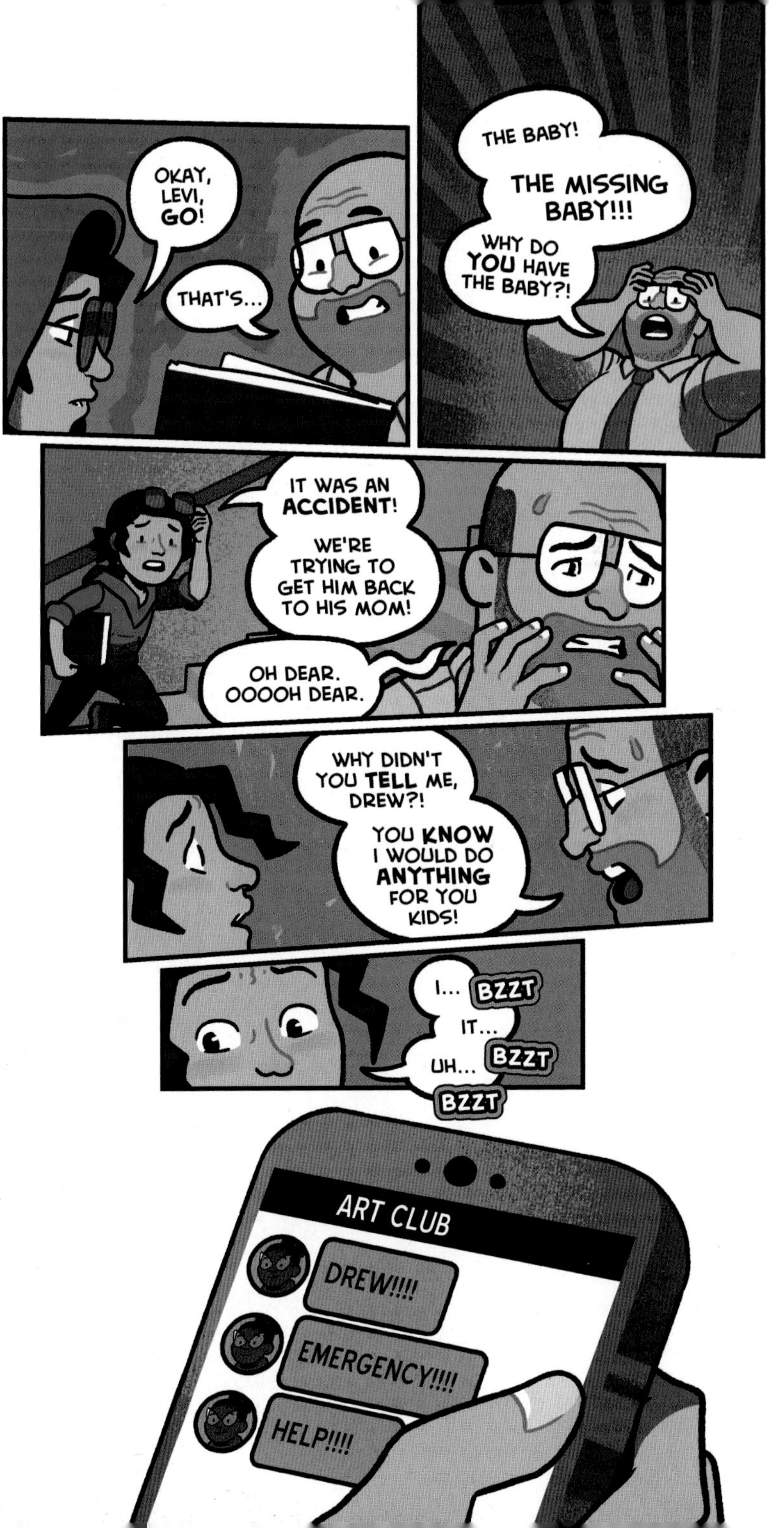
OKAY, LEVI, GO!
THAT'S...
THE BABY!
THE MISSING BABY!!!
WHY DO YOU HAVE THE BABY?!
IT WAS AN ACCIDENT!
WE'RE TRYING TO GET HIM BACK TO HIS MOM!
OH DEAR. OOOOH DEAR.
WHY DIDN'T YOU TELL ME, DREW?!
YOU KNOW I WOULD DO ANYTHING FOR YOU KIDS!
I...
BZZT
IT...
UH...
BZZT
BZZT
ART CLUB
DREW!!!!
EMERGENCY!!!!
HELP!!!!

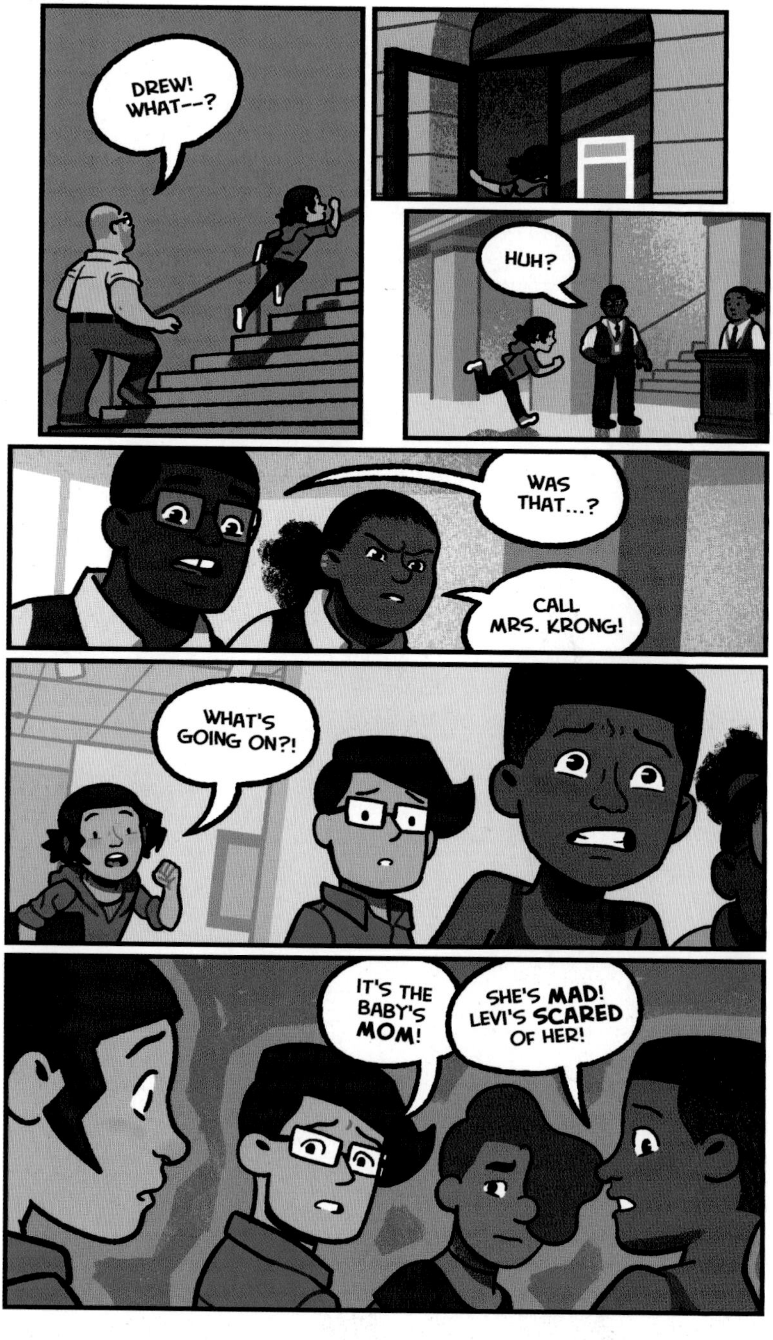
DREW! WHAT--?
HUH?
WAS THAT...?
CALL MRS. KRONG!
WHAT'S GOING ON?!
IT'S THE BABY'S MOM!
SHE'S MAD! LEVI'S SCARED OF HER!

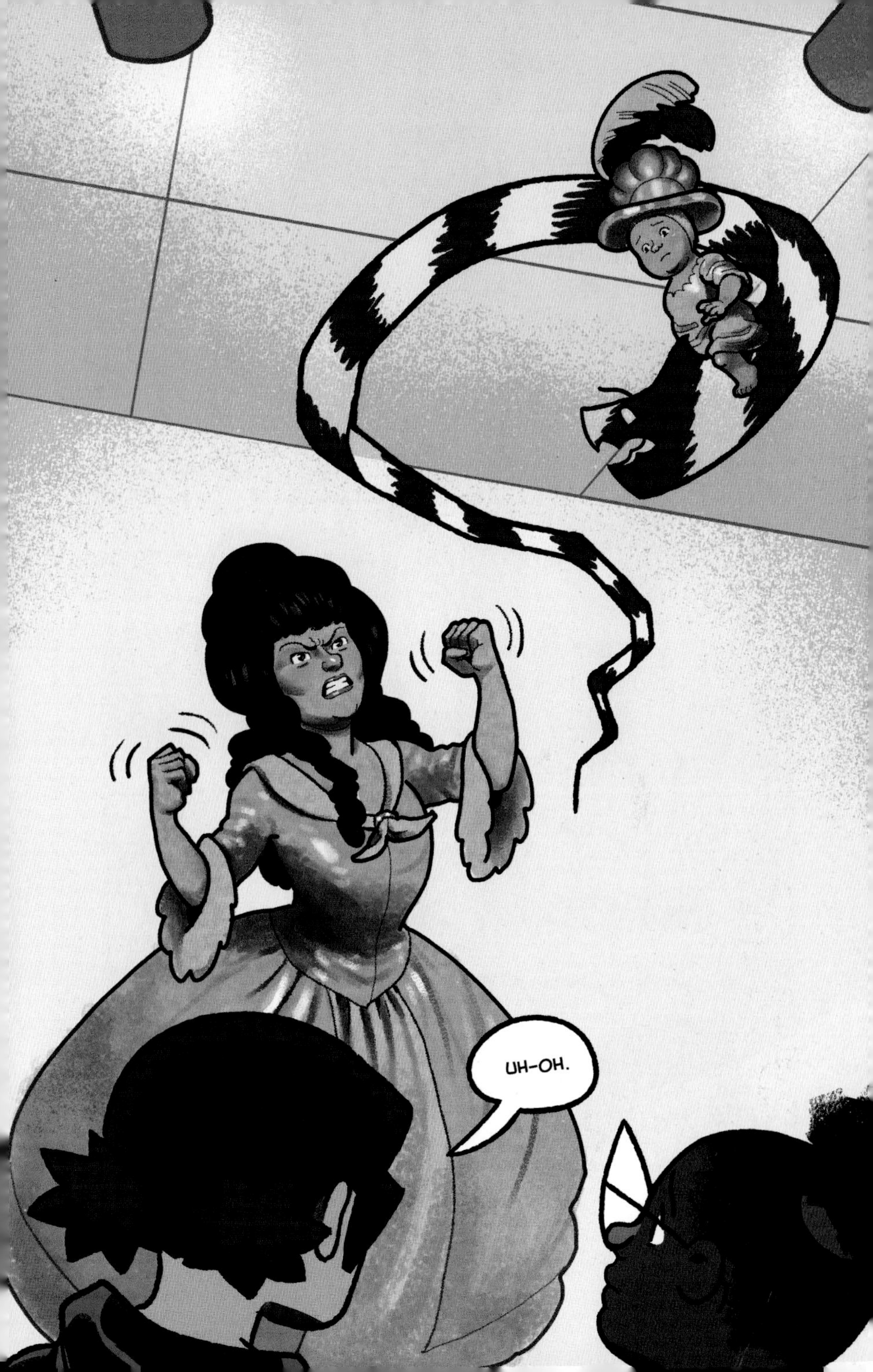
UH-OH.

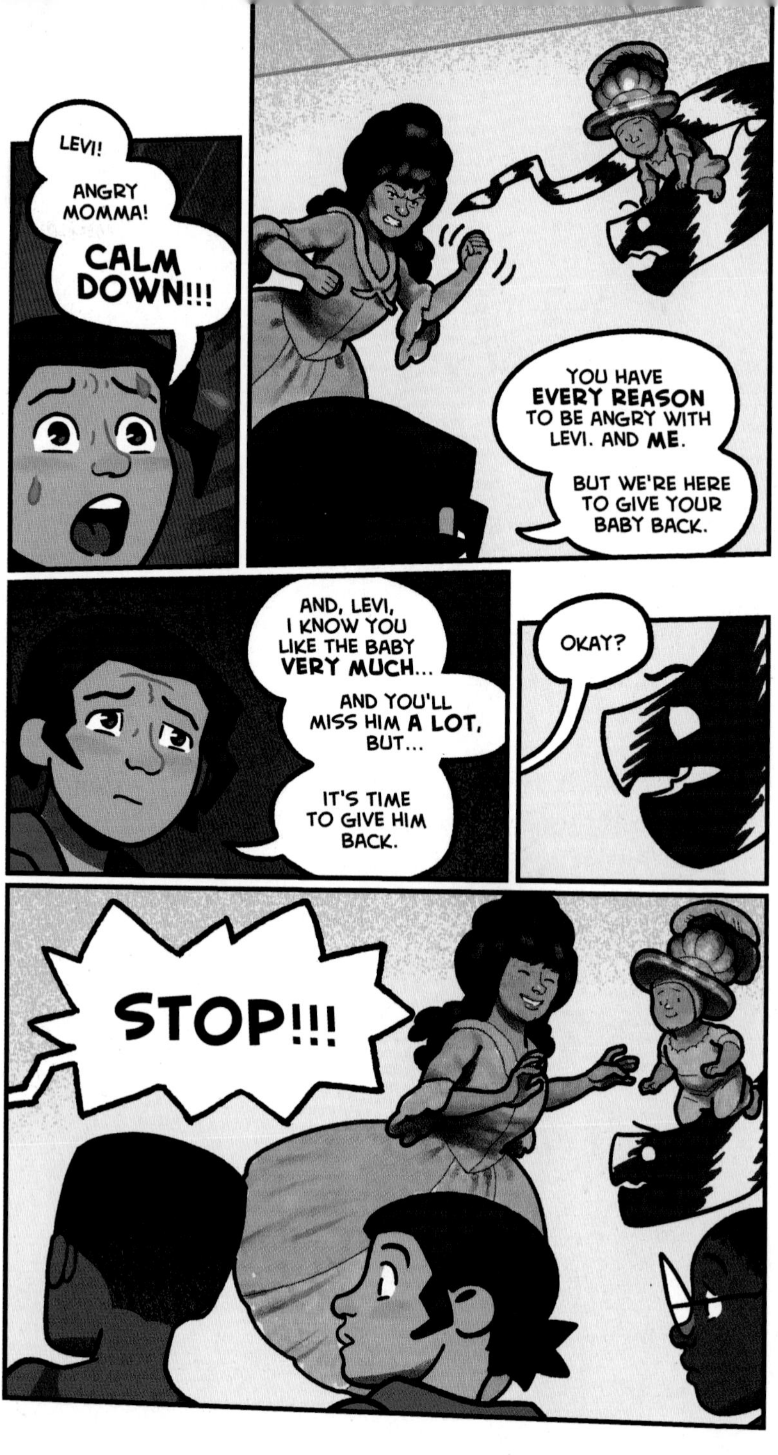
LEVI!
ANGRY MOMMA!
CALM DOWN!!!
YOU HAVE EVERY REASON TO BE ANGRY WITH LEVI. AND ME.
BUT WE'RE HERE TO GIVE YOUR BABY BACK.
AND, LEVI, I KNOW YOU LIKE THE BABY VERY MUCH...
AND YOU'LL MISS HIM A LOT, BUT...
IT'S TIME TO GIVE HIM BACK.
OKAY?
STOP!!!

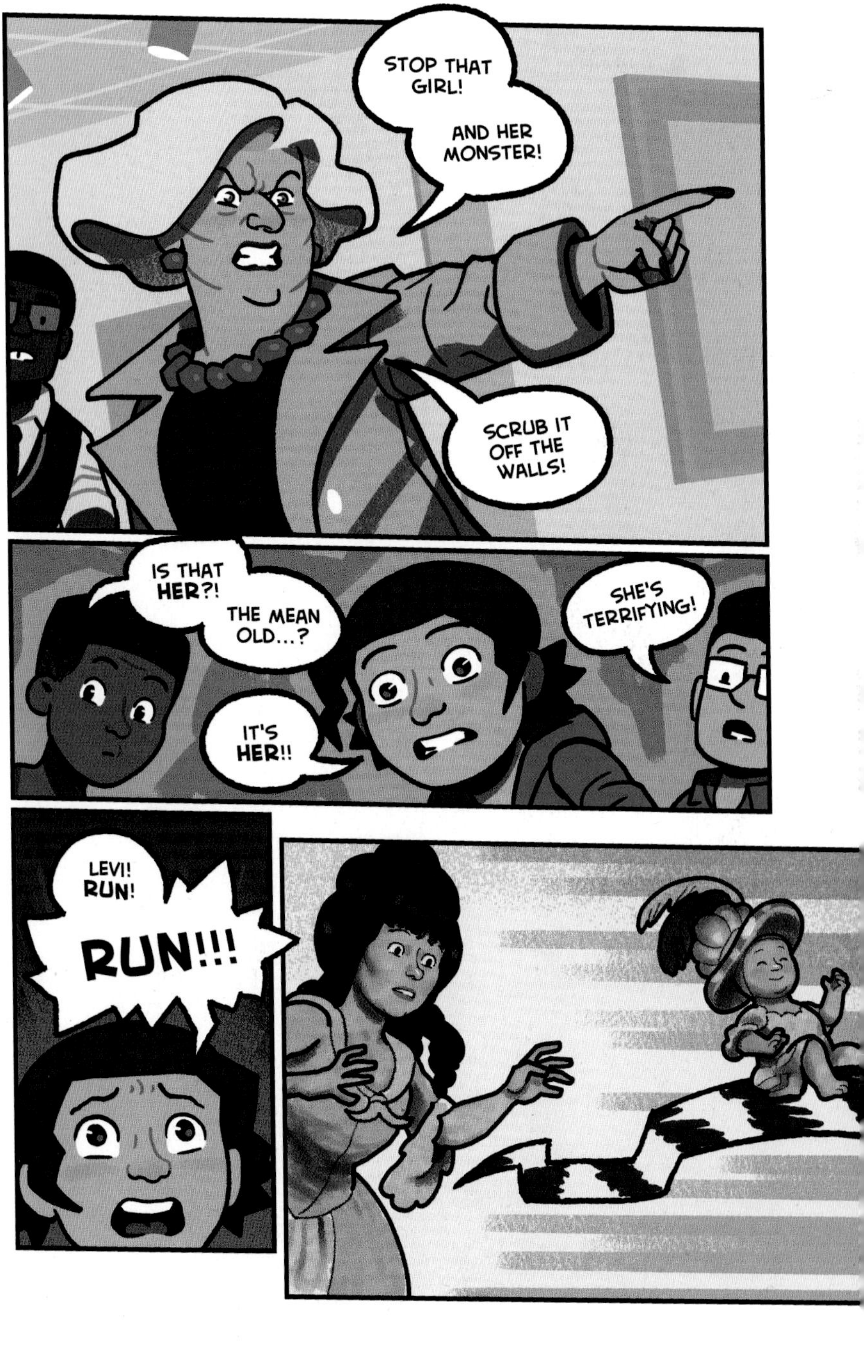
STOP THAT GIRL!
AND HER MONSTER!
SCRUB IT OFF THE WALLS!
IS THAT **HER**?!
THE MEAN OLD...?
SHE'S TERRIFYING!
IT'S **HER**!!
LEVI! **RUN**!
RUN!!!

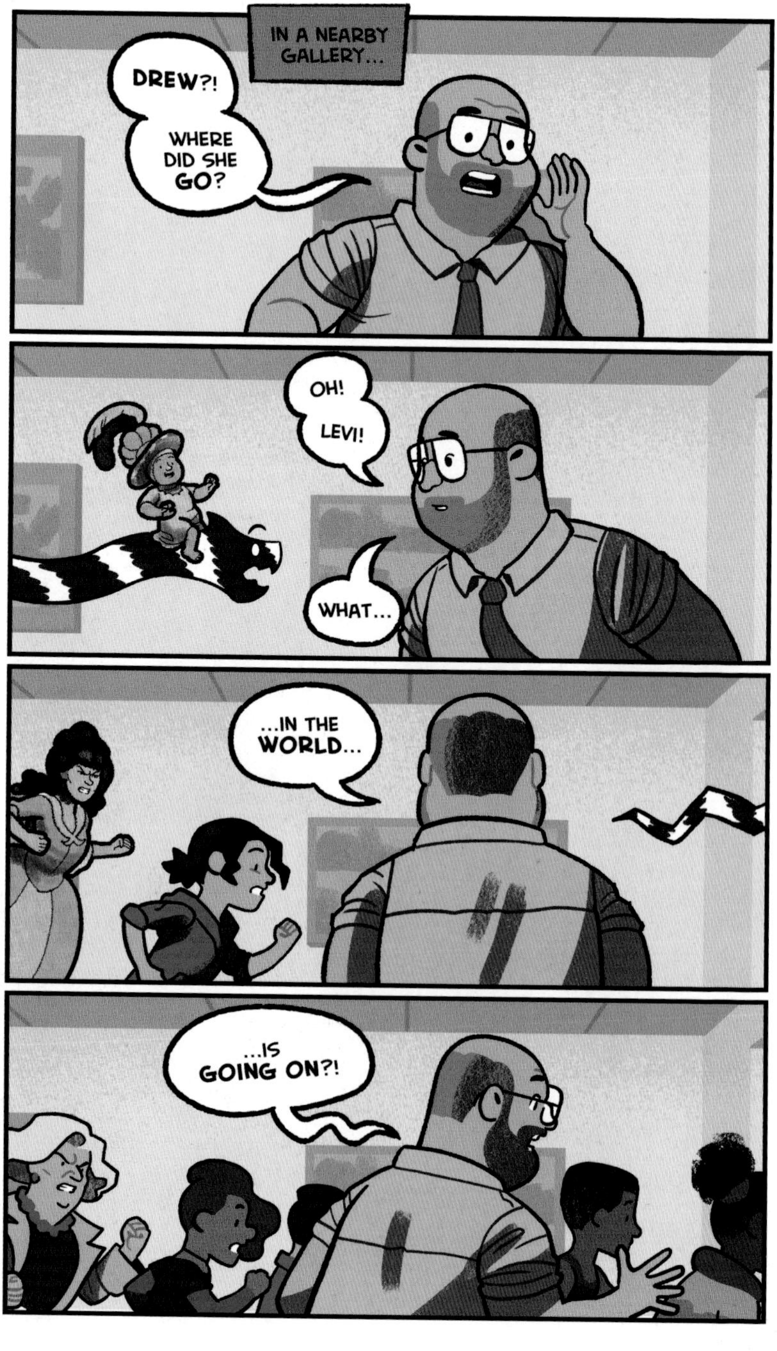
IN A NEARBY GALLERY...
DREW?!
WHERE DID SHE GO?
OH!
LEVI!
WHAT...
...IN THE WORLD...
...IS GOING ON?!

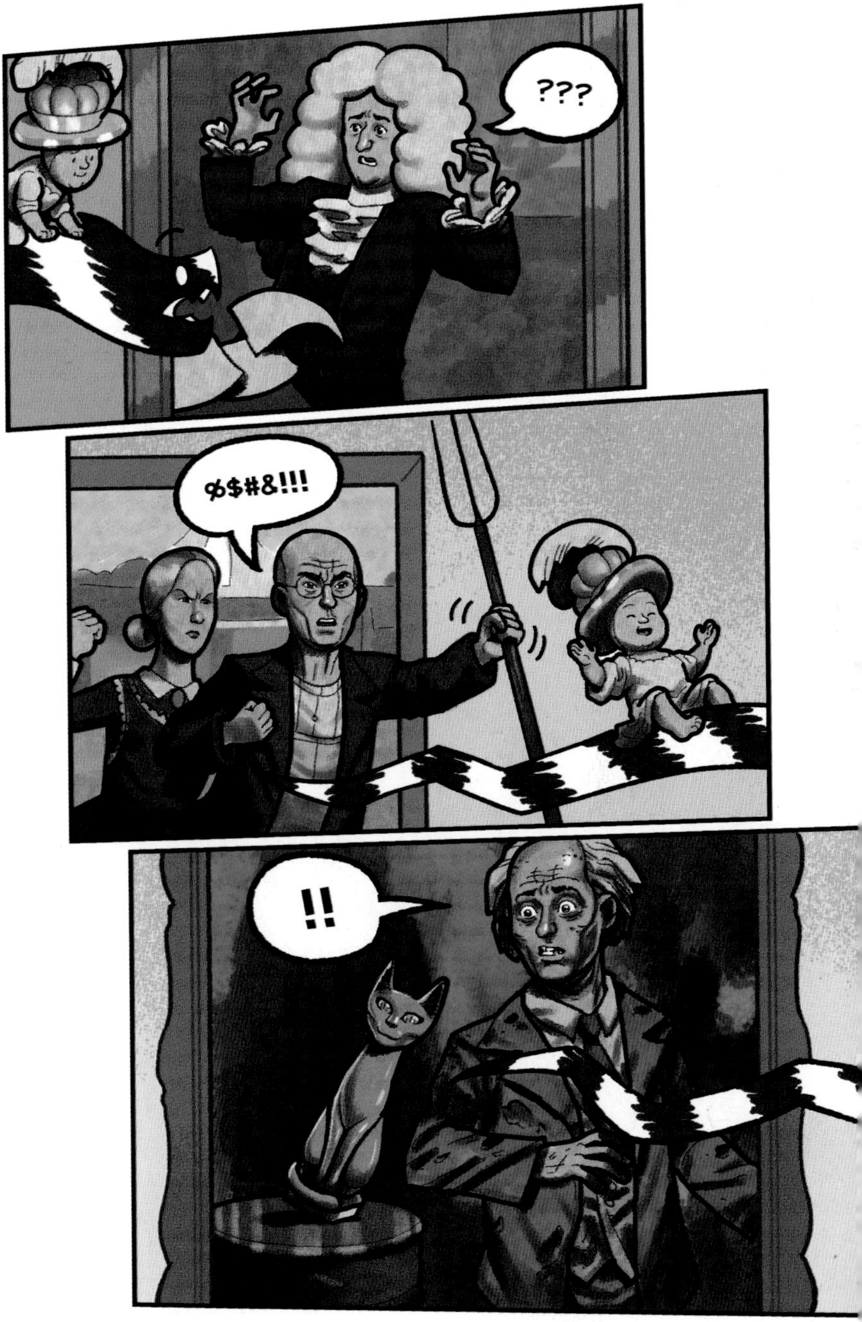
???
%$#&!!!
!!

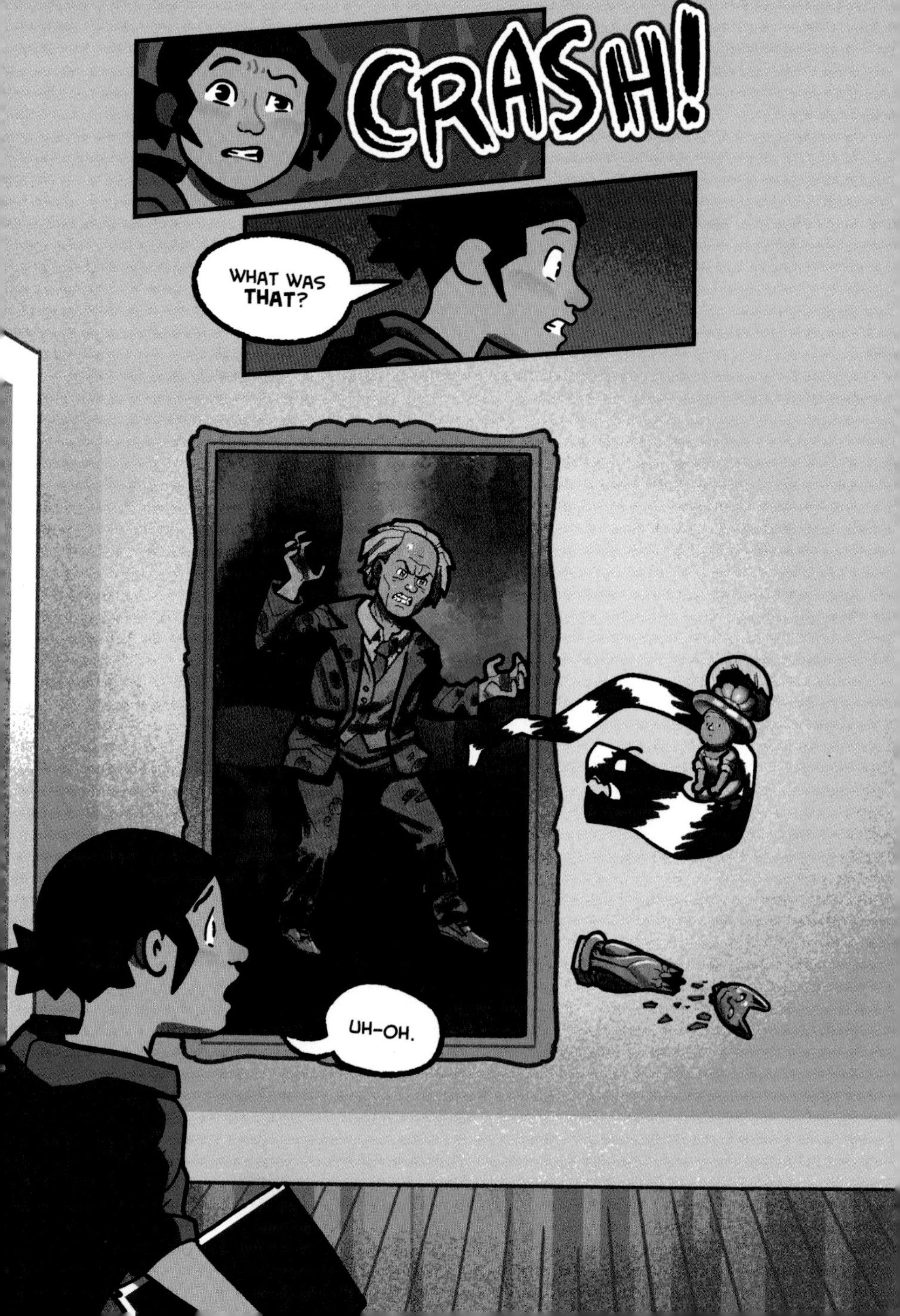
CRASH!
WHAT WAS THAT?
UH-OH.

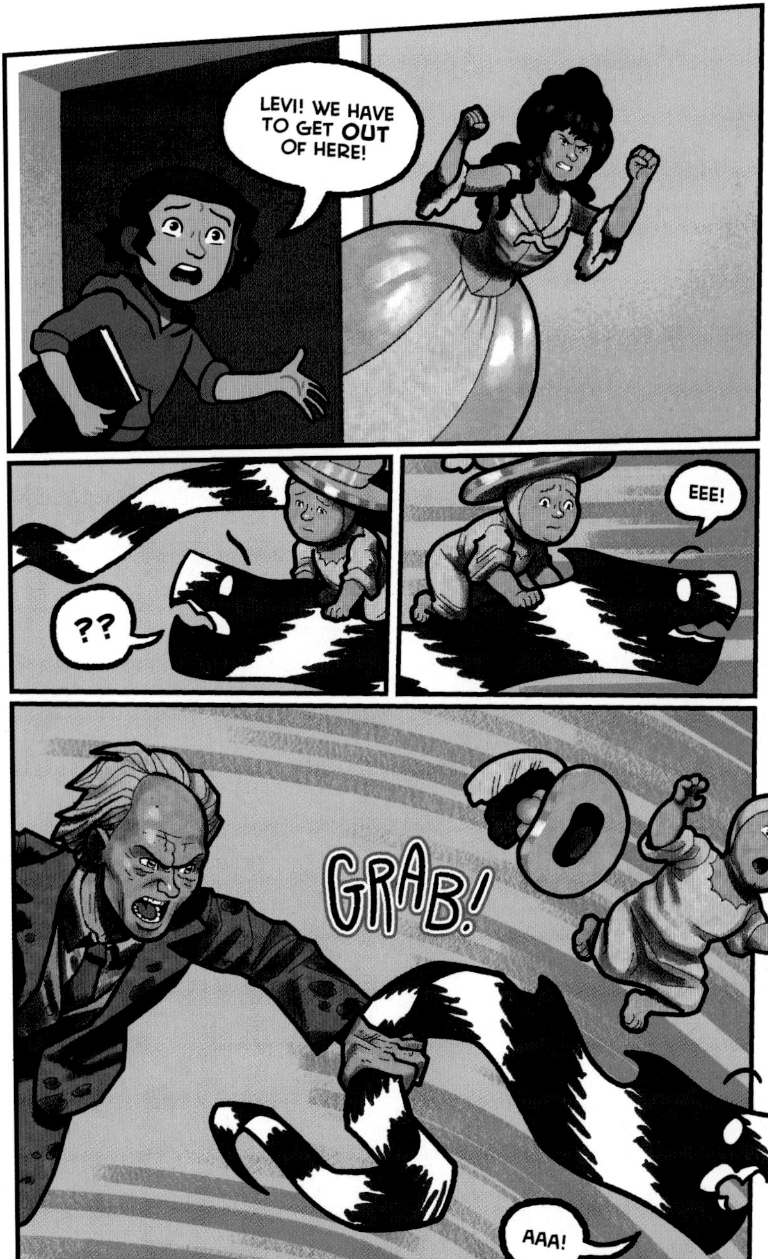
LEVI! WE HAVE TO GET OUT OF HERE!
??
EEE!
GRAB!
AAA!

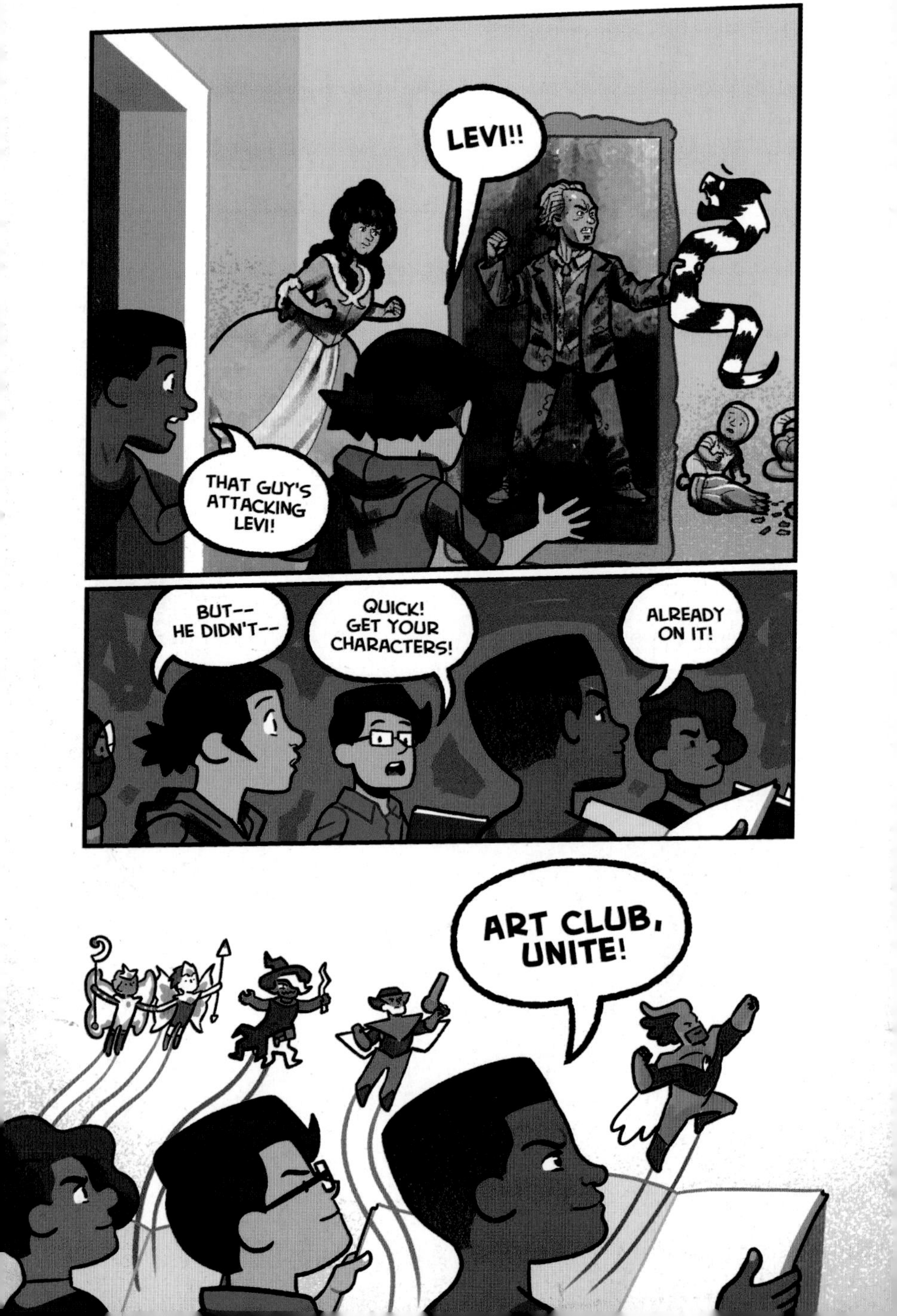
LEVI!!
THAT GUY'S ATTACKING LEVI!
BUT-- HE DIDN'T--
QUICK! GET YOUR CHARACTERS!
ALREADY ON IT!
ART CLUB, UNITE!

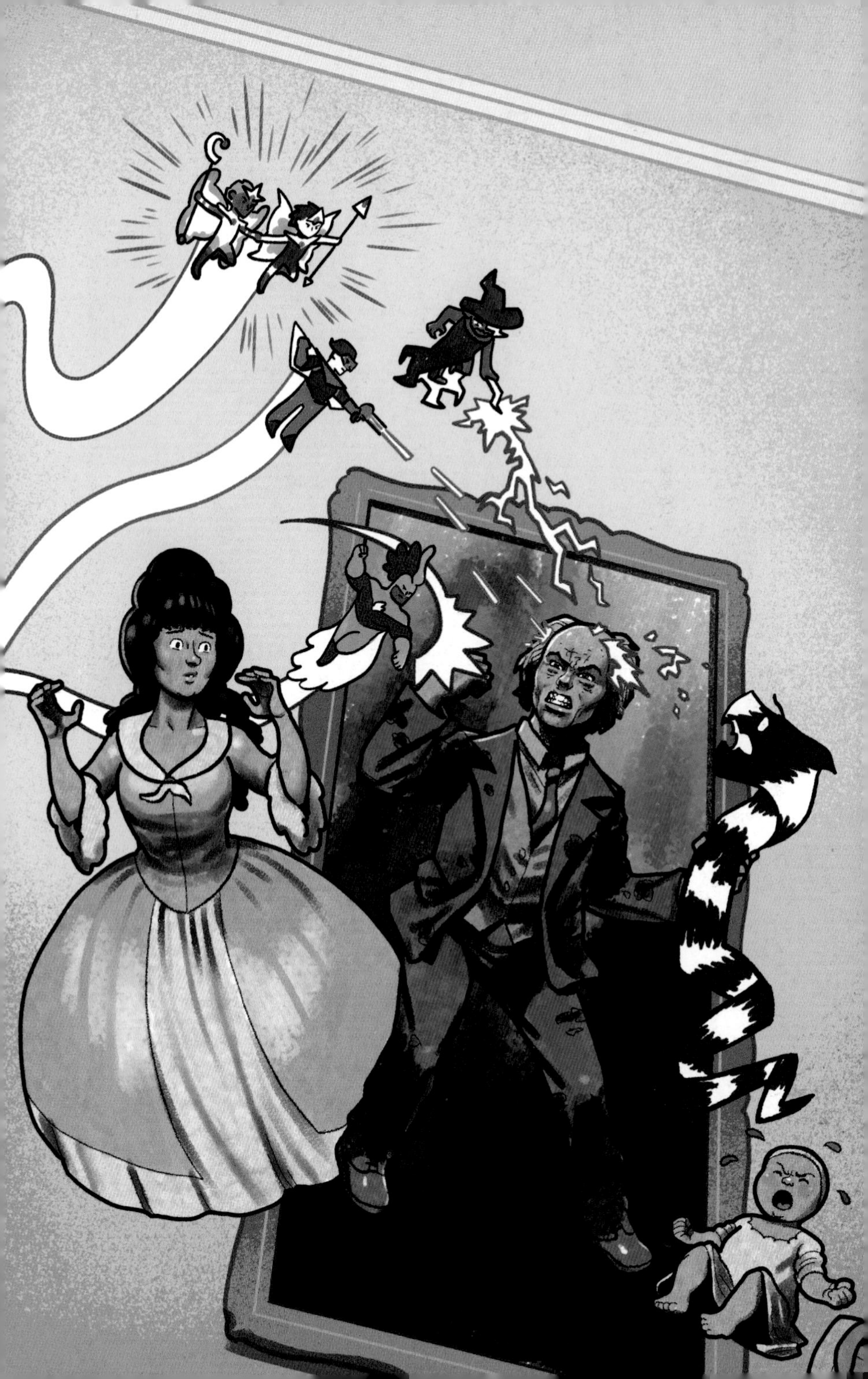

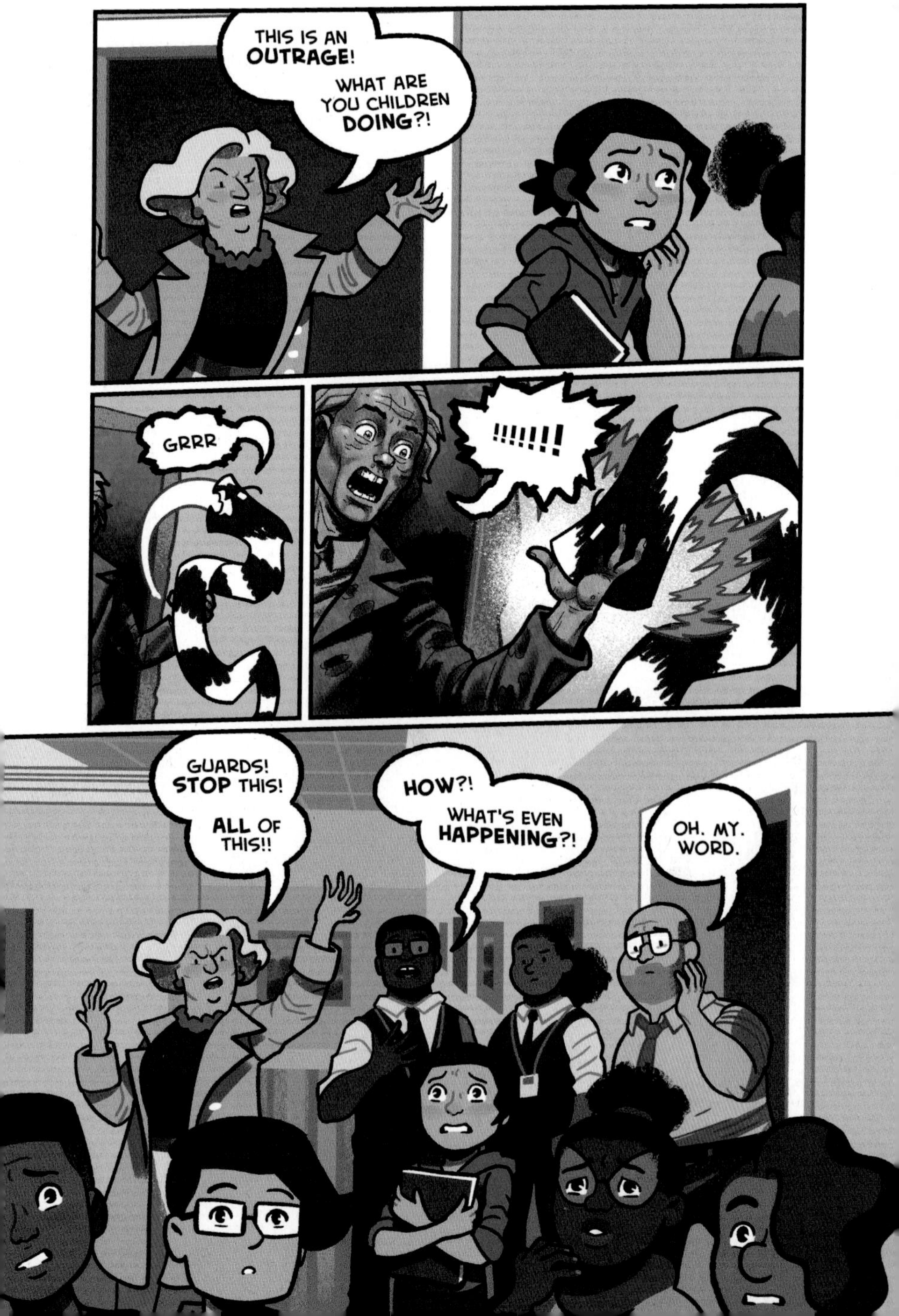
THIS IS AN OUTRAGE!
WHAT ARE YOU CHILDREN DOING?!
GRRR
!!!!!!!
GUARDS! STOP THIS!
ALL OF THIS!!
HOW?!
WHAT'S EVEN HAPPENING?!
OH. MY. WORD.

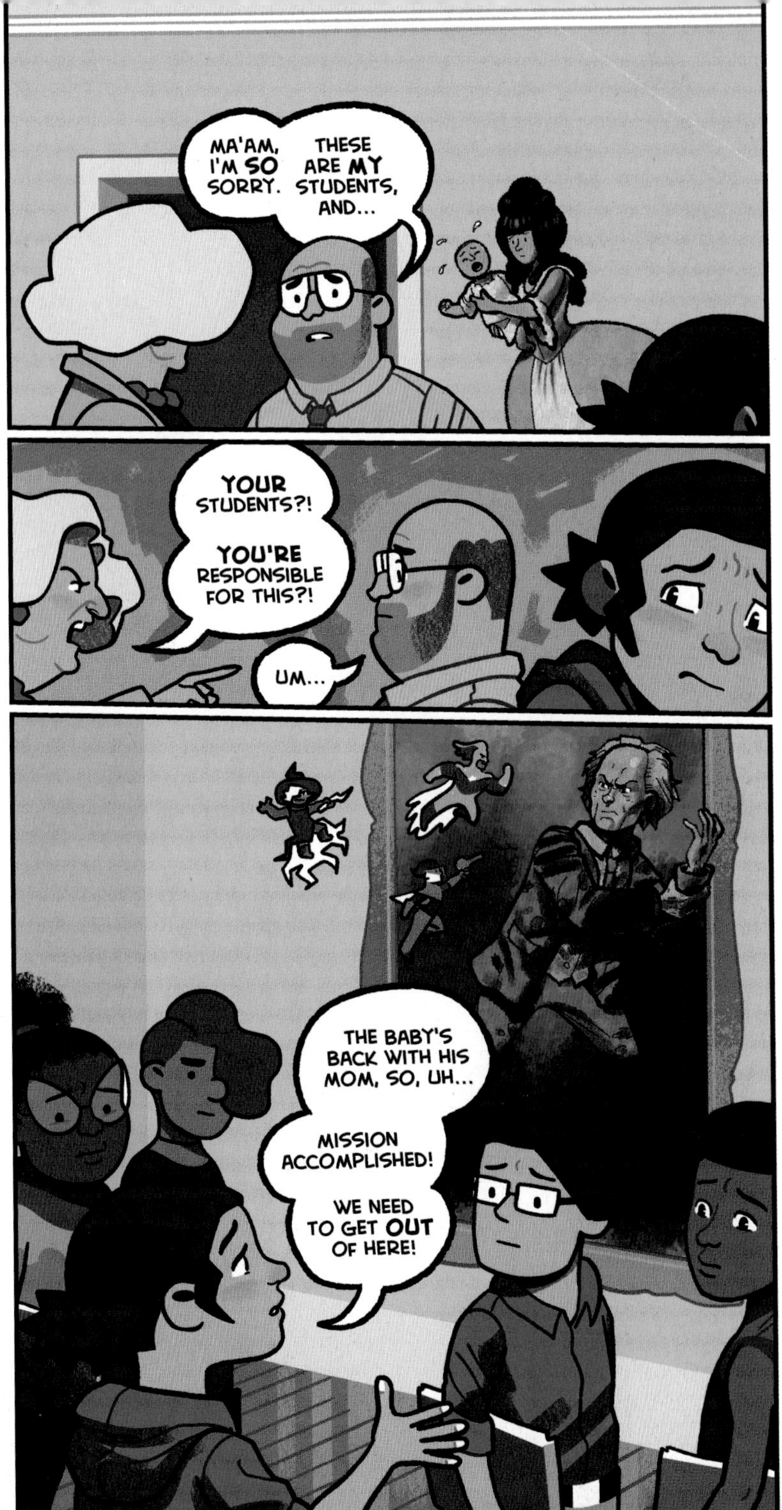
MA'AM, I'M SO SORRY.
THESE ARE MY STUDENTS, AND...
YOUR STUDENTS?! YOU'RE RESPONSIBLE FOR THIS?!
UM...
THE BABY'S BACK WITH HIS MOM, SO, UH...
MISSION ACCOMPLISHED!
WE NEED TO GET OUT OF HERE!

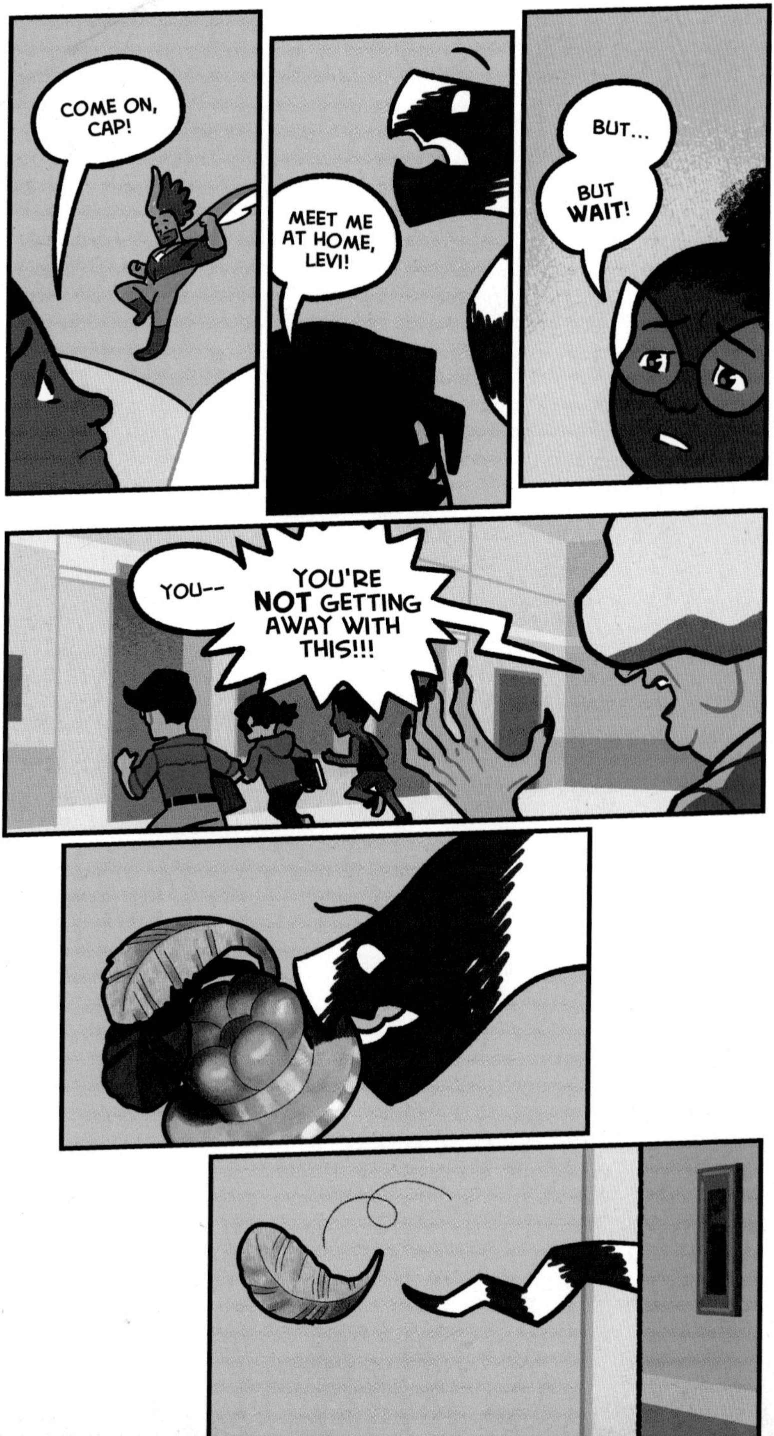
COME ON, CAP!
MEET ME AT HOME, LEVI!
BUT...
BUT WAIT!
YOU--
YOU'RE NOT GETTING AWAY WITH THIS!!!

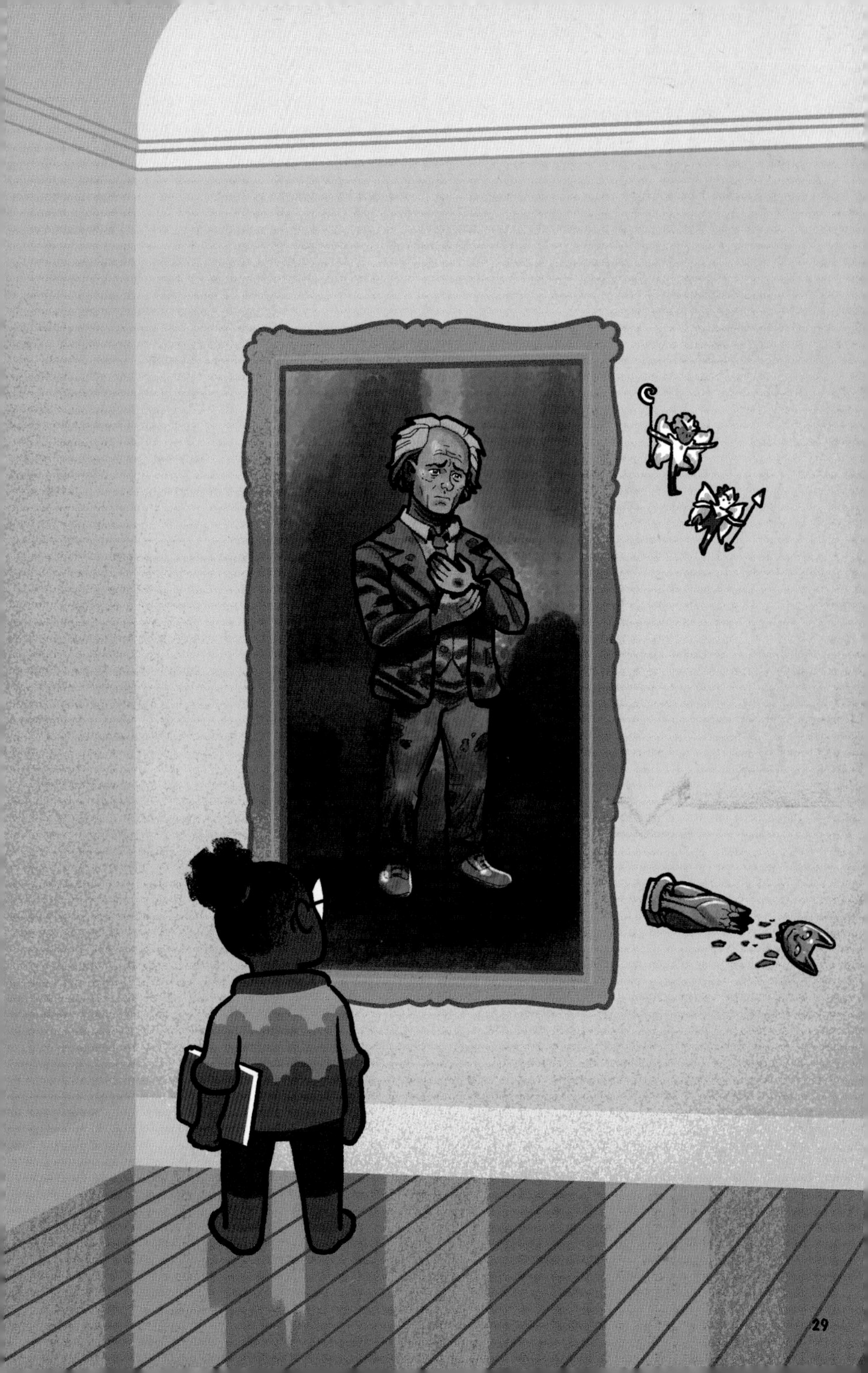

CHAPTER 2: MISSION... ACCOMPLISHED?

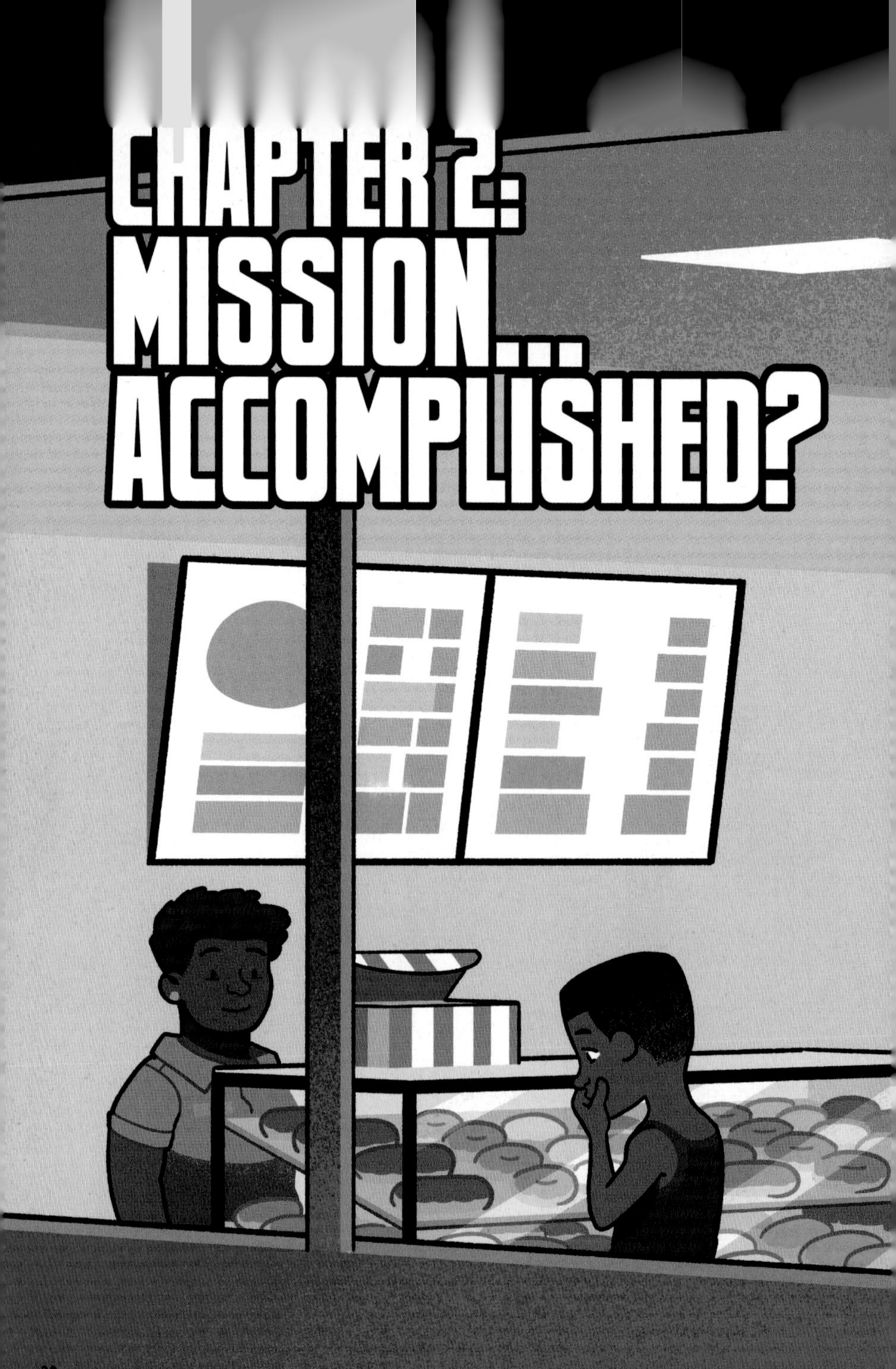

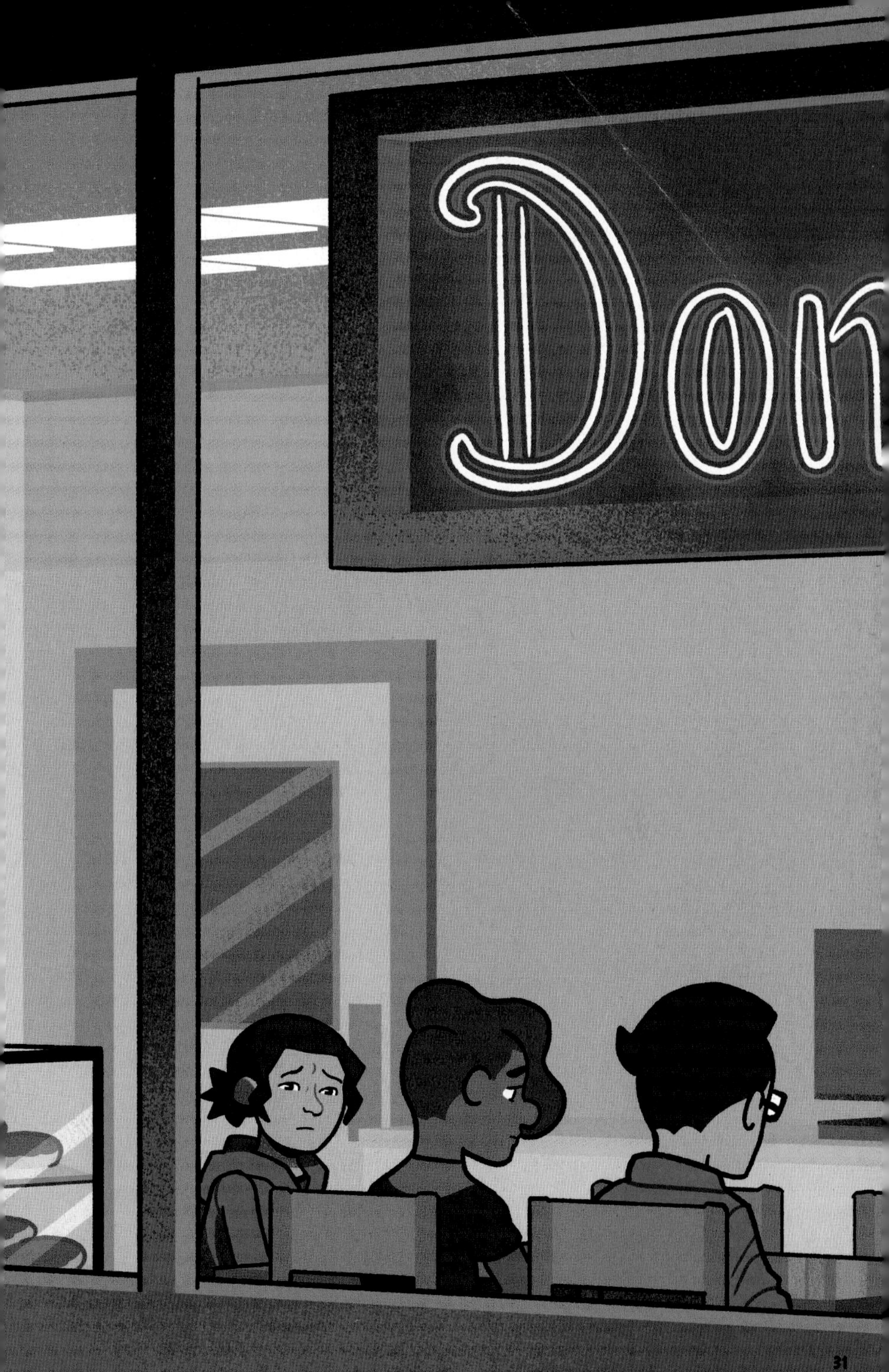
Don

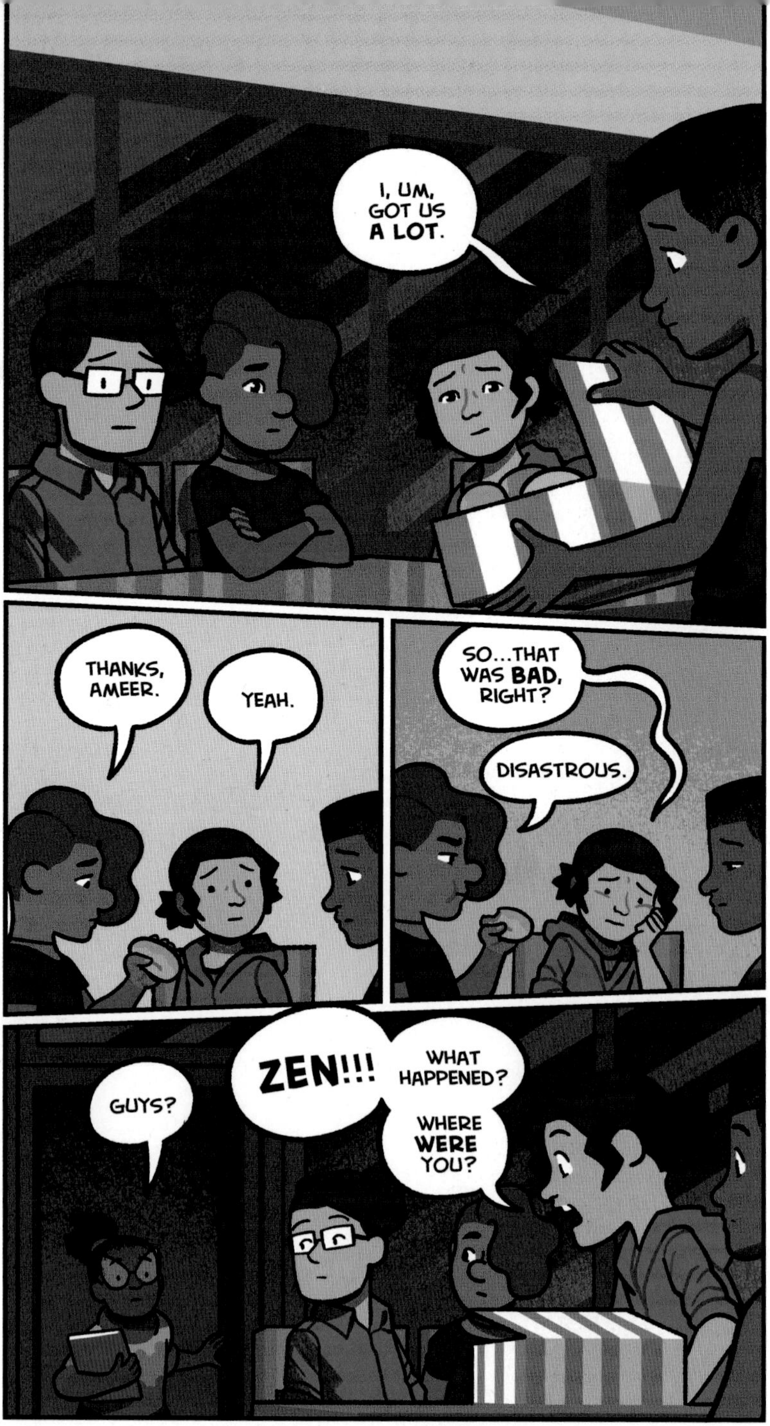

I, UM, GOT US **A LOT**.
THANKS, AMEER.
YEAH.
SO...THAT WAS **BAD**, RIGHT?
DISASTROUS.
GUYS?
ZEN!!!
WHAT HAPPENED?
WHERE **WERE** YOU?

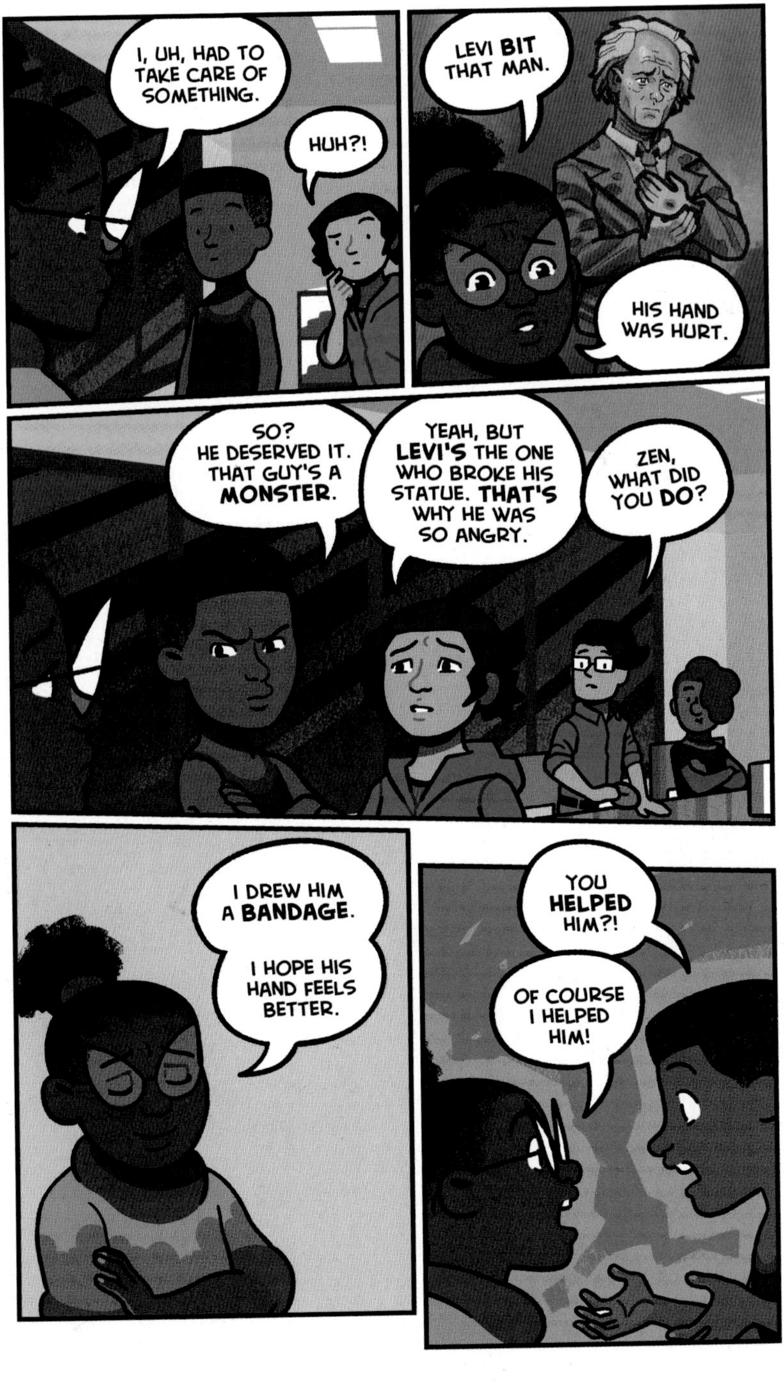
I, UH, HAD TO TAKE CARE OF SOMETHING.
HUH?!
LEVI BIT THAT MAN.
HIS HAND WAS HURT.
SO? HE DESERVED IT. THAT GUY'S A MONSTER.
YEAH, BUT LEVI'S THE ONE WHO BROKE HIS STATUE. THAT'S WHY HE WAS SO ANGRY.
ZEN, WHAT DID YOU DO?
I DREW HIM A BANDAGE.
I HOPE HIS HAND FEELS BETTER.
YOU HELPED HIM?!
OF COURSE I HELPED HIM!

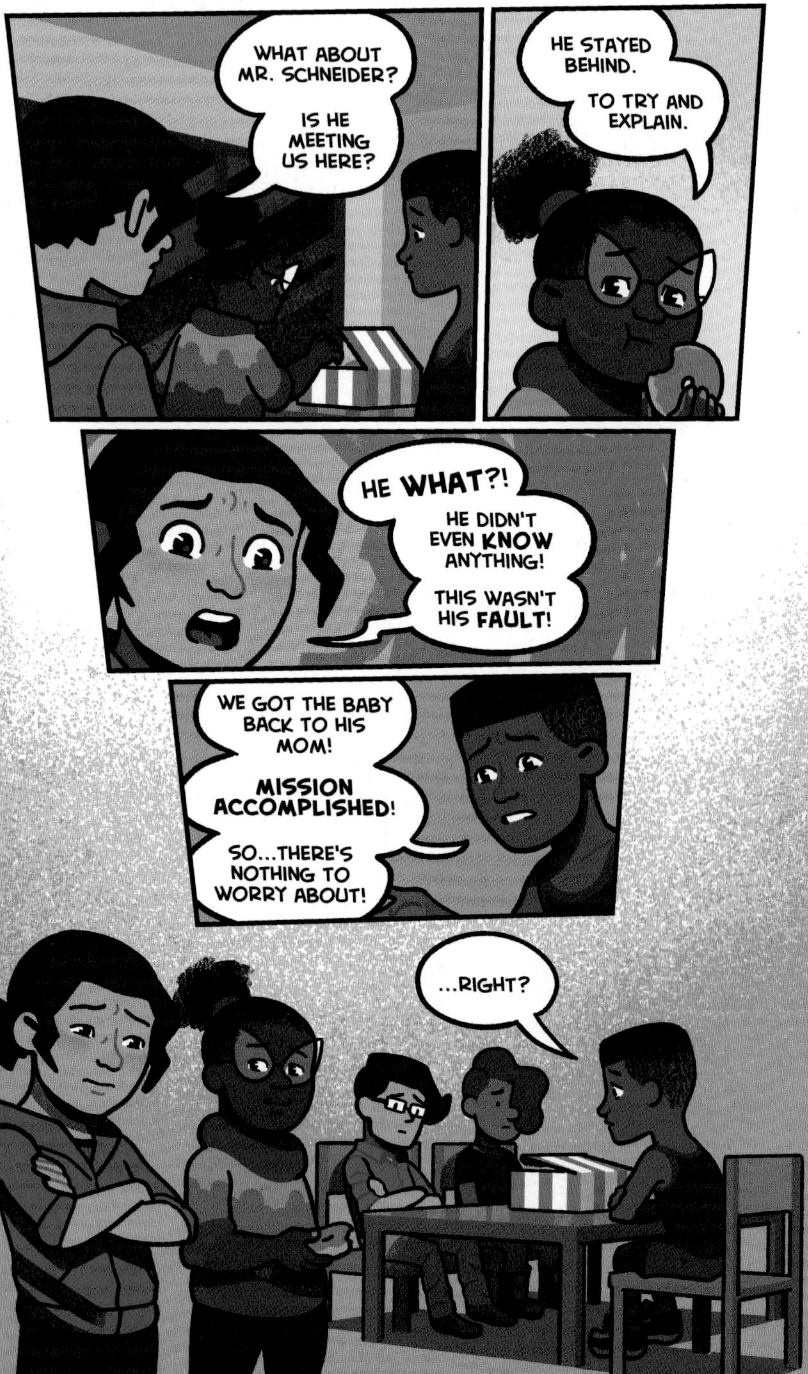
WHAT ABOUT MR. SCHNEIDER?
IS HE MEETING US HERE?
HE STAYED BEHIND.
TO TRY AND EXPLAIN.
HE WHAT?!
HE DIDN'T EVEN KNOW ANYTHING!
THIS WASN'T HIS FAULT!
WE GOT THE BABY BACK TO HIS MOM!
MISSION ACCOMPLISHED!
SO...THERE'S NOTHING TO WORRY ABOUT!
...RIGHT?

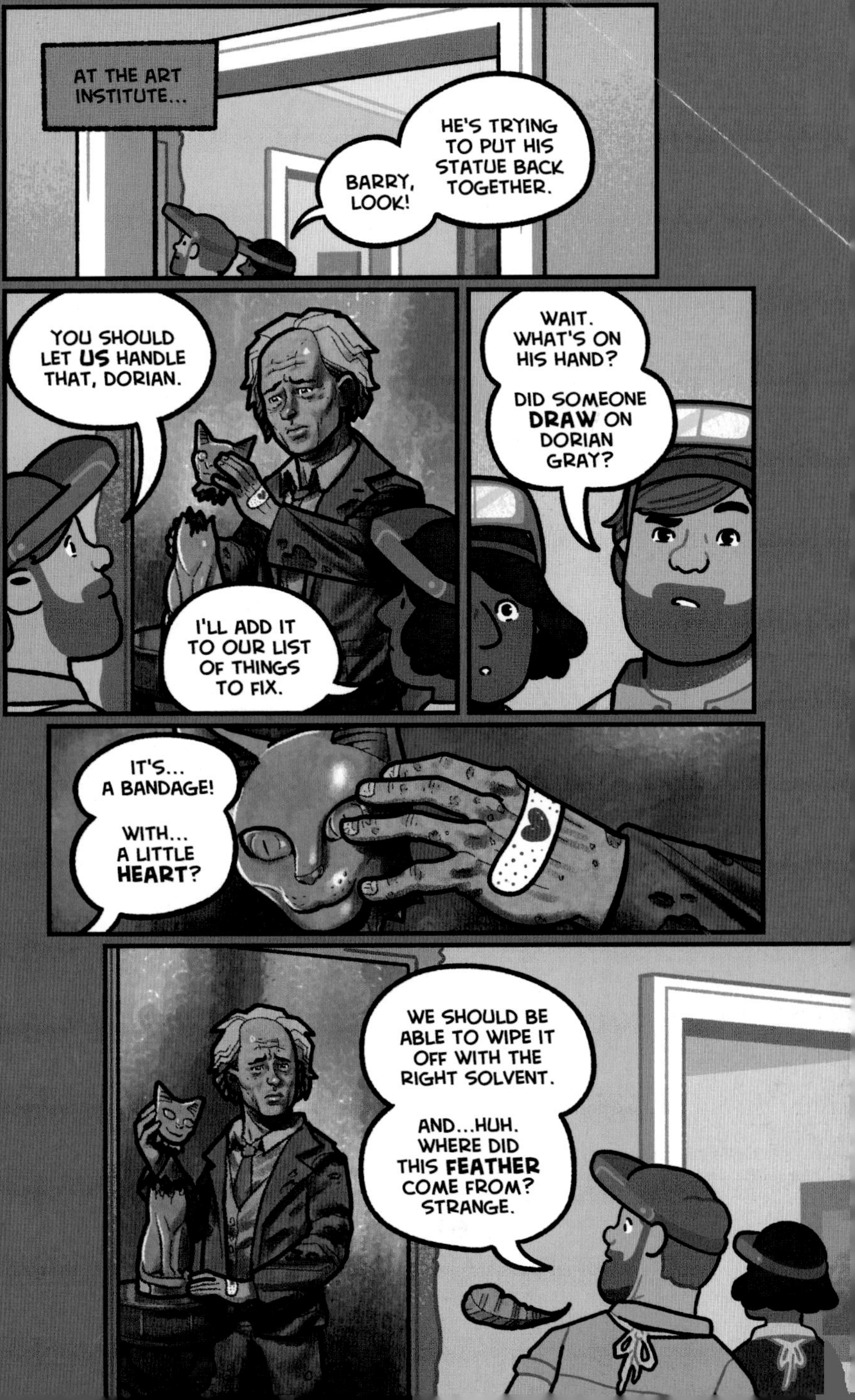
AT THE ART INSTITUTE...
BARRY, LOOK!
HE'S TRYING TO PUT HIS STATUE BACK TOGETHER.
YOU SHOULD LET **US** HANDLE THAT, DORIAN.
I'LL ADD IT TO OUR LIST OF THINGS TO FIX.
WAIT. WHAT'S ON HIS HAND?
DID SOMEONE **DRAW** ON DORIAN GRAY?
IT'S... A BANDAGE!
WITH... A LITTLE **HEART**?
WE SHOULD BE ABLE TO WIPE IT OFF WITH THE RIGHT SOLVENT.
AND...HUH. WHERE DID THIS **FEATHER** COME FROM? STRANGE.

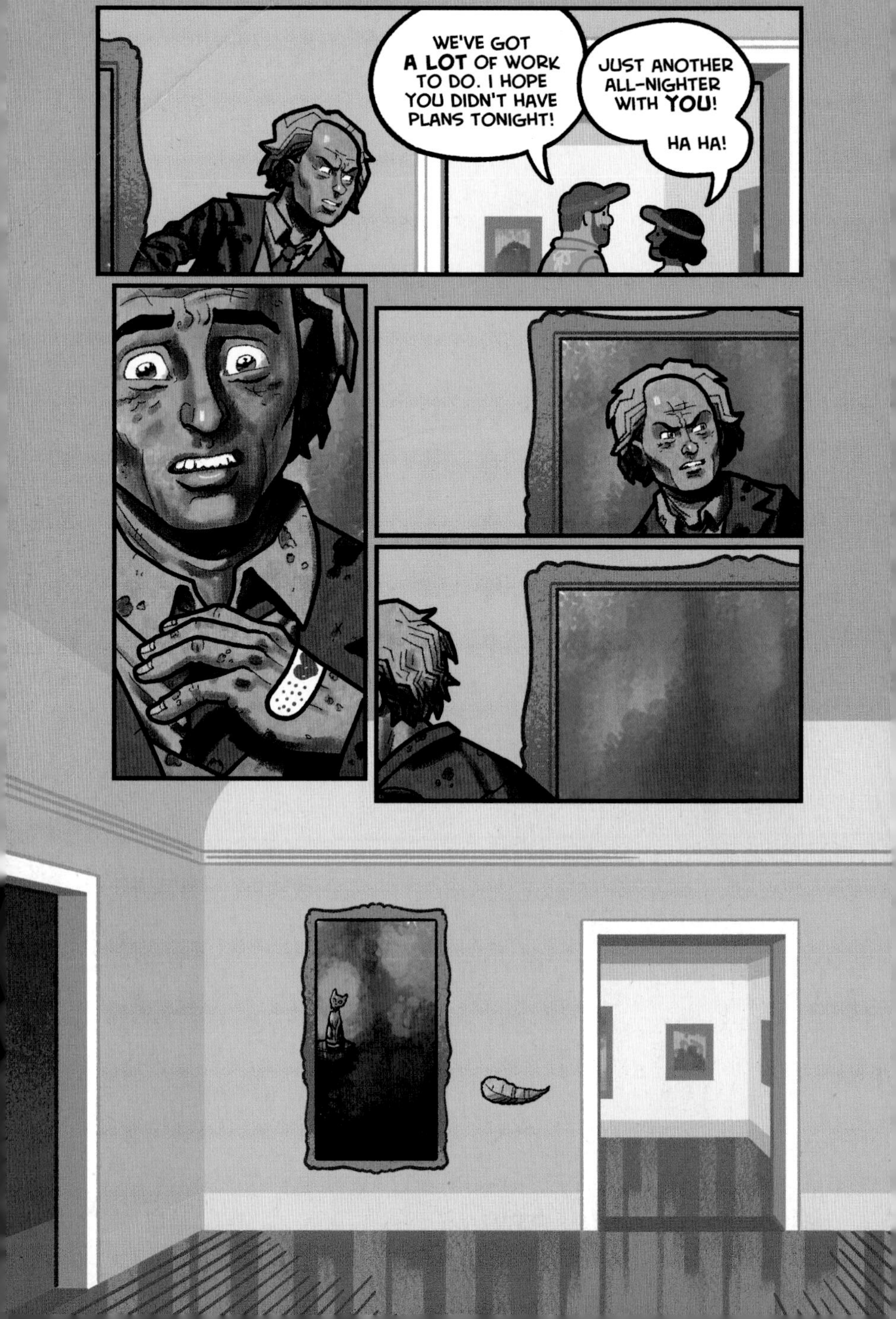
WE'VE GOT A LOT OF WORK TO DO. I HOPE YOU DIDN'T HAVE PLANS TONIGHT!
JUST ANOTHER ALL-NIGHTER WITH YOU!
HA HA!

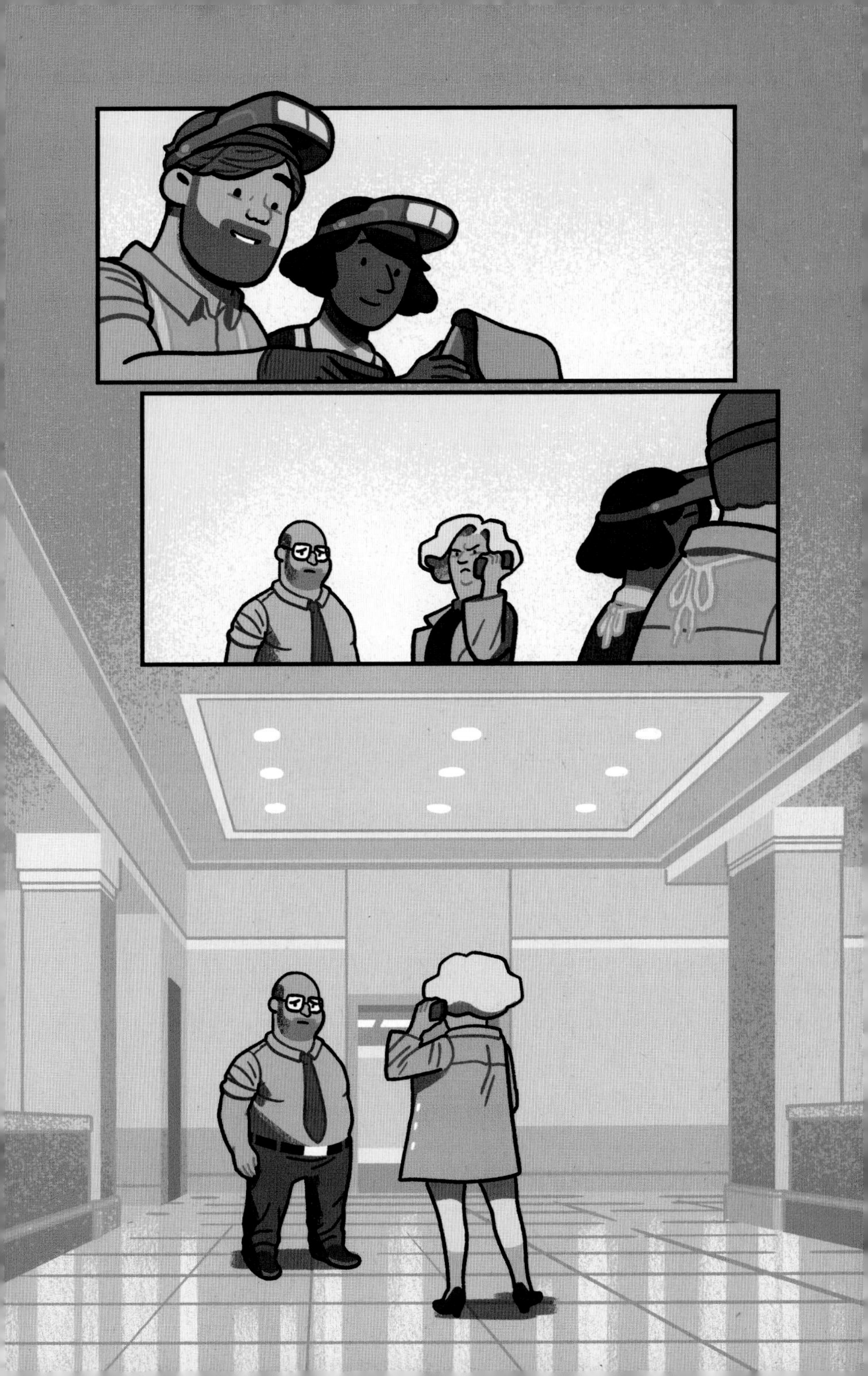

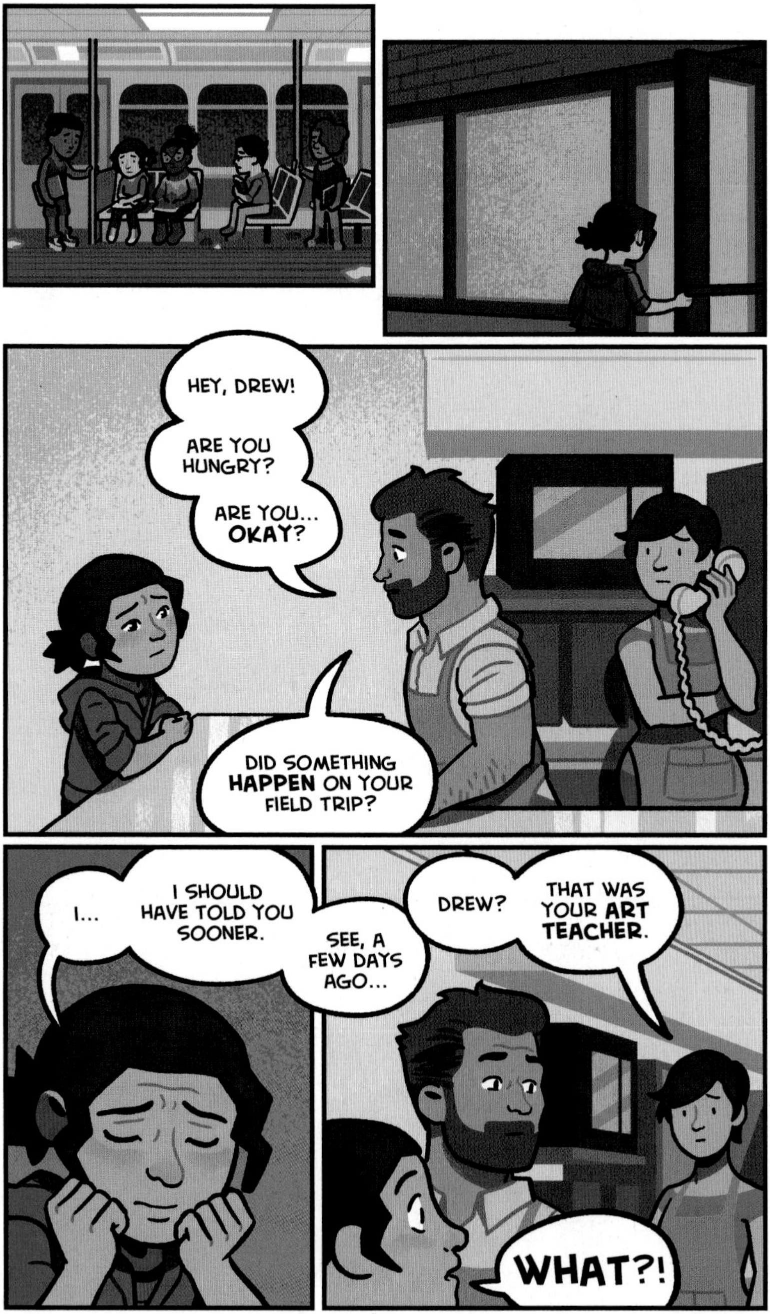
HEY, DREW!
ARE YOU HUNGRY?
ARE YOU... **OKAY**?
DID SOMETHING **HAPPEN** ON YOUR FIELD TRIP?
I...
I SHOULD HAVE TOLD YOU SOONER.
SEE, A FEW DAYS AGO...
DREW?
THAT WAS YOUR **ART TEACHER**.
WHAT?!

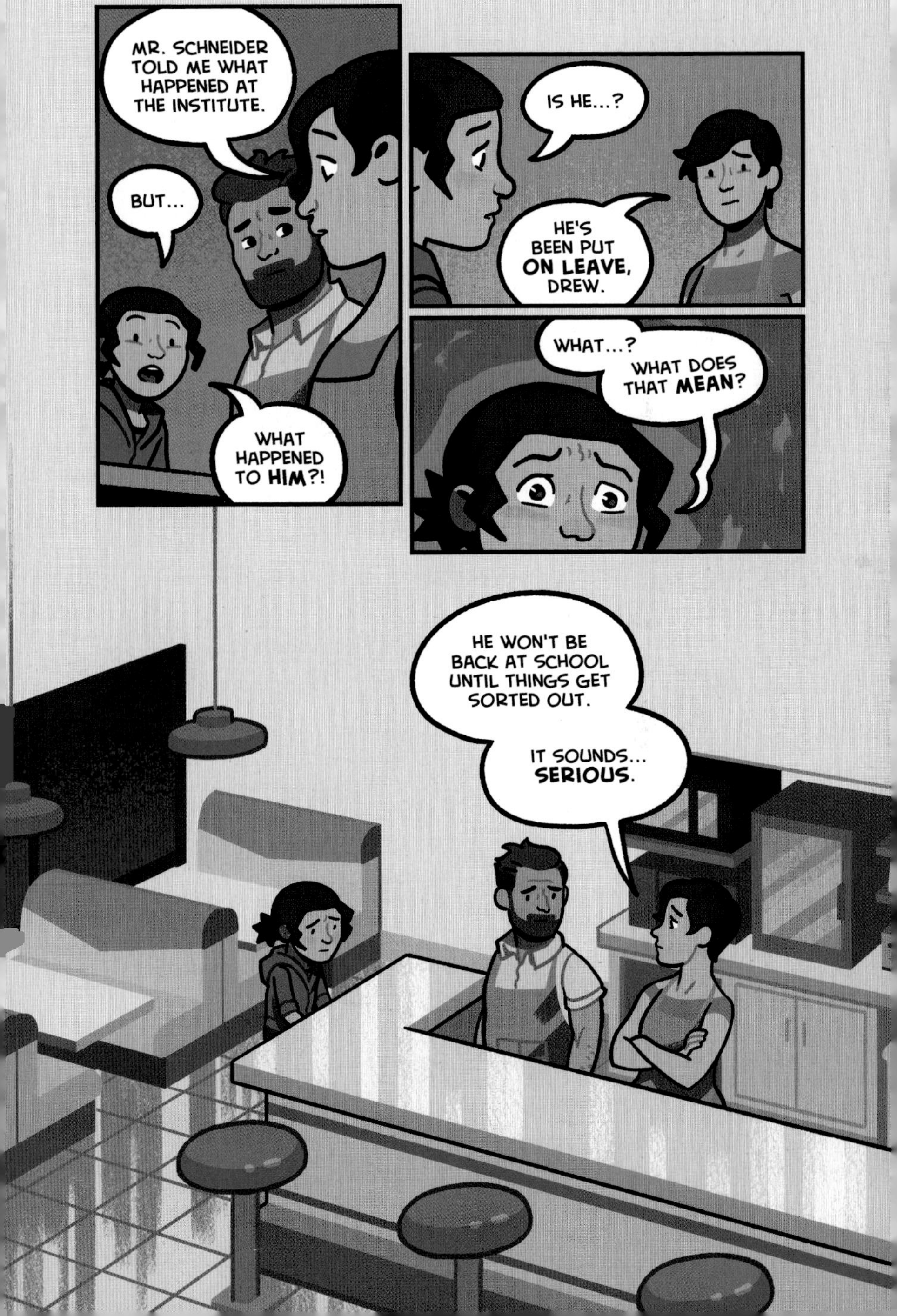
MR. SCHNEIDER TOLD ME WHAT HAPPENED AT THE INSTITUTE.
BUT...
WHAT HAPPENED TO **HIM**?!
IS HE...?
HE'S BEEN PUT **ON LEAVE**, DREW.
WHAT...?
WHAT DOES THAT **MEAN**?
HE WON'T BE BACK AT SCHOOL UNTIL THINGS GET SORTED OUT.
IT SOUNDS... **SERIOUS**.

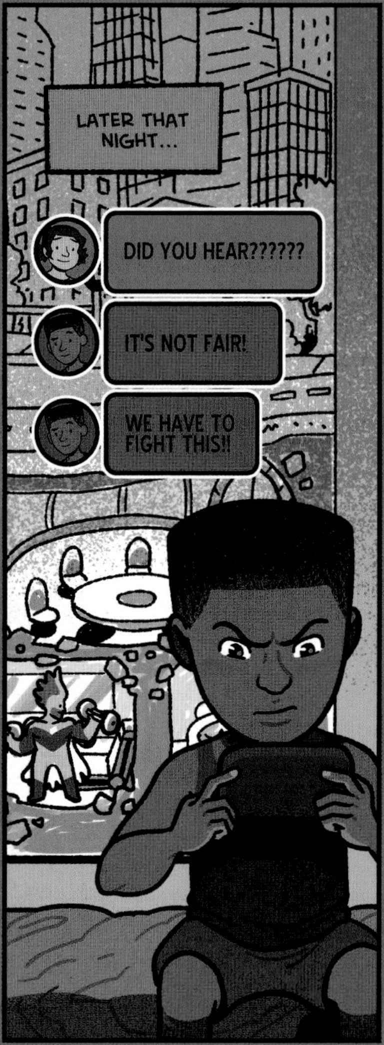
LATER THAT NIGHT...
DID YOU HEAR??????
IT'S NOT FAIR!
WE HAVE TO FIGHT THIS!!

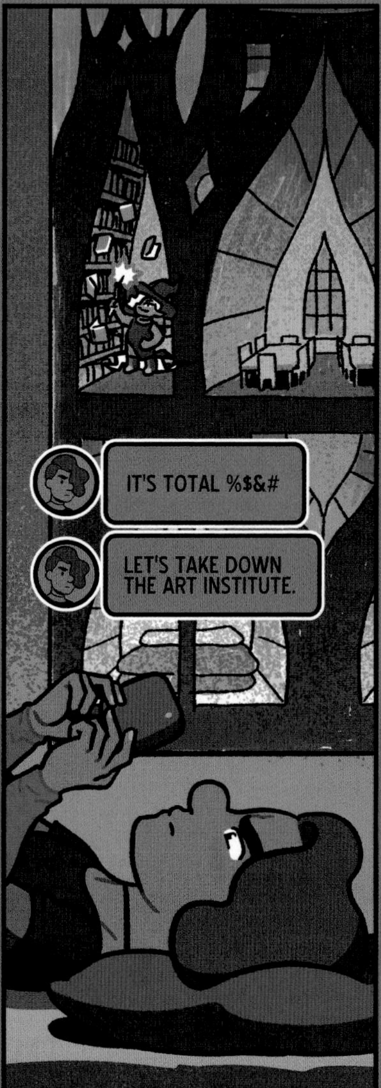
IT'S TOTAL %$&#
LET'S TAKE DOWN THE ART INSTITUTE.

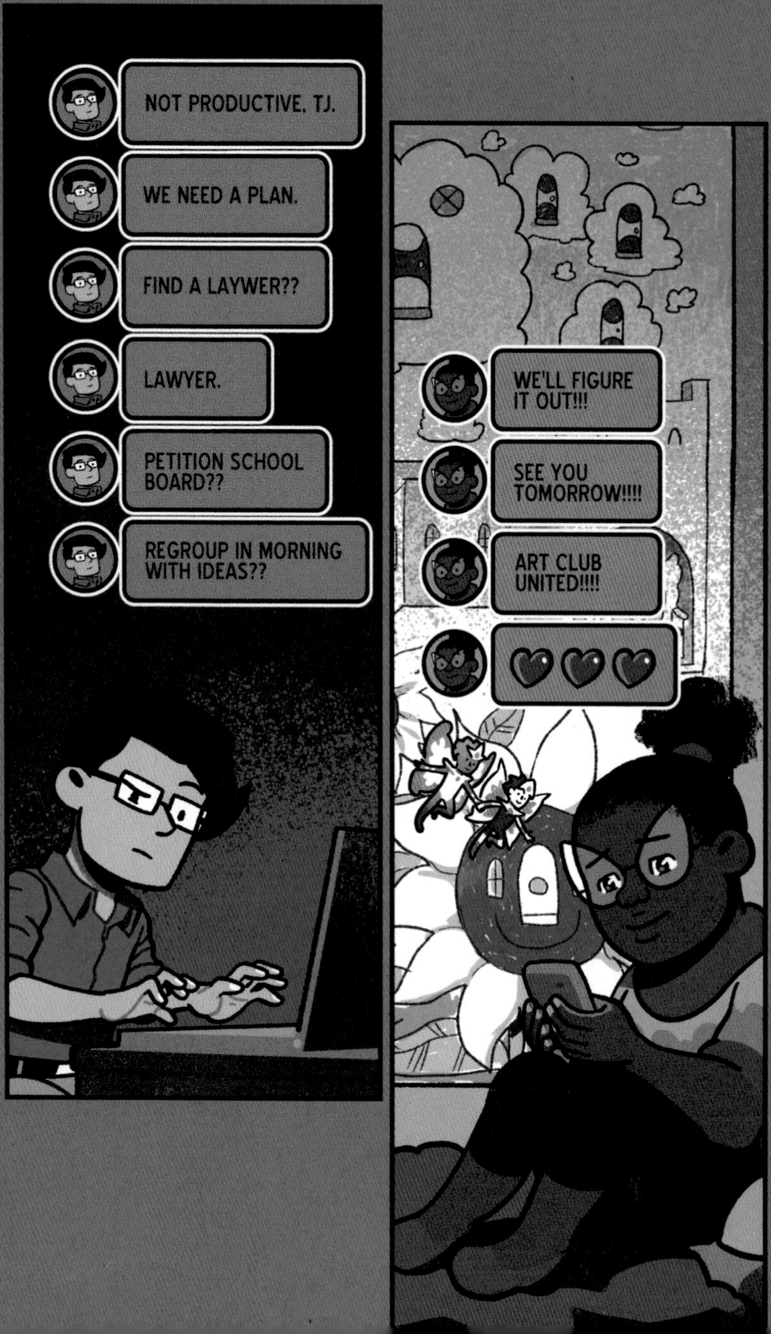
NOT PRODUCTIVE, TJ.
WE NEED A PLAN.
FIND A LAYWER??
LAWYER.
PETITION SCHOOL BOARD??
REGROUP IN MORNING WITH IDEAS??
WE'LL FIGURE IT OUT!!!
SEE YOU TOMORROW!!!!
ART CLUB UNITED!!!!

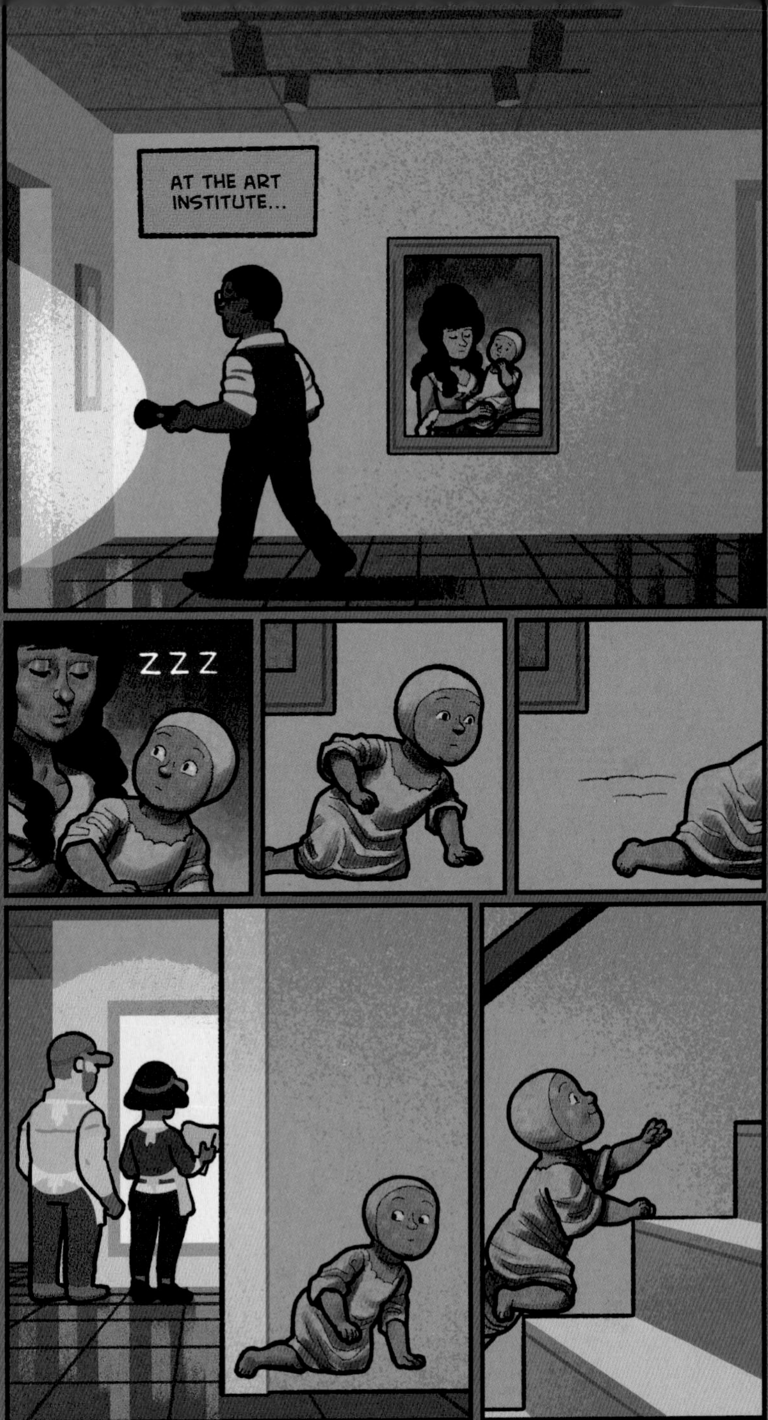
AT THE ART INSTITUTE...
ZZZ

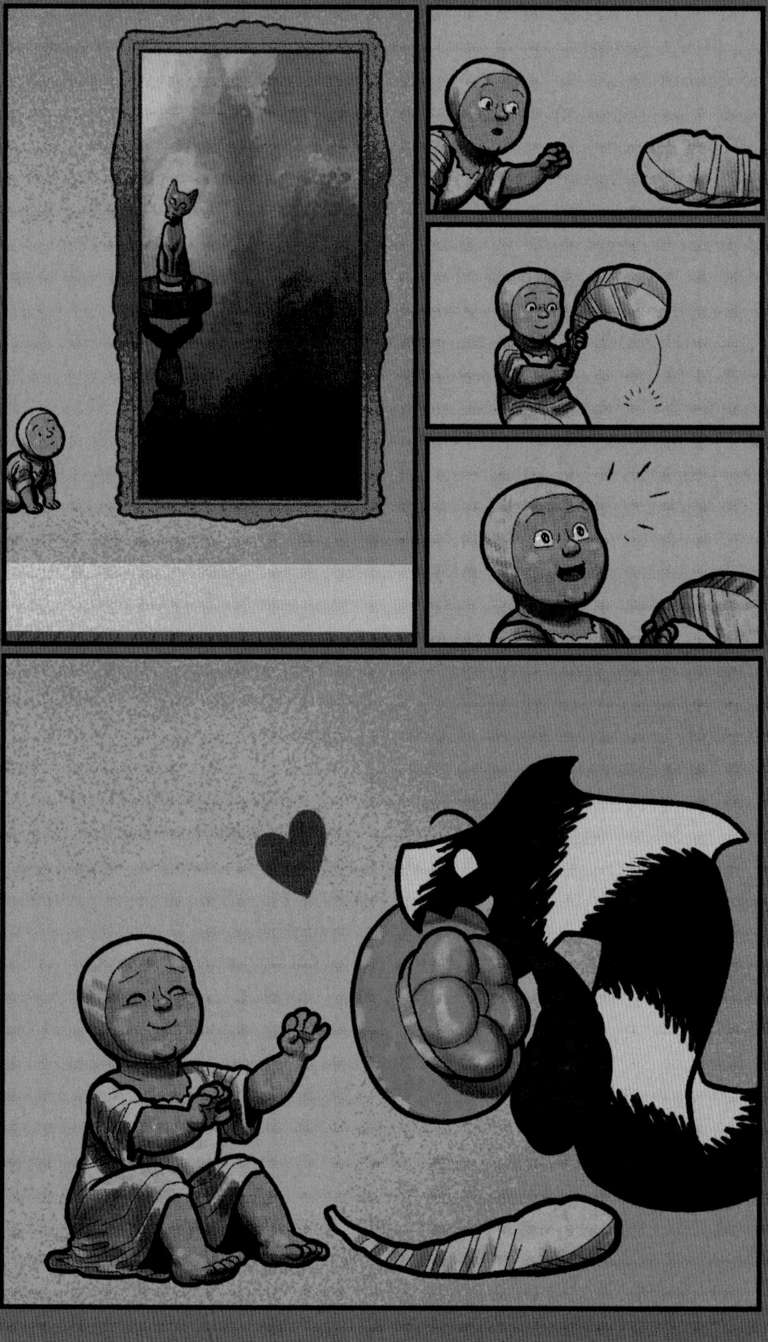

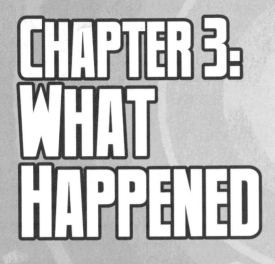

CHAPTER 3:
WHAT
HAPPENED

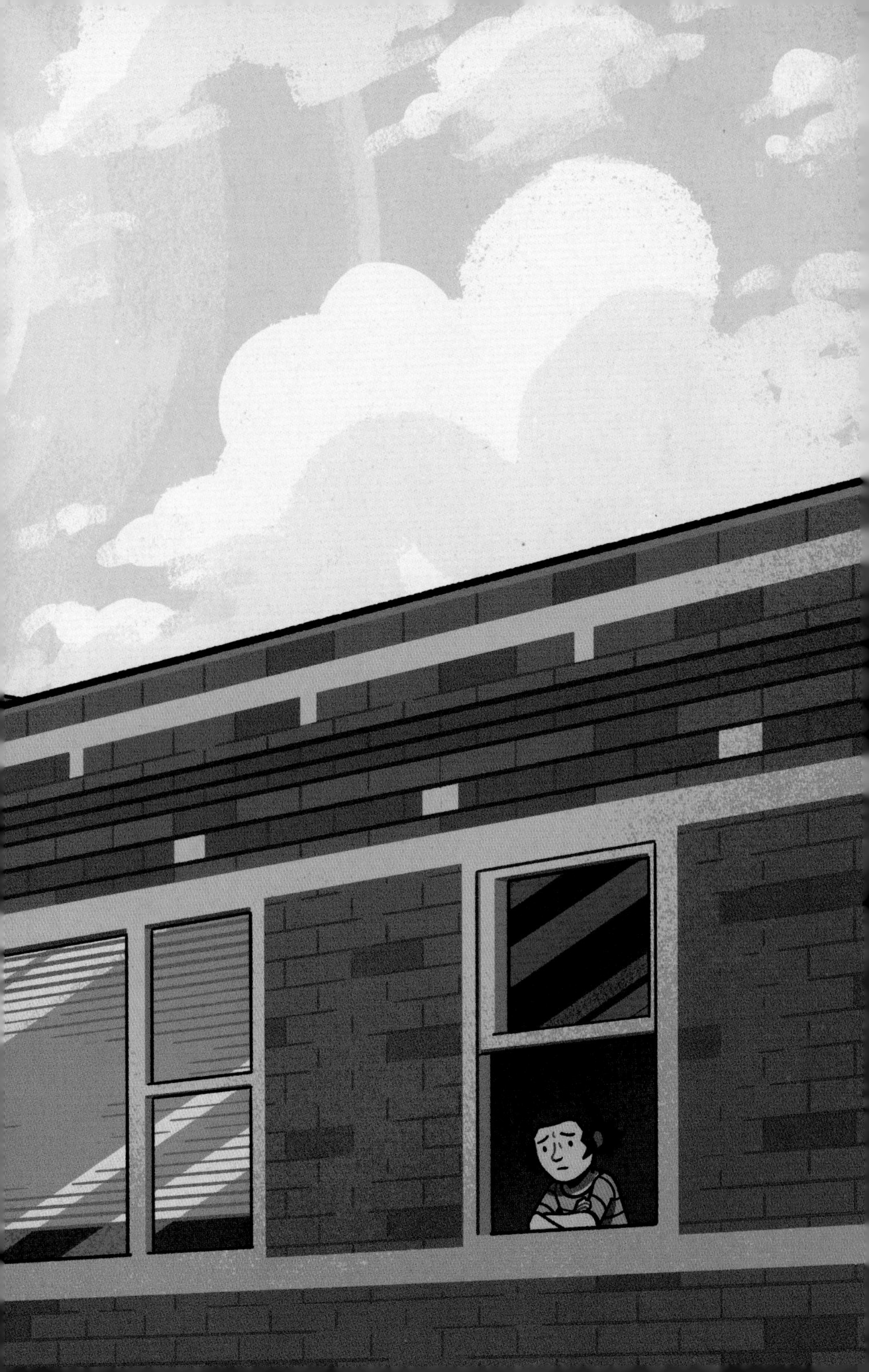

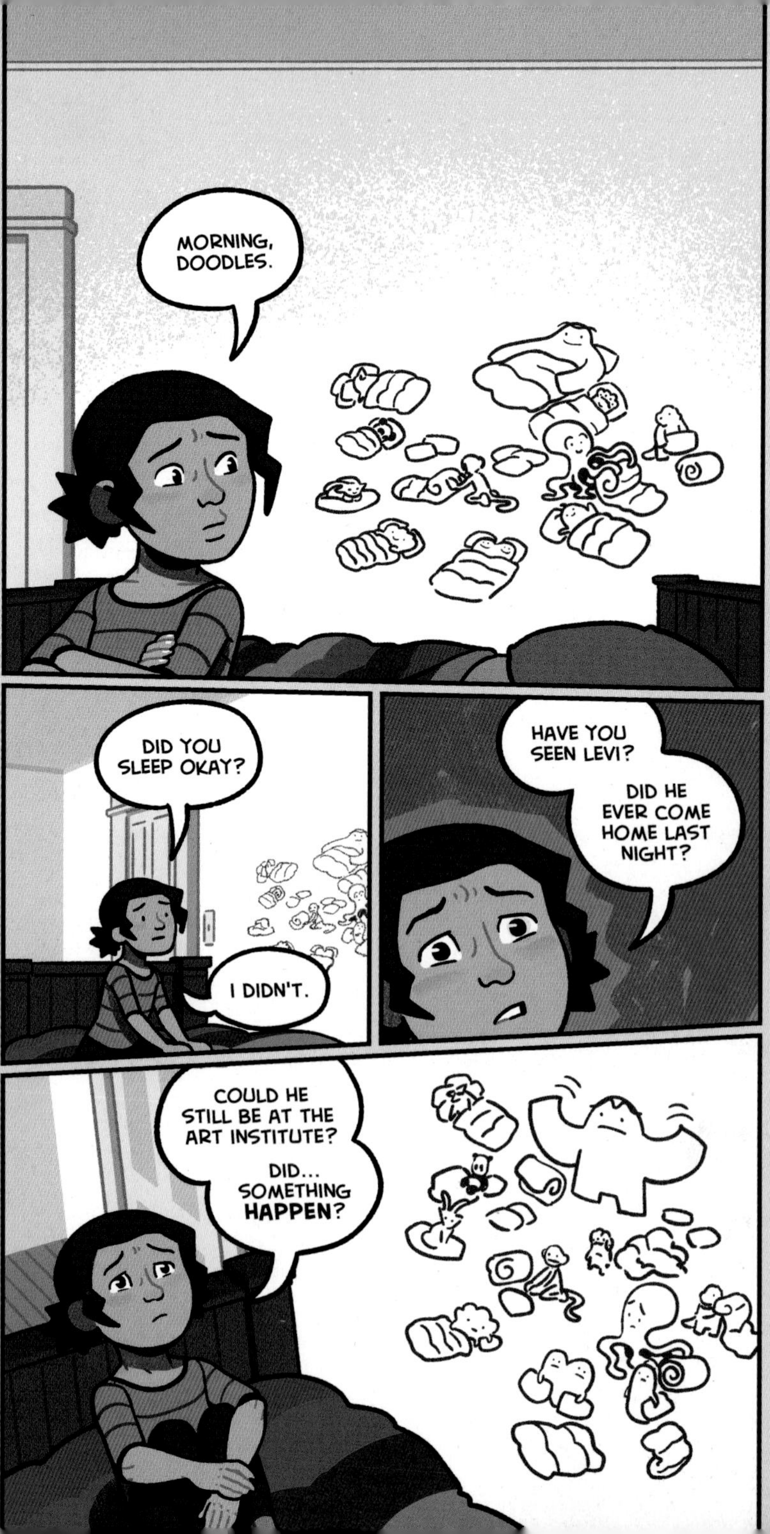
MORNING, DOODLES.
DID YOU SLEEP OKAY?
I DIDN'T.
HAVE YOU SEEN LEVI?
DID HE EVER COME HOME LAST NIGHT?
COULD HE STILL BE AT THE ART INSTITUTE?
DID... SOMETHING **HAPPEN**?

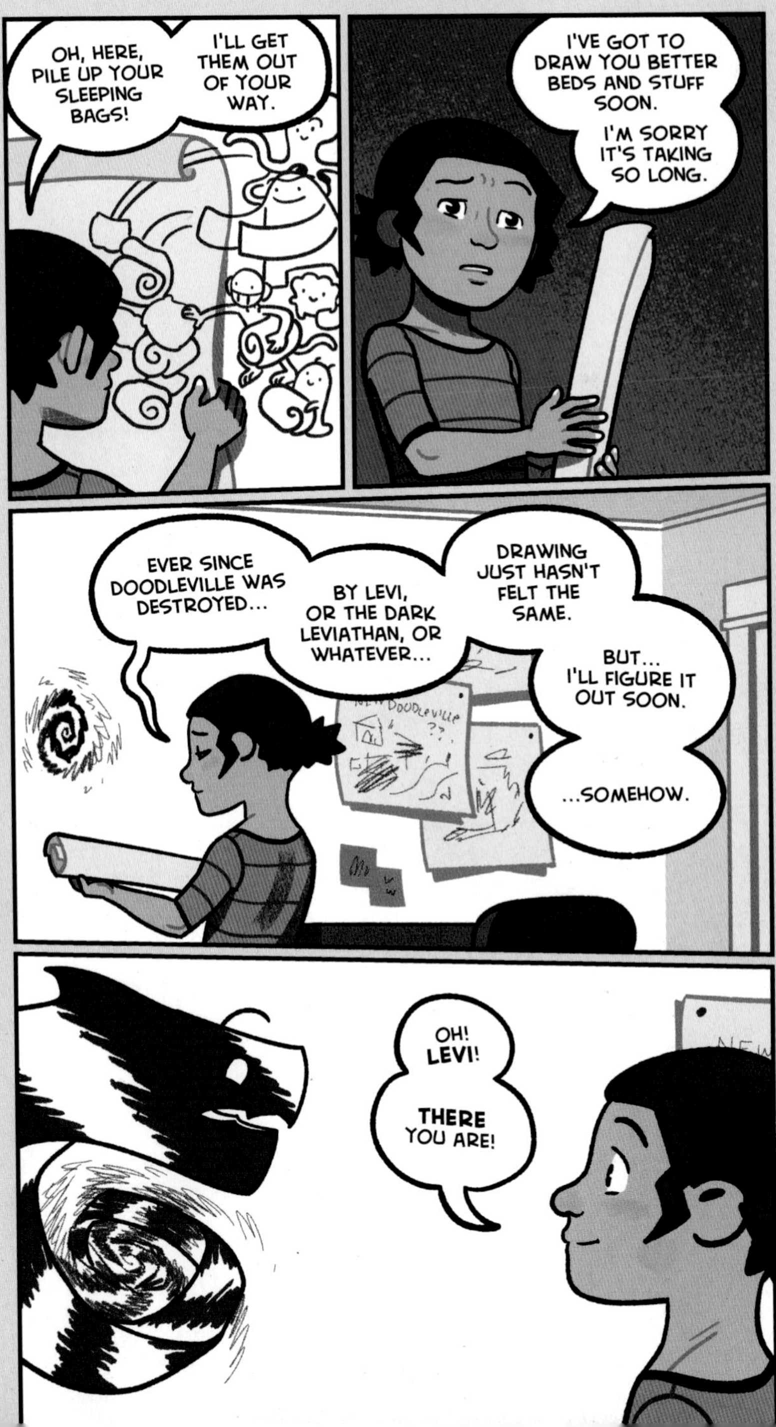
OH, HERE, PILE UP YOUR SLEEPING BAGS!
I'LL GET THEM OUT OF YOUR WAY.
I'VE GOT TO DRAW YOU BETTER BEDS AND STUFF SOON.
I'M SORRY IT'S TAKING SO LONG.
EVER SINCE DOODLEVILLE WAS DESTROYED...
BY LEVI, OR THE DARK LEVIATHAN, OR WHATEVER...
DRAWING JUST HASN'T FELT THE SAME.
BUT... I'LL FIGURE IT OUT SOON.
...SOMEHOW.
OH! LEVI!
THERE YOU ARE!

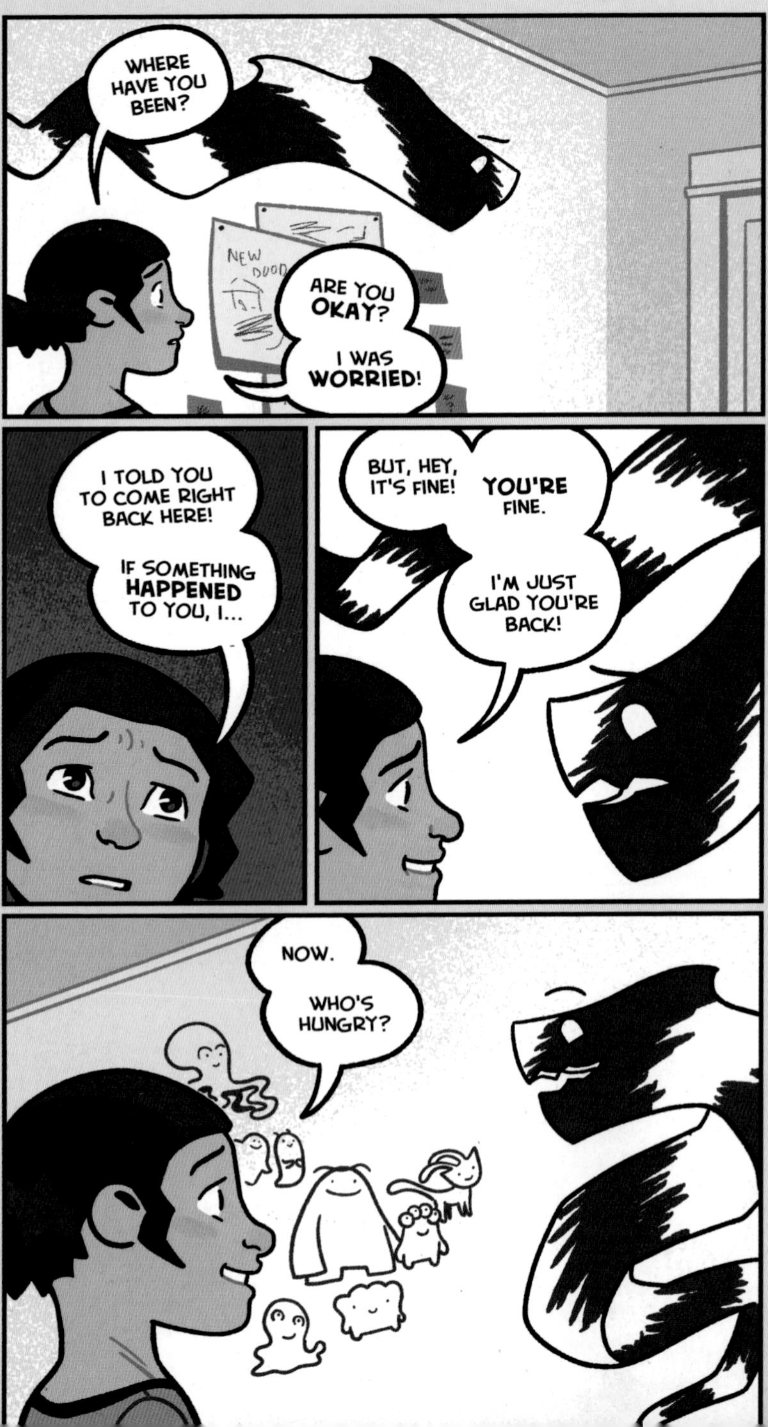
WHERE HAVE YOU BEEN?
ARE YOU OKAY?
I WAS WORRIED!
I TOLD YOU TO COME RIGHT BACK HERE!
IF SOMETHING HAPPENED TO YOU, I...
BUT, HEY, IT'S FINE!
YOU'RE FINE.
I'M JUST GLAD YOU'RE BACK!
NOW.
WHO'S HUNGRY?

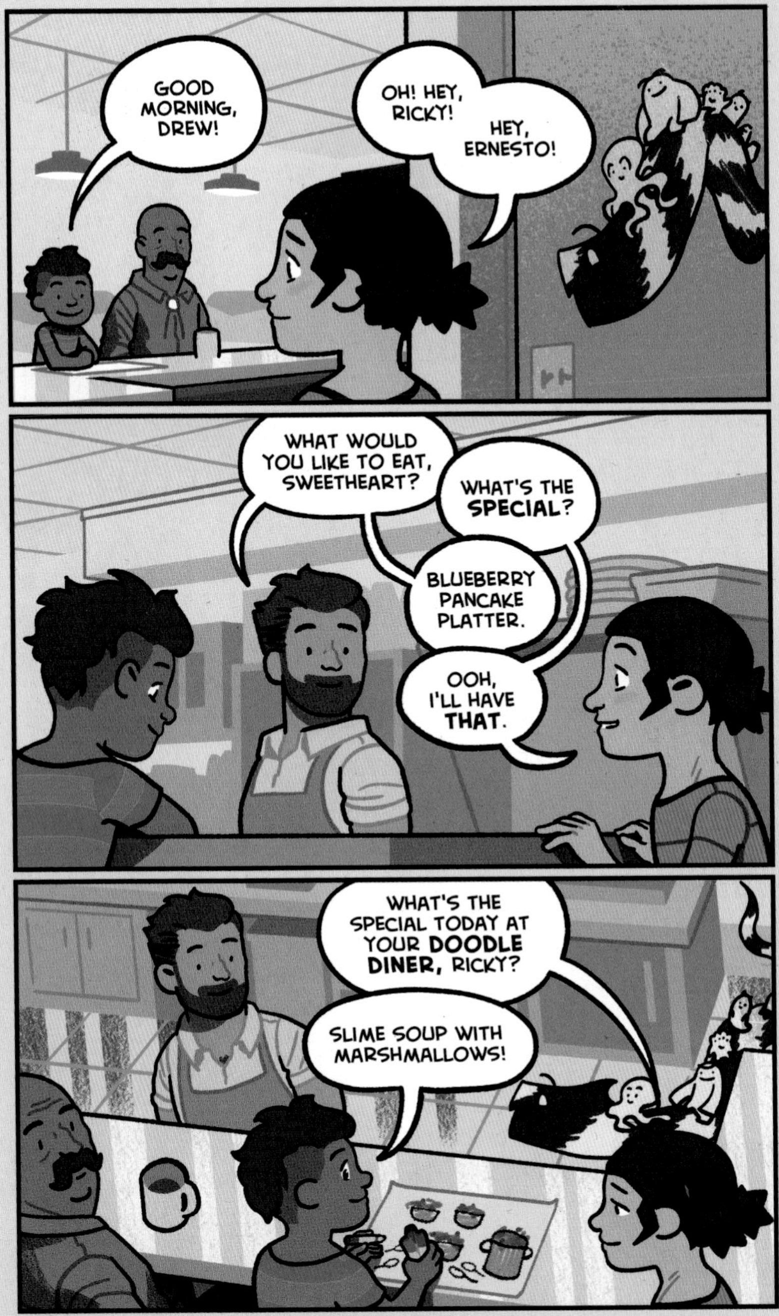
GOOD MORNING, DREW!
OH! HEY, RICKY!
HEY, ERNESTO!
WHAT WOULD YOU LIKE TO EAT, SWEETHEART?
WHAT'S THE SPECIAL?
BLUEBERRY PANCAKE PLATTER.
OOH, I'LL HAVE THAT.
WHAT'S THE SPECIAL TODAY AT YOUR DOODLE DINER, RICKY?
SLIME SOUP WITH MARSHMALLOWS!

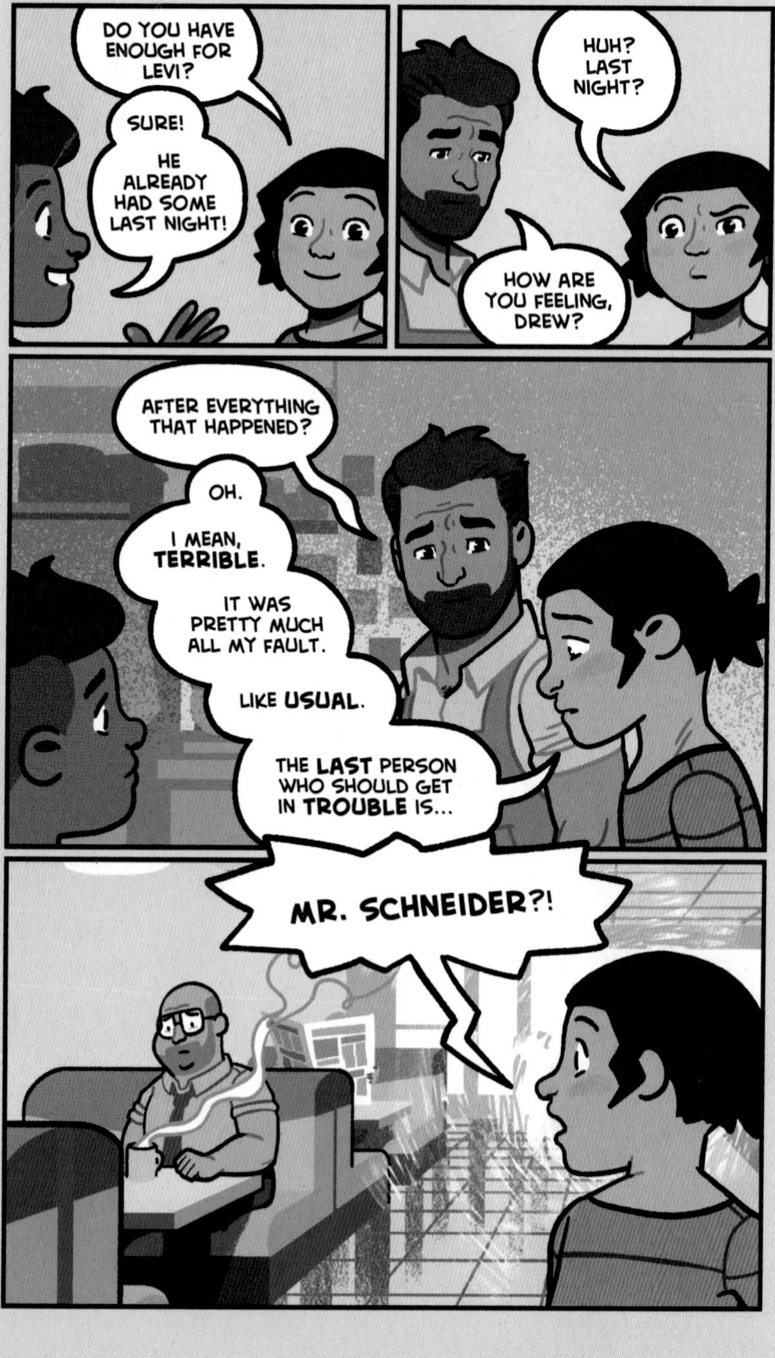
DO YOU HAVE ENOUGH FOR LEVI?
SURE!
HE ALREADY HAD SOME LAST NIGHT!
HUH? LAST NIGHT?
HOW ARE YOU FEELING, DREW?
AFTER EVERYTHING THAT HAPPENED?
OH.
I MEAN, TERRIBLE.
IT WAS PRETTY MUCH ALL MY FAULT.
LIKE USUAL.
THE LAST PERSON WHO SHOULD GET IN TROUBLE IS...
MR. SCHNEIDER?!

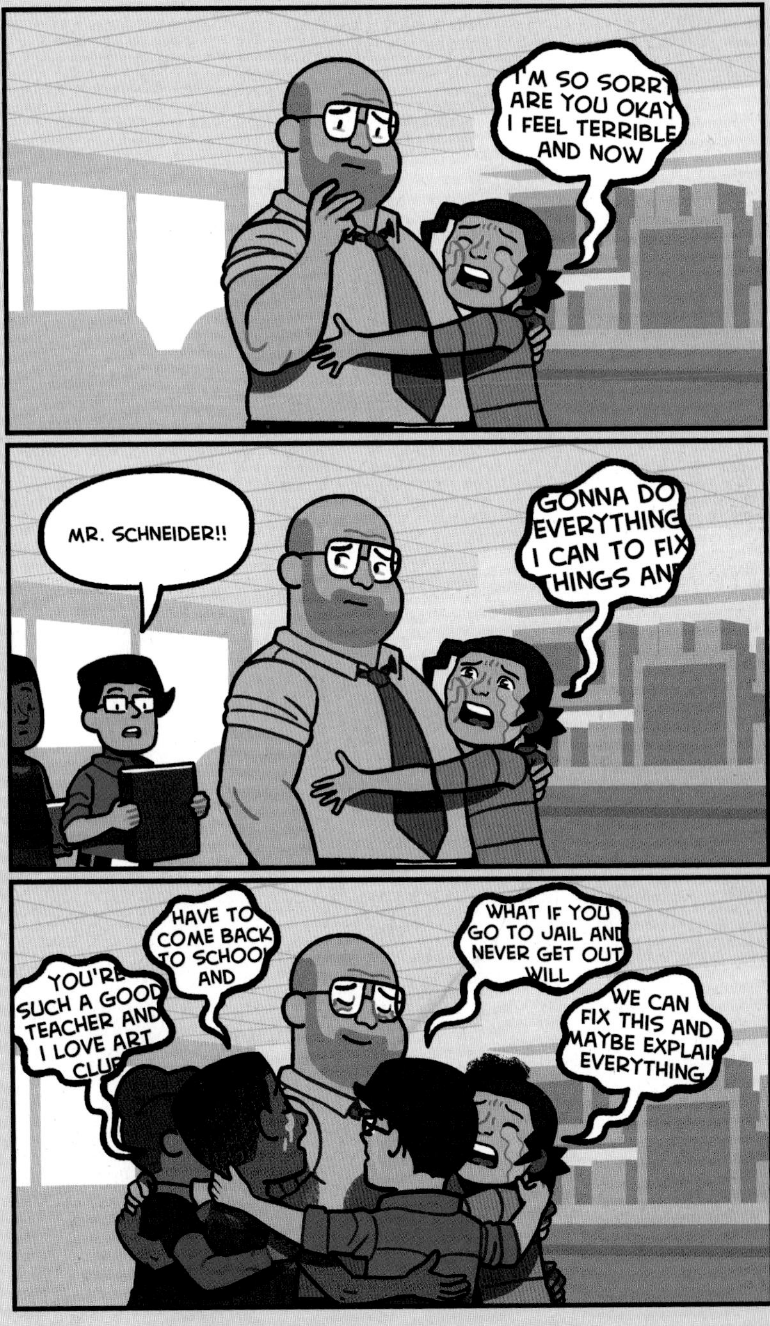
I'M SO SORRY ARE YOU OKAY I FEEL TERRIBLE AND NOW
MR. SCHNEIDER!!
GONNA DO EVERYTHING I CAN TO FIX THINGS AN
YOU'RE SUCH A GOOD TEACHER AND I LOVE ART CLUB
HAVE TO COME BACK TO SCHOOL AND
WHAT IF YOU GO TO JAIL AND NEVER GET OUT WILL
WE CAN FIX THIS AND MAYBE EXPLAIN EVERYTHING

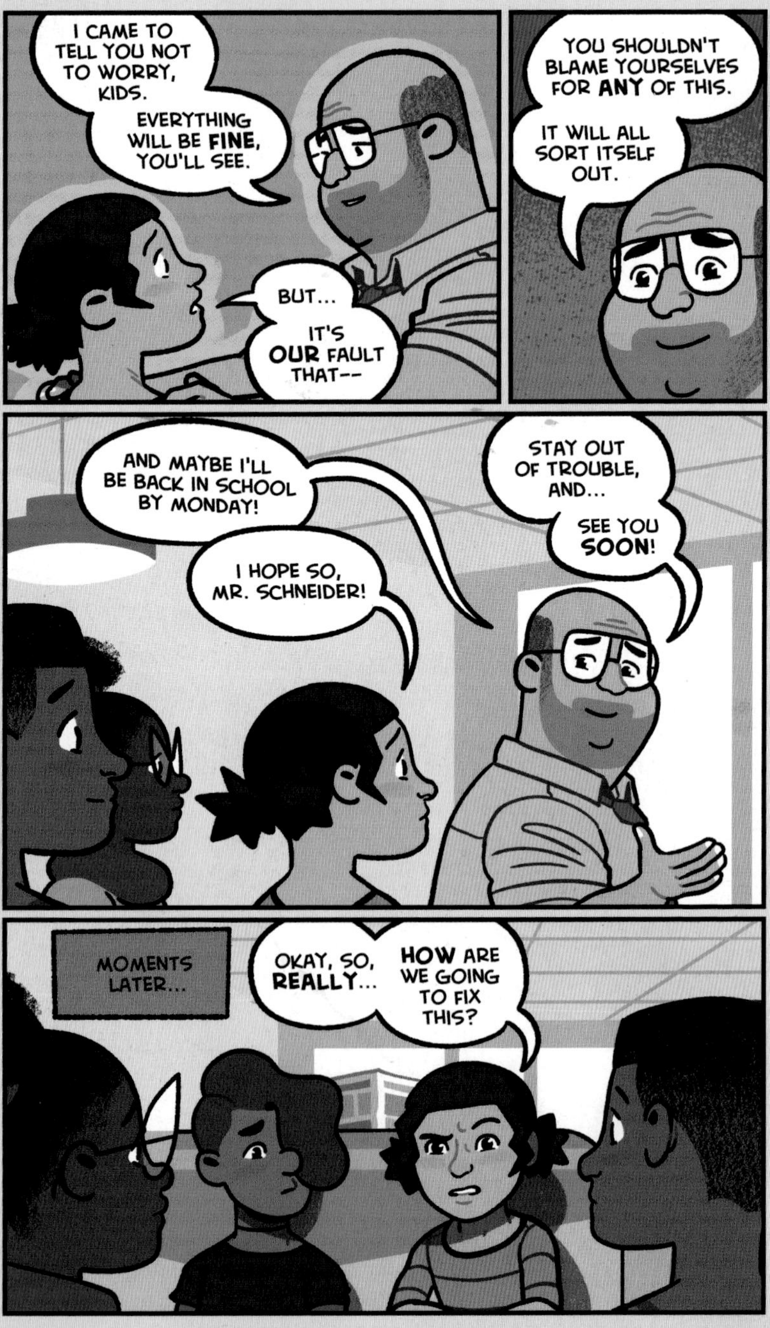
I CAME TO TELL YOU NOT TO WORRY, KIDS.
EVERYTHING WILL BE FINE, YOU'LL SEE.
BUT...
IT'S OUR FAULT THAT--
YOU SHOULDN'T BLAME YOURSELVES FOR ANY OF THIS.
IT WILL ALL SORT ITSELF OUT.
AND MAYBE I'LL BE BACK IN SCHOOL BY MONDAY!
I HOPE SO, MR. SCHNEIDER!
STAY OUT OF TROUBLE, AND...
SEE YOU SOON!
MOMENTS LATER...
OKAY, SO, REALLY...
HOW ARE WE GOING TO FIX THIS?

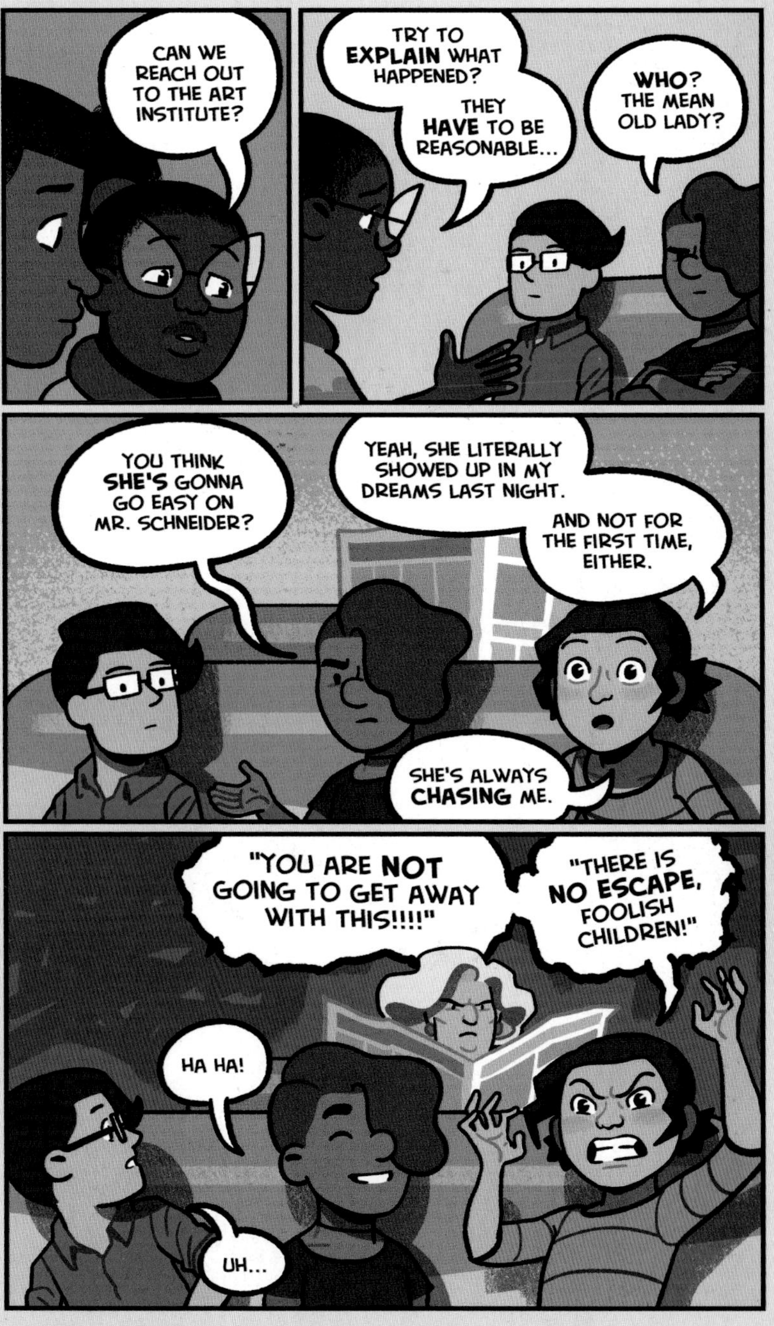
CAN WE REACH OUT TO THE ART INSTITUTE?
TRY TO EXPLAIN WHAT HAPPENED?
THEY HAVE TO BE REASONABLE...
WHO? THE MEAN OLD LADY?
YOU THINK SHE'S GONNA GO EASY ON MR. SCHNEIDER?
YEAH, SHE LITERALLY SHOWED UP IN MY DREAMS LAST NIGHT.
AND NOT FOR THE FIRST TIME, EITHER.
SHE'S ALWAYS CHASING ME.
"YOU ARE NOT GOING TO GET AWAY WITH THIS!!!!"
"THERE IS NO ESCAPE, FOOLISH CHILDREN!"
HA HA!
UH...

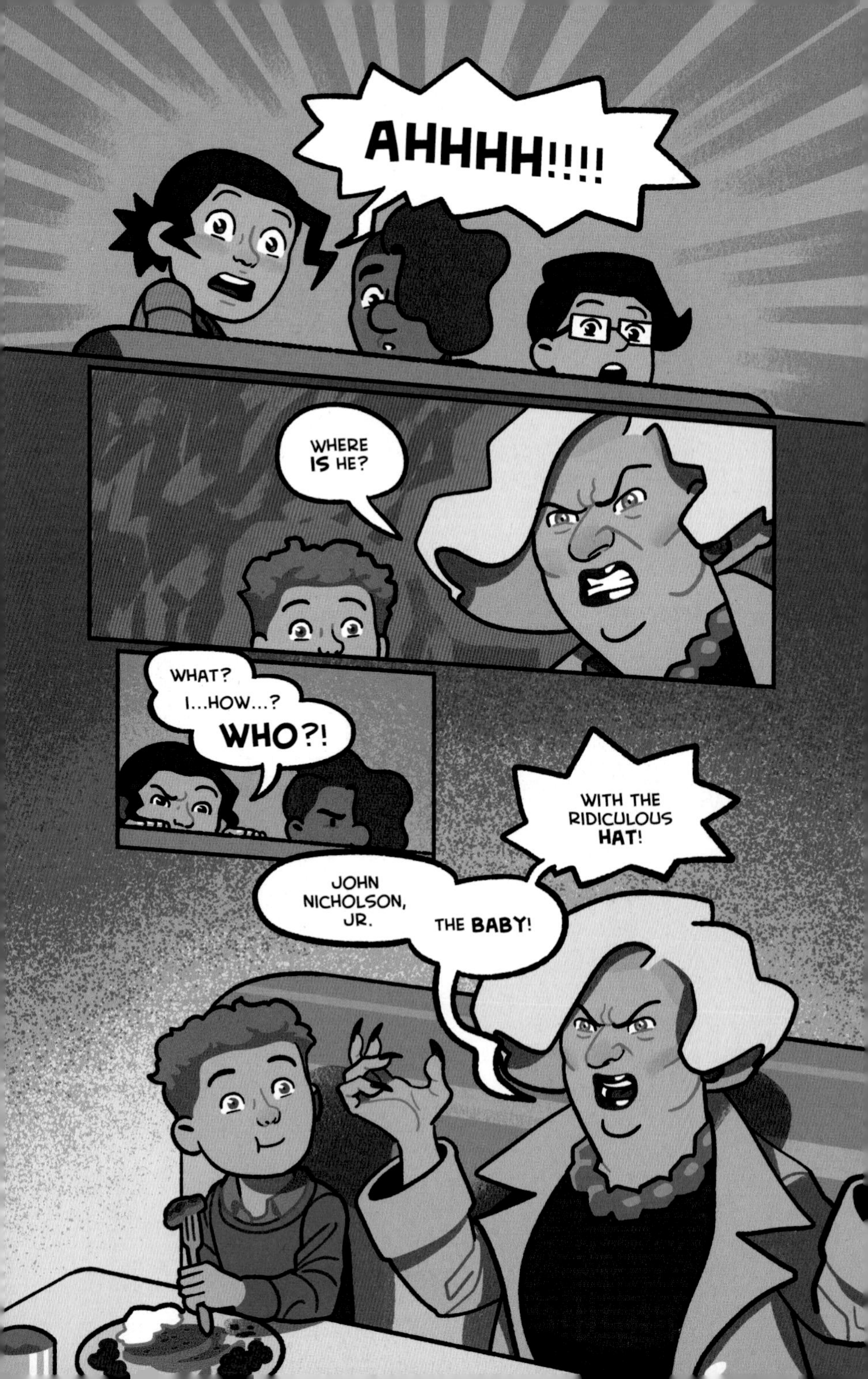
AHHHH!!!!
WHERE IS HE?
WHAT?
I...HOW...?
WHO?!
WITH THE RIDICULOUS HAT!
JOHN NICHOLSON, JR.
THE BABY!

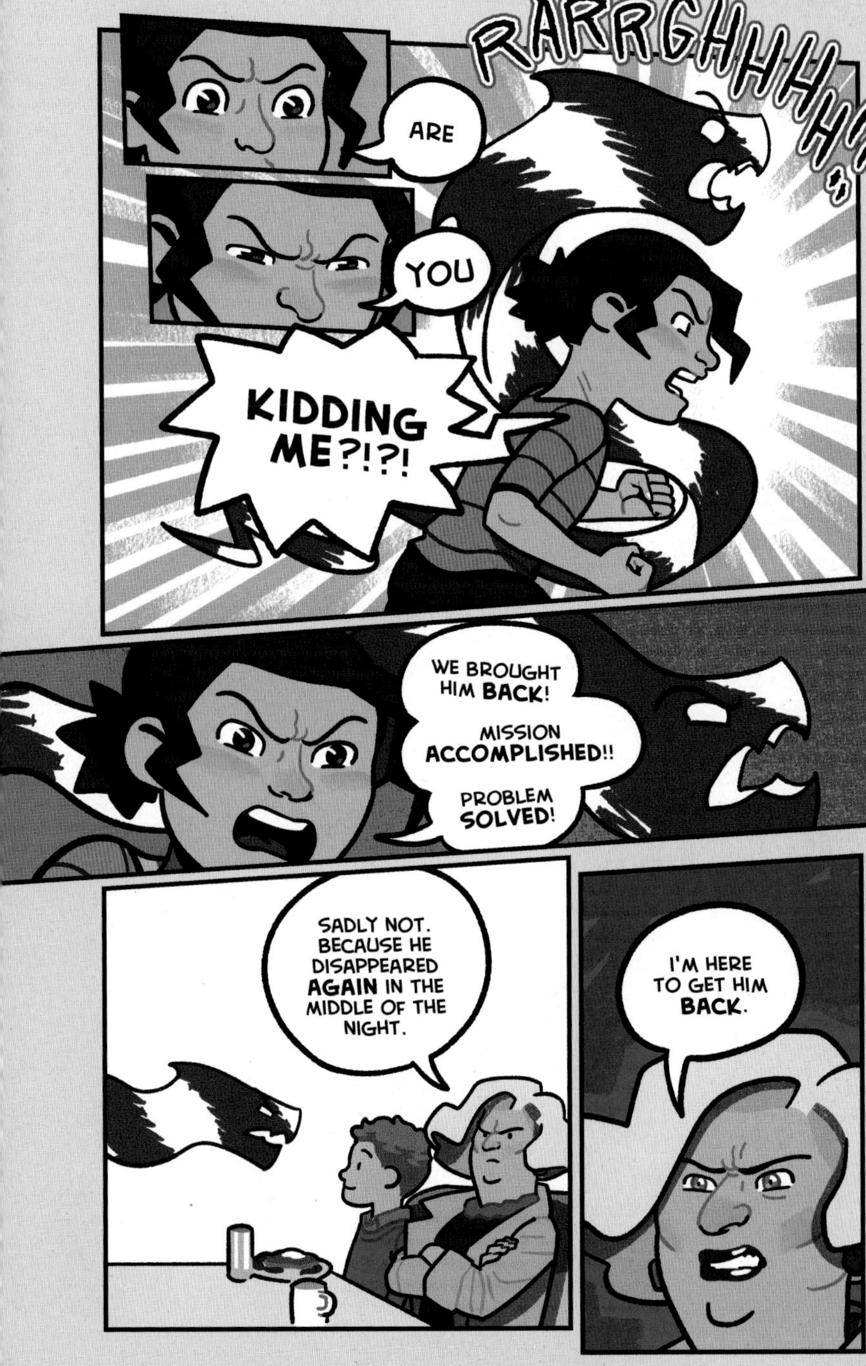
RARRGHHHHH!!
ARE
YOU
KIDDING ME?!?!
WE BROUGHT HIM BACK!
MISSION ACCOMPLISHED!!
PROBLEM SOLVED!
SADLY NOT. BECAUSE HE DISAPPEARED AGAIN IN THE MIDDLE OF THE NIGHT.
I'M HERE TO GET HIM BACK.

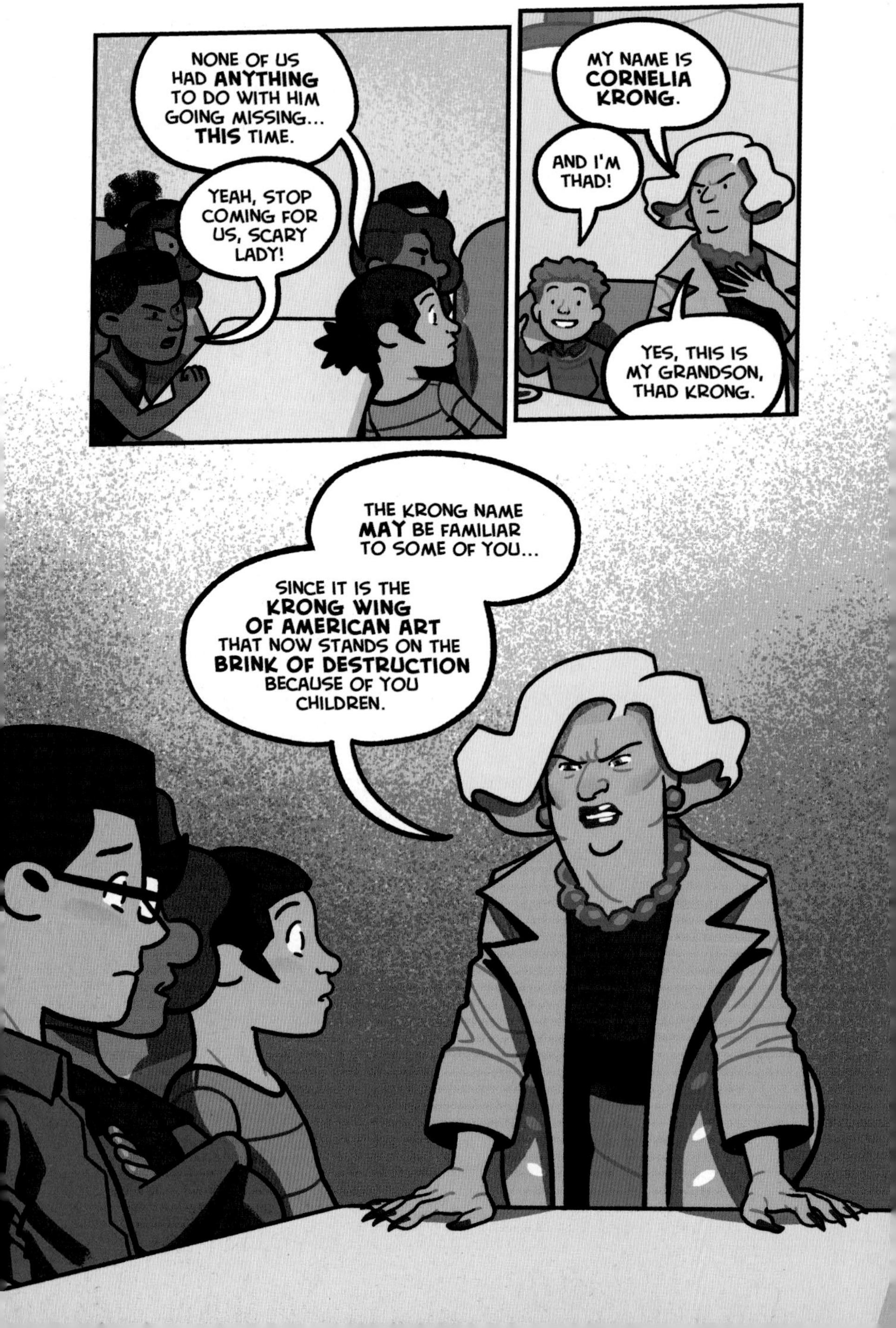
NONE OF US HAD ANYTHING TO DO WITH HIM GOING MISSING... THIS TIME.
YEAH, STOP COMING FOR US, SCARY LADY!
MY NAME IS CORNELIA KRONG.
AND I'M THAD!
YES, THIS IS MY GRANDSON, THAD KRONG.
THE KRONG NAME MAY BE FAMILIAR TO SOME OF YOU...
SINCE IT IS THE KRONG WING OF AMERICAN ART THAT NOW STANDS ON THE BRINK OF DESTRUCTION BECAUSE OF YOU CHILDREN.

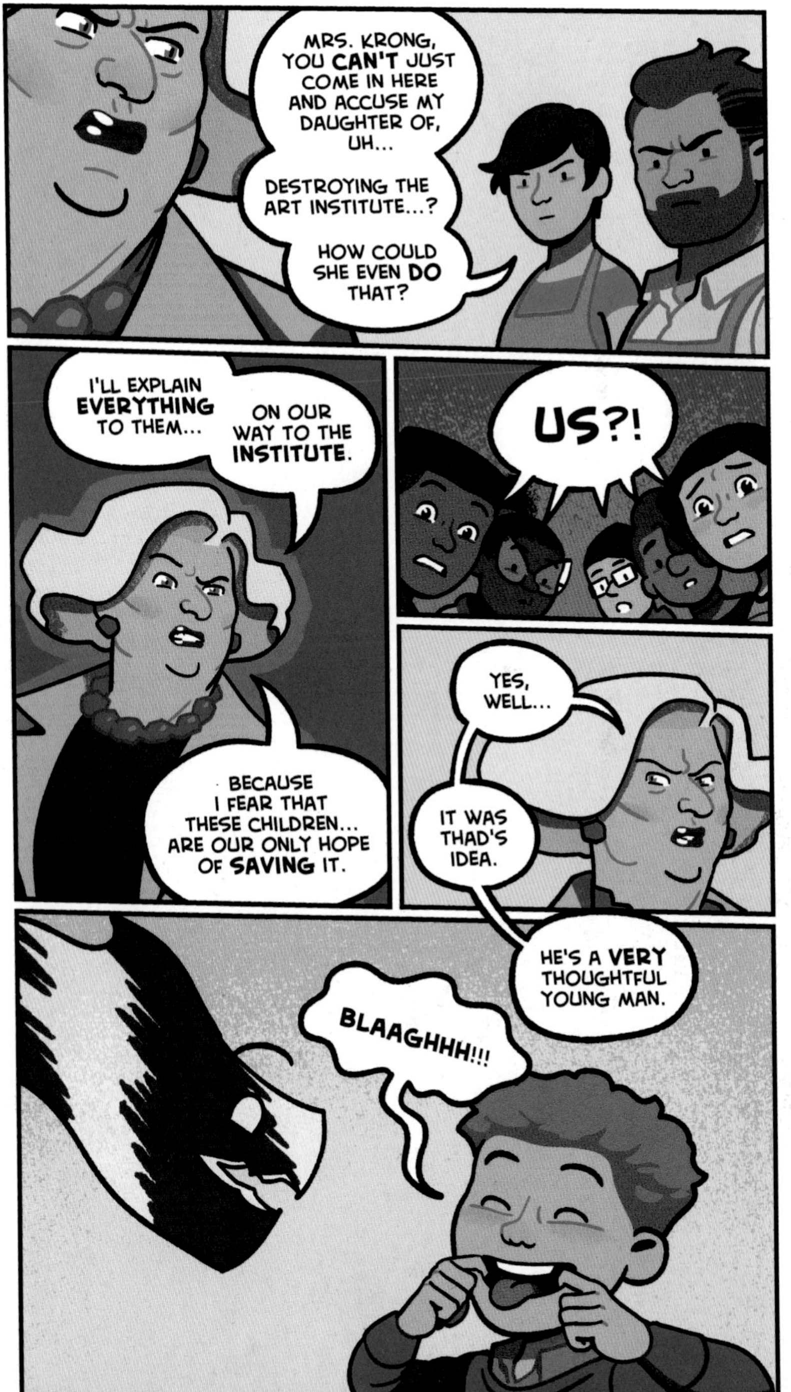
MRS. KRONG, YOU CAN'T JUST COME IN HERE AND ACCUSE MY DAUGHTER OF, UH...
DESTROYING THE ART INSTITUTE...?
HOW COULD SHE EVEN DO THAT?
I'LL EXPLAIN EVERYTHING TO THEM...
ON OUR WAY TO THE INSTITUTE.
BECAUSE I FEAR THAT THESE CHILDREN... ARE OUR ONLY HOPE OF SAVING IT.
US?!
YES, WELL...
IT WAS THAD'S IDEA.
HE'S A VERY THOUGHTFUL YOUNG MAN.
BLAAGHHH!!!

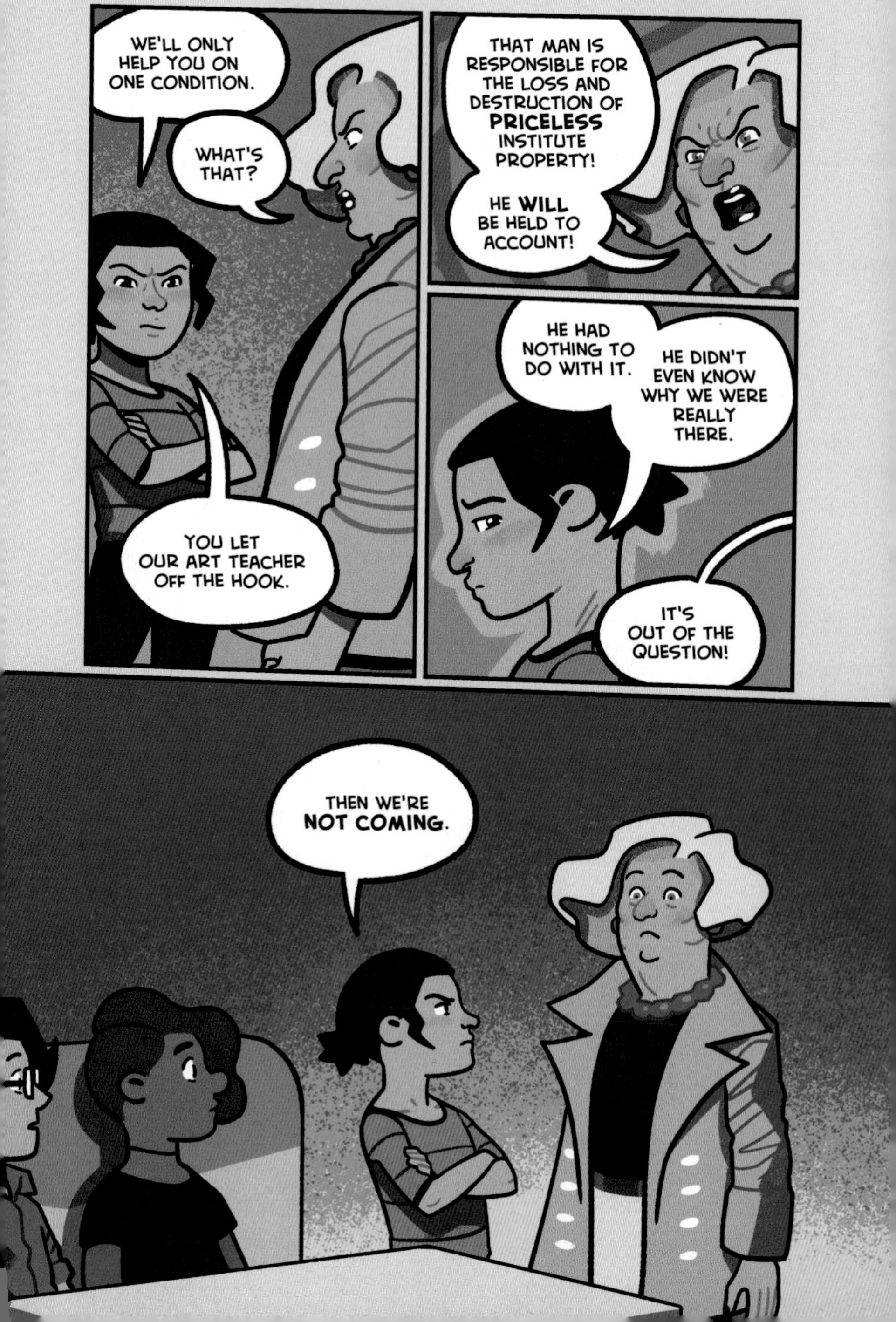

WE'LL ONLY HELP YOU ON ONE CONDITION.
WHAT'S THAT?
YOU LET OUR ART TEACHER OFF THE HOOK.
THAT MAN IS RESPONSIBLE FOR THE LOSS AND DESTRUCTION OF PRICELESS INSTITUTE PROPERTY!
HE WILL BE HELD TO ACCOUNT!
HE HAD NOTHING TO DO WITH IT.
HE DIDN'T EVEN KNOW WHY WE WERE REALLY THERE.
IT'S OUT OF THE QUESTION!
THEN WE'RE NOT COMING.

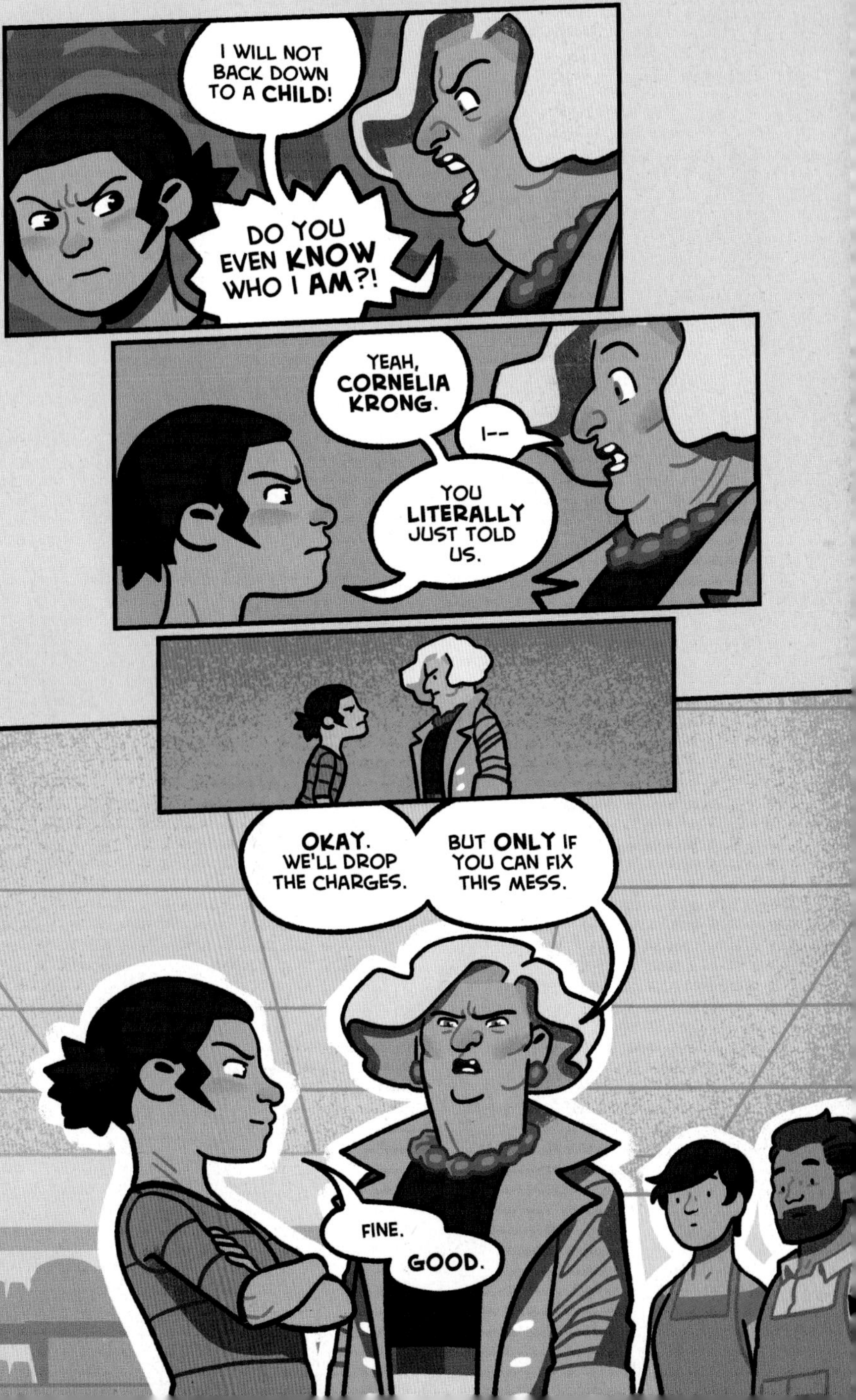
I WILL NOT BACK DOWN TO A CHILD!
DO YOU EVEN KNOW WHO I AM?!
YEAH, CORNELIA KRONG.
I--
YOU LITERALLY JUST TOLD US.
OKAY. WE'LL DROP THE CHARGES.
BUT ONLY IF YOU CAN FIX THIS MESS.
FINE.
GOOD.

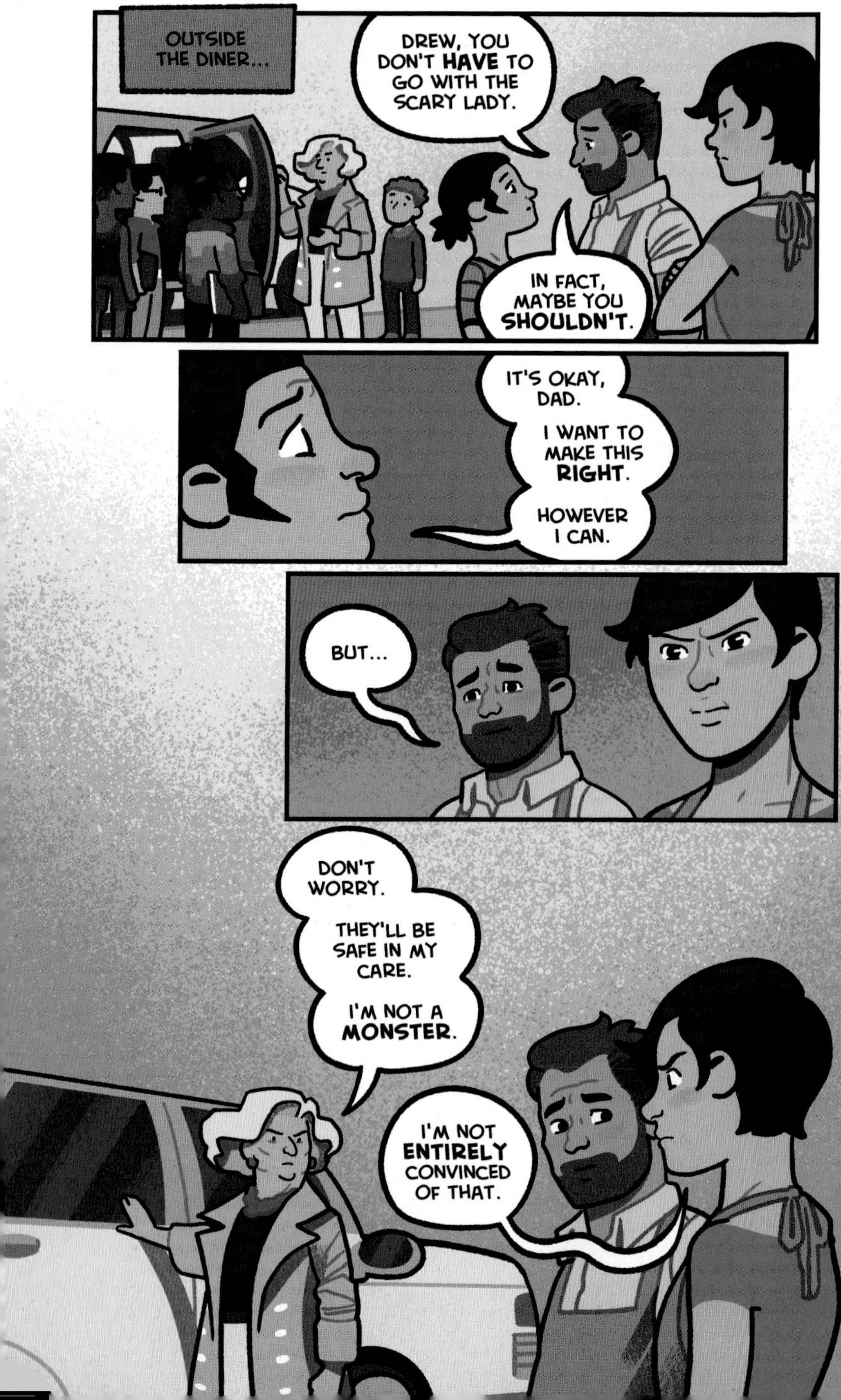
OUTSIDE THE DINER...
DREW, YOU DON'T HAVE TO GO WITH THE SCARY LADY.
IN FACT, MAYBE YOU SHOULDN'T.
IT'S OKAY, DAD.
I WANT TO MAKE THIS RIGHT.
HOWEVER I CAN.
BUT...
DON'T WORRY.
THEY'LL BE SAFE IN MY CARE.
I'M NOT A MONSTER.
I'M NOT ENTIRELY CONVINCED OF THAT.

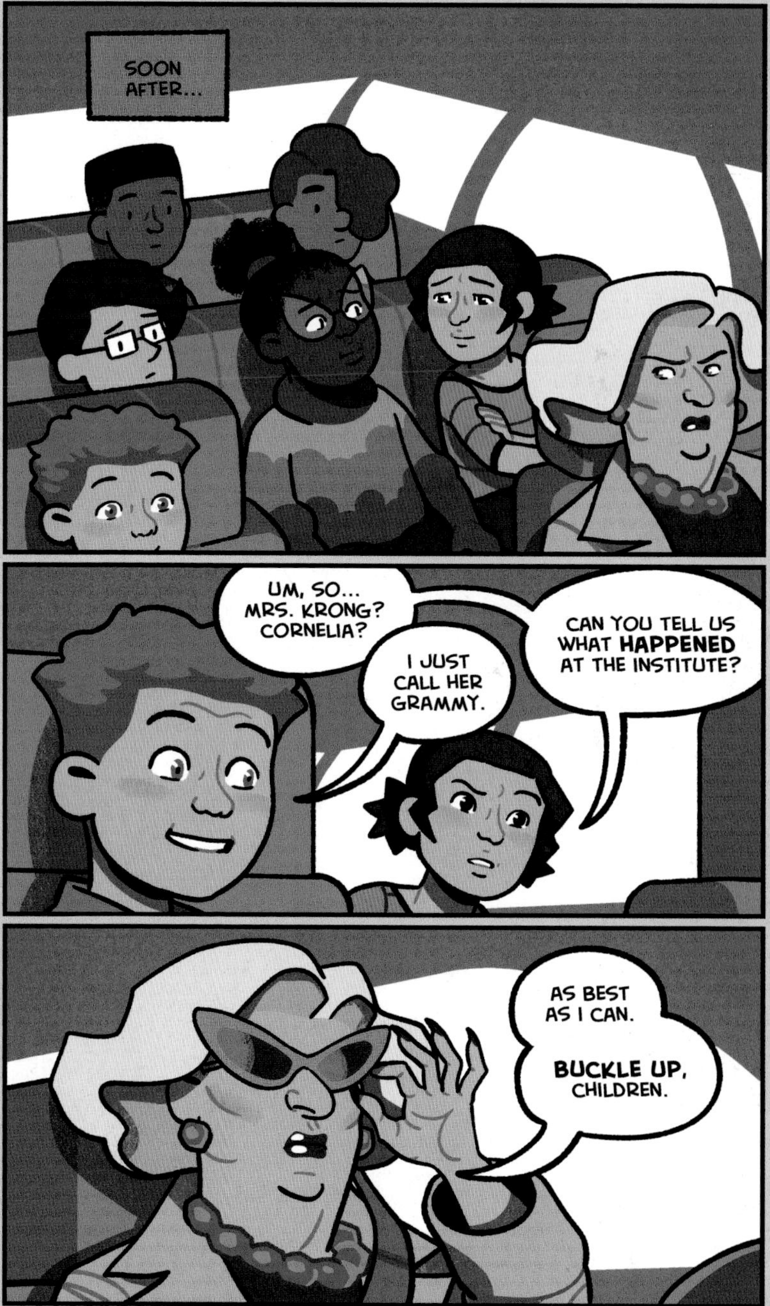
SOON AFTER...
UM, SO... MRS. KRONG? CORNELIA?
I JUST CALL HER GRAMMY.
CAN YOU TELL US WHAT **HAPPENED** AT THE INSTITUTE?
AS BEST AS I CAN.
BUCKLE UP, CHILDREN.

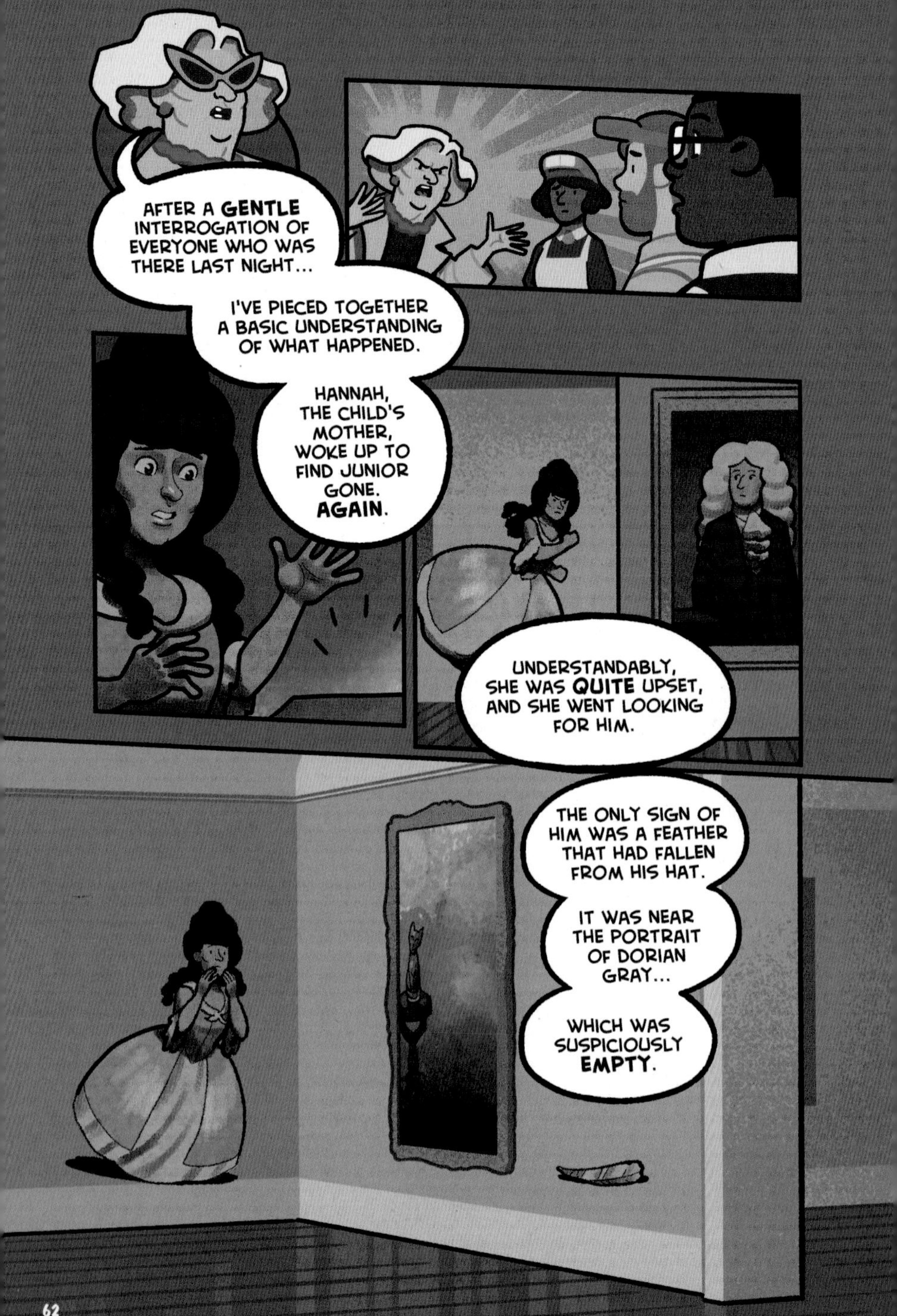
AFTER A GENTLE INTERROGATION OF EVERYONE WHO WAS THERE LAST NIGHT...
I'VE PIECED TOGETHER A BASIC UNDERSTANDING OF WHAT HAPPENED.
HANNAH, THE CHILD'S MOTHER, WOKE UP TO FIND JUNIOR GONE. AGAIN.
UNDERSTANDABLY, SHE WAS QUITE UPSET, AND SHE WENT LOOKING FOR HIM.
THE ONLY SIGN OF HIM WAS A FEATHER THAT HAD FALLEN FROM HIS HAT.
IT WAS NEAR THE PORTRAIT OF DORIAN GRAY...
WHICH WAS SUSPICIOUSLY EMPTY.

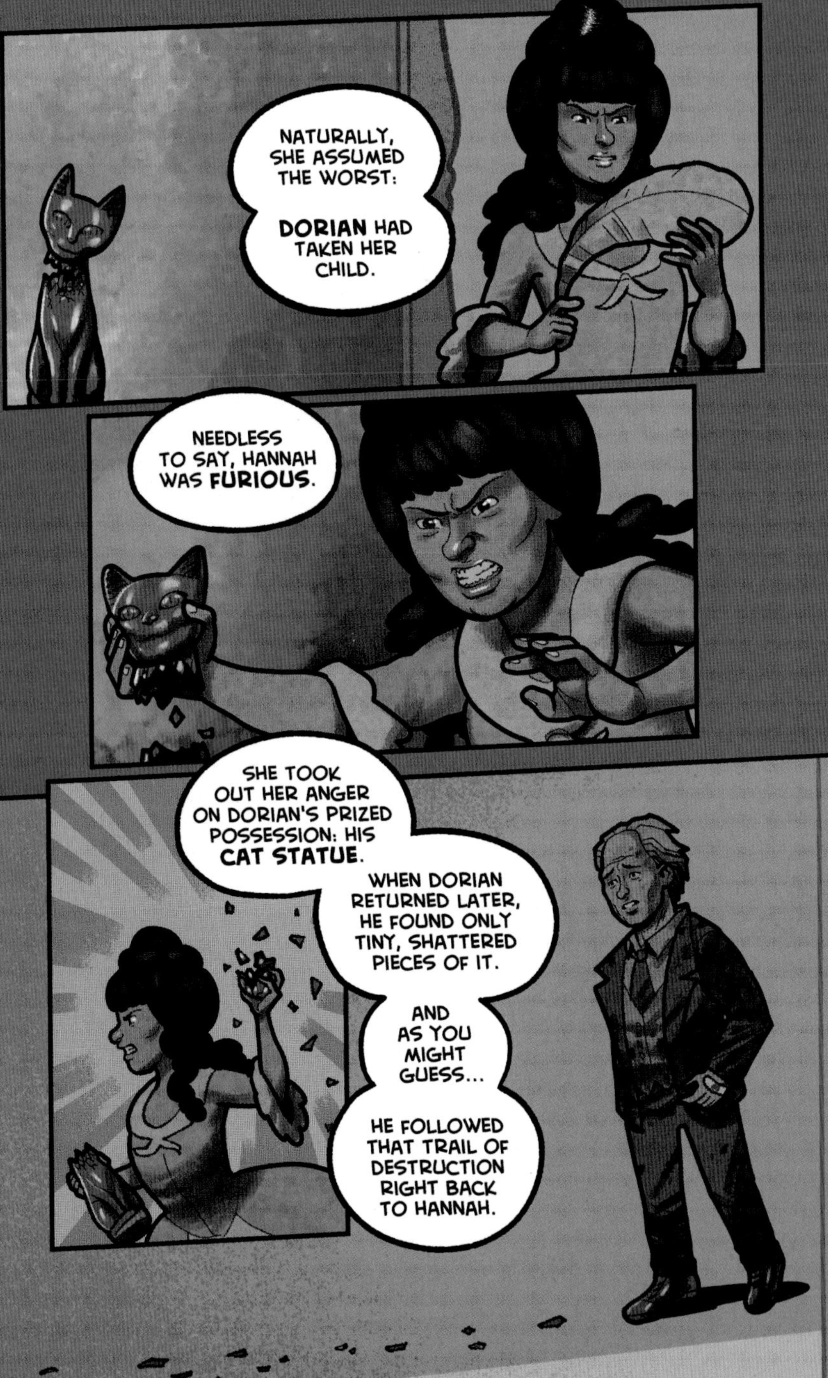
NATURALLY, SHE ASSUMED THE WORST:
DORIAN HAD TAKEN HER CHILD.
NEEDLESS TO SAY, HANNAH WAS FURIOUS.
SHE TOOK OUT HER ANGER ON DORIAN'S PRIZED POSSESSION: HIS CAT STATUE.
WHEN DORIAN RETURNED LATER, HE FOUND ONLY TINY, SHATTERED PIECES OF IT.
AND AS YOU MIGHT GUESS...
HE FOLLOWED THAT TRAIL OF DESTRUCTION RIGHT BACK TO HANNAH.

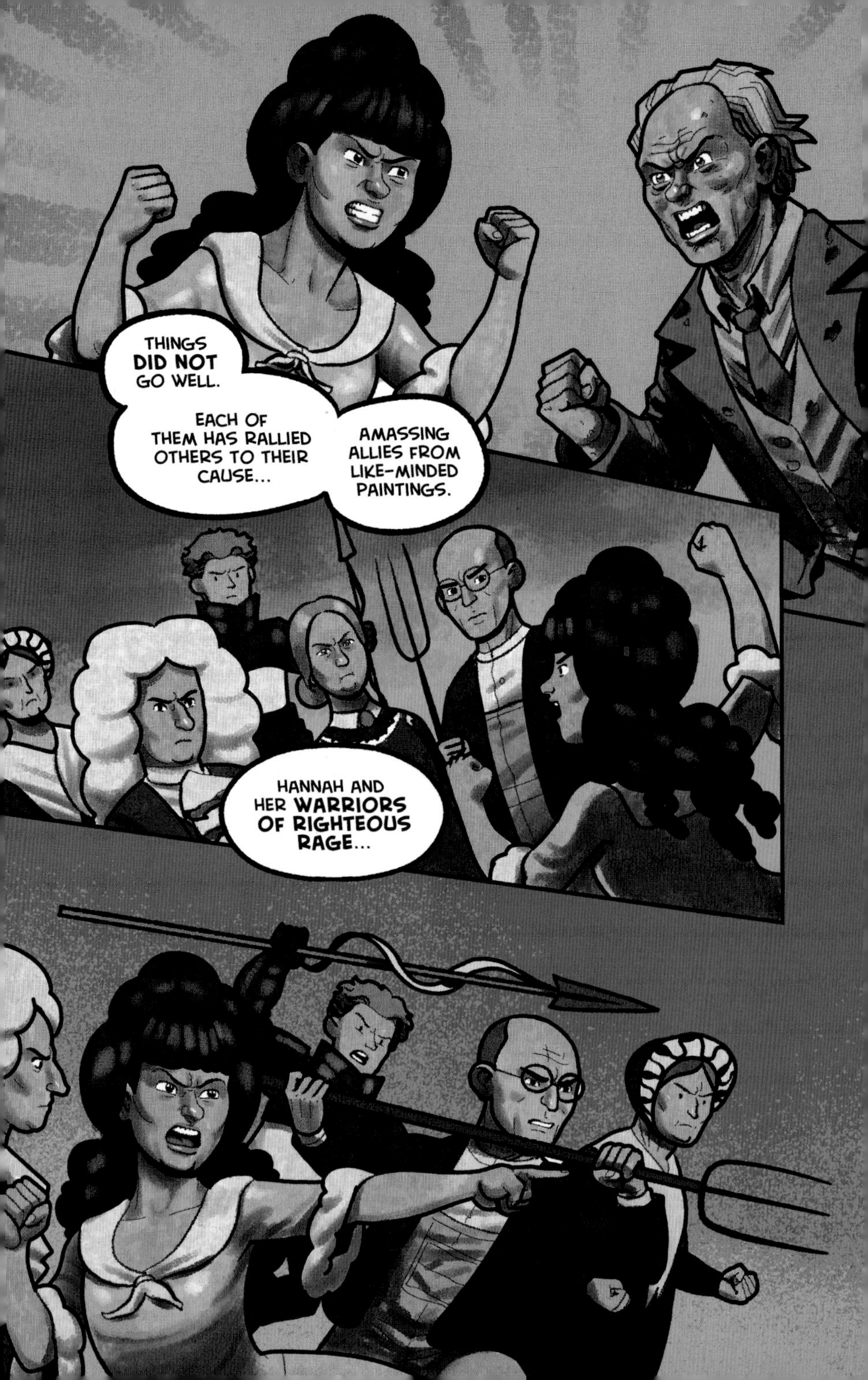
THINGS **DID NOT** GO WELL.
EACH OF THEM HAS RALLIED OTHERS TO THEIR CAUSE...
AMASSING ALLIES FROM LIKE-MINDED PAINTINGS.
HANNAH AND HER **WARRIORS OF RIGHTEOUS RAGE...**

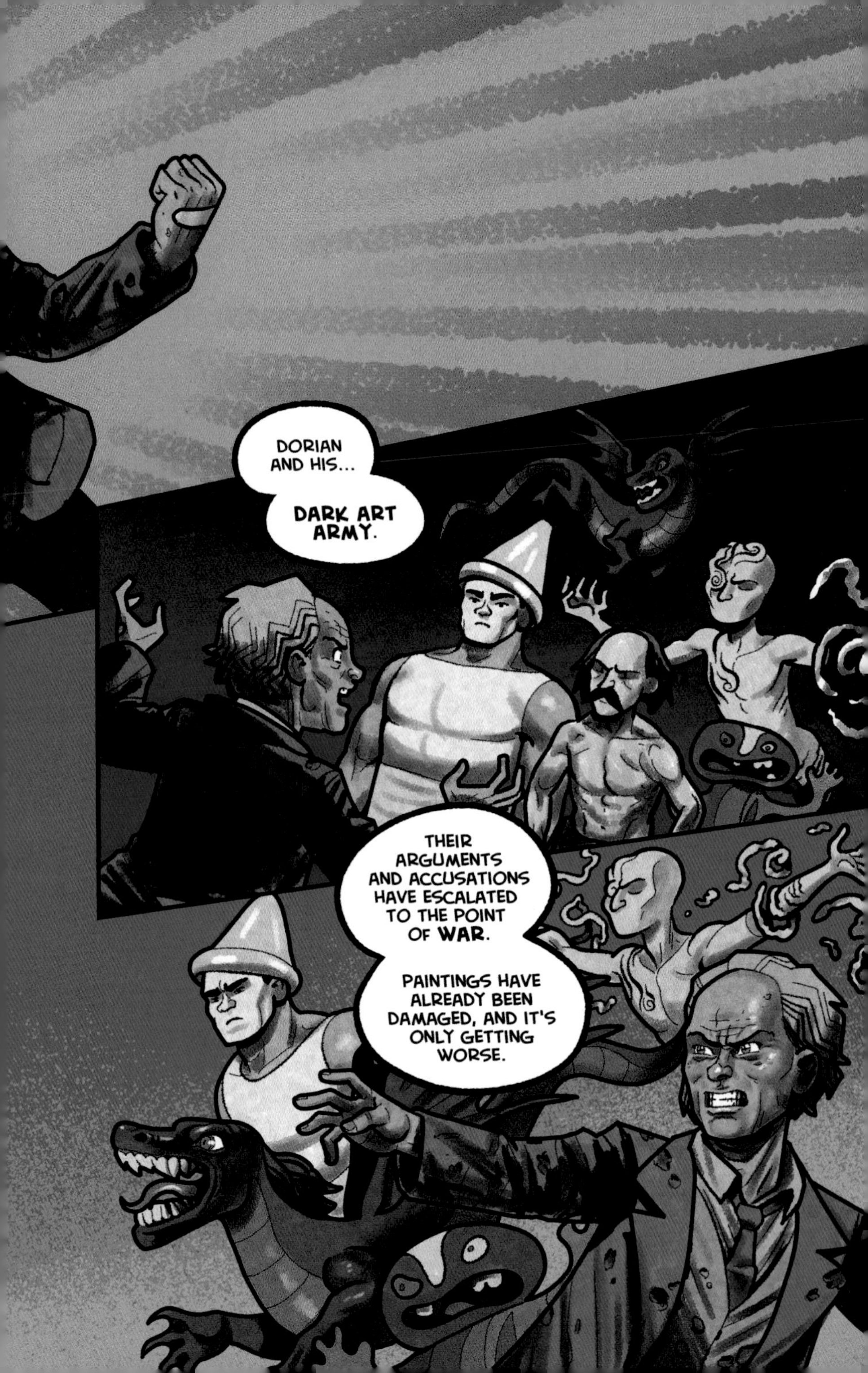
DORIAN AND HIS...
DARK ART ARMY.
THEIR ARGUMENTS AND ACCUSATIONS HAVE ESCALATED TO THE POINT OF WAR.
PAINTINGS HAVE ALREADY BEEN DAMAGED, AND IT'S ONLY GETTING WORSE.

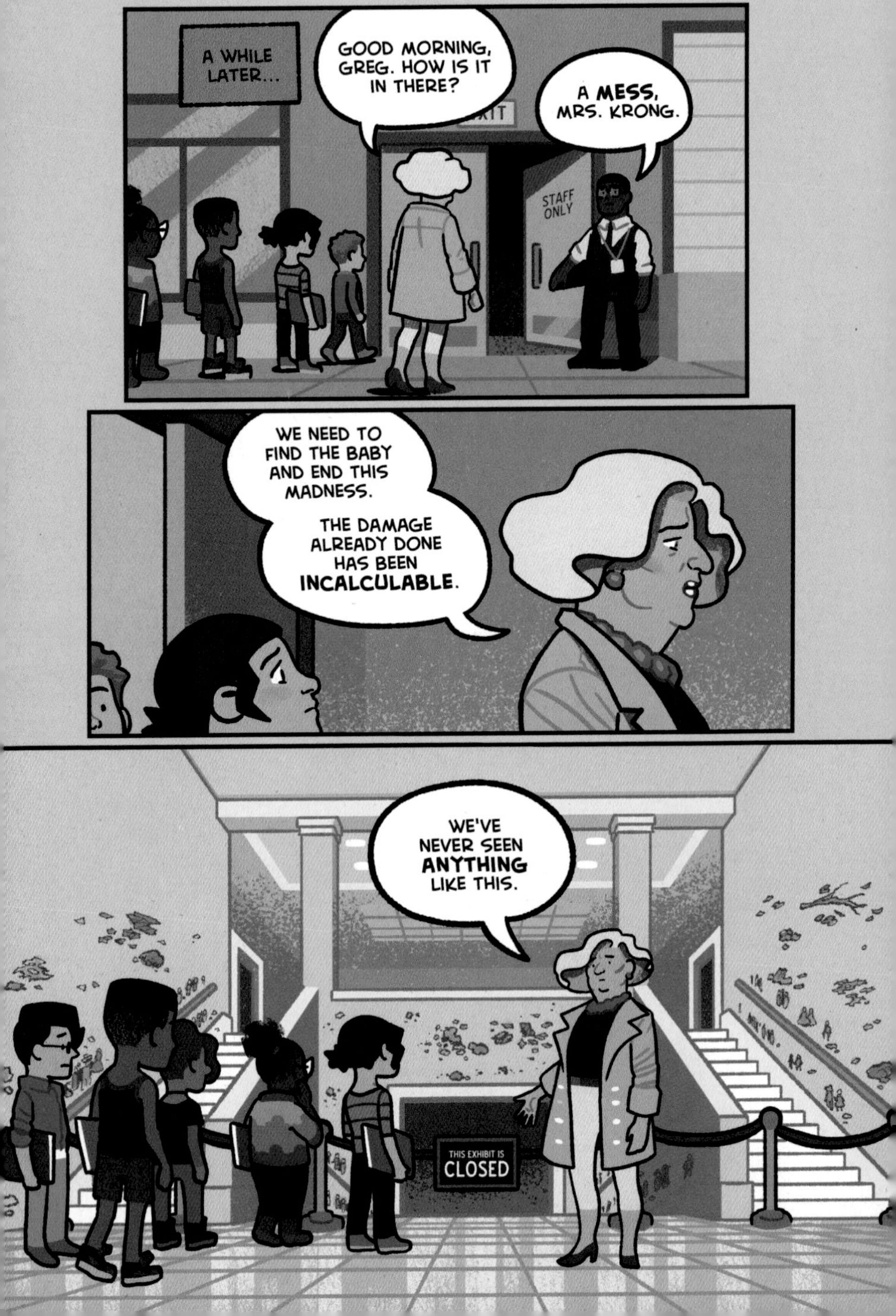
A WHILE LATER...
GOOD MORNING, GREG. HOW IS IT IN THERE?
A MESS, MRS. KRONG.
STAFF ONLY
WE NEED TO FIND THE BABY AND END THIS MADNESS.
THE DAMAGE ALREADY DONE HAS BEEN INCALCULABLE.
WE'VE NEVER SEEN ANYTHING LIKE THIS.
THIS EXHIBIT IS CLOSED

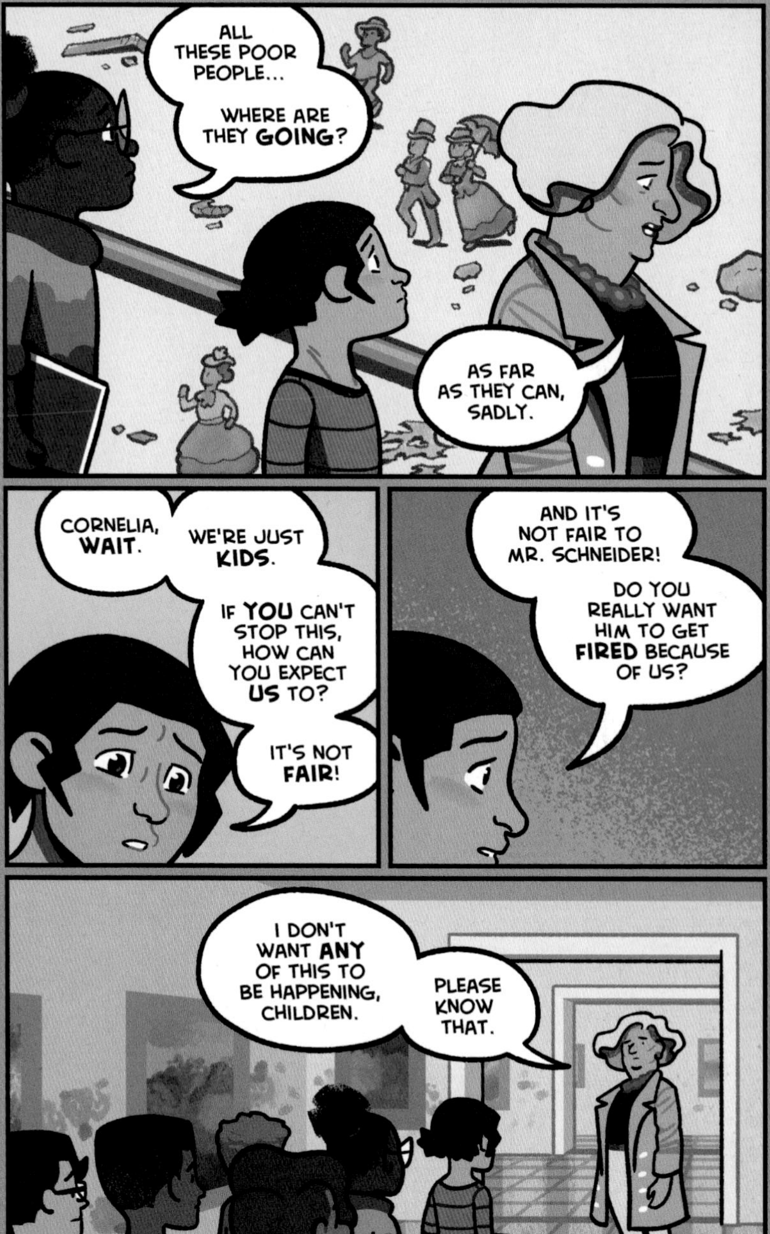
ALL THESE POOR PEOPLE...
WHERE ARE THEY GOING?
AS FAR AS THEY CAN, SADLY.
CORNELIA, WAIT.
WE'RE JUST KIDS.
IF YOU CAN'T STOP THIS, HOW CAN YOU EXPECT US TO?
IT'S NOT FAIR!
AND IT'S NOT FAIR TO MR. SCHNEIDER!
DO YOU REALLY WANT HIM TO GET FIRED BECAUSE OF US?
I DON'T WANT ANY OF THIS TO BE HAPPENING, CHILDREN.
PLEASE KNOW THAT.

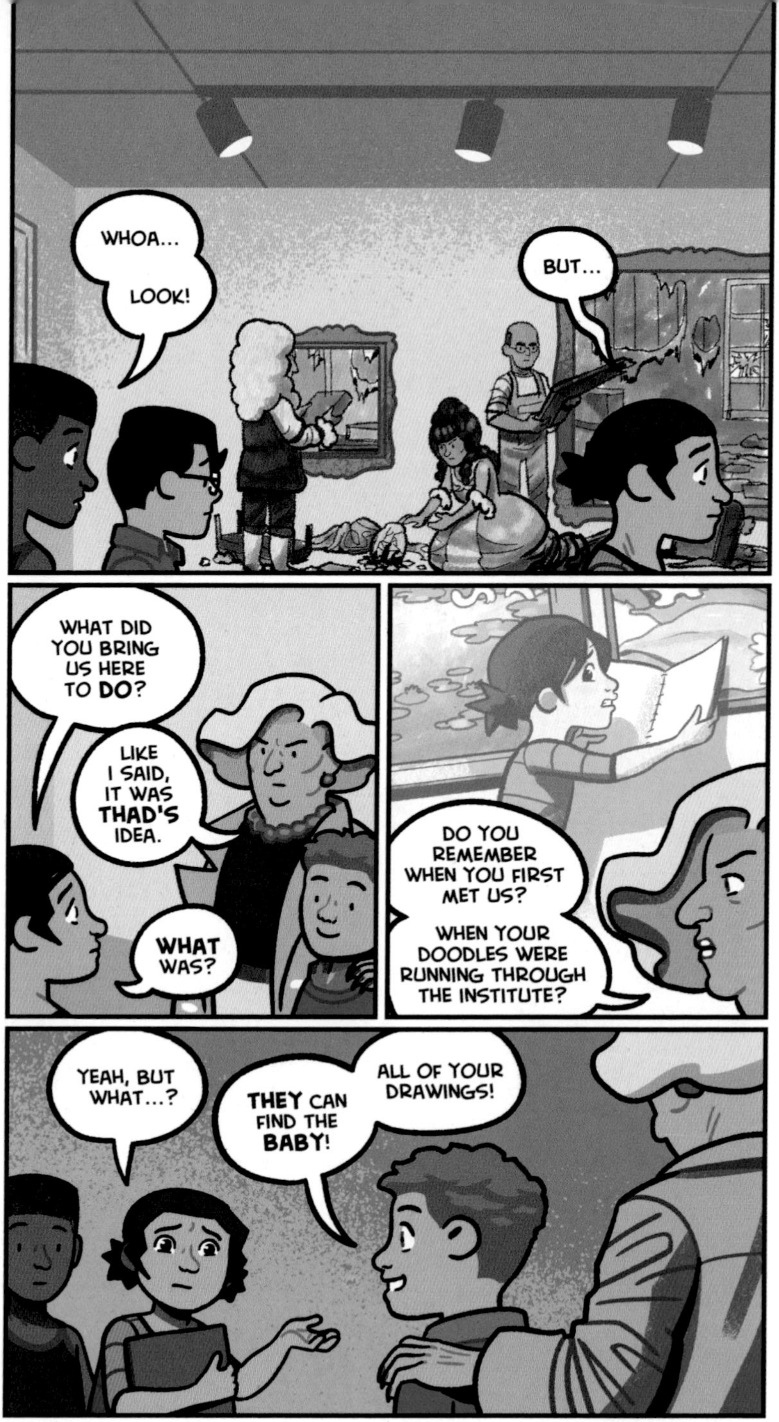
WHOA...
LOOK!
BUT...
WHAT DID YOU BRING US HERE TO DO?
LIKE I SAID, IT WAS THAD'S IDEA.
WHAT WAS?
DO YOU REMEMBER WHEN YOU FIRST MET US?
WHEN YOUR DOODLES WERE RUNNING THROUGH THE INSTITUTE?
YEAH, BUT WHAT...?
ALL OF YOUR DRAWINGS!
THEY CAN FIND THE BABY!

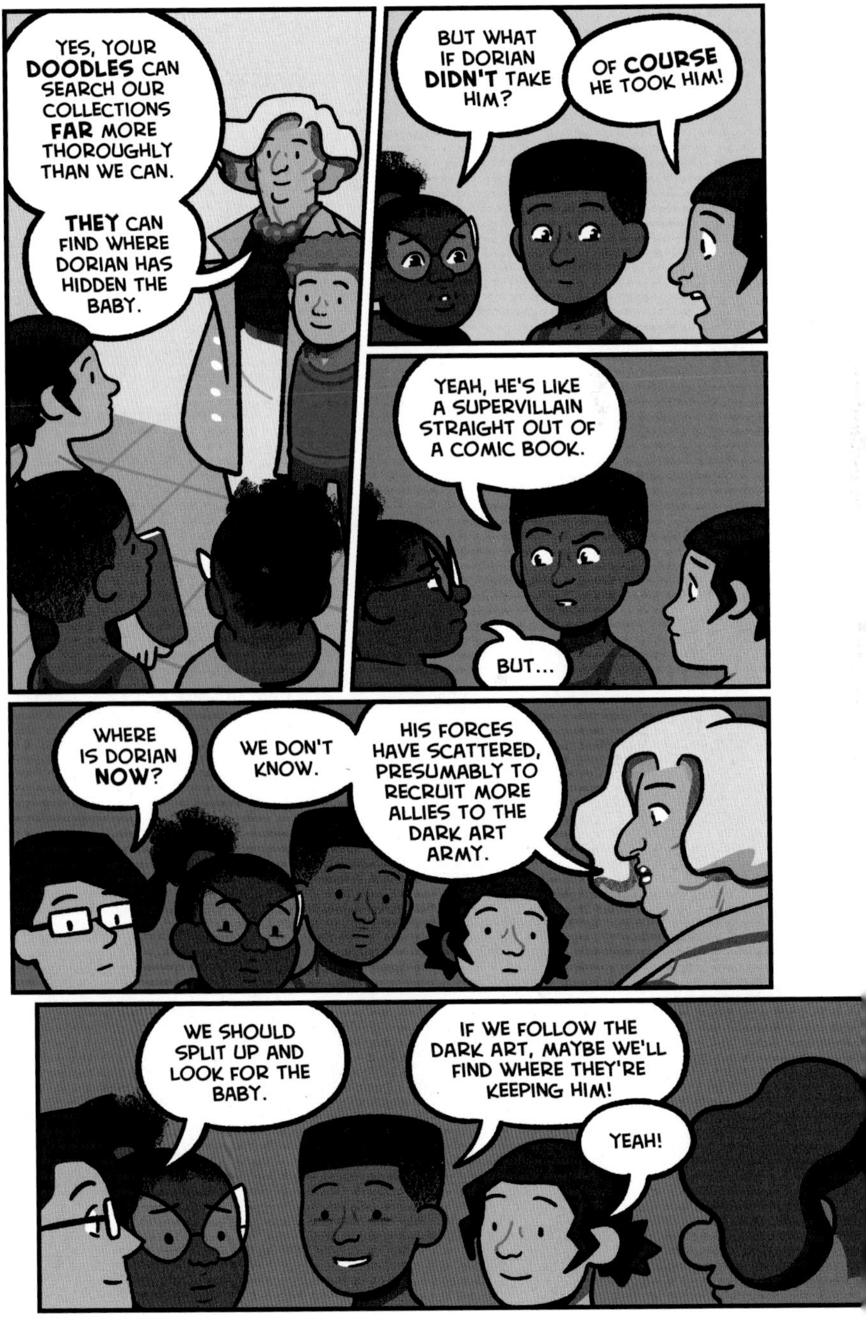
YES, YOUR **DOODLES** CAN SEARCH OUR COLLECTIONS **FAR** MORE THOROUGHLY THAN WE CAN.
THEY CAN FIND WHERE DORIAN HAS HIDDEN THE BABY.
BUT WHAT IF DORIAN **DIDN'T** TAKE HIM?
OF **COURSE** HE TOOK HIM!
YEAH, HE'S LIKE A SUPERVILLAIN STRAIGHT OUT OF A COMIC BOOK.
BUT...
WHERE IS DORIAN **NOW**?
WE DON'T KNOW.
HIS FORCES HAVE SCATTERED, PRESUMABLY TO RECRUIT MORE ALLIES TO THE DARK ART ARMY.
WE SHOULD SPLIT UP AND LOOK FOR THE BABY.
IF WE FOLLOW THE DARK ART, MAYBE WE'LL FIND WHERE THEY'RE KEEPING HIM!
YEAH!

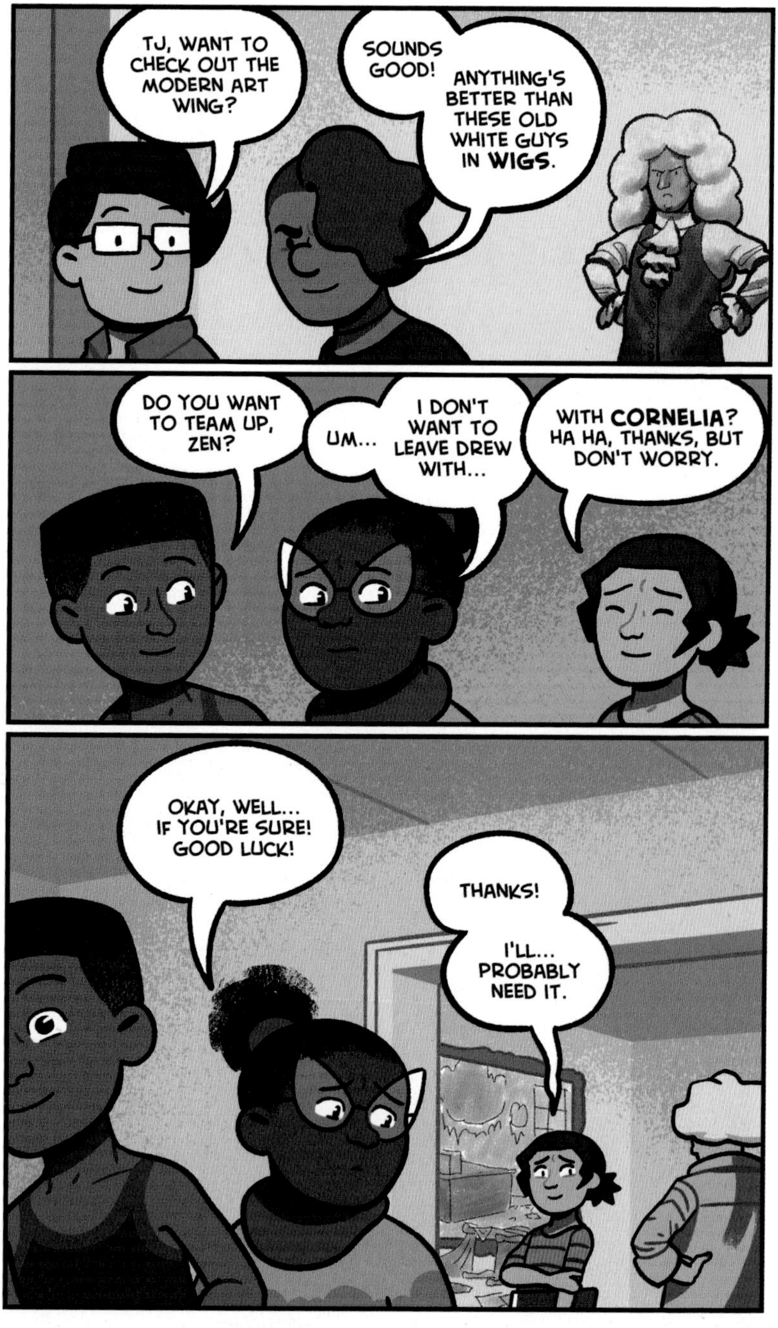
TJ, WANT TO CHECK OUT THE MODERN ART WING?
SOUNDS GOOD!
ANYTHING'S BETTER THAN THESE OLD WHITE GUYS IN **WIGS**.
DO YOU WANT TO TEAM UP, ZEN?
UM...
I DON'T WANT TO LEAVE DREW WITH...
WITH **CORNELIA**? HA HA, THANKS, BUT DON'T WORRY.
OKAY, WELL... IF YOU'RE SURE! GOOD LUCK!
THANKS!
I'LL... PROBABLY NEED IT.

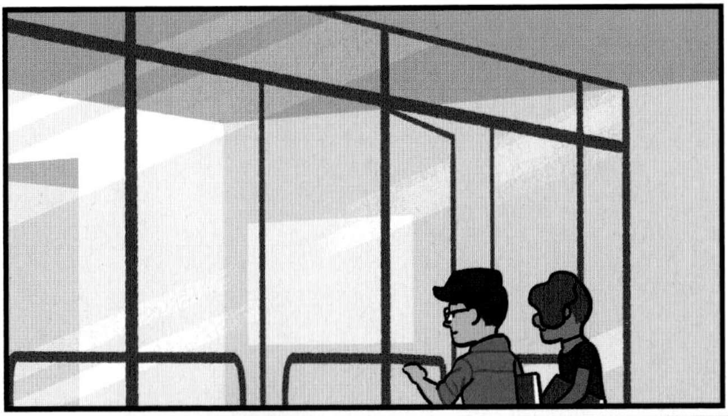

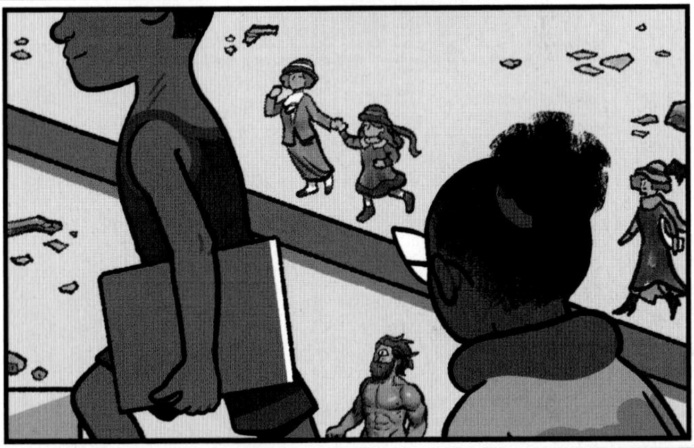

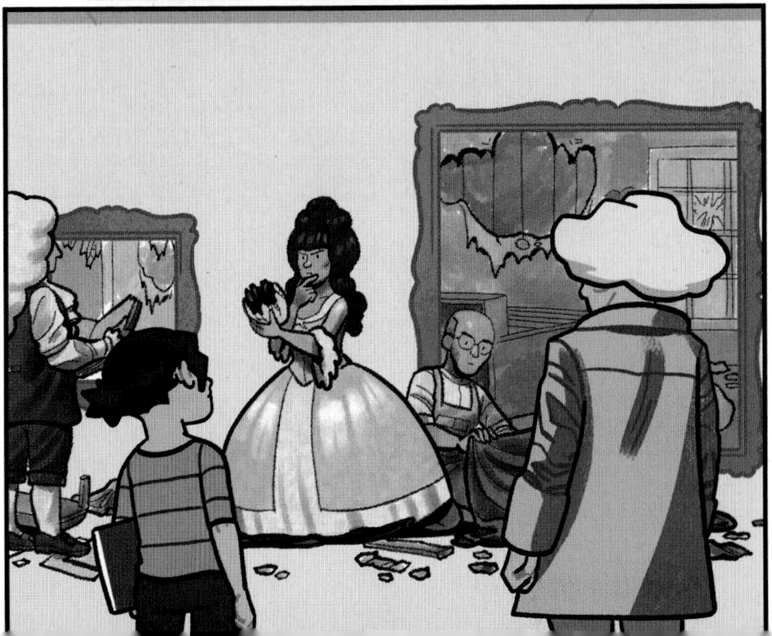

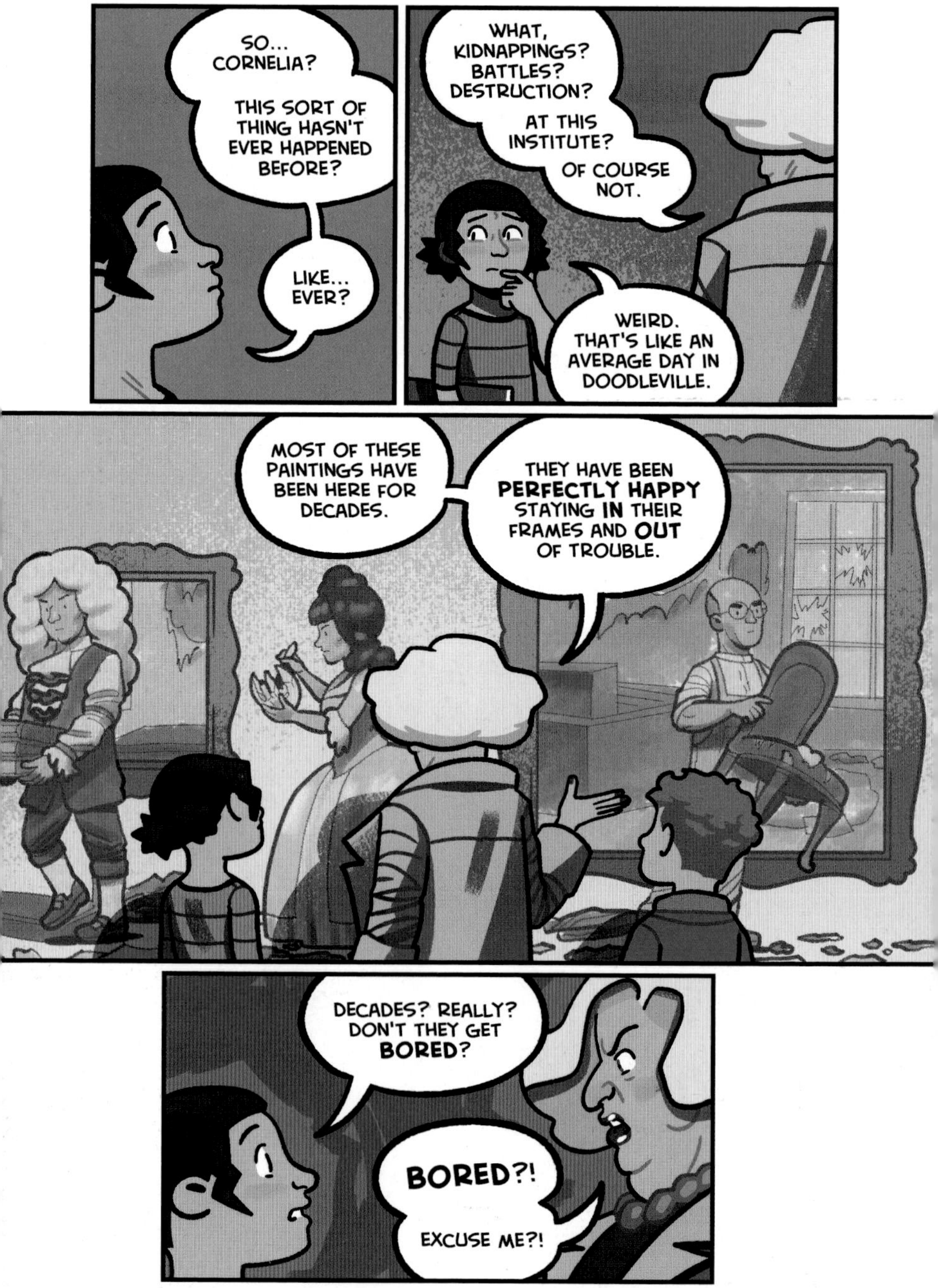
SO... CORNELIA?
THIS SORT OF THING HASN'T EVER HAPPENED BEFORE?
LIKE... EVER?
WHAT, KIDNAPPINGS? BATTLES? DESTRUCTION?
AT THIS INSTITUTE?
OF COURSE NOT.
WEIRD. THAT'S LIKE AN AVERAGE DAY IN DOODLEVILLE.
MOST OF THESE PAINTINGS HAVE BEEN HERE FOR DECADES.
THEY HAVE BEEN **PERFECTLY HAPPY** STAYING **IN** THEIR FRAMES AND **OUT** OF TROUBLE.
DECADES? REALLY? DON'T THEY GET **BORED**?
BORED?!
EXCUSE ME?!

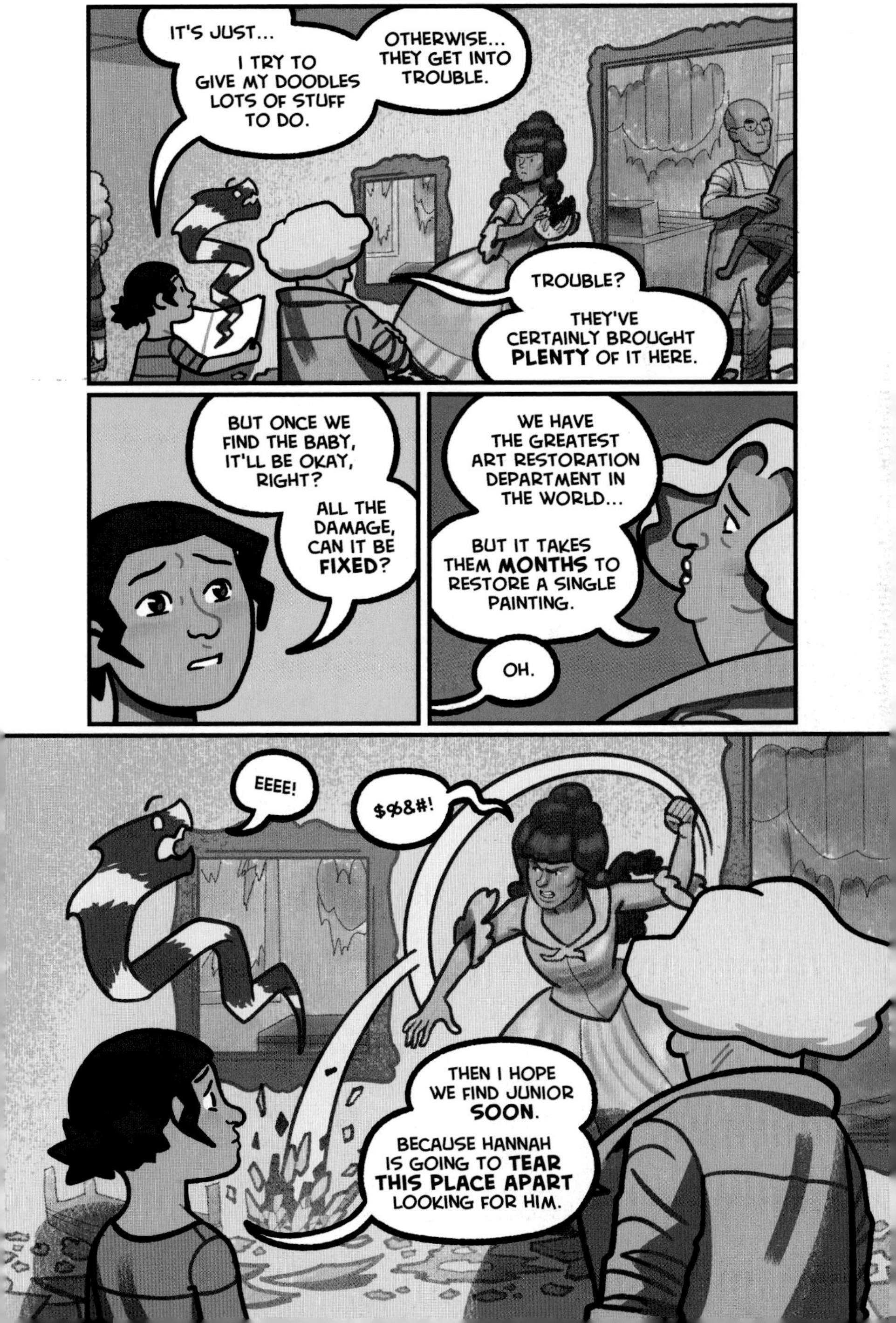
IT'S JUST...
I TRY TO GIVE MY DOODLES LOTS OF STUFF TO DO.
OTHERWISE... THEY GET INTO TROUBLE.
TROUBLE?
THEY'VE CERTAINLY BROUGHT **PLENTY** OF IT HERE.
BUT ONCE WE FIND THE BABY, IT'LL BE OKAY, RIGHT?
ALL THE DAMAGE, CAN IT BE **FIXED**?
WE HAVE THE GREATEST ART RESTORATION DEPARTMENT IN THE WORLD...
BUT IT TAKES THEM **MONTHS** TO RESTORE A SINGLE PAINTING.
OH.
EEEE!
$¢&#!
THEN I HOPE WE FIND JUNIOR **SOON**.
BECAUSE HANNAH IS GOING TO **TEAR THIS PLACE APART** LOOKING FOR HIM.

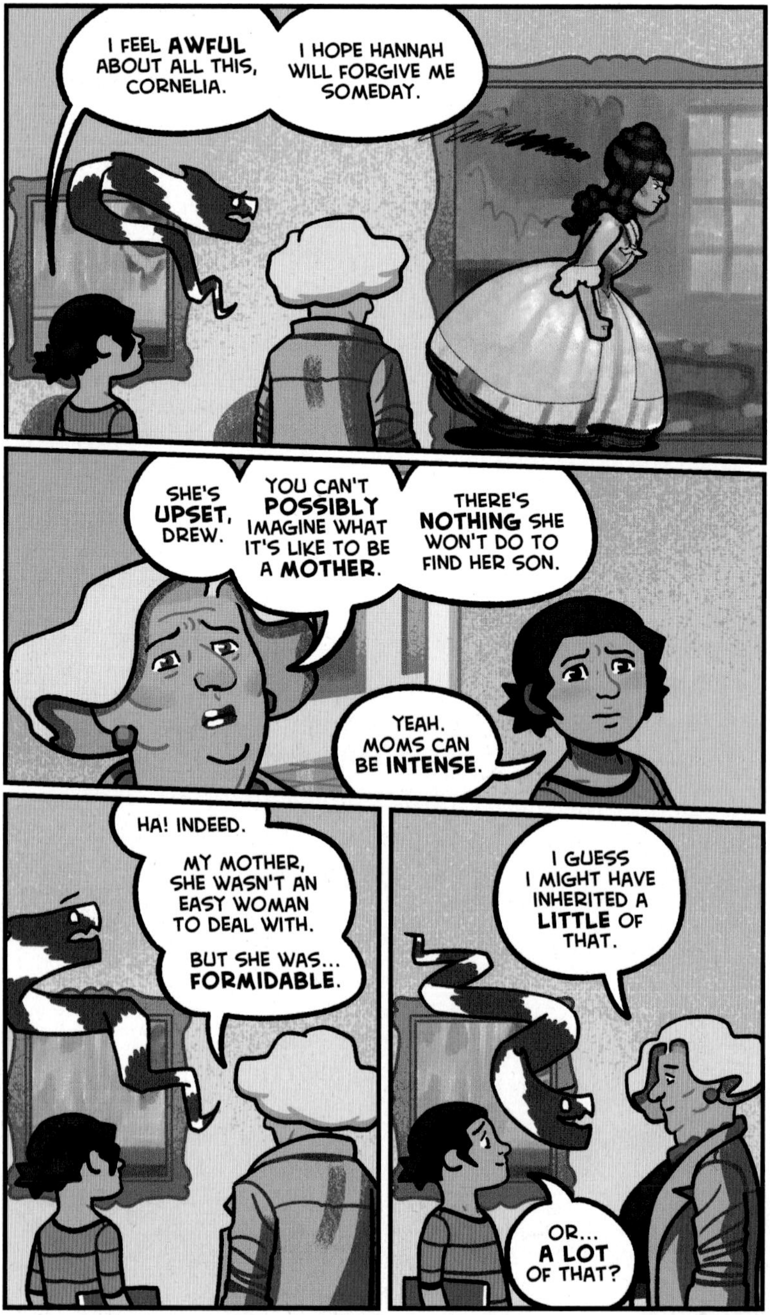

I FEEL AWFUL ABOUT ALL THIS, CORNELIA.
I HOPE HANNAH WILL FORGIVE ME SOMEDAY.
SHE'S UPSET, DREW.
YOU CAN'T POSSIBLY IMAGINE WHAT IT'S LIKE TO BE A MOTHER.
THERE'S NOTHING SHE WON'T DO TO FIND HER SON.
YEAH. MOMS CAN BE INTENSE.
HA! INDEED.
MY MOTHER, SHE WASN'T AN EASY WOMAN TO DEAL WITH.
BUT SHE WAS... FORMIDABLE.
I GUESS I MIGHT HAVE INHERITED A LITTLE OF THAT.
OR... A LOT OF THAT?

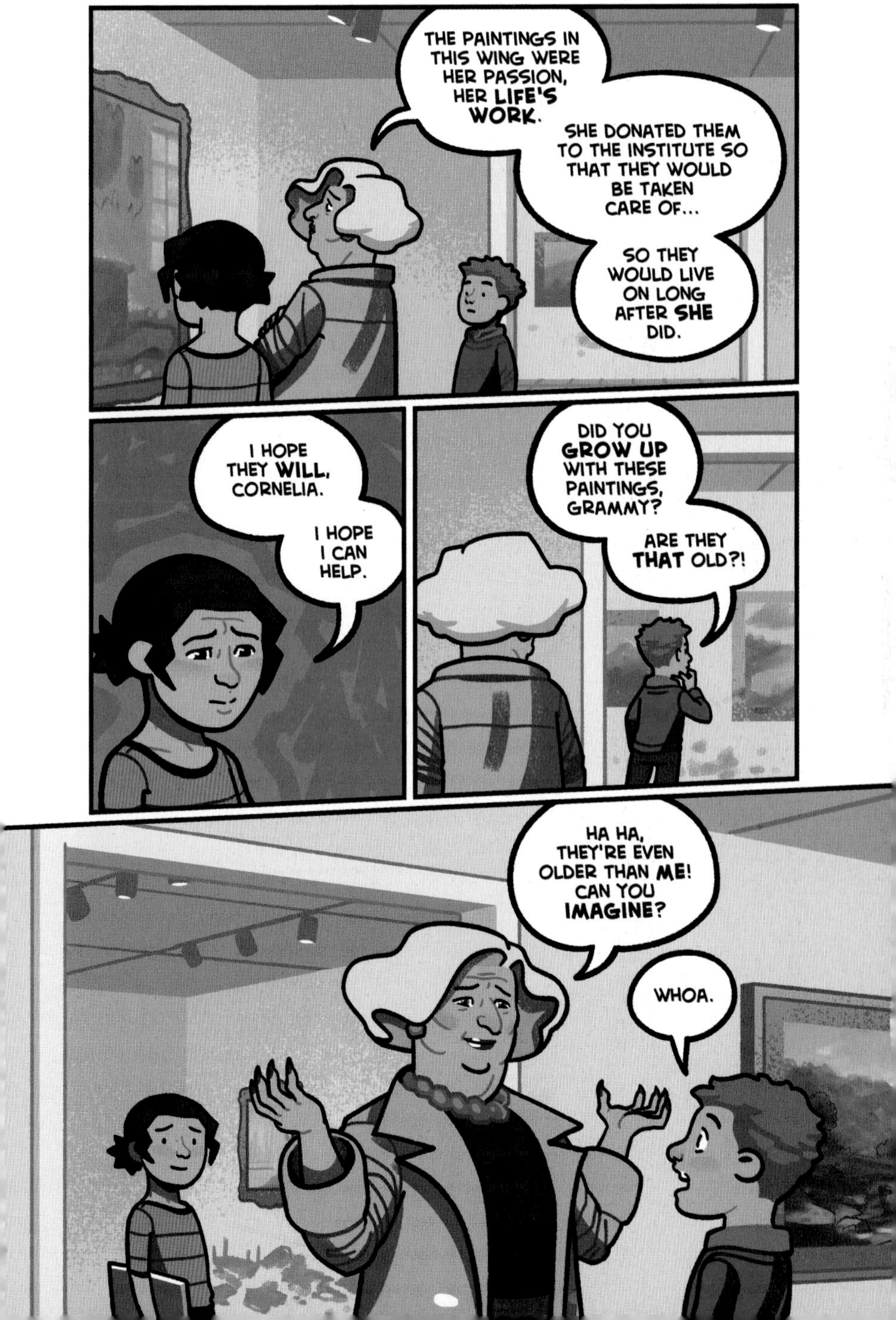
THE PAINTINGS IN THIS WING WERE HER PASSION, HER LIFE'S WORK.
SHE DONATED THEM TO THE INSTITUTE SO THAT THEY WOULD BE TAKEN CARE OF...
SO THEY WOULD LIVE ON LONG AFTER SHE DID.
I HOPE THEY WILL, CORNELIA.
I HOPE I CAN HELP.
DID YOU GROW UP WITH THESE PAINTINGS, GRAMMY?
ARE THEY THAT OLD?!
HA HA, THEY'RE EVEN OLDER THAN ME! CAN YOU IMAGINE?
WHOA.

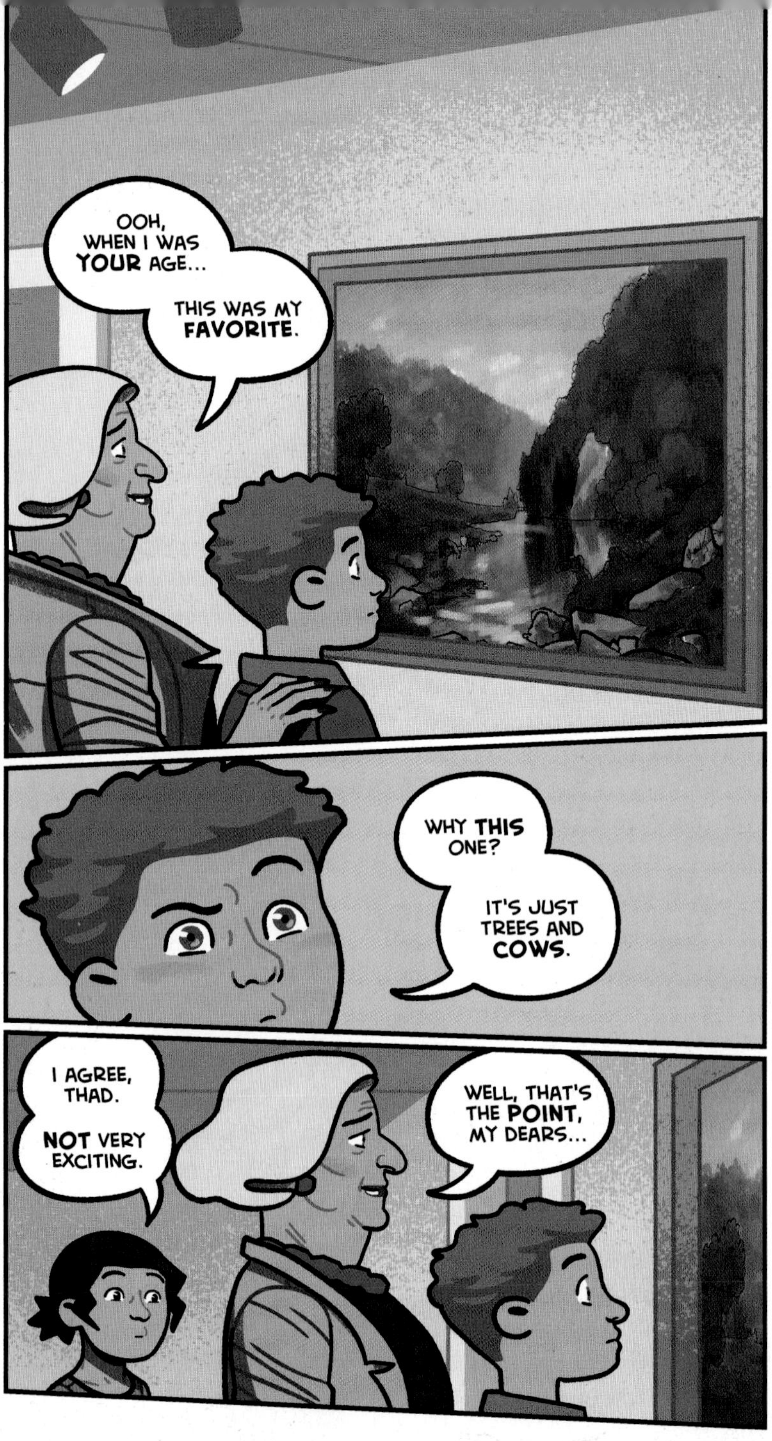
OOH, WHEN I WAS YOUR AGE...
THIS WAS MY FAVORITE.
WHY THIS ONE?
IT'S JUST TREES AND COWS.
I AGREE, THAD.
NOT VERY EXCITING.
WELL, THAT'S THE POINT, MY DEARS...

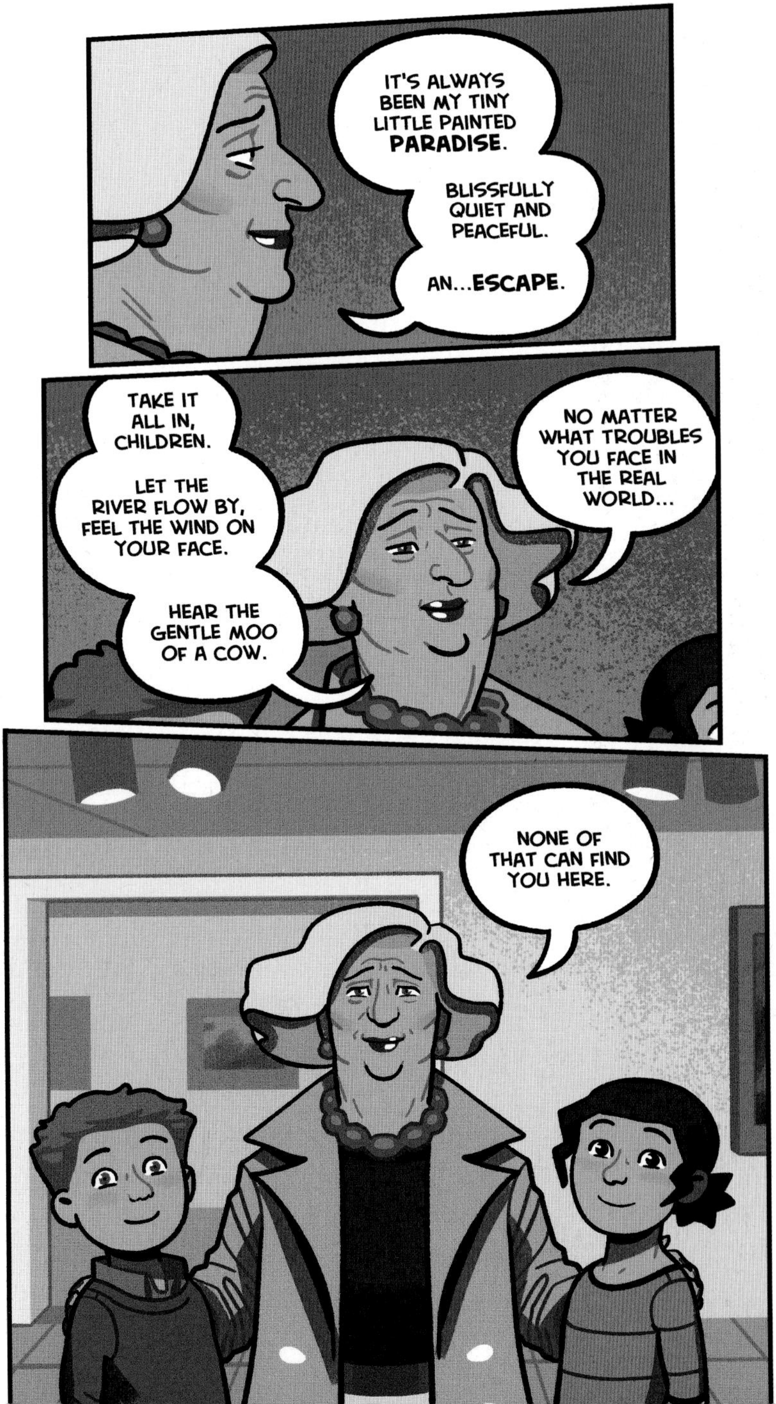
IT'S ALWAYS BEEN MY TINY LITTLE PAINTED PARADISE.
BLISSFULLY QUIET AND PEACEFUL.
AN...ESCAPE.
TAKE IT ALL IN, CHILDREN.
LET THE RIVER FLOW BY, FEEL THE WIND ON YOUR FACE.
HEAR THE GENTLE MOO OF A COW.
NO MATTER WHAT TROUBLES YOU FACE IN THE REAL WORLD...
NONE OF THAT CAN FIND YOU HERE.

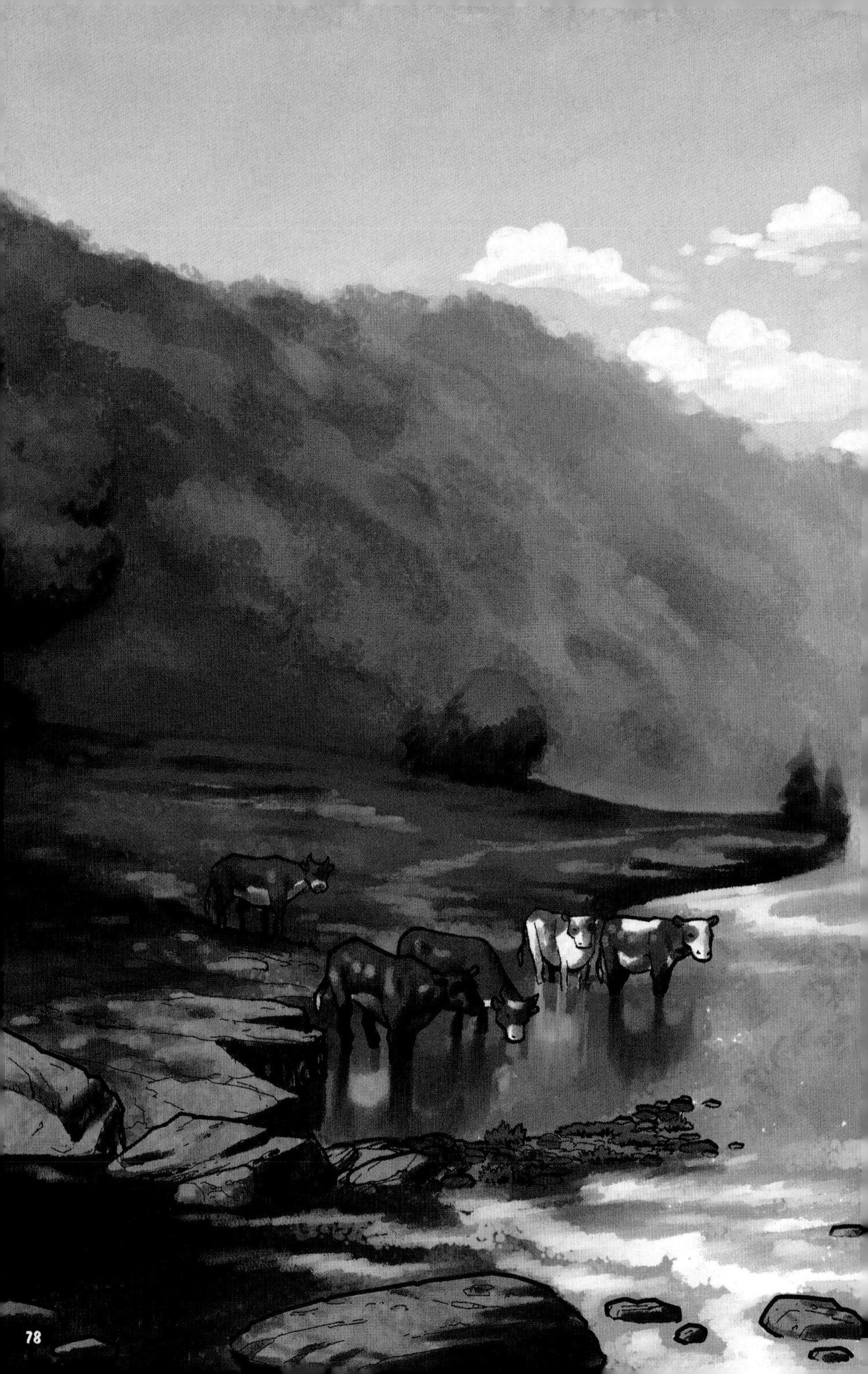

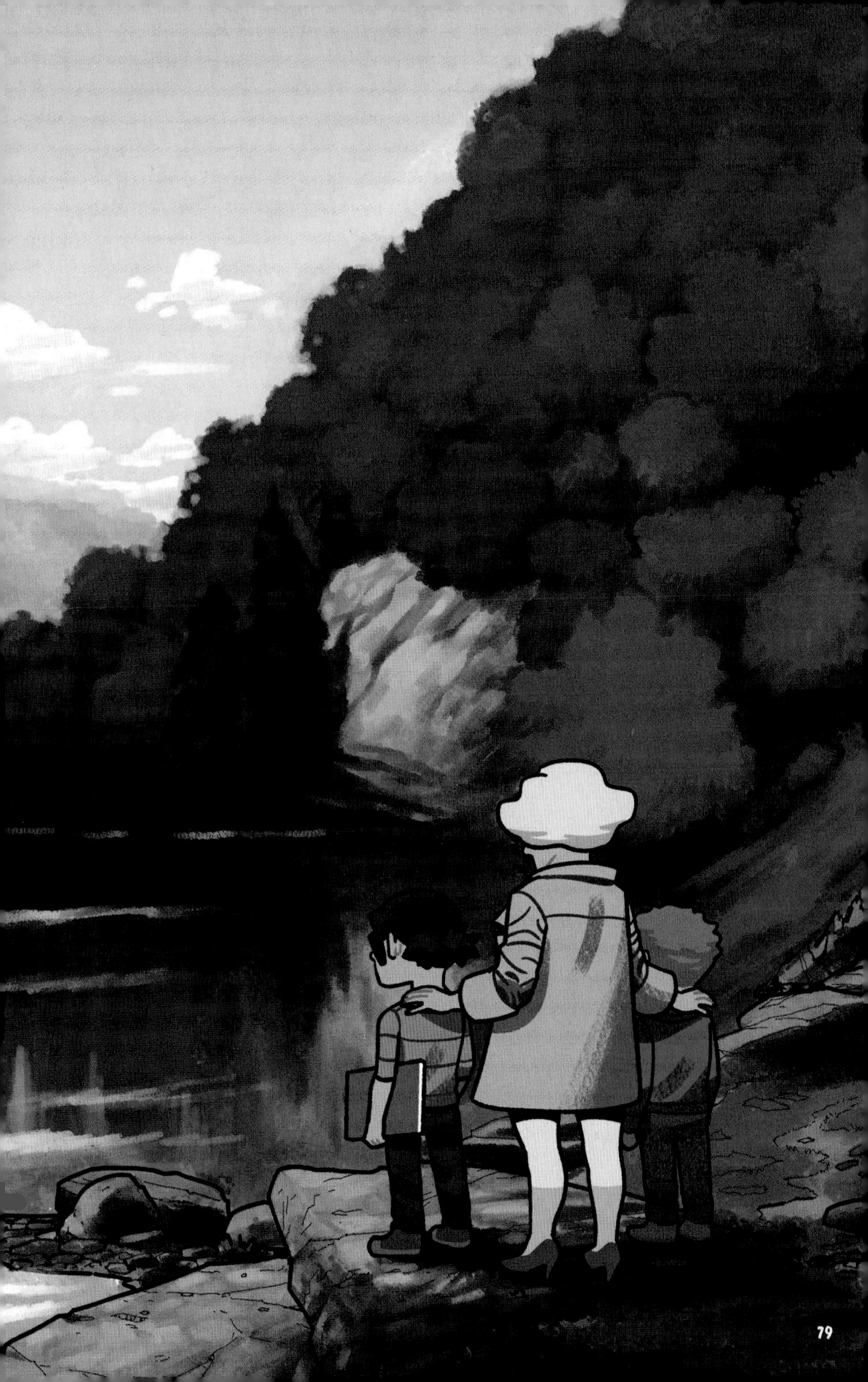

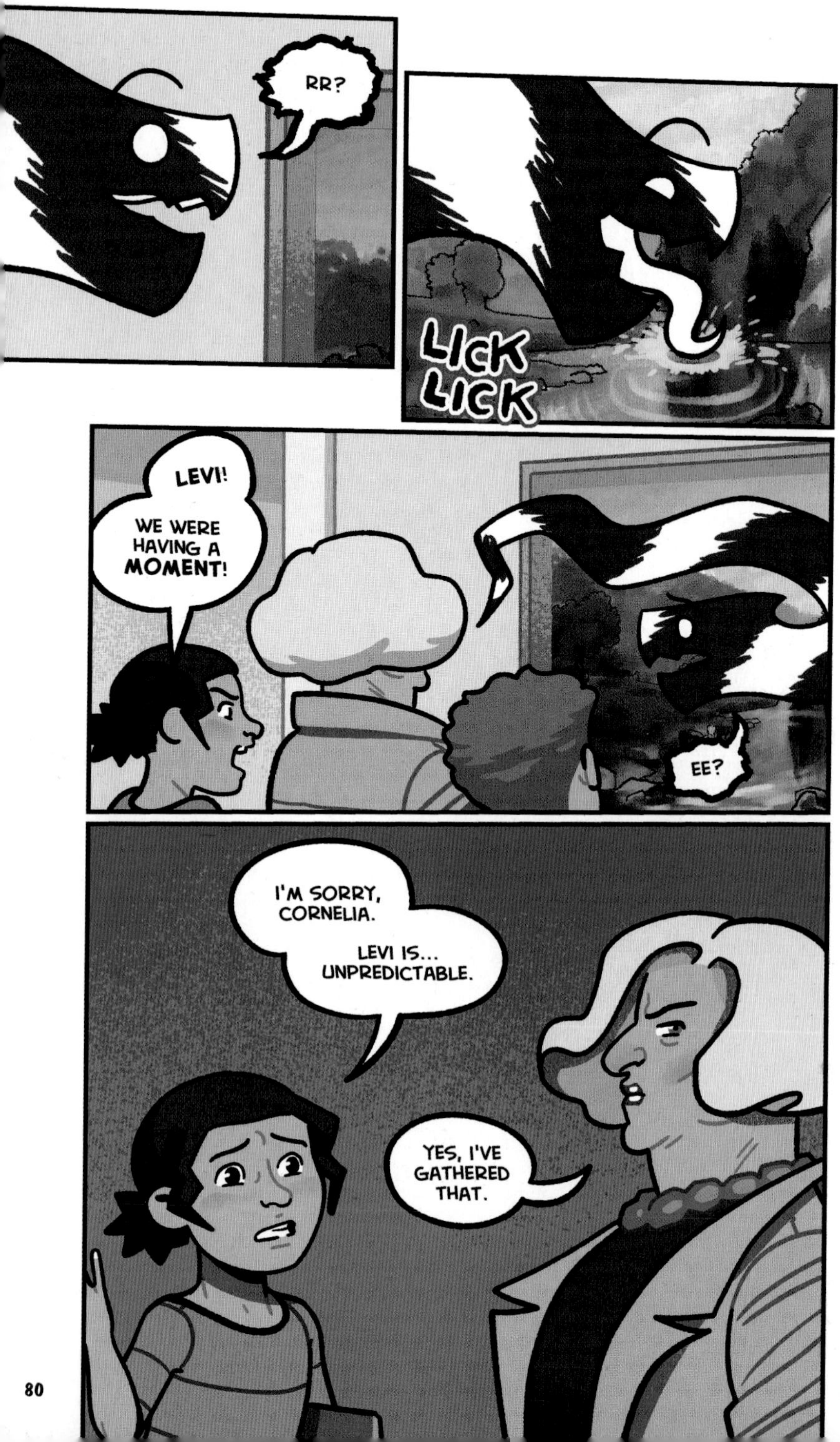

RR?
LICK LICK
LEVI!
WE WERE HAVING A MOMENT!
EE?
I'M SORRY, CORNELIA.
LEVI IS... UNPREDICTABLE.
YES, I'VE GATHERED THAT.

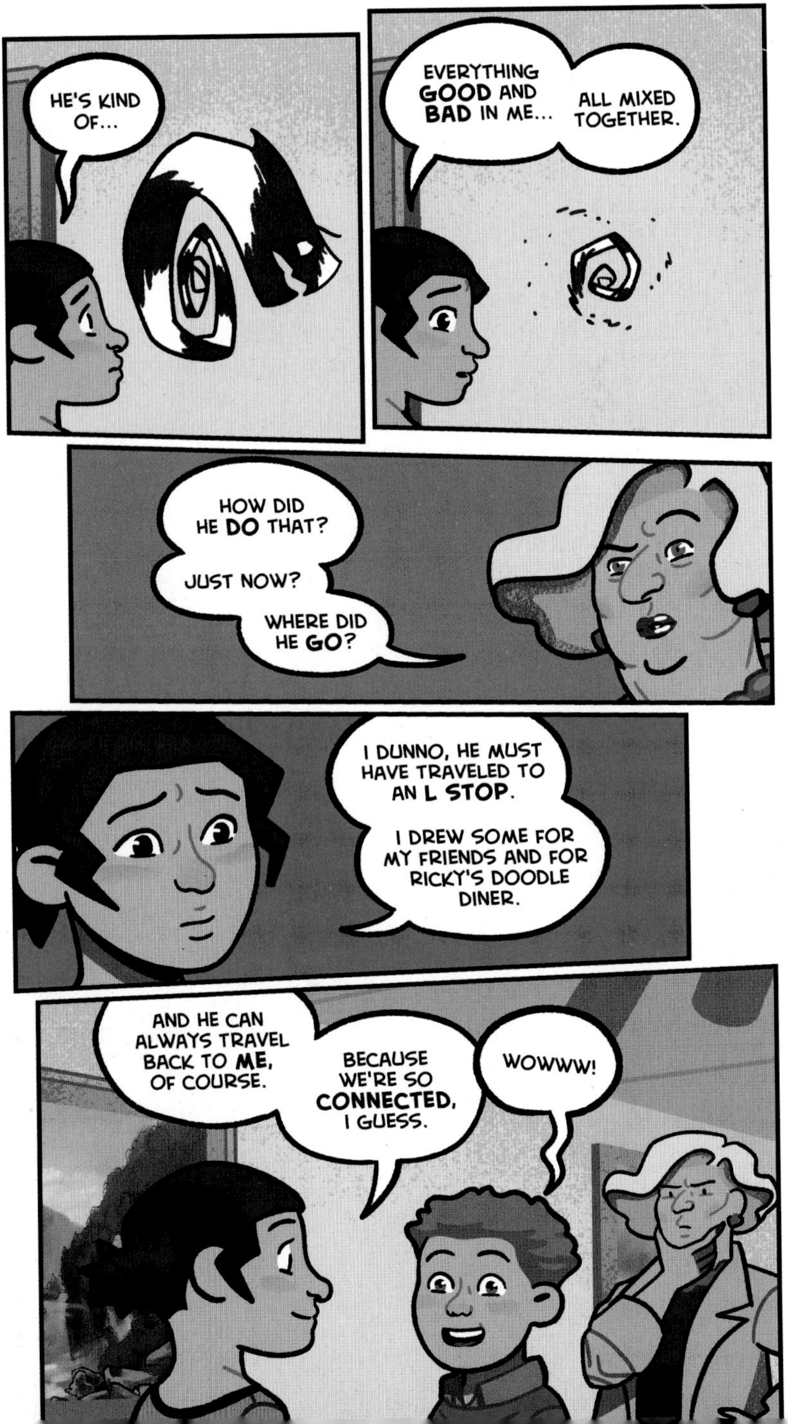
HE'S KIND OF...
EVERYTHING GOOD AND BAD IN ME...
ALL MIXED TOGETHER.
HOW DID HE DO THAT?
JUST NOW?
WHERE DID HE GO?
I DUNNO, HE MUST HAVE TRAVELED TO AN L STOP.
I DREW SOME FOR MY FRIENDS AND FOR RICKY'S DOODLE DINER.
AND HE CAN ALWAYS TRAVEL BACK TO ME, OF COURSE.
BECAUSE WE'RE SO CONNECTED, I GUESS.
WOWWW!

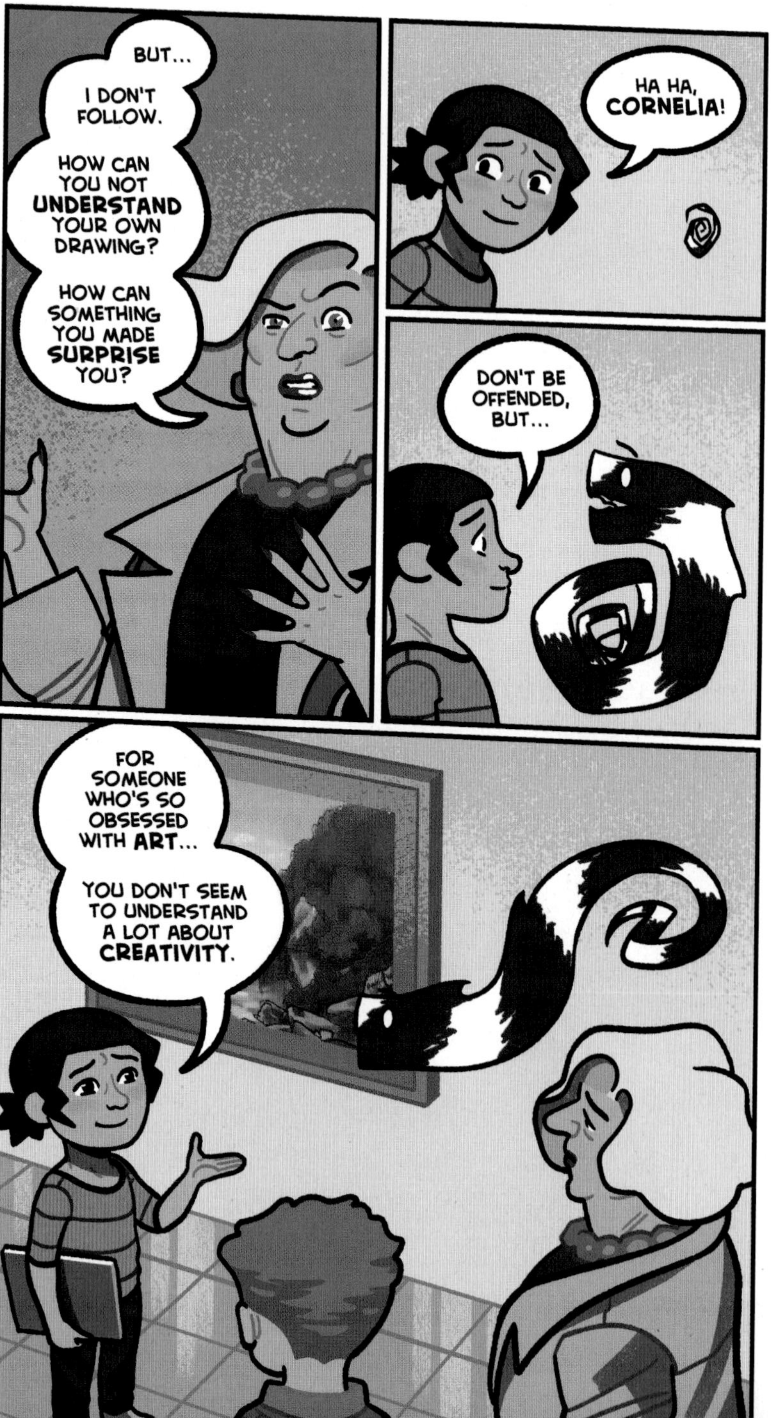
BUT...
I DON'T FOLLOW.
HOW CAN YOU NOT **UNDERSTAND** YOUR OWN DRAWING?
HOW CAN SOMETHING YOU MADE **SURPRISE** YOU?
HA HA, **CORNELIA**!
DON'T BE OFFENDED, BUT...
FOR SOMEONE WHO'S SO OBSESSED WITH **ART**...
YOU DON'T SEEM TO UNDERSTAND A LOT ABOUT **CREATIVITY**.

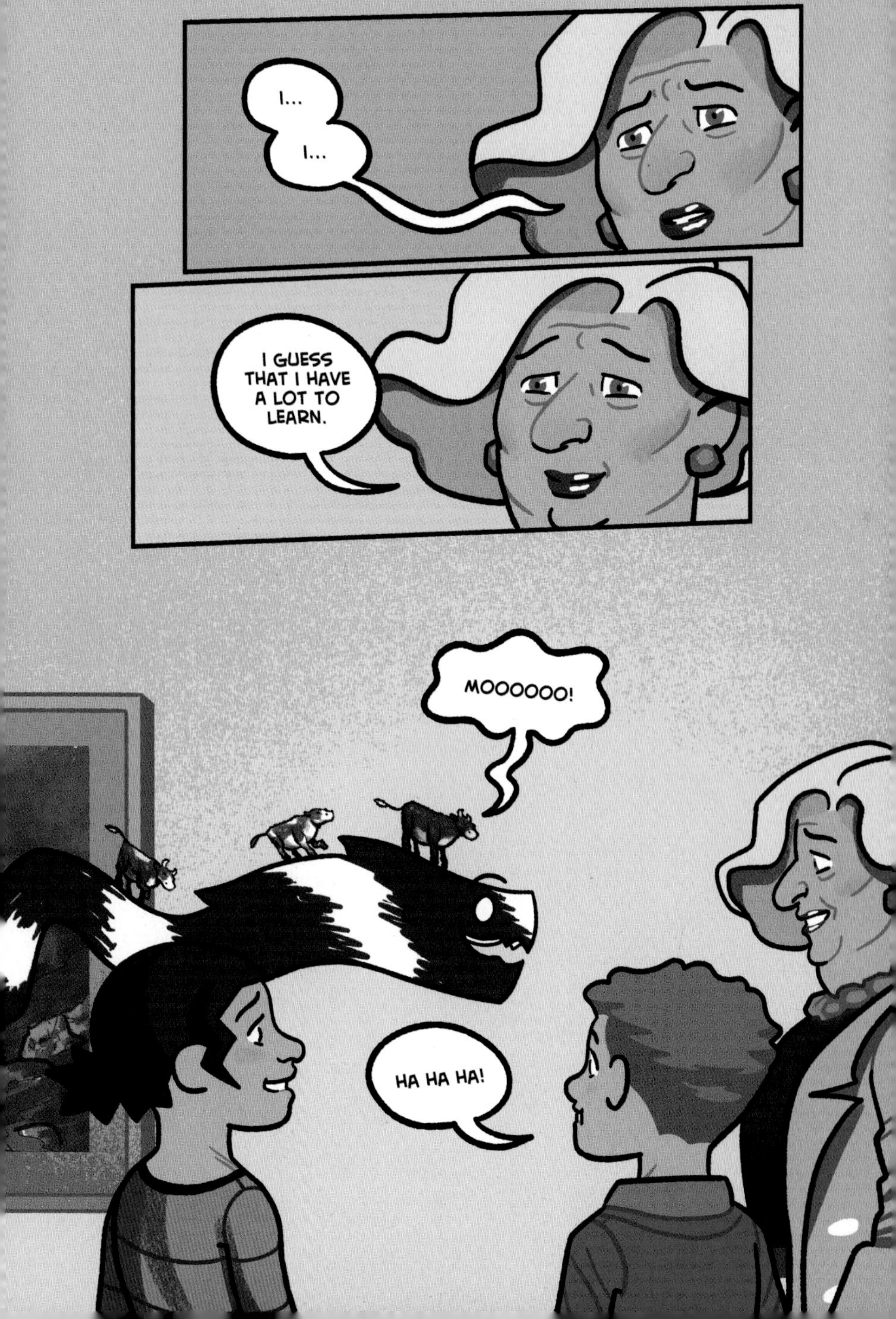
I...
I...
I GUESS THAT I HAVE A LOT TO LEARN.
MOOOOOO!
HA HA HA!

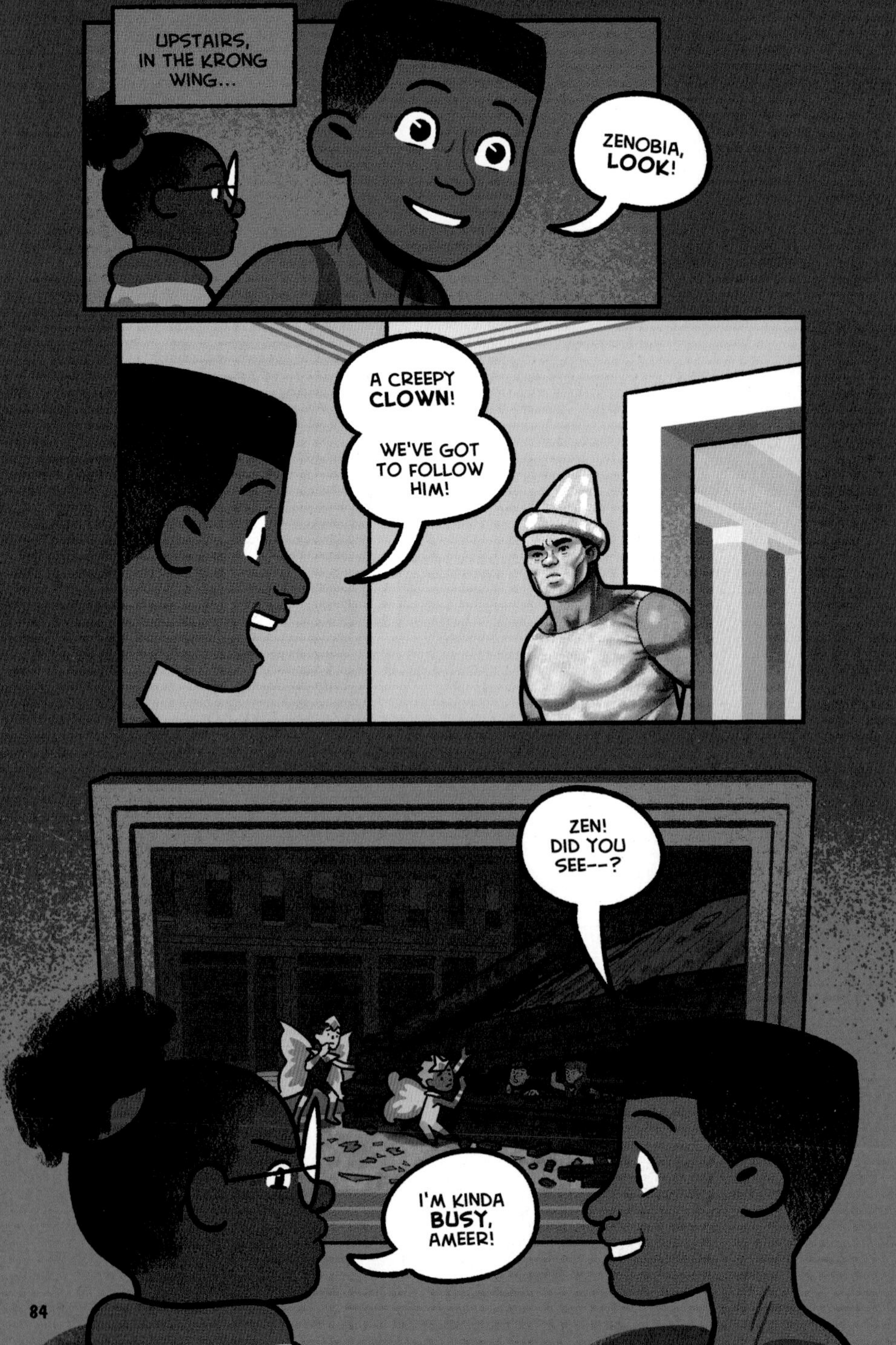
UPSTAIRS, IN THE KRONG WING...
ZENOBIA, LOOK!
A CREEPY CLOWN!
WE'VE GOT TO FOLLOW HIM!
ZEN! DID YOU SEE--?
I'M KINDA BUSY, AMEER!

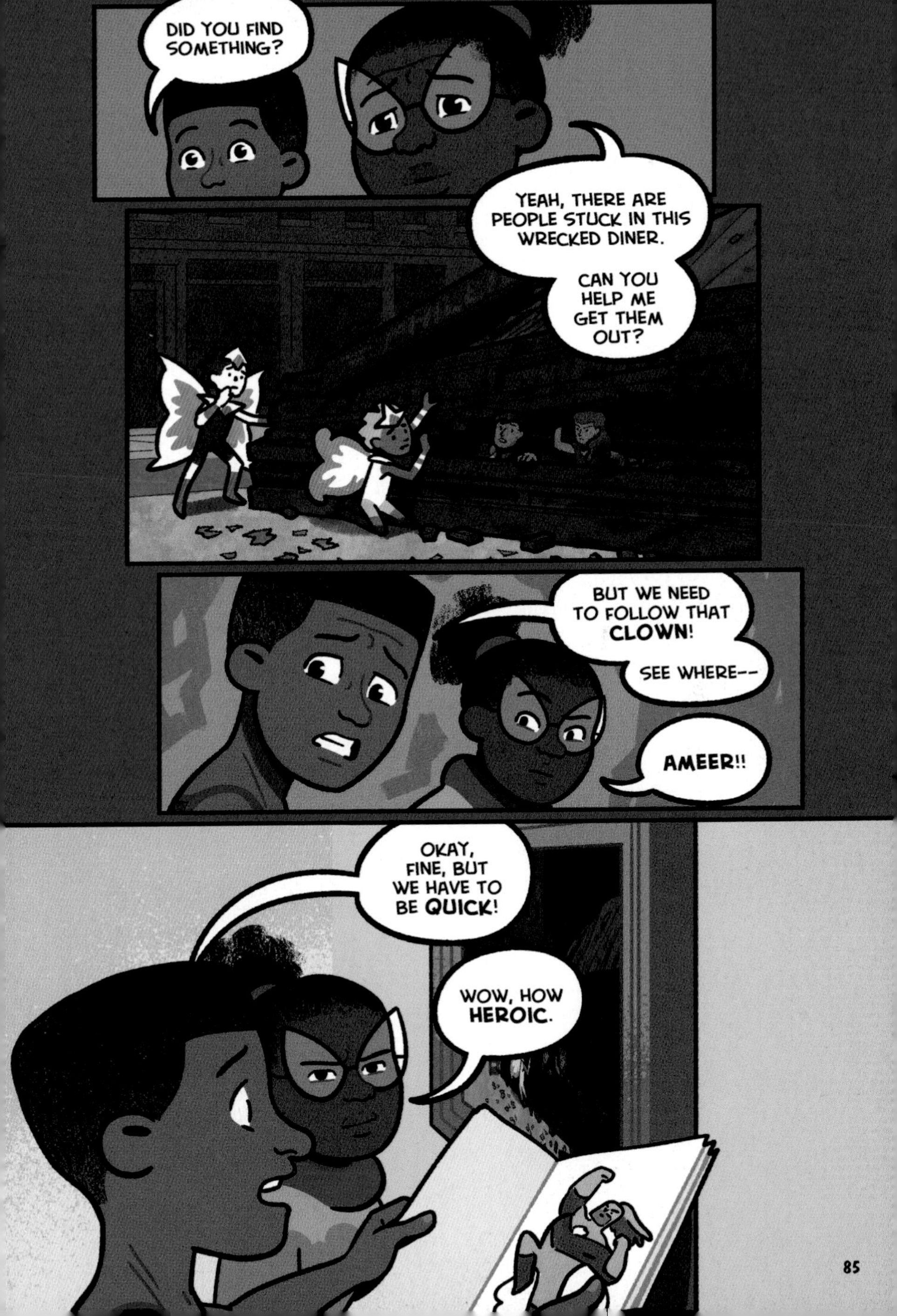
DID YOU FIND SOMETHING?
YEAH, THERE ARE PEOPLE STUCK IN THIS WRECKED DINER.
CAN YOU HELP ME GET THEM OUT?
BUT WE NEED TO FOLLOW THAT **CLOWN**!
SEE WHERE--
AMEER!!
OKAY, FINE, BUT WE HAVE TO BE **QUICK**!
WOW, HOW **HEROIC**.

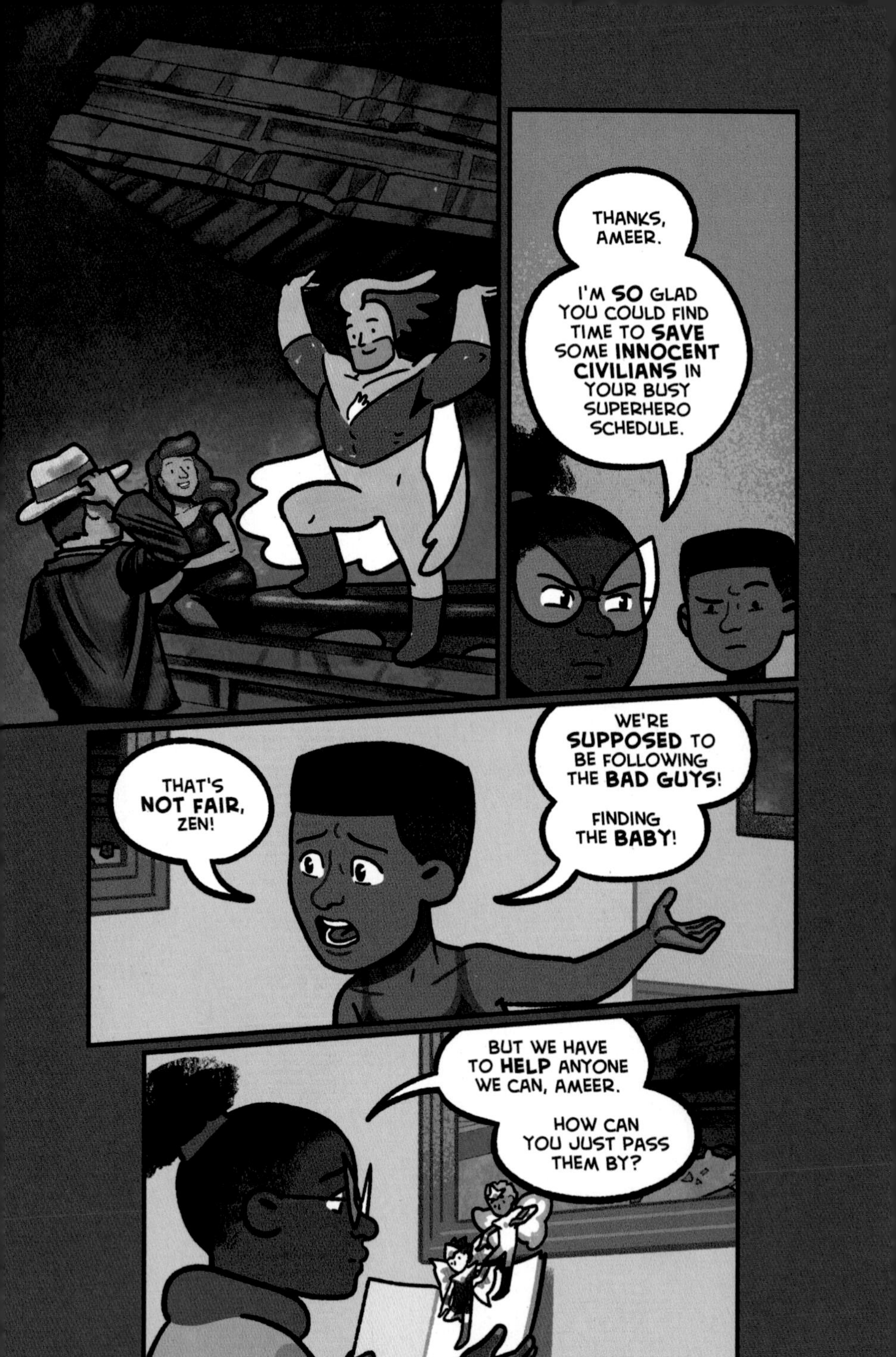
THANKS, AMEER.
I'M SO GLAD YOU COULD FIND TIME TO SAVE SOME INNOCENT CIVILIANS IN YOUR BUSY SUPERHERO SCHEDULE.
THAT'S NOT FAIR, ZEN!
WE'RE SUPPOSED TO BE FOLLOWING THE BAD GUYS!
FINDING THE BABY!
BUT WE HAVE TO HELP ANYONE WE CAN, AMEER.
HOW CAN YOU JUST PASS THEM BY?

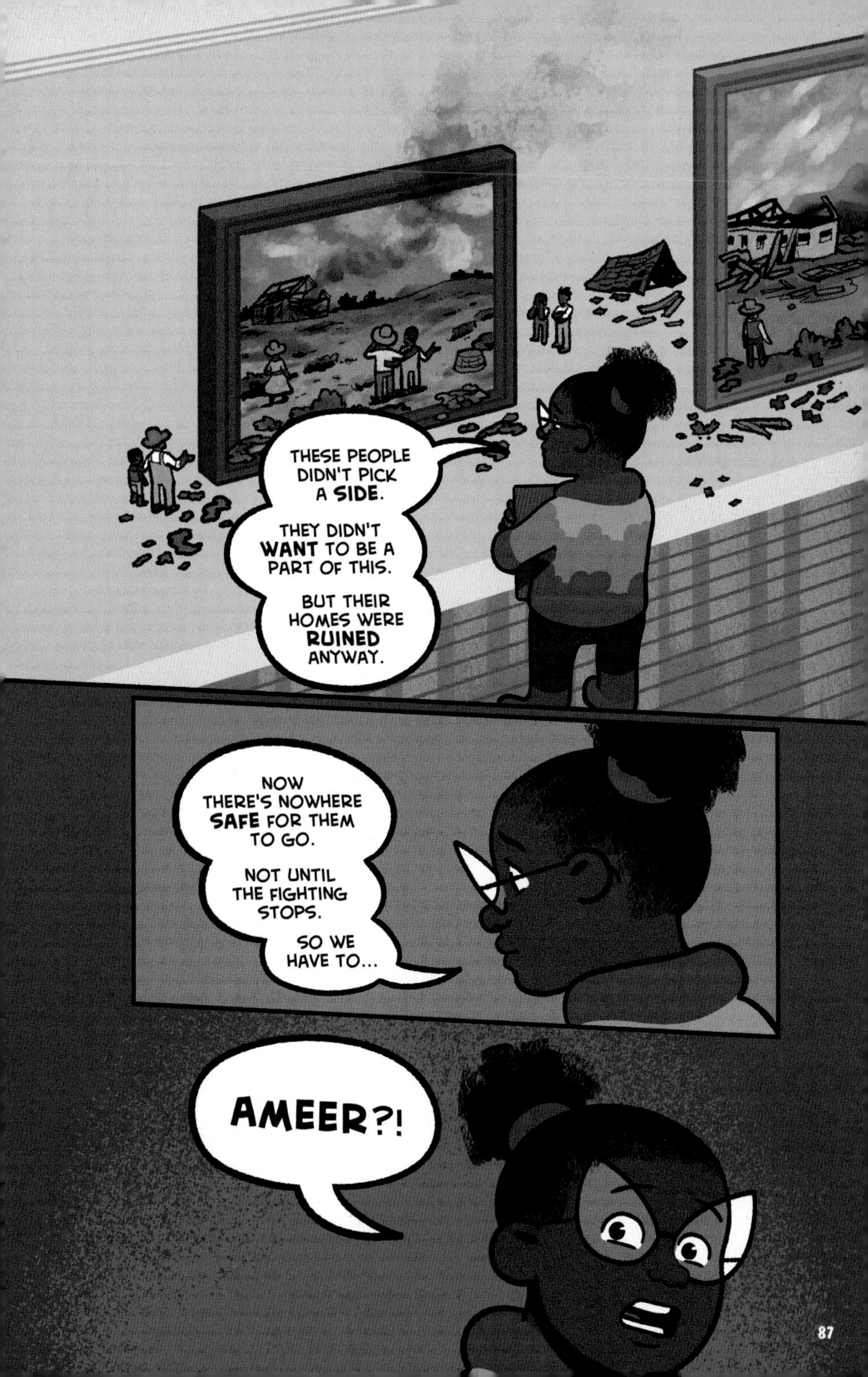
THESE PEOPLE DIDN'T PICK A **SIDE**.
THEY DIDN'T **WANT** TO BE A PART OF THIS.
BUT THEIR HOMES WERE **RUINED** ANYWAY.
NOW THERE'S NOWHERE **SAFE** FOR THEM TO GO.
NOT UNTIL THE FIGHTING STOPS.
SO WE HAVE TO...
AMEER?!

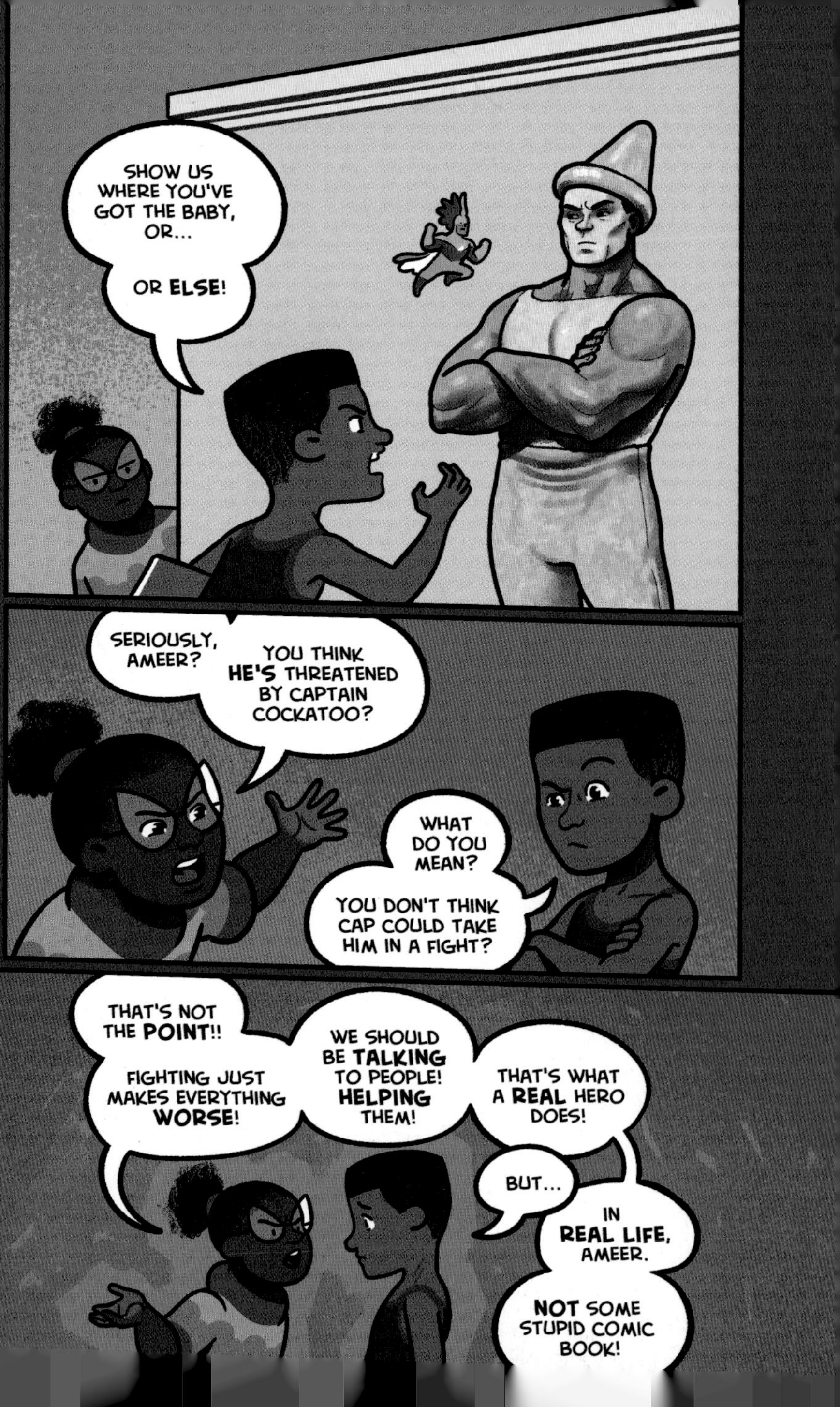
SHOW US WHERE YOU'VE GOT THE BABY, OR...
OR ELSE!
SERIOUSLY, AMEER?
YOU THINK HE'S THREATENED BY CAPTAIN COCKATOO?
WHAT DO YOU MEAN?
YOU DON'T THINK CAP COULD TAKE HIM IN A FIGHT?
THAT'S NOT THE POINT!!
FIGHTING JUST MAKES EVERYTHING WORSE!
WE SHOULD BE TALKING TO PEOPLE! HELPING THEM!
THAT'S WHAT A REAL HERO DOES!
BUT...
IN REAL LIFE, AMEER.
NOT SOME STUPID COMIC BOOK!

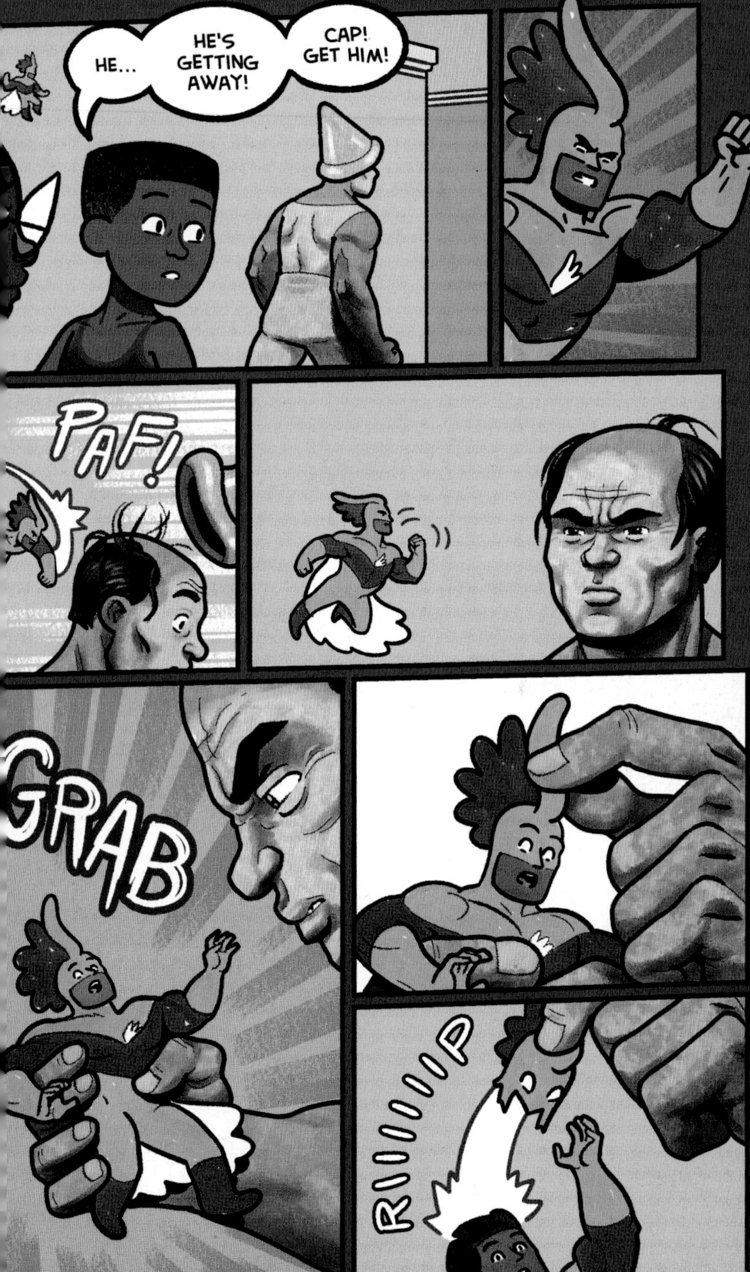
HE...
HE'S GETTING AWAY!
CAP! GET HIM!
PAF!
GRAB
RIIIIIIP

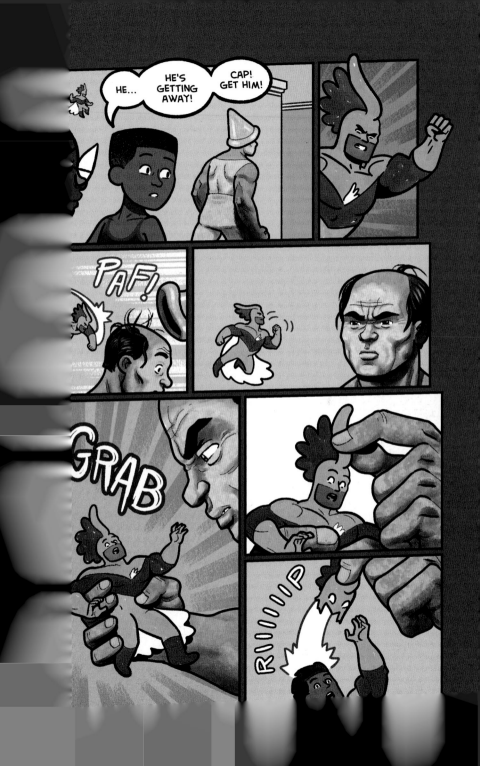

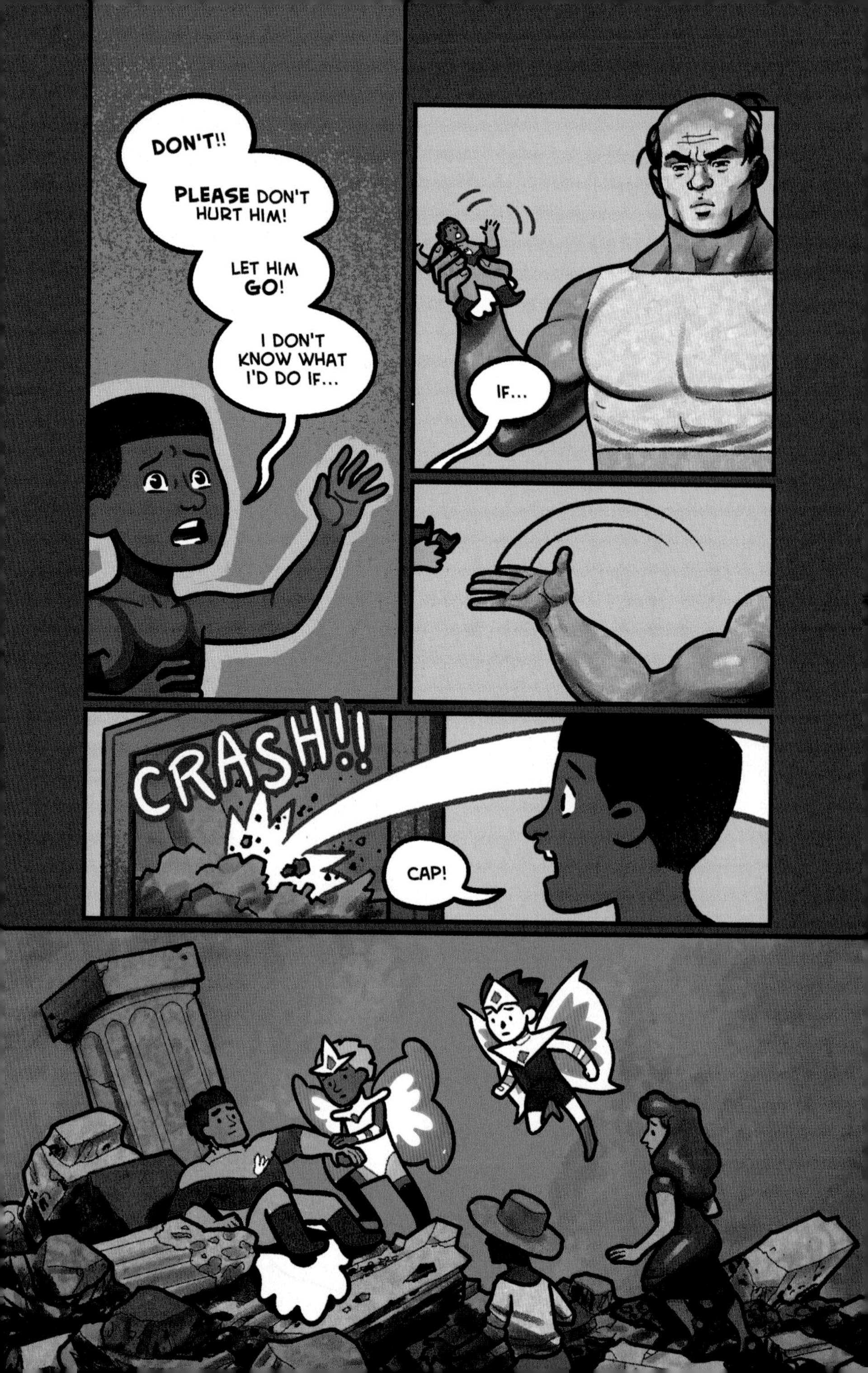
DON'T!!
PLEASE DON'T HURT HIM!
LET HIM GO!
I DON'T KNOW WHAT I'D DO IF...
IF...
CRASH!!
CAP!

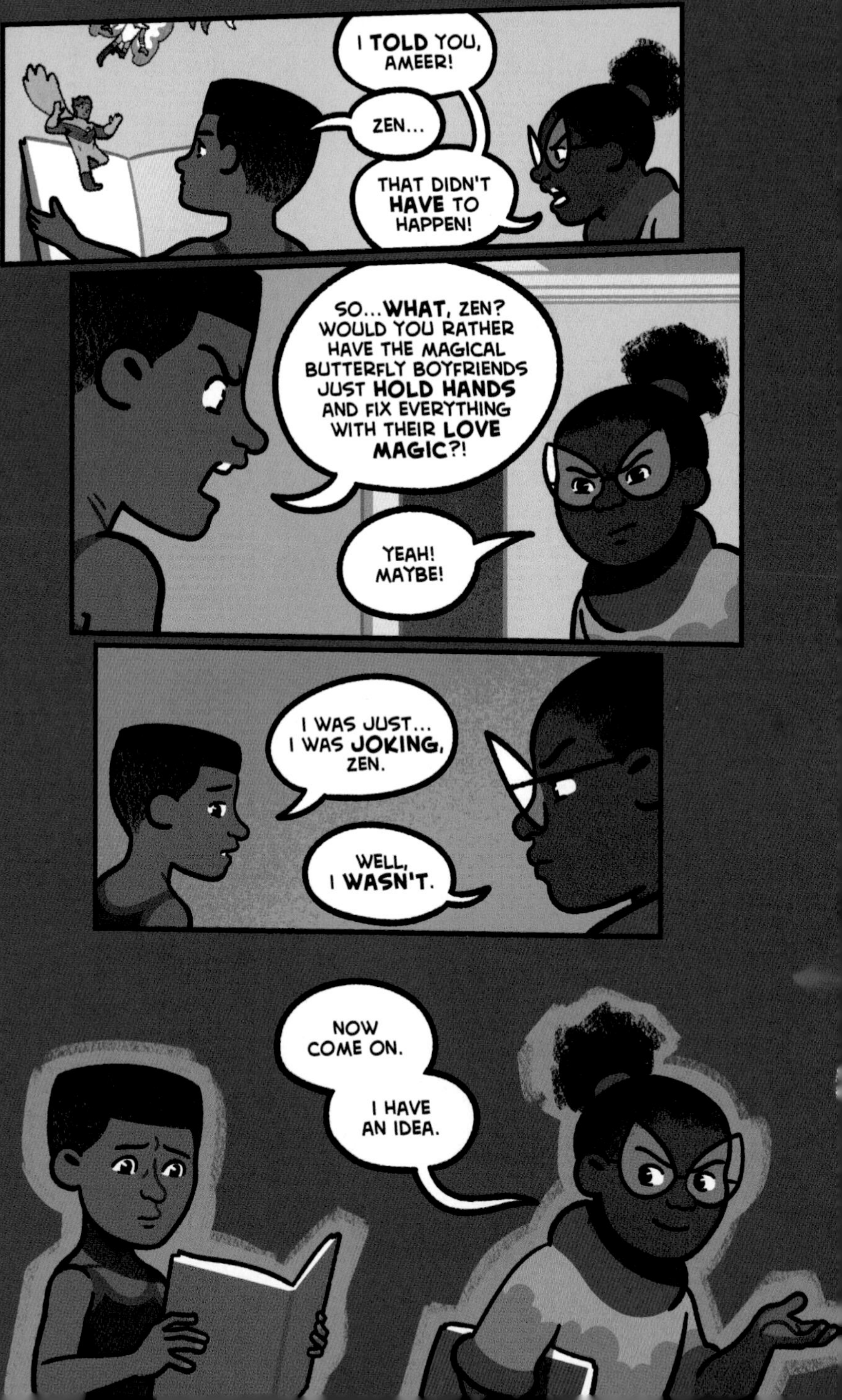
I TOLD YOU, AMEER!
ZEN...
THAT DIDN'T HAVE TO HAPPEN!
SO...WHAT, ZEN? WOULD YOU RATHER HAVE THE MAGICAL BUTTERFLY BOYFRIENDS JUST HOLD HANDS AND FIX EVERYTHING WITH THEIR LOVE MAGIC?!
YEAH! MAYBE!
I WAS JUST... I WAS JOKING, ZEN.
WELL, I WASN'T.
NOW COME ON.
I HAVE AN IDEA.

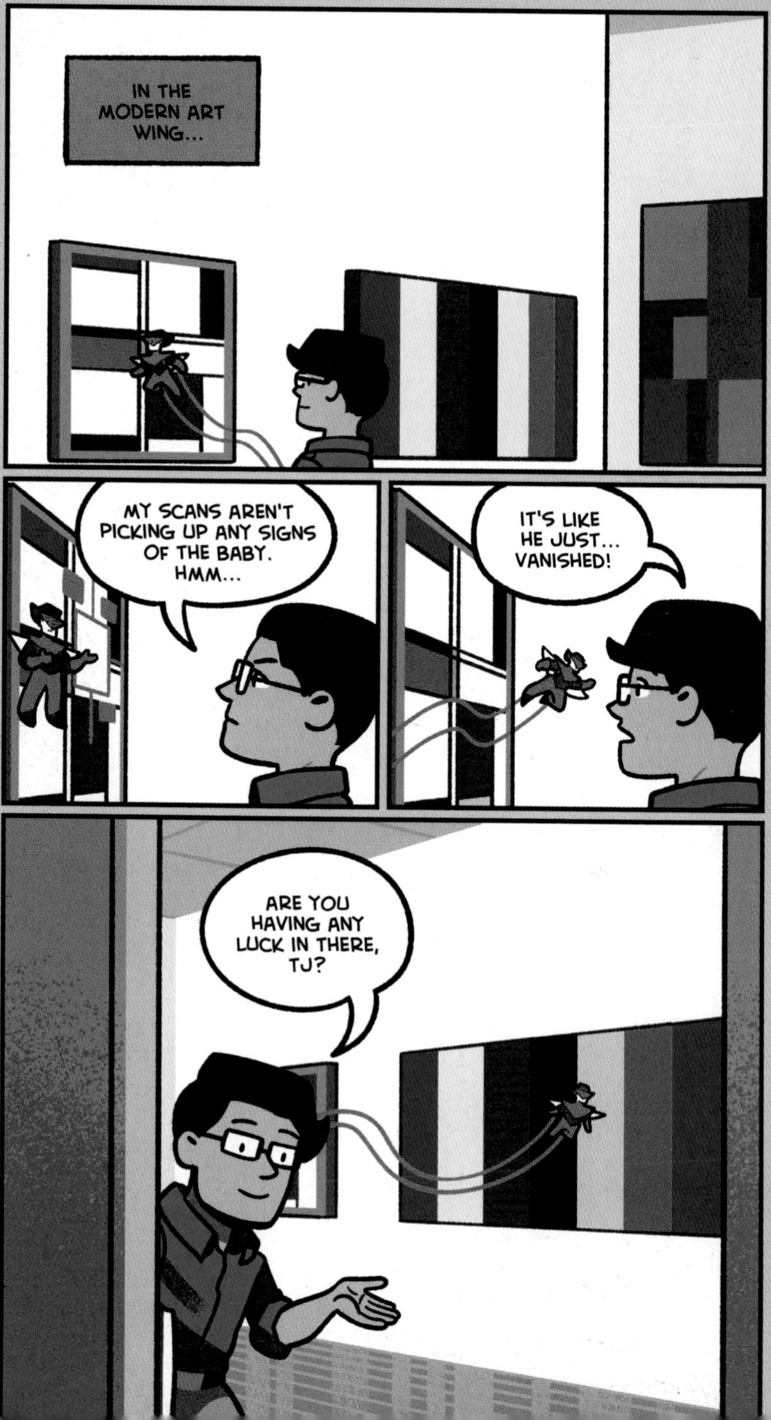
IN THE MODERN ART WING...
MY SCANS AREN'T PICKING UP ANY SIGNS OF THE BABY. HMM...
IT'S LIKE HE JUST... VANISHED!
ARE YOU HAVING ANY LUCK IN THERE, TJ?

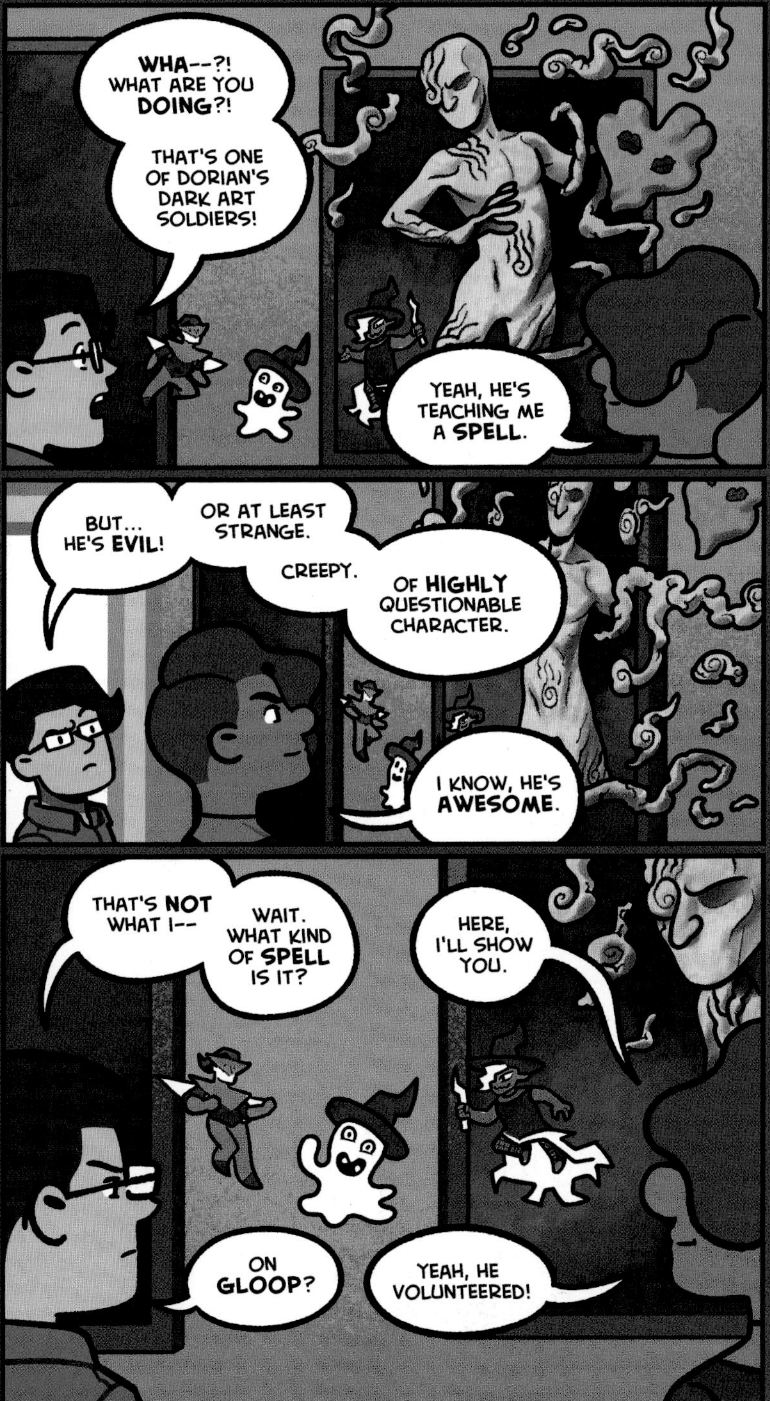
WHA--?! WHAT ARE YOU DOING?!
THAT'S ONE OF DORIAN'S DARK ART SOLDIERS!
YEAH, HE'S TEACHING ME A SPELL.
BUT... HE'S EVIL!
OR AT LEAST STRANGE.
CREEPY.
OF HIGHLY QUESTIONABLE CHARACTER.
I KNOW, HE'S AWESOME.
THAT'S NOT WHAT I--
WAIT. WHAT KIND OF SPELL IS IT?
HERE, I'LL SHOW YOU.
ON GLOOP?
YEAH, HE VOLUNTEERED!

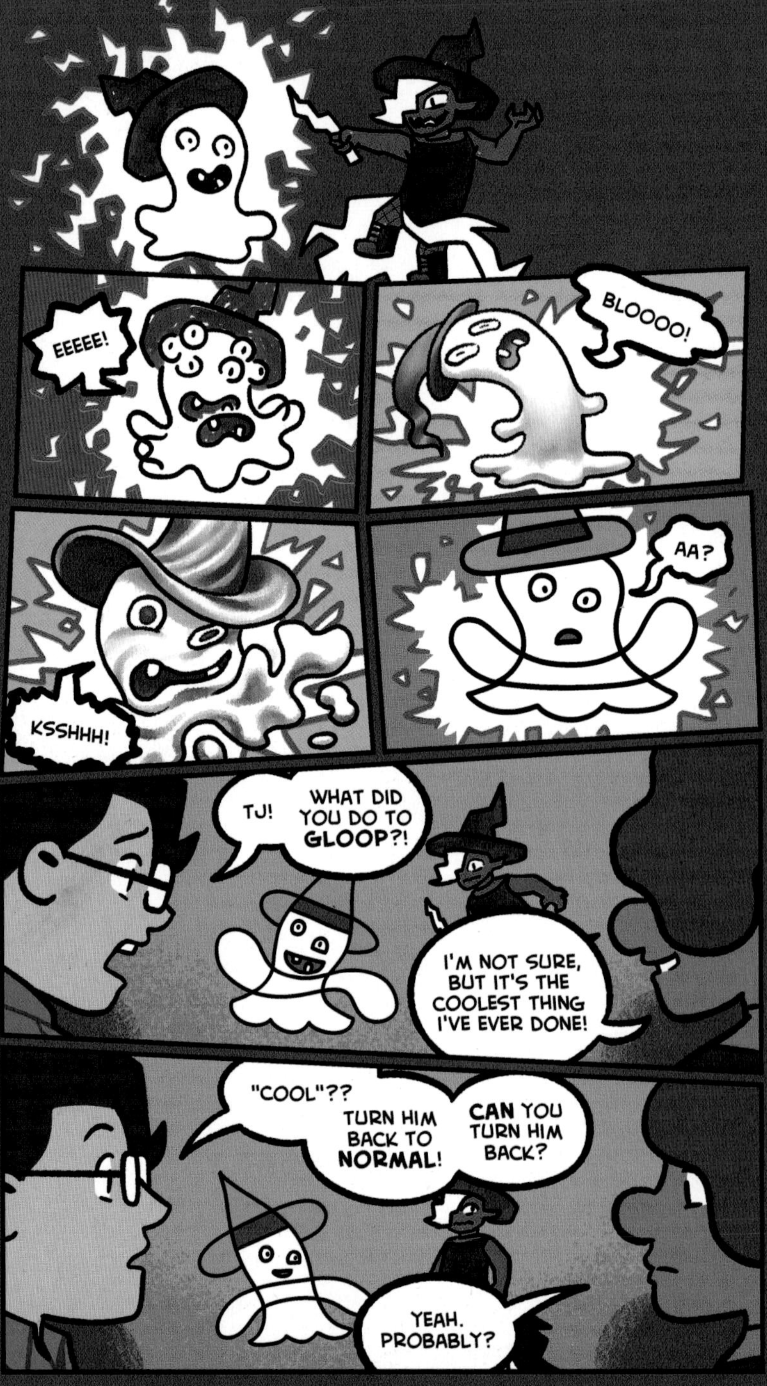
EEEEE!
BLOOOO!
KSSHHH!
AA?
TJ!
WHAT DID YOU DO TO GLOOP?!
I'M NOT SURE, BUT IT'S THE COOLEST THING I'VE EVER DONE!
"COOL"??
TURN HIM BACK TO NORMAL!
CAN YOU TURN HIM BACK?
YEAH. PROBABLY?

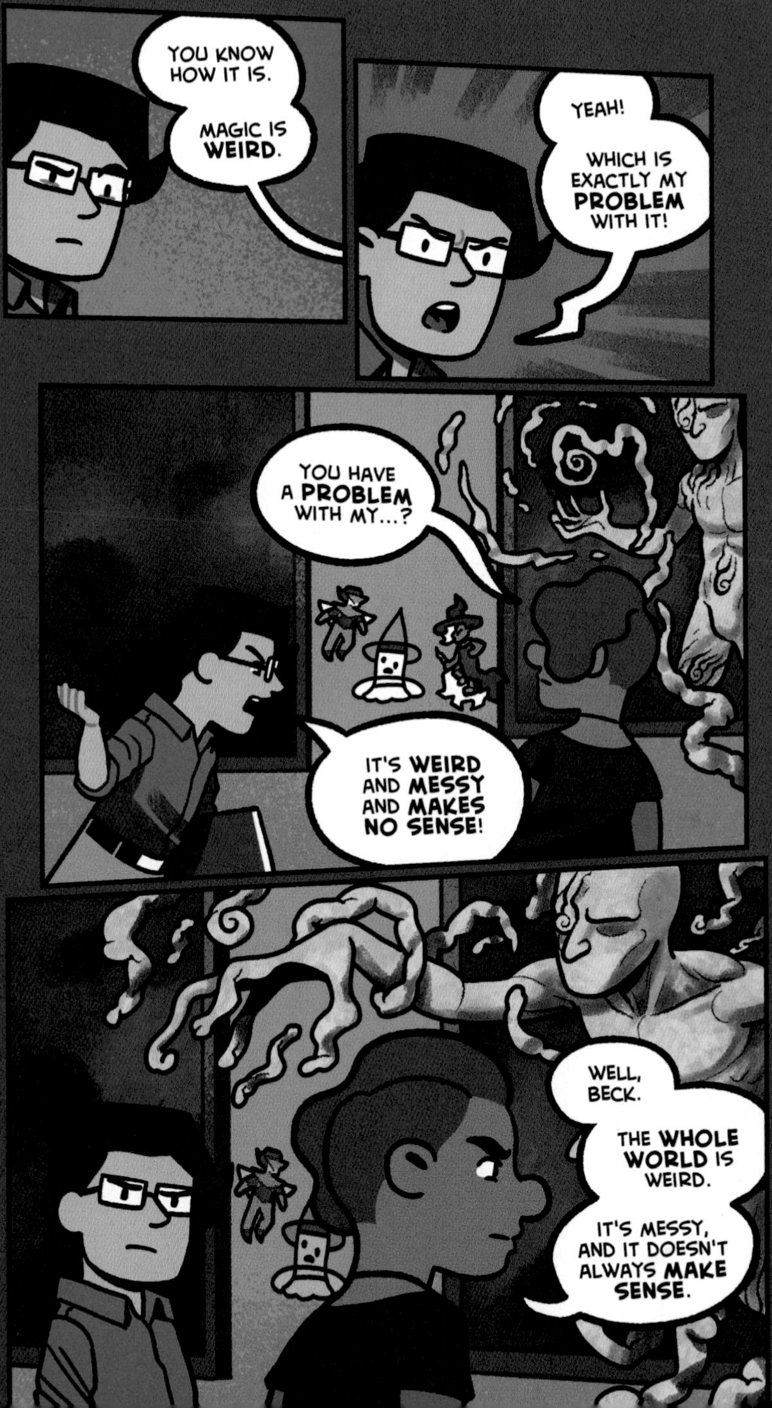
YOU KNOW HOW IT IS.
MAGIC IS WEIRD.
YEAH!
WHICH IS EXACTLY MY PROBLEM WITH IT!
YOU HAVE A PROBLEM WITH MY...?
IT'S WEIRD AND MESSY AND MAKES NO SENSE!
WELL, BECK.
THE WHOLE WORLD IS WEIRD.
IT'S MESSY, AND IT DOESN'T ALWAYS MAKE SENSE.

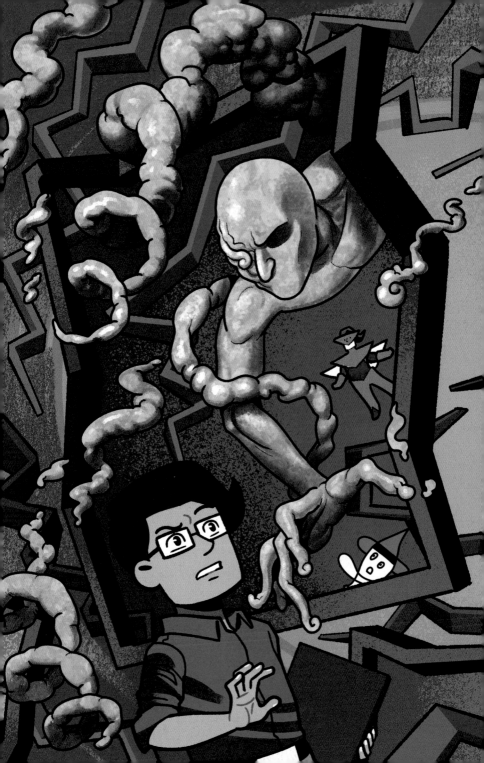

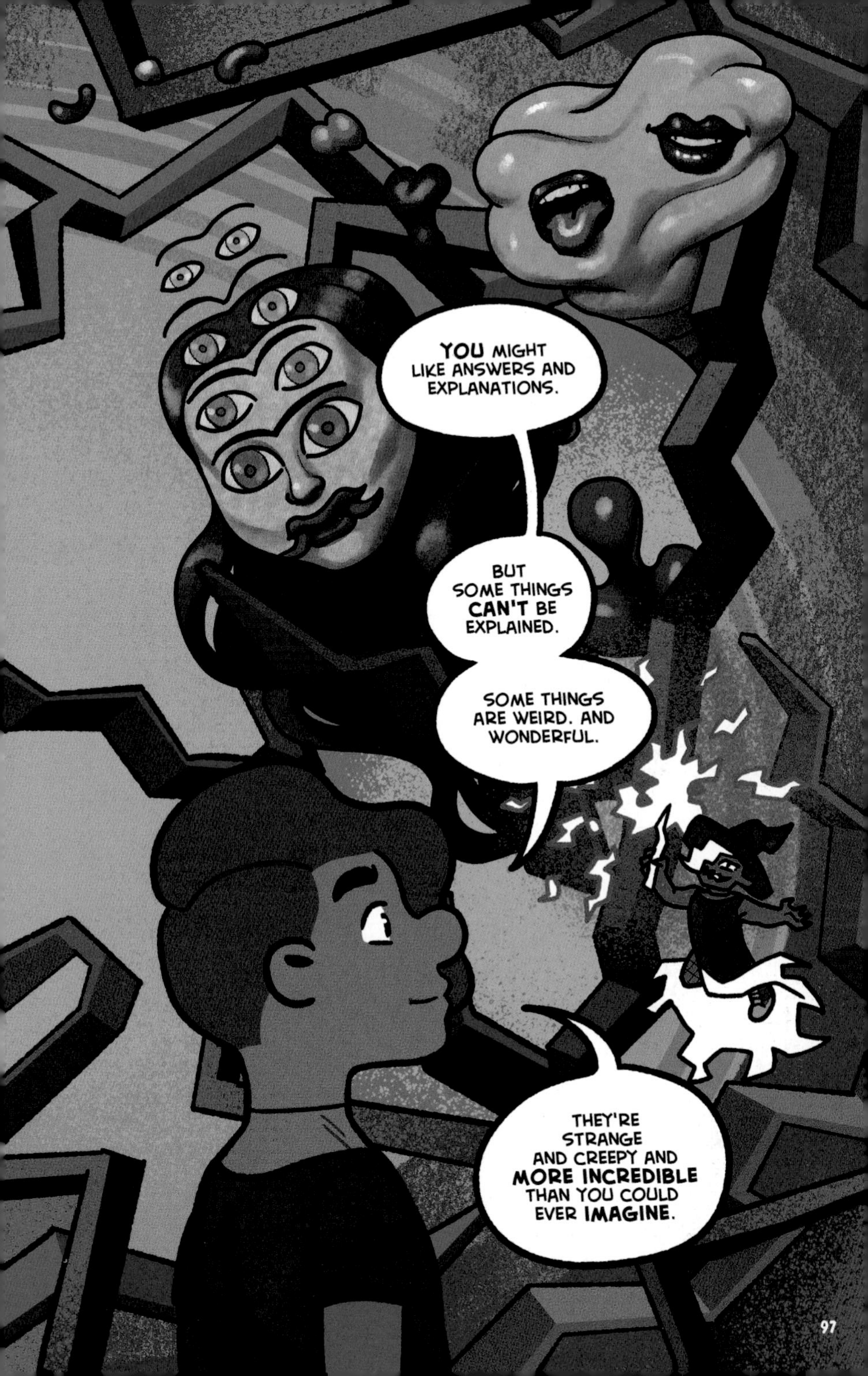
YOU MIGHT LIKE ANSWERS AND EXPLANATIONS.
BUT SOME THINGS CAN'T BE EXPLAINED.
SOME THINGS ARE WEIRD. AND WONDERFUL.
THEY'RE STRANGE AND CREEPY AND MORE INCREDIBLE THAN YOU COULD EVER IMAGINE.

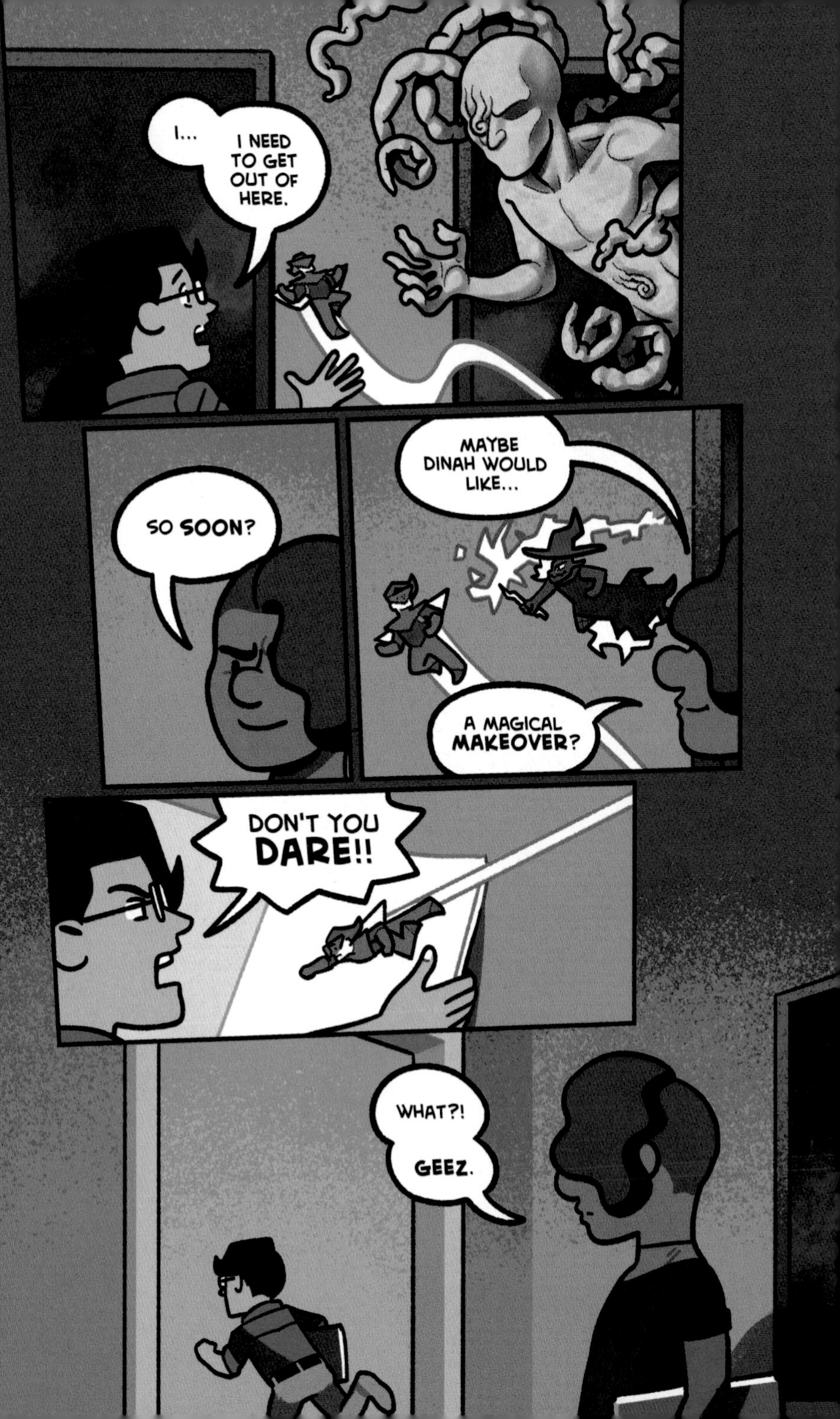
I...
I NEED TO GET OUT OF HERE.
SO SOON?
MAYBE DINAH WOULD LIKE...
A MAGICAL MAKEOVER?
DON'T YOU DARE!!
WHAT?!
GEEZ.

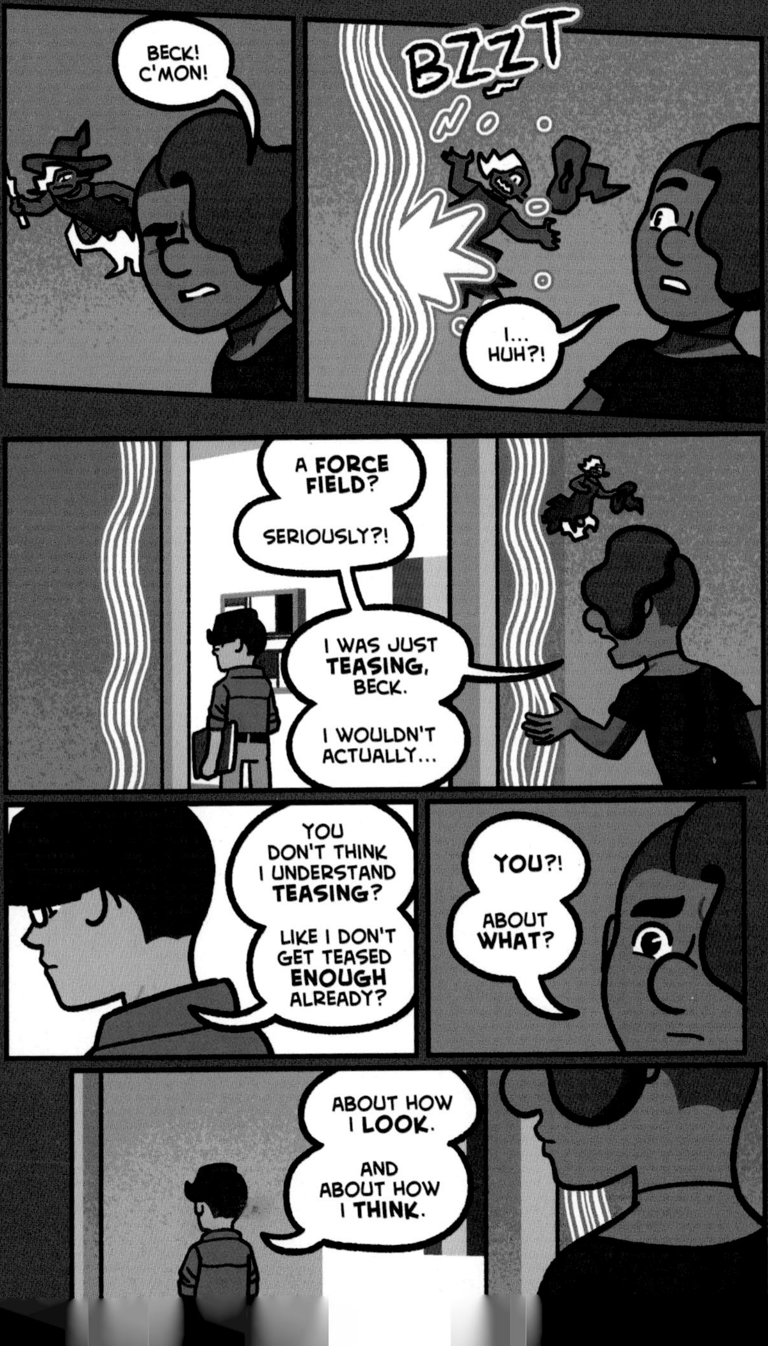
BECK! C'MON!
BZZT
I... HUH?!
A FORCE FIELD?
SERIOUSLY?!
I WAS JUST TEASING, BECK.
I WOULDN'T ACTUALLY...
YOU DON'T THINK I UNDERSTAND TEASING?
LIKE I DON'T GET TEASED ENOUGH ALREADY?
YOU?!
ABOUT WHAT?
ABOUT HOW I LOOK.
AND ABOUT HOW I THINK.

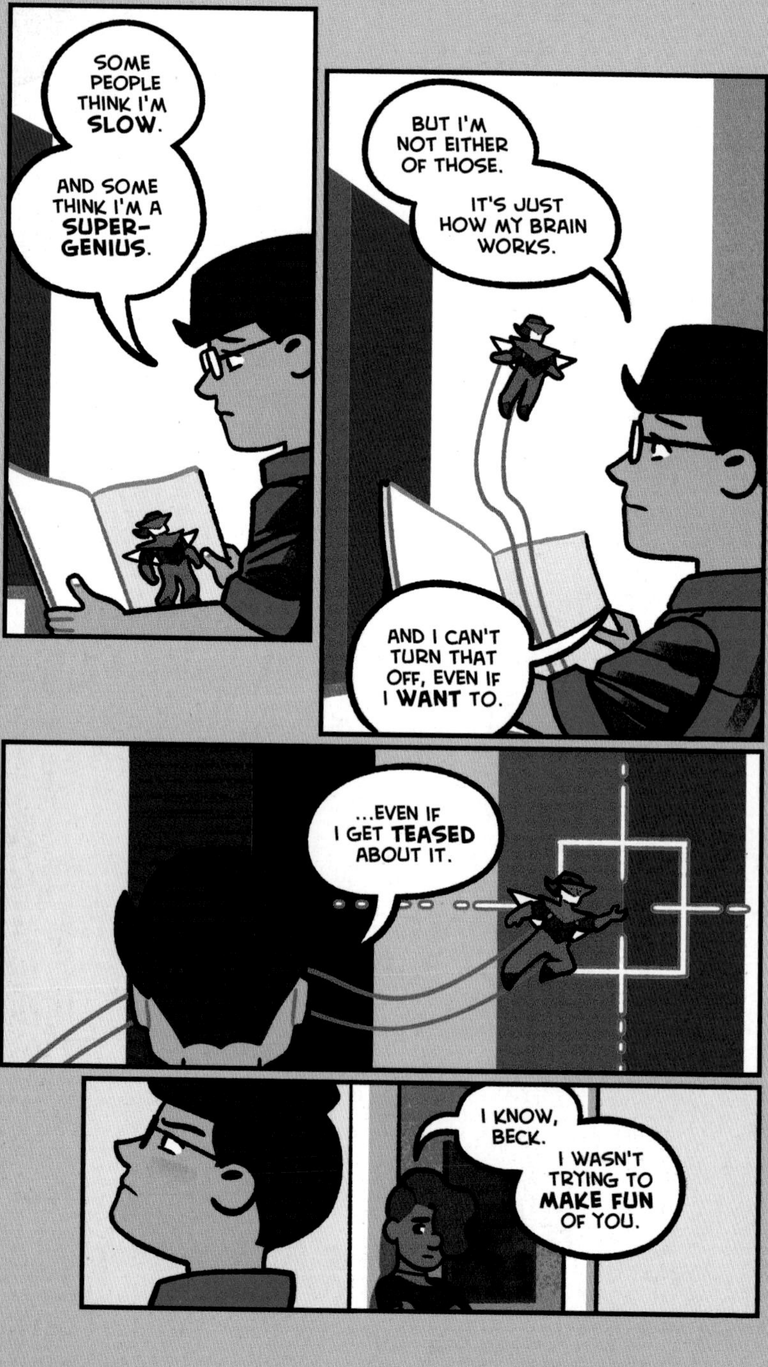
SOME PEOPLE THINK I'M **SLOW**.
AND SOME THINK I'M A **SUPER-GENIUS**.
BUT I'M NOT EITHER OF THOSE.
IT'S JUST HOW MY BRAIN WORKS.
AND I CAN'T TURN THAT OFF, EVEN IF I **WANT** TO.
...EVEN IF I GET **TEASED** ABOUT IT.
I KNOW, BECK.
I WASN'T TRYING TO **MAKE FUN** OF YOU.

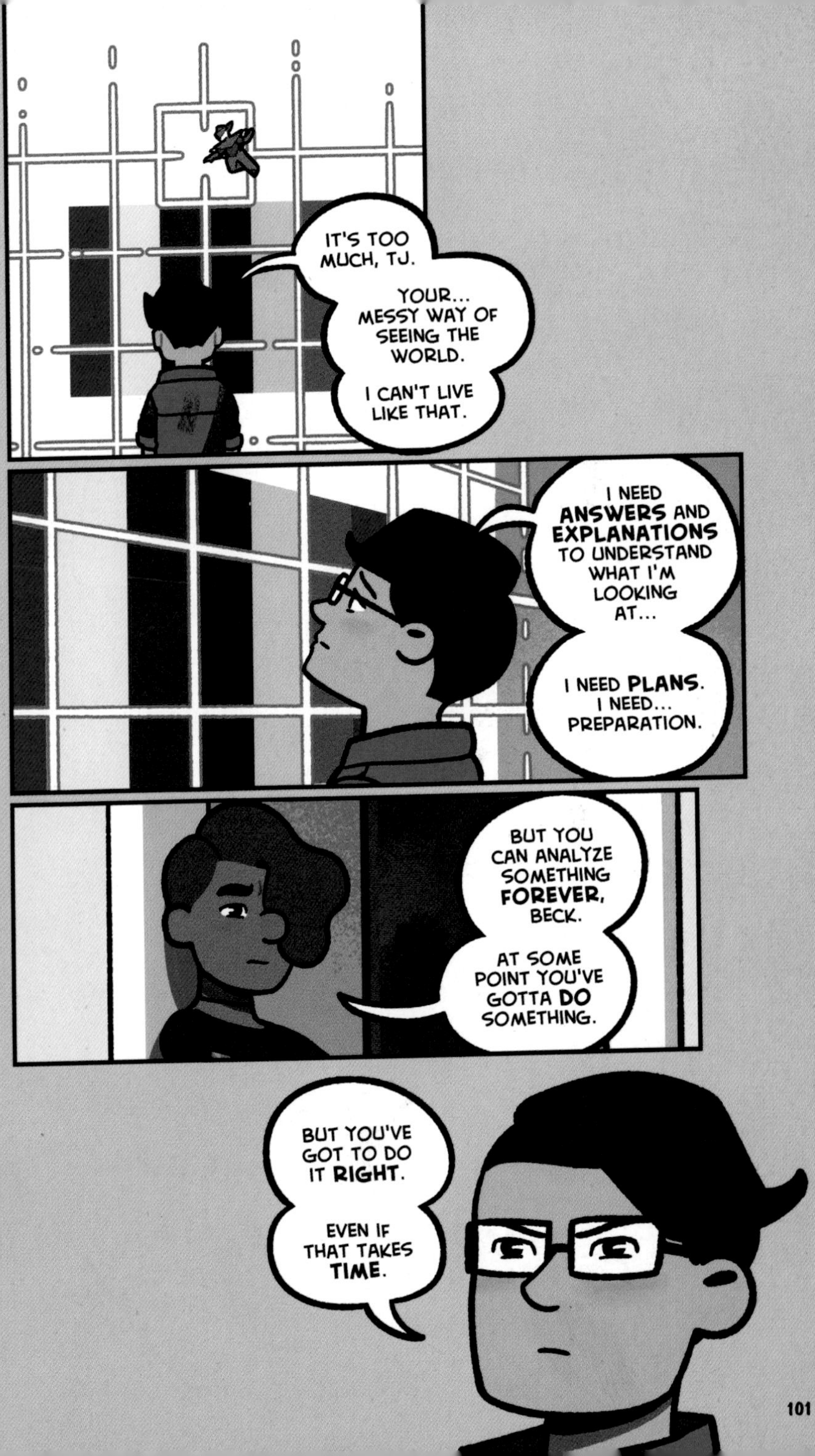
IT'S TOO MUCH, TJ.
YOUR... MESSY WAY OF SEEING THE WORLD.
I CAN'T LIVE LIKE THAT.
I NEED ANSWERS AND EXPLANATIONS TO UNDERSTAND WHAT I'M LOOKING AT...
I NEED PLANS. I NEED... PREPARATION.
BUT YOU CAN ANALYZE SOMETHING FOREVER, BECK.
AT SOME POINT YOU'VE GOTTA DO SOMETHING.
BUT YOU'VE GOT TO DO IT RIGHT.
EVEN IF THAT TAKES TIME.

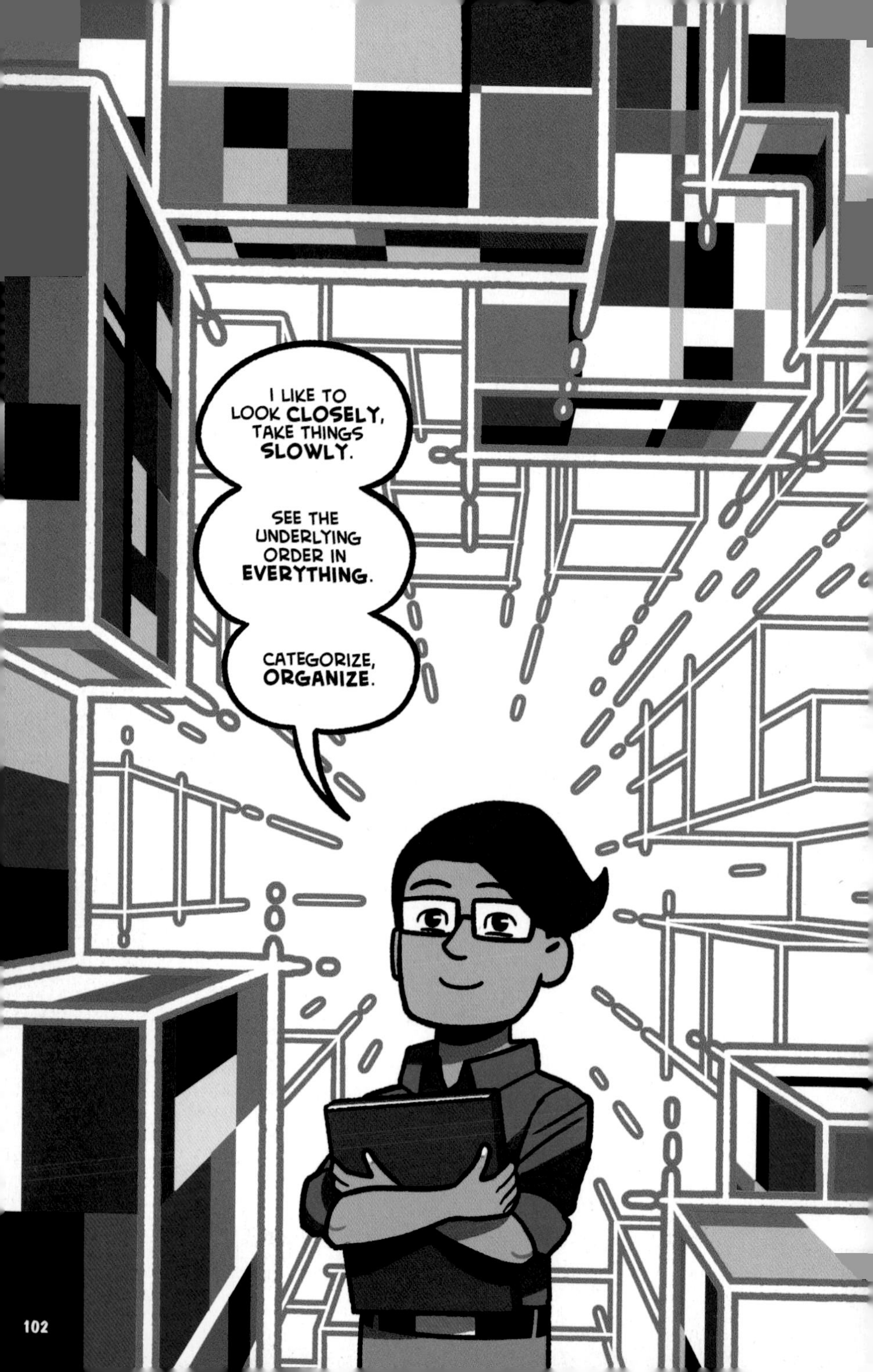
I LIKE TO LOOK CLOSELY, TAKE THINGS SLOWLY.
SEE THE UNDERLYING ORDER IN EVERYTHING.
CATEGORIZE, ORGANIZE.

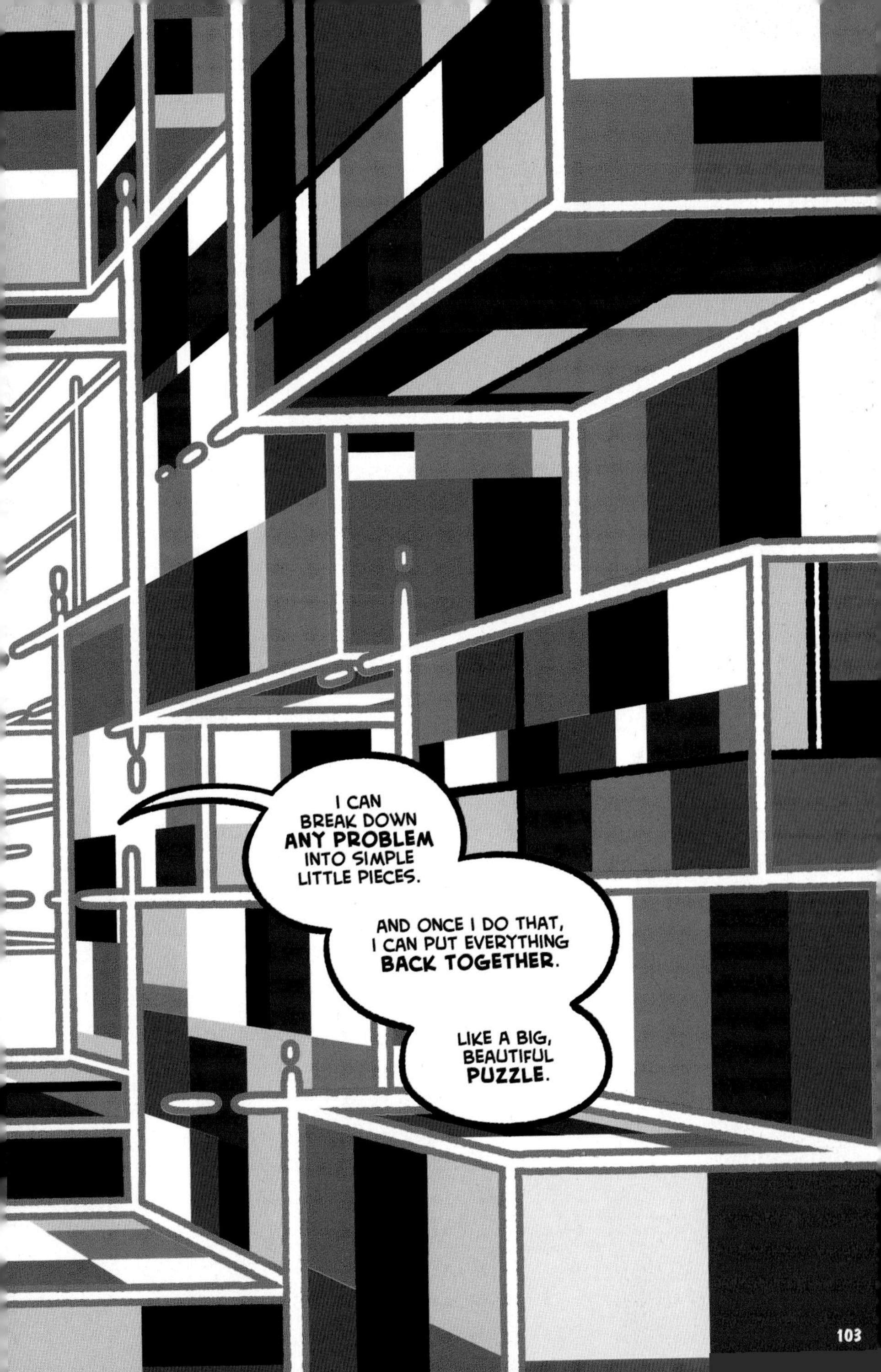
I CAN BREAK DOWN **ANY PROBLEM** INTO SIMPLE LITTLE PIECES.
AND ONCE I DO THAT, I CAN PUT EVERYTHING **BACK TOGETHER**.
LIKE A BIG, BEAUTIFUL **PUZZLE**.

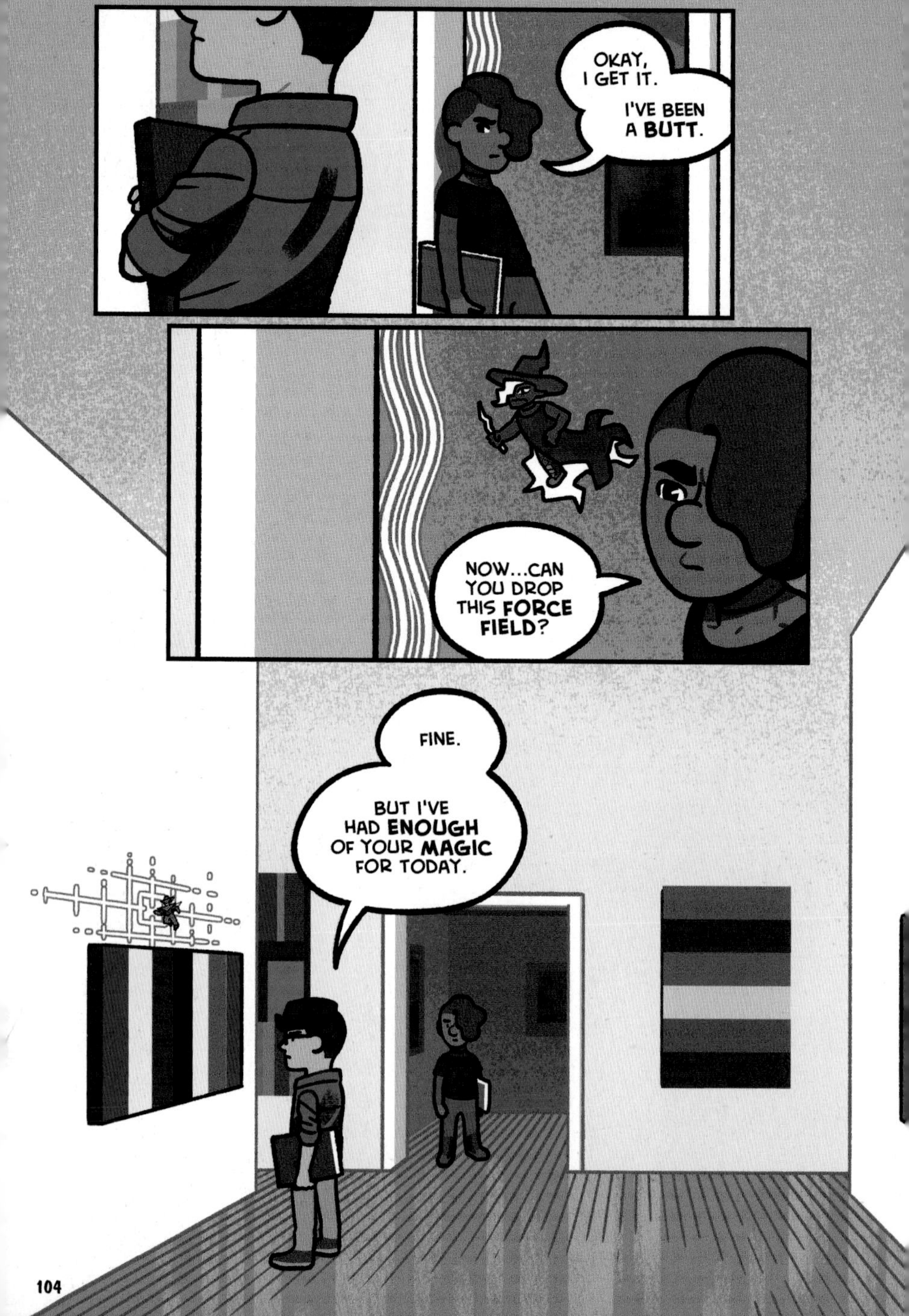
OKAY, I GET IT.
I'VE BEEN A BUTT.
NOW...CAN YOU DROP THIS FORCE FIELD?
FINE.
BUT I'VE HAD ENOUGH OF YOUR MAGIC FOR TODAY.

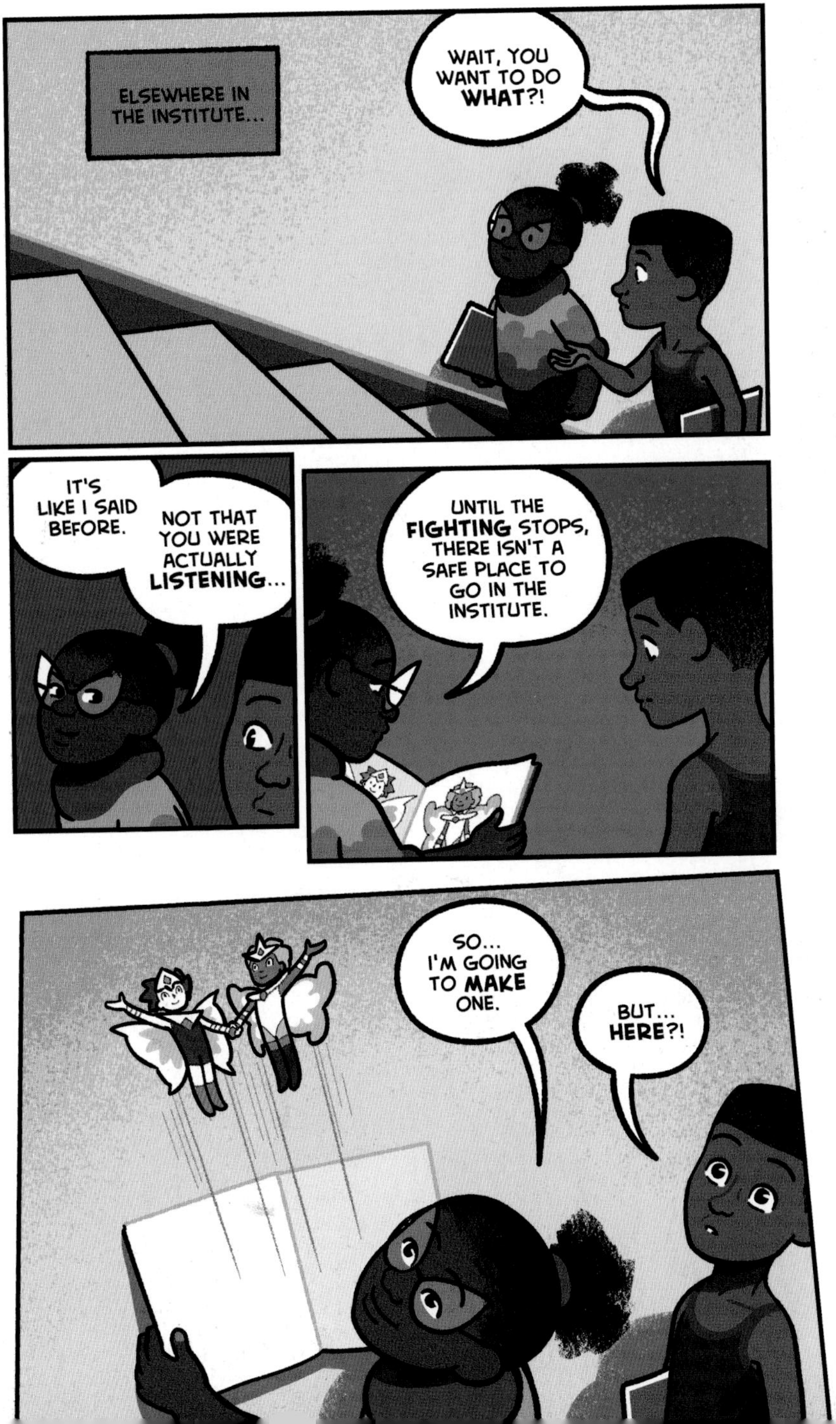
ELSEWHERE IN THE INSTITUTE...
WAIT, YOU WANT TO DO WHAT?!
IT'S LIKE I SAID BEFORE.
NOT THAT YOU WERE ACTUALLY LISTENING...
UNTIL THE FIGHTING STOPS, THERE ISN'T A SAFE PLACE TO GO IN THE INSTITUTE.
SO... I'M GOING TO MAKE ONE.
BUT... HERE?!

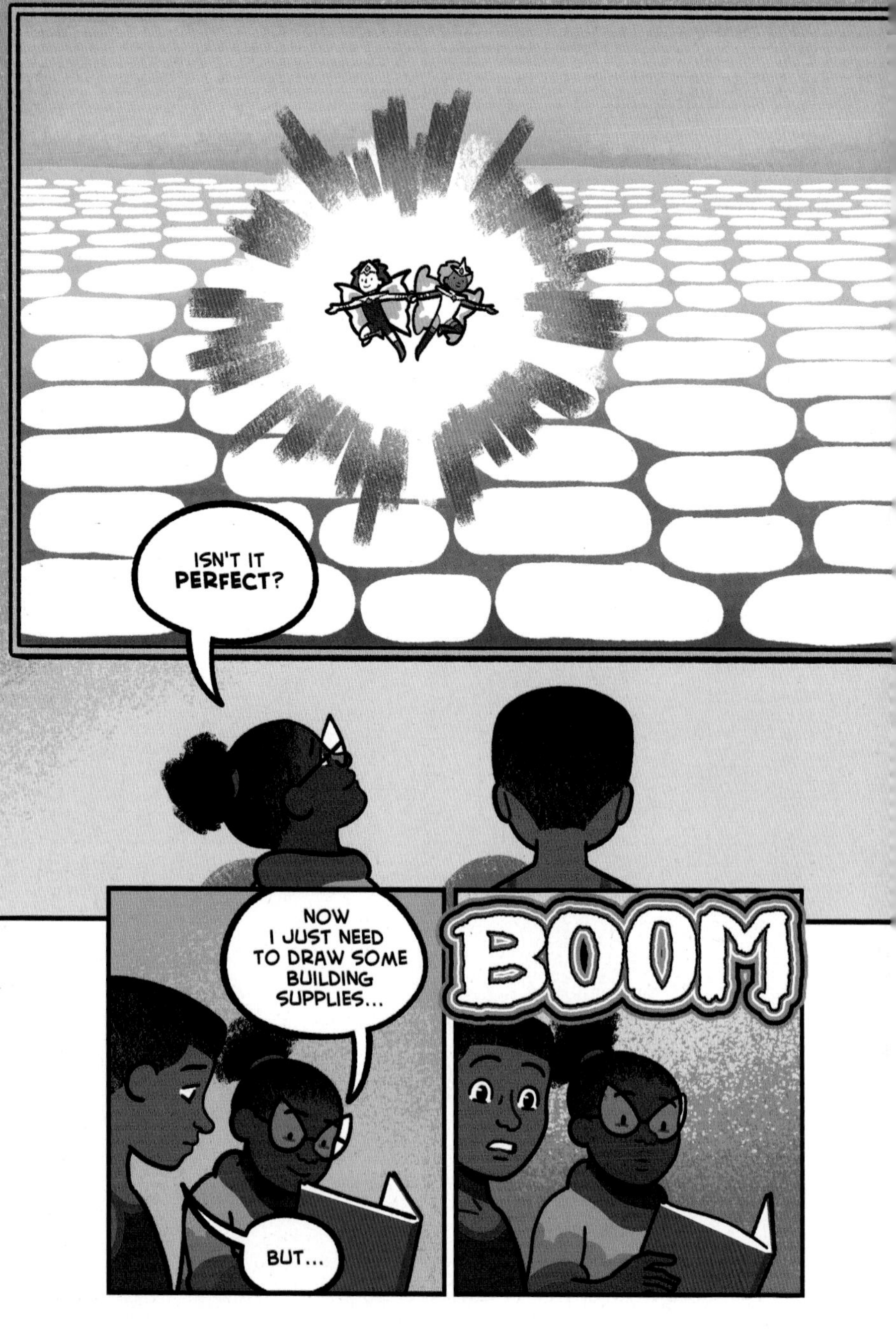
ISN'T IT PERFECT?
NOW I JUST NEED TO DRAW SOME BUILDING SUPPLIES...
BUT...
BOOM

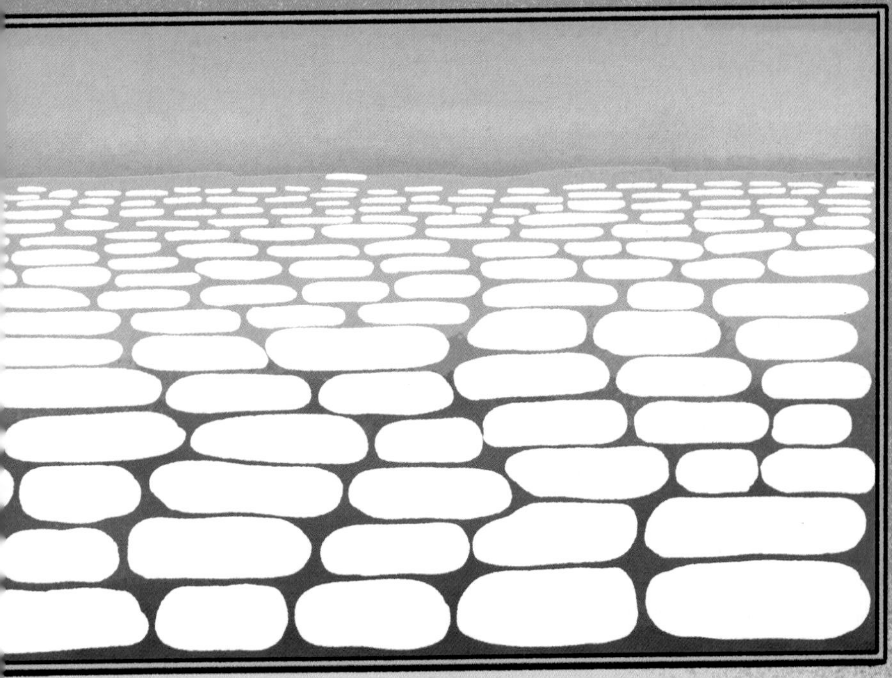

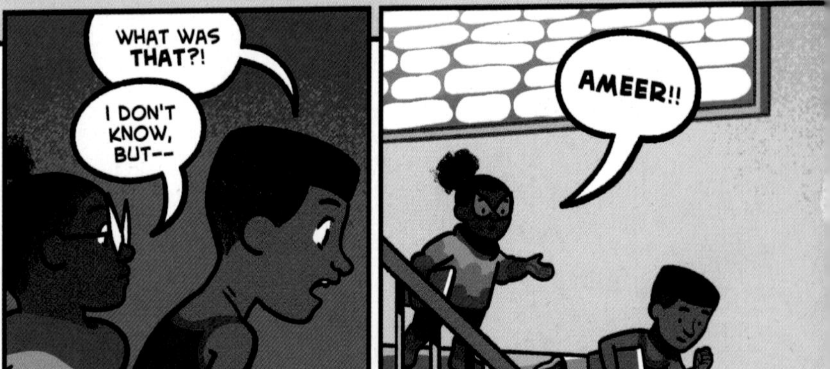
WHAT WAS THAT?!
I DON'T KNOW, BUT--
AMEER!!

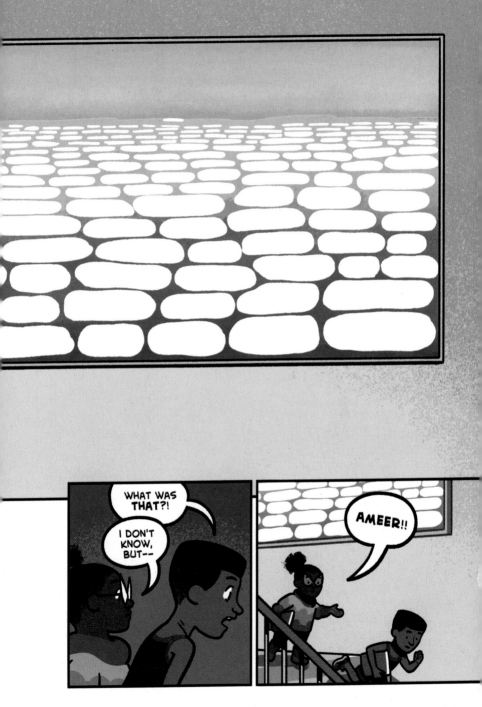

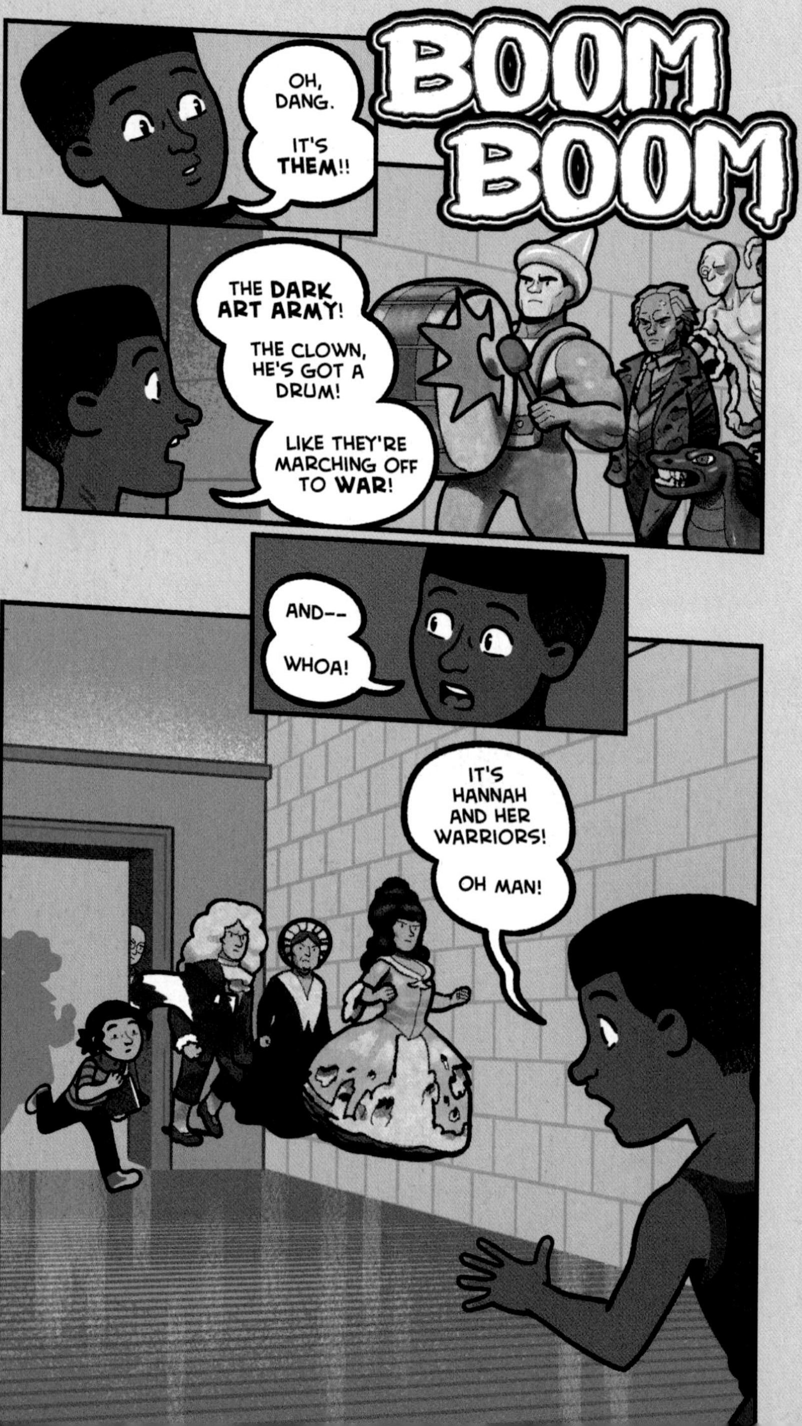

OH, DANG.
IT'S THEM!!
BOOM BOOM
THE DARK ART ARMY!
THE CLOWN, HE'S GOT A DRUM!
LIKE THEY'RE MARCHING OFF TO WAR!
AND--
WHOA!
IT'S HANNAH AND HER WARRIORS!
OH MAN!

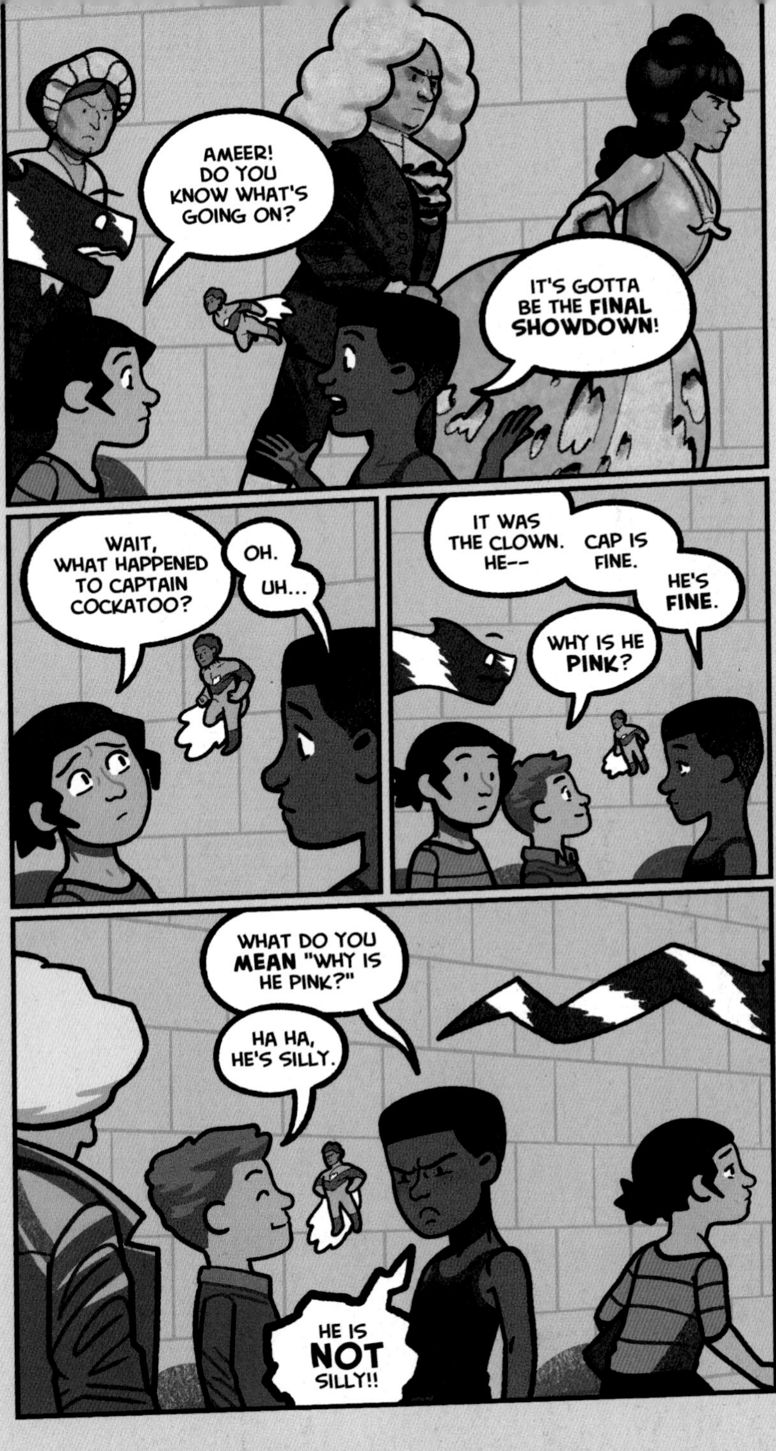
AMEER! DO YOU KNOW WHAT'S GOING ON?
IT'S GOTTA BE THE **FINAL SHOWDOWN**!
WAIT, WHAT HAPPENED TO CAPTAIN COCKATOO?
OH.
UH...
IT WAS THE CLOWN. HE--
CAP IS FINE.
HE'S **FINE**.
WHY IS HE **PINK**?
WHAT DO YOU **MEAN** "WHY IS HE PINK?"
HA HA, HE'S SILLY.
HE IS **NOT** SILLY!!

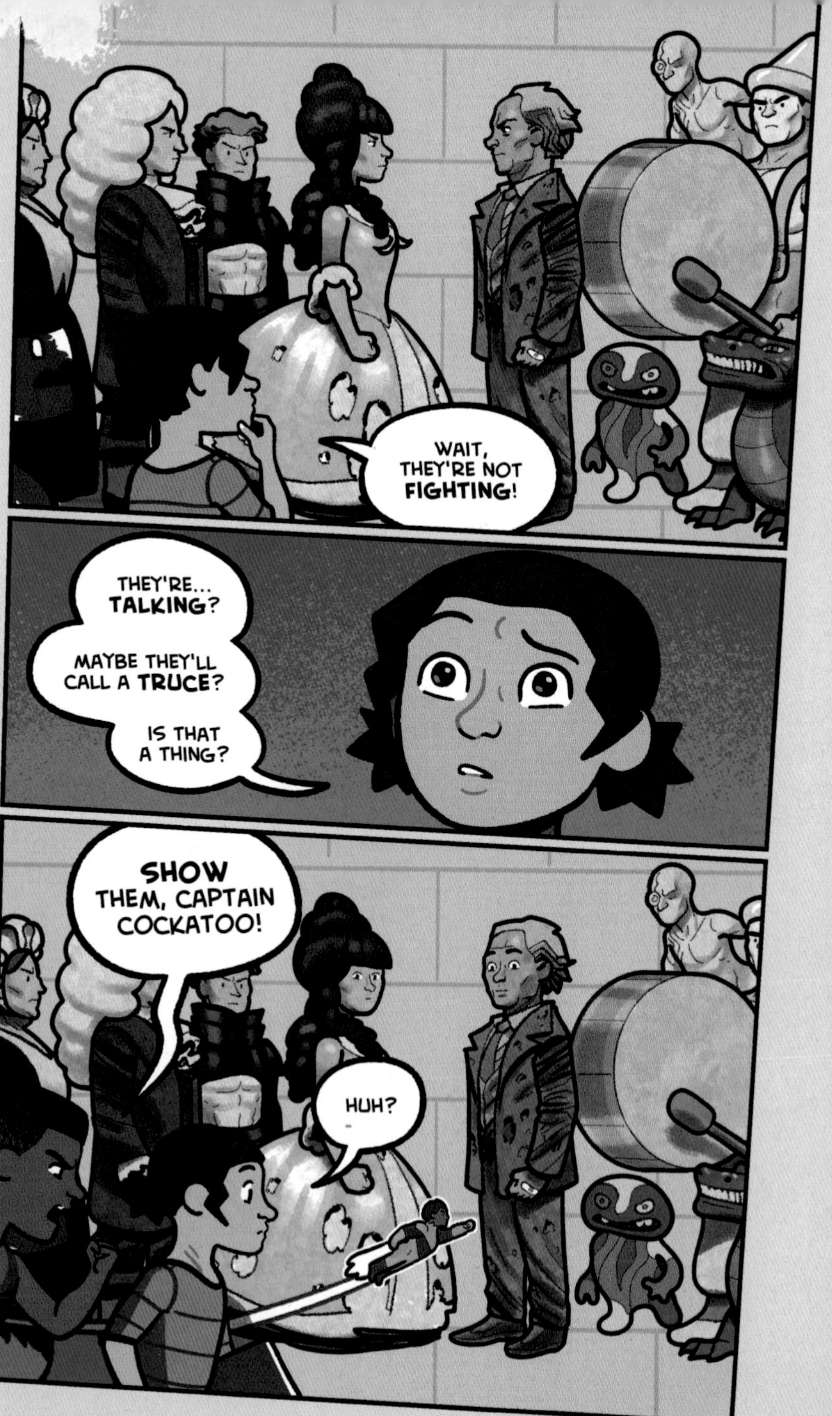
WAIT, THEY'RE NOT FIGHTING!
THEY'RE... TALKING?
MAYBE THEY'LL CALL A TRUCE?
IS THAT A THING?
SHOW THEM, CAPTAIN COCKATOO!
HUH?

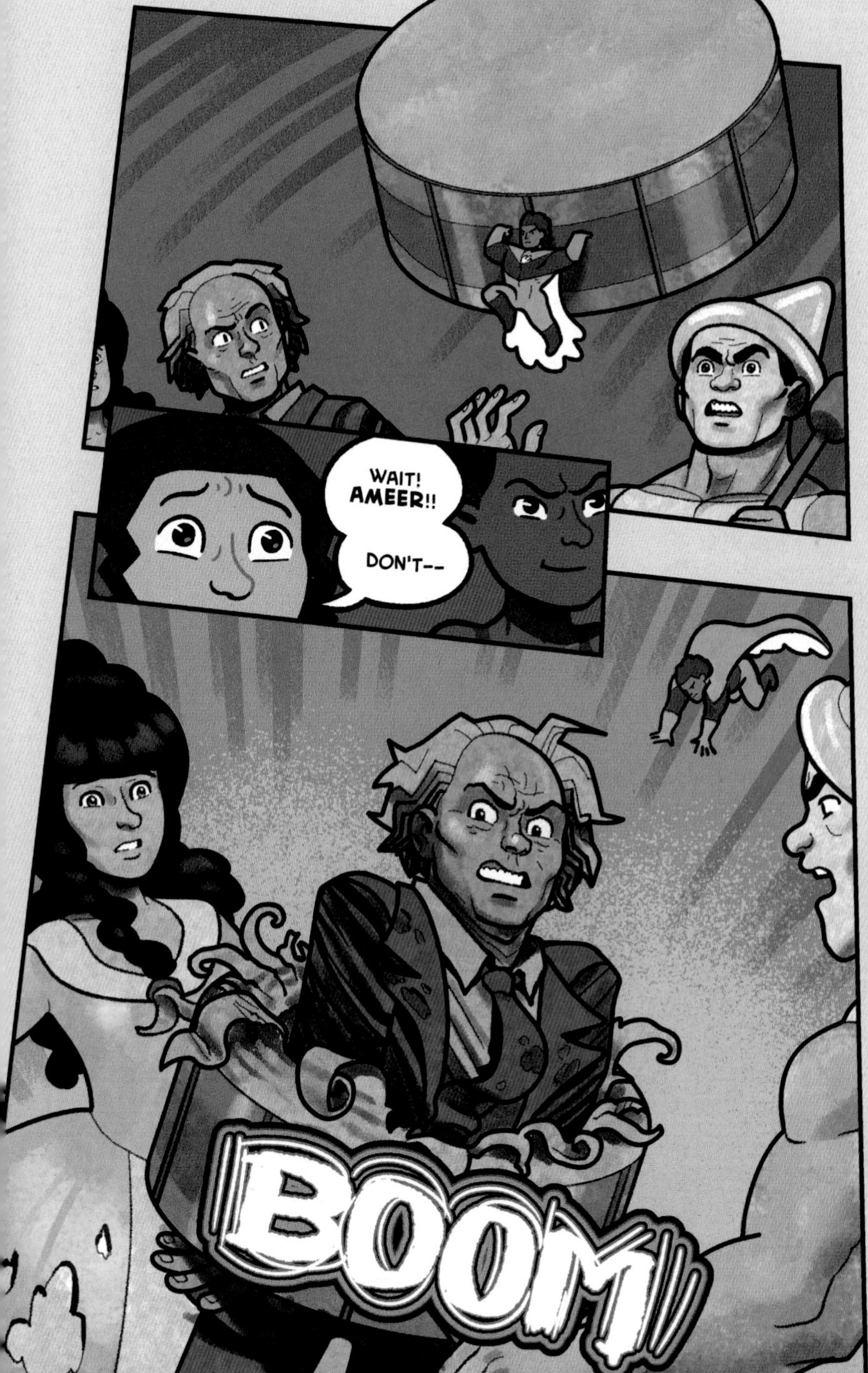
WAIT! AMEER!!
DON'T--
BOOM

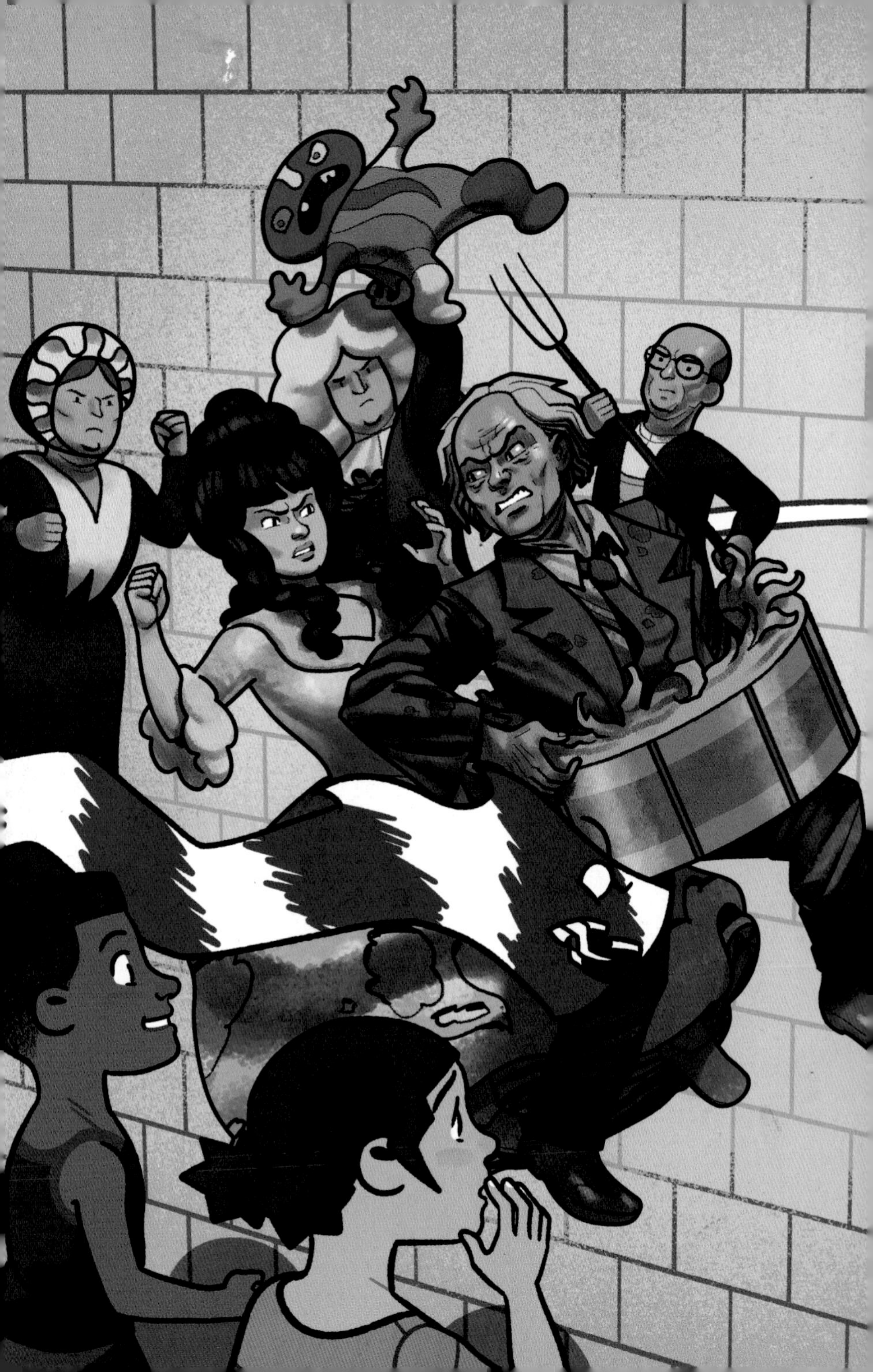

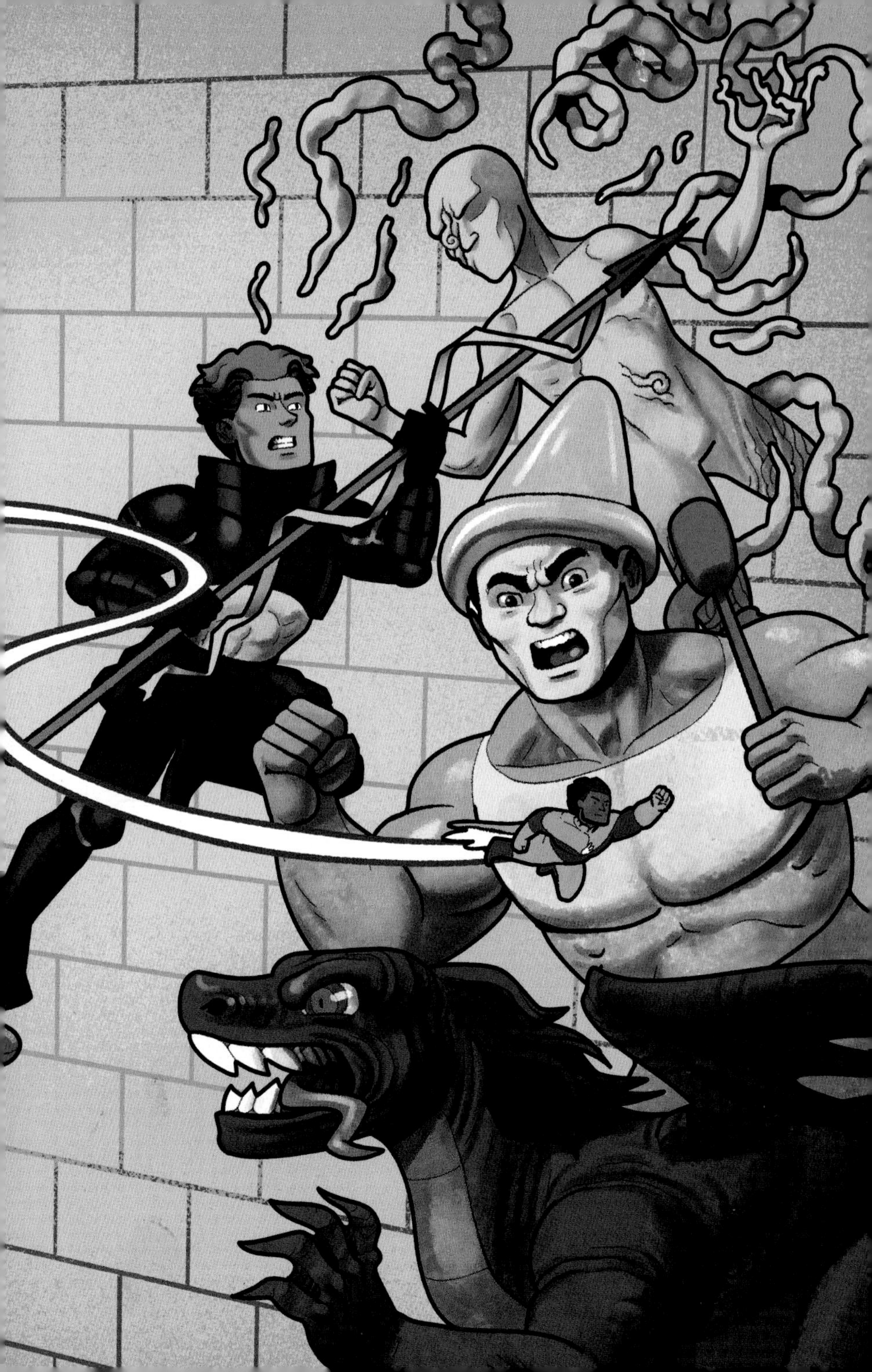

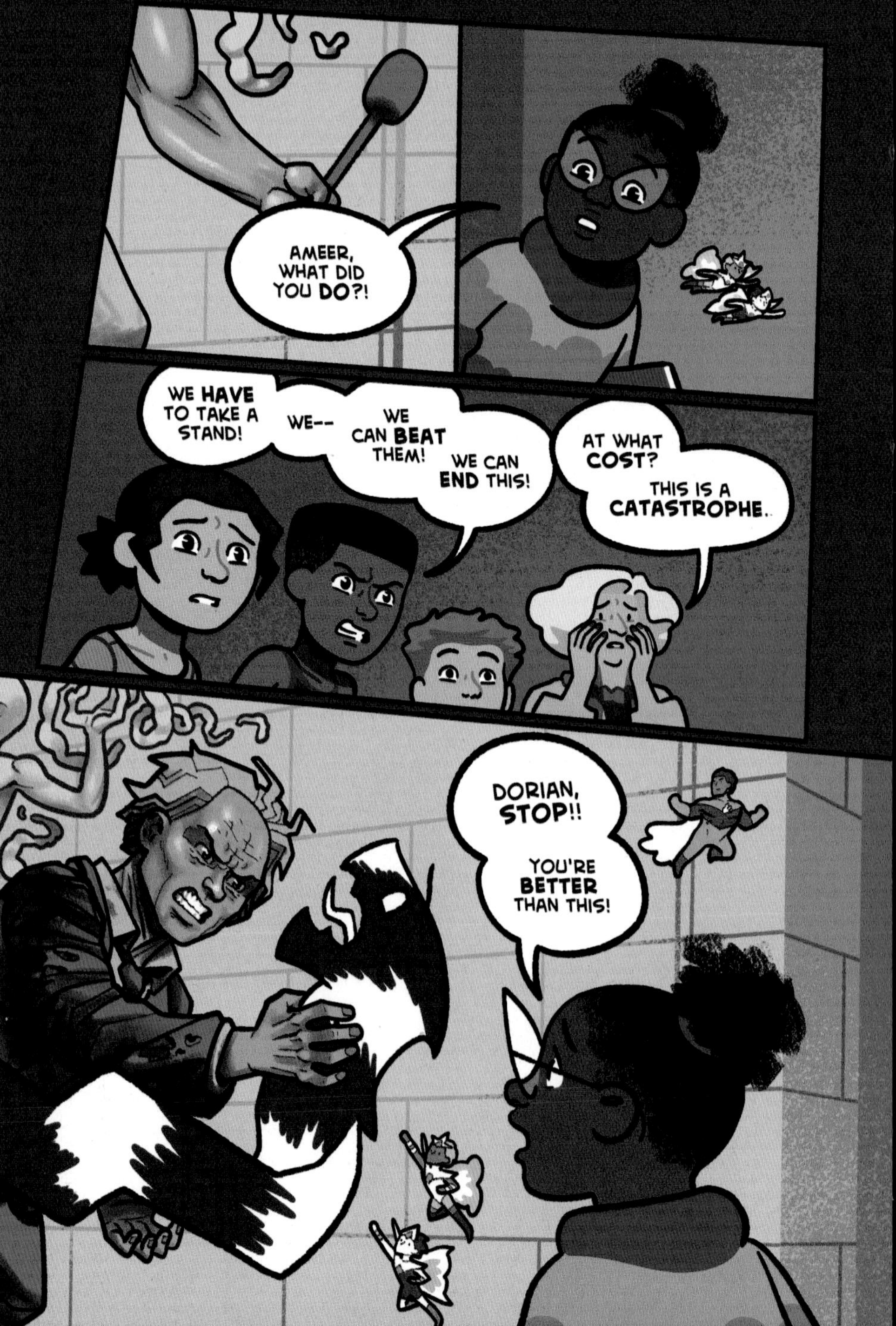
AMEER, WHAT DID YOU DO?!
WE HAVE TO TAKE A STAND!
WE--
WE CAN BEAT THEM!
WE CAN END THIS!
AT WHAT COST?
THIS IS A CATASTROPHE..
DORIAN, STOP!!
YOU'RE BETTER THAN THIS!

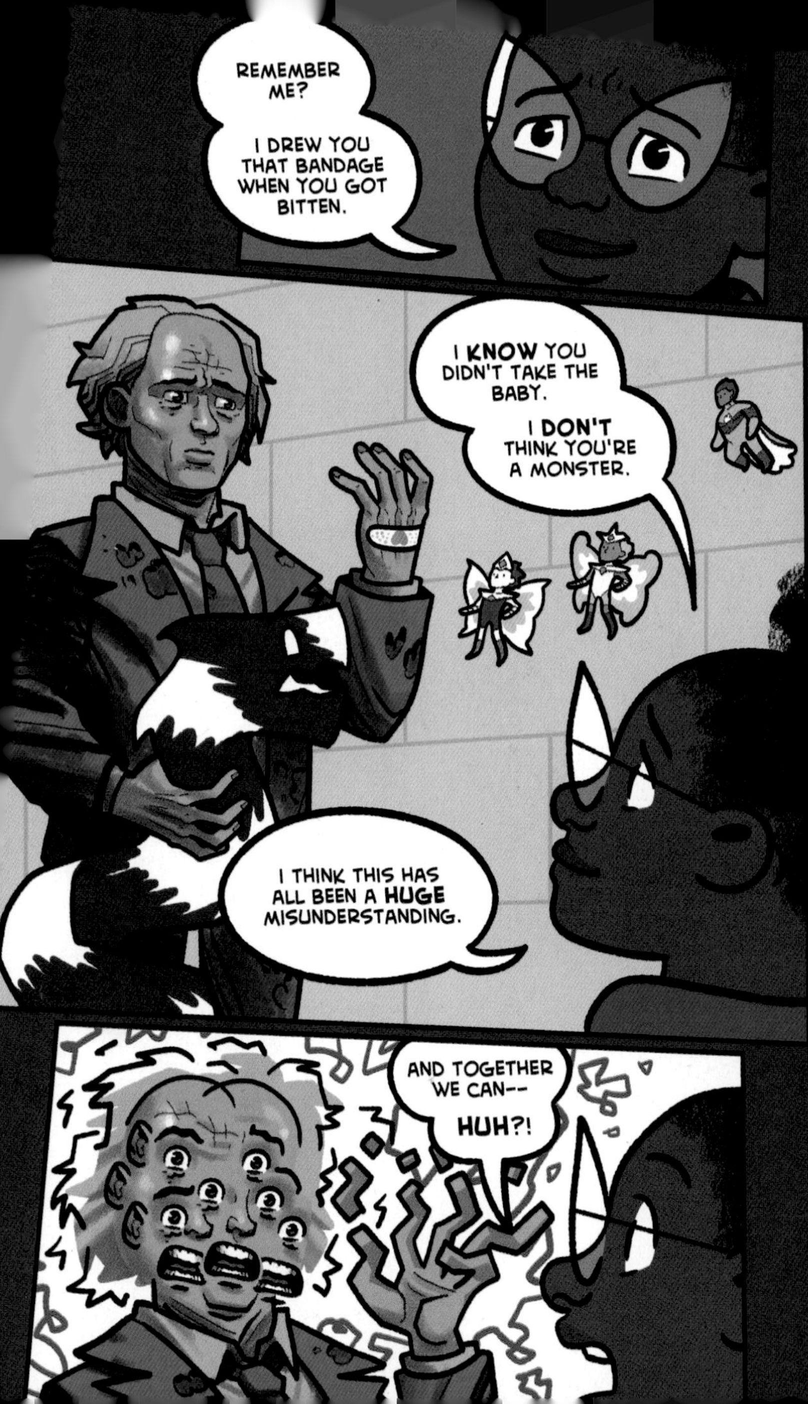
REMEMBER ME?
I DREW YOU THAT BANDAGE WHEN YOU GOT BITTEN.
I **KNOW** YOU DIDN'T TAKE THE BABY.
I **DON'T** THINK YOU'RE A MONSTER.
I THINK THIS HAS ALL BEEN A **HUGE** MISUNDERSTANDING.
AND TOGETHER WE CAN--
HUH?!

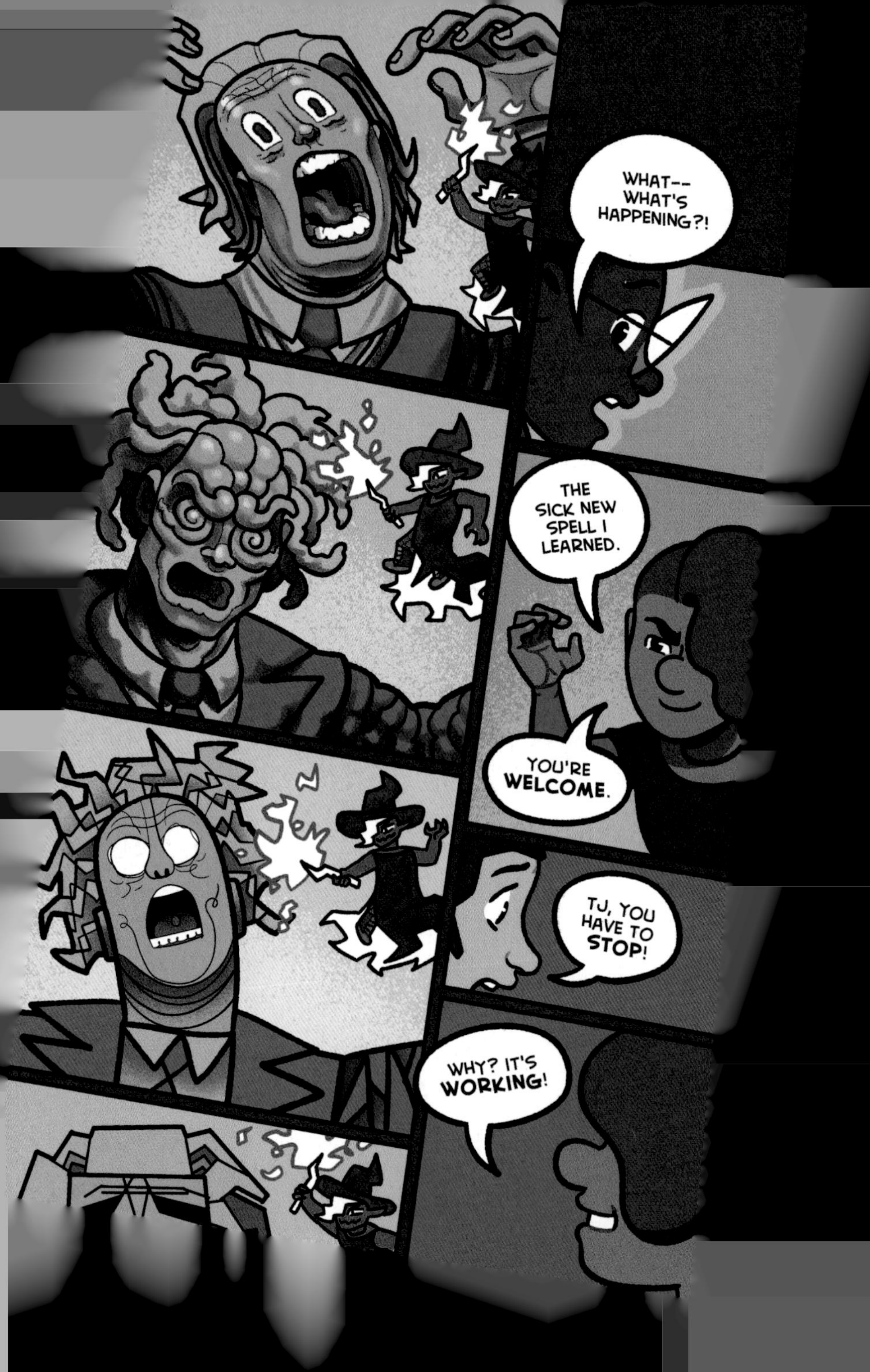

WHAT--
WHAT'S
HAPPENING?!
THE
SICK NEW
SPELL I
LEARNED.
YOU'RE
WELCOME.
TJ, YOU
HAVE TO
STOP!
WHY? IT'S
WORKING!

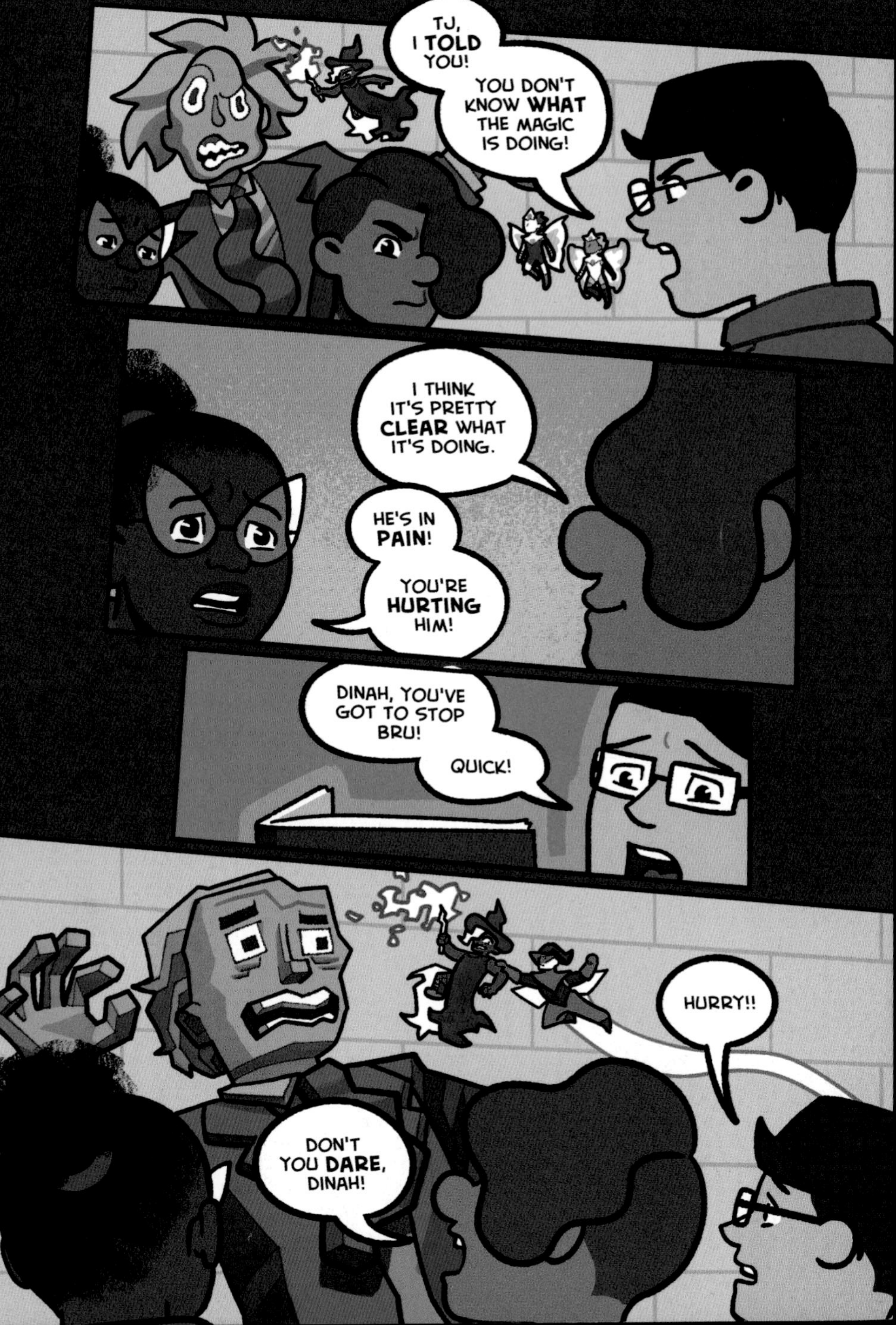
TJ, I TOLD YOU!
YOU DON'T KNOW WHAT THE MAGIC IS DOING!
I THINK IT'S PRETTY CLEAR WHAT IT'S DOING.
HE'S IN PAIN!
YOU'RE HURTING HIM!
DINAH, YOU'VE GOT TO STOP BRU!
QUICK!
HURRY!!
DON'T YOU DARE, DINAH!

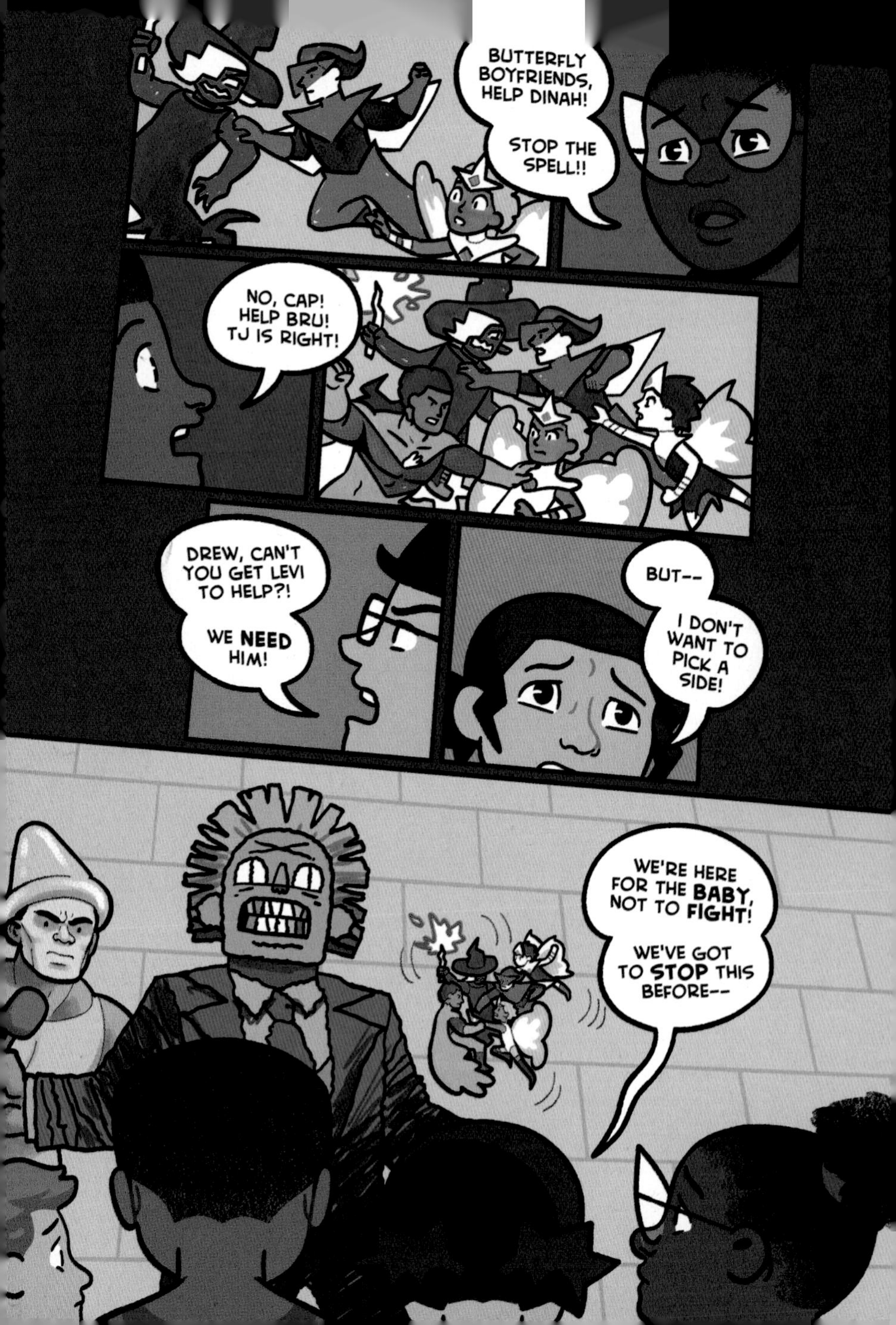
BUTTERFLY BOYFRIENDS, HELP DINAH!
STOP THE SPELL!!
NO, CAP! HELP BRU! TJ IS RIGHT!
DREW, CAN'T YOU GET LEVI TO HELP?!
WE NEED HIM!
BUT--
I DON'T WANT TO PICK A SIDE!
WE'RE HERE FOR THE BABY, NOT TO FIGHT!
WE'VE GOT TO STOP THIS BEFORE--

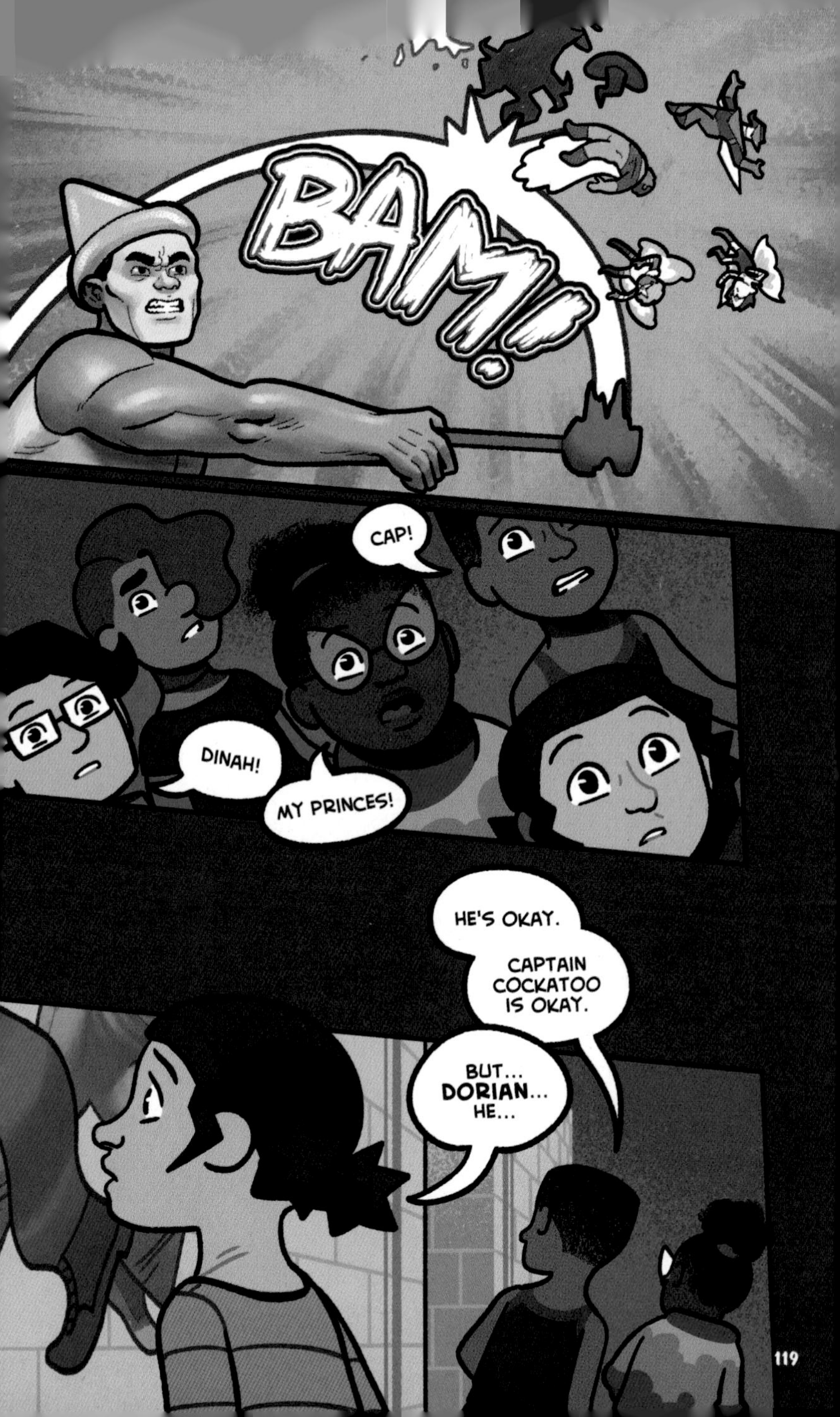
BAM!!
CAP!
DINAH!
MY PRINCES!
HE'S OKAY.
CAPTAIN COCKATOO IS OKAY.
BUT… DORIAN… HE…

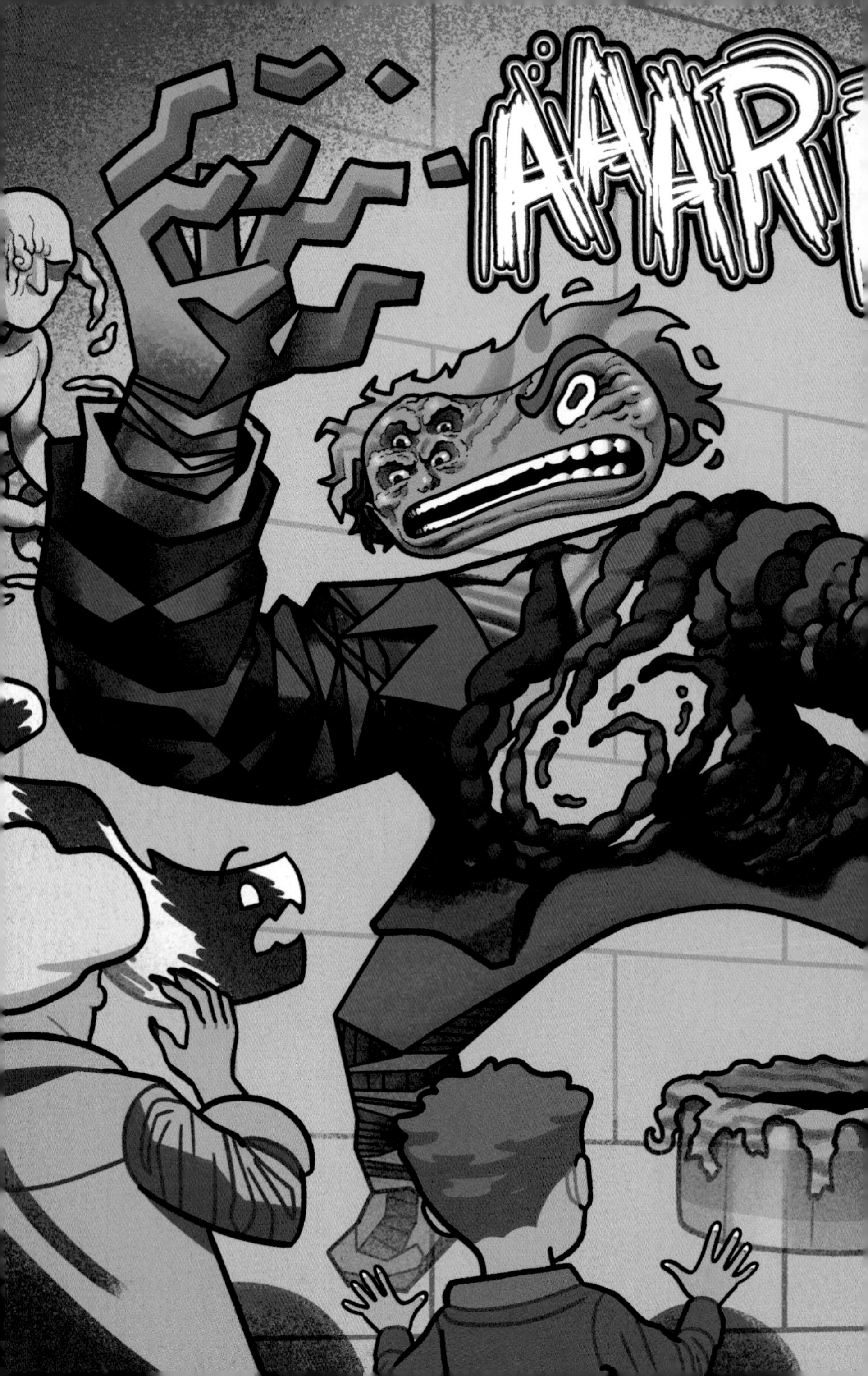
AAAR

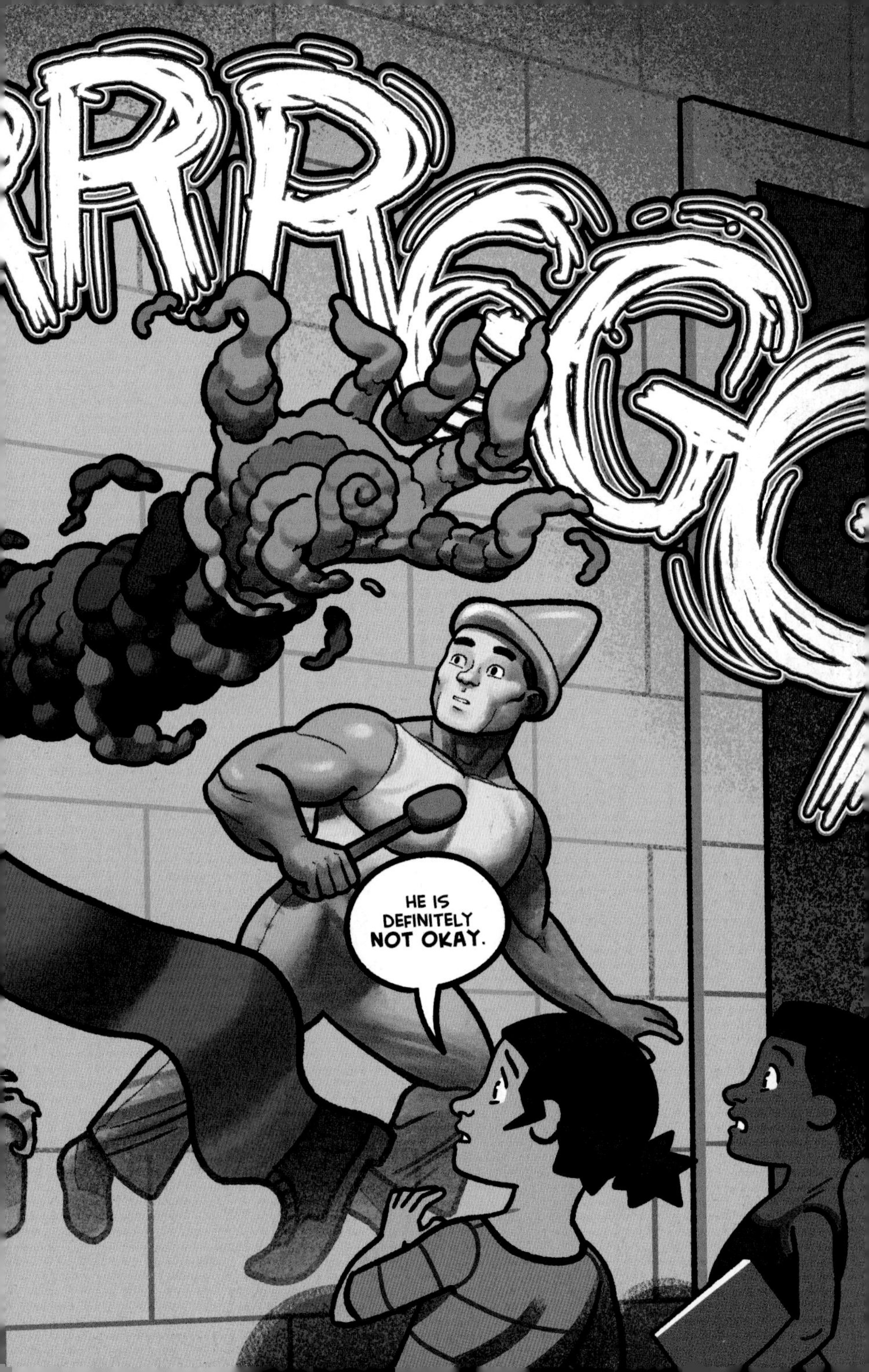

RRRRGG
HE IS DEFINITELY NOT OKAY.

CHAPTER 4: DEFINITELY NOT OKAY

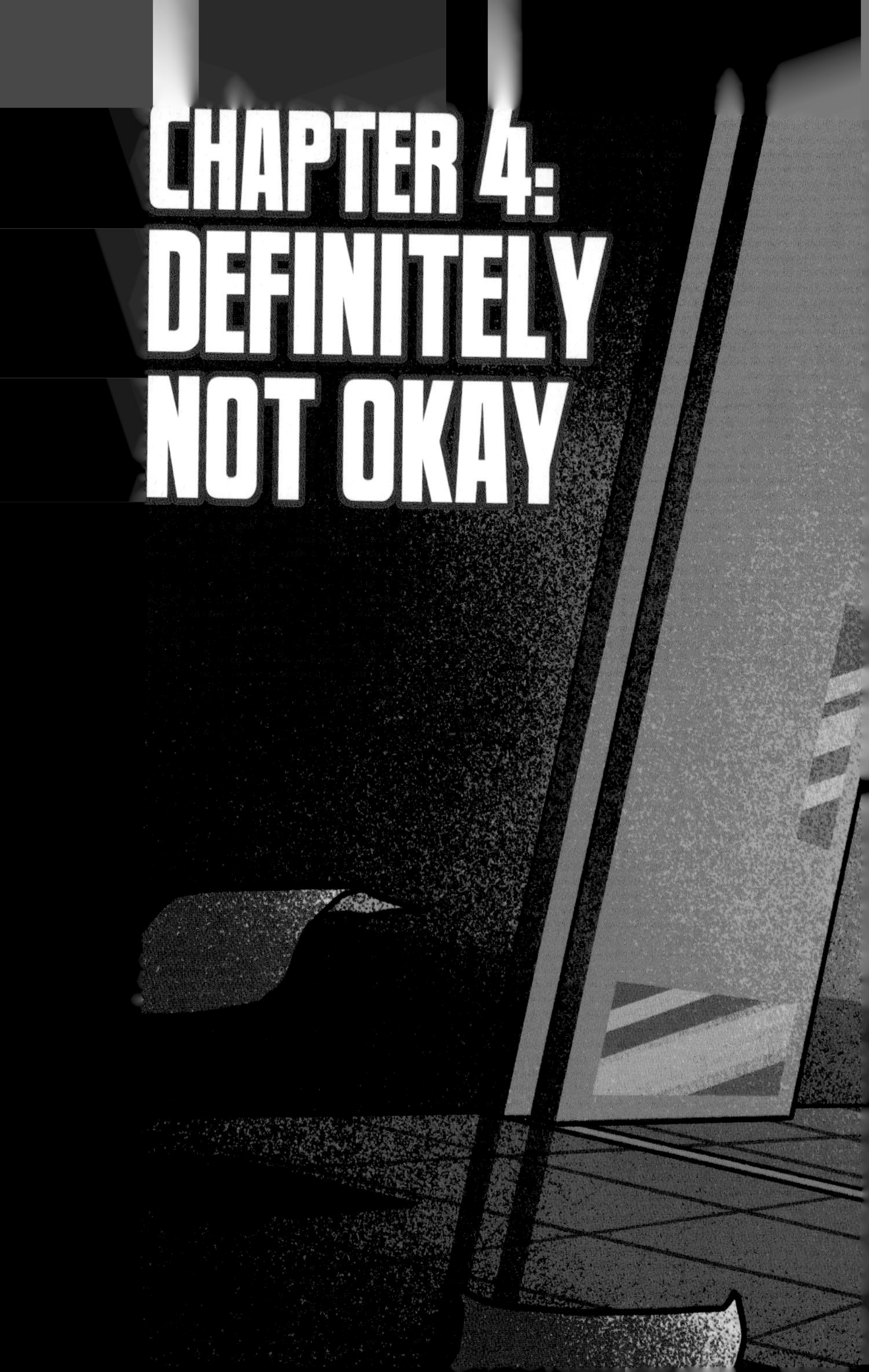

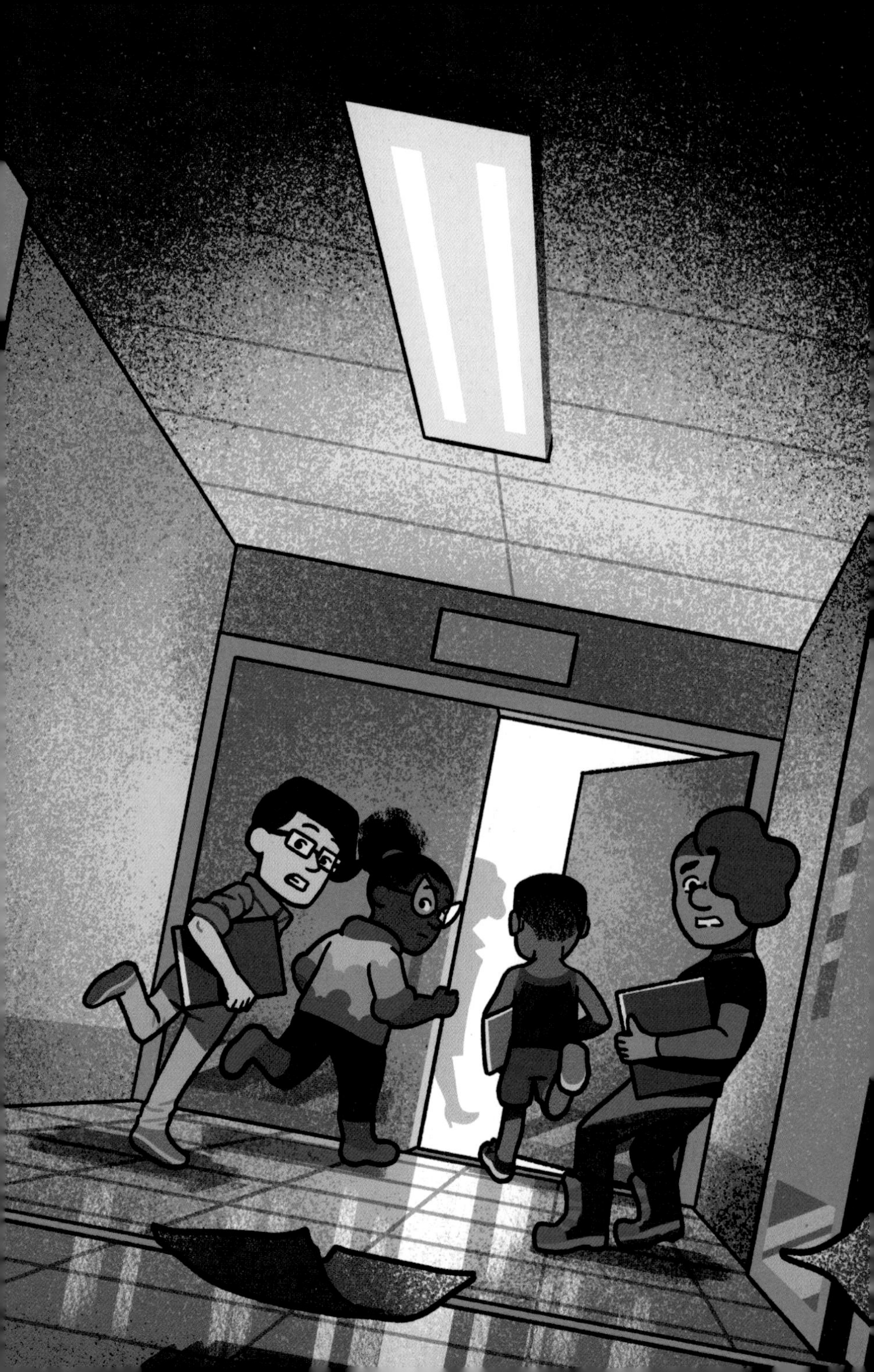

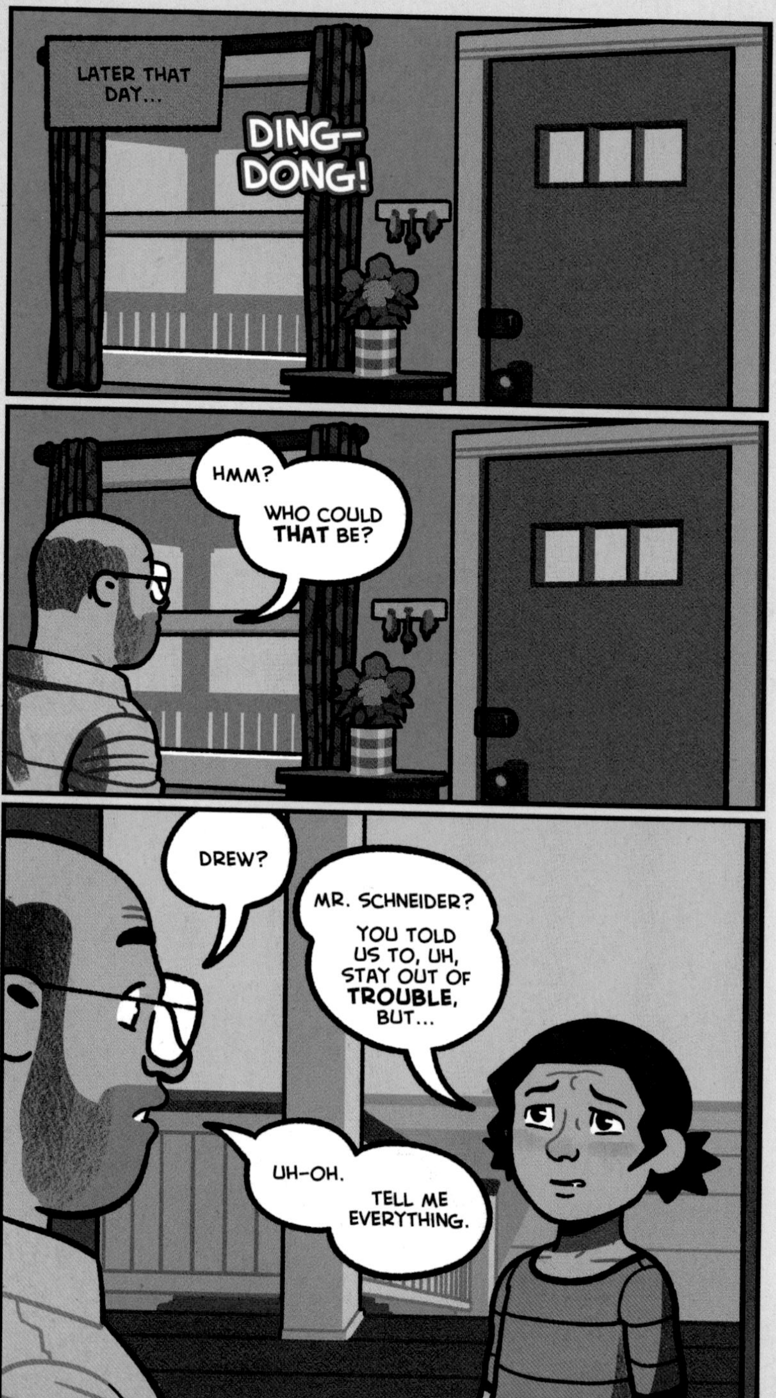
LATER THAT DAY...
DING-DONG!
HMM?
WHO COULD THAT BE?
DREW?
MR. SCHNEIDER?
YOU TOLD US TO, UH, STAY OUT OF TROUBLE, BUT...
UH-OH.
TELL ME EVERYTHING.

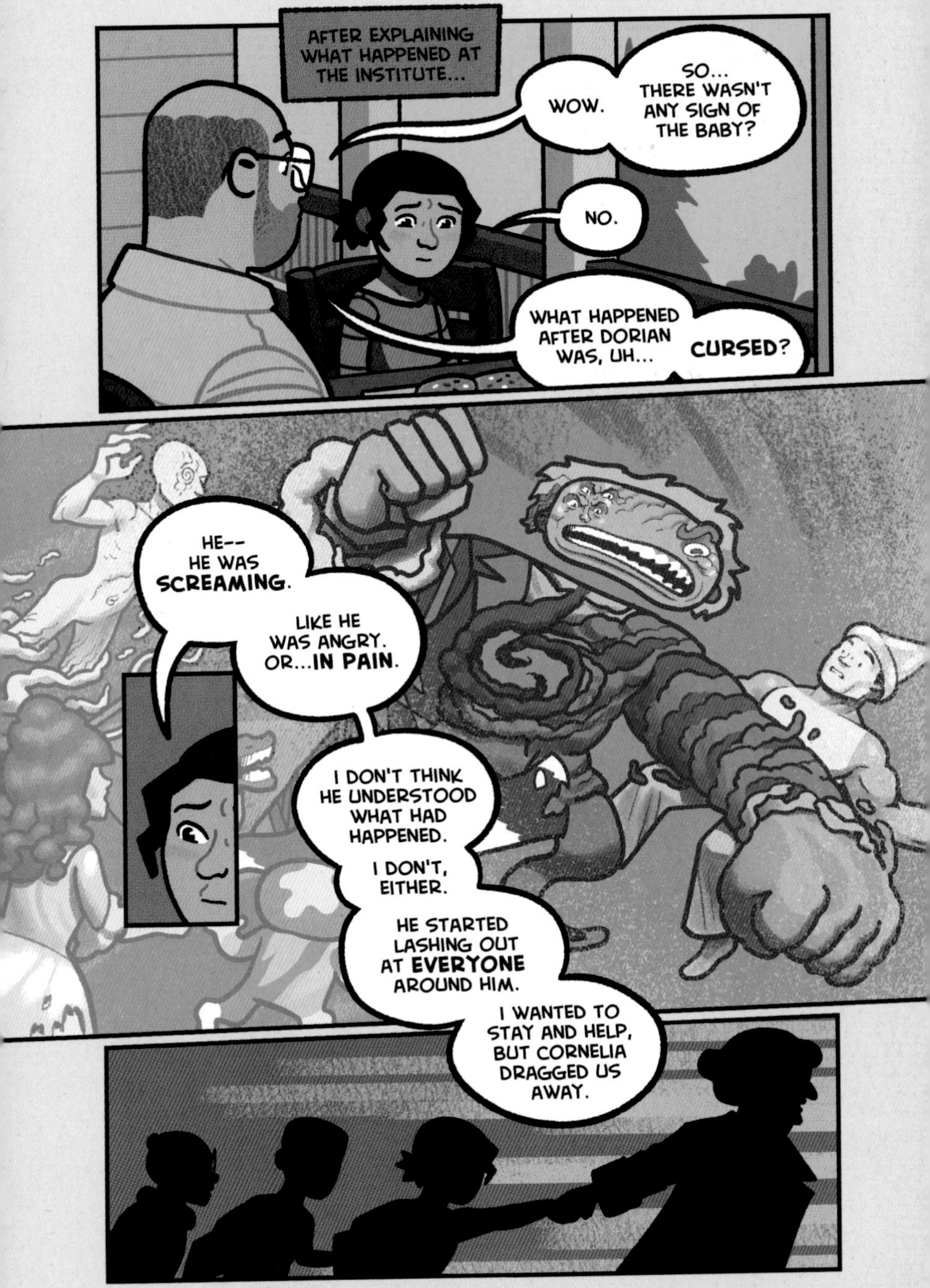
AFTER EXPLAINING WHAT HAPPENED AT THE INSTITUTE...
WOW.
SO... THERE WASN'T ANY SIGN OF THE BABY?
NO.
WHAT HAPPENED AFTER DORIAN WAS, UH... **CURSED**?
HE-- HE WAS **SCREAMING**.
LIKE HE WAS ANGRY. OR...**IN PAIN**.
I DON'T THINK HE UNDERSTOOD WHAT HAD HAPPENED.
I DON'T, EITHER.
HE STARTED LASHING OUT AT **EVERYONE** AROUND HIM.
I WANTED TO STAY AND HELP, BUT CORNELIA DRAGGED US AWAY.

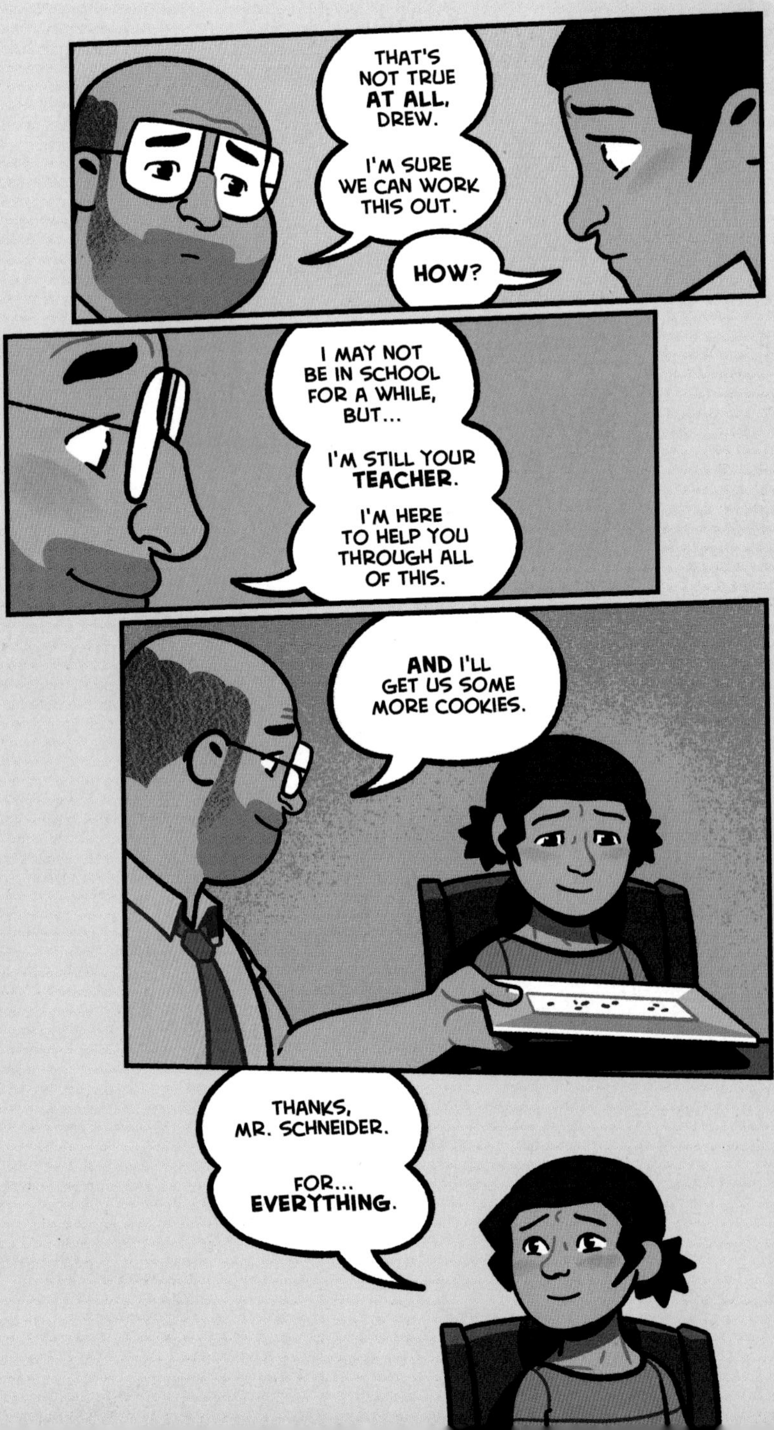
THAT'S NOT TRUE AT ALL, DREW.
I'M SURE WE CAN WORK THIS OUT.
HOW?
I MAY NOT BE IN SCHOOL FOR A WHILE, BUT...
I'M STILL YOUR TEACHER.
I'M HERE TO HELP YOU THROUGH ALL OF THIS.
AND I'LL GET US SOME MORE COOKIES.
THANKS, MR. SCHNEIDER.
FOR... EVERYTHING.

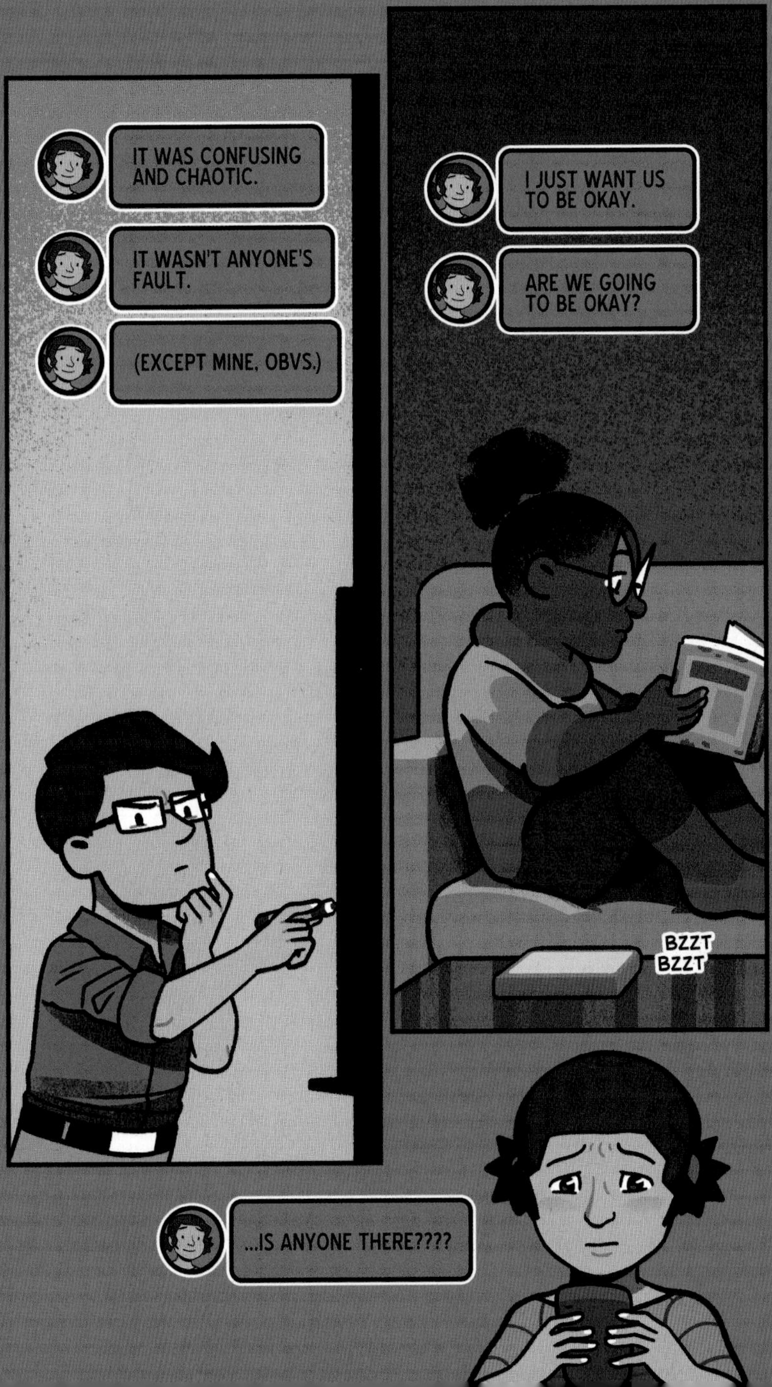
IT WAS CONFUSING AND CHAOTIC.
IT WASN'T ANYONE'S FAULT.
(EXCEPT MINE, OBVS.)
I JUST WANT US TO BE OKAY.
ARE WE GOING TO BE OKAY?
BZZT BZZT
...IS ANYONE THERE????

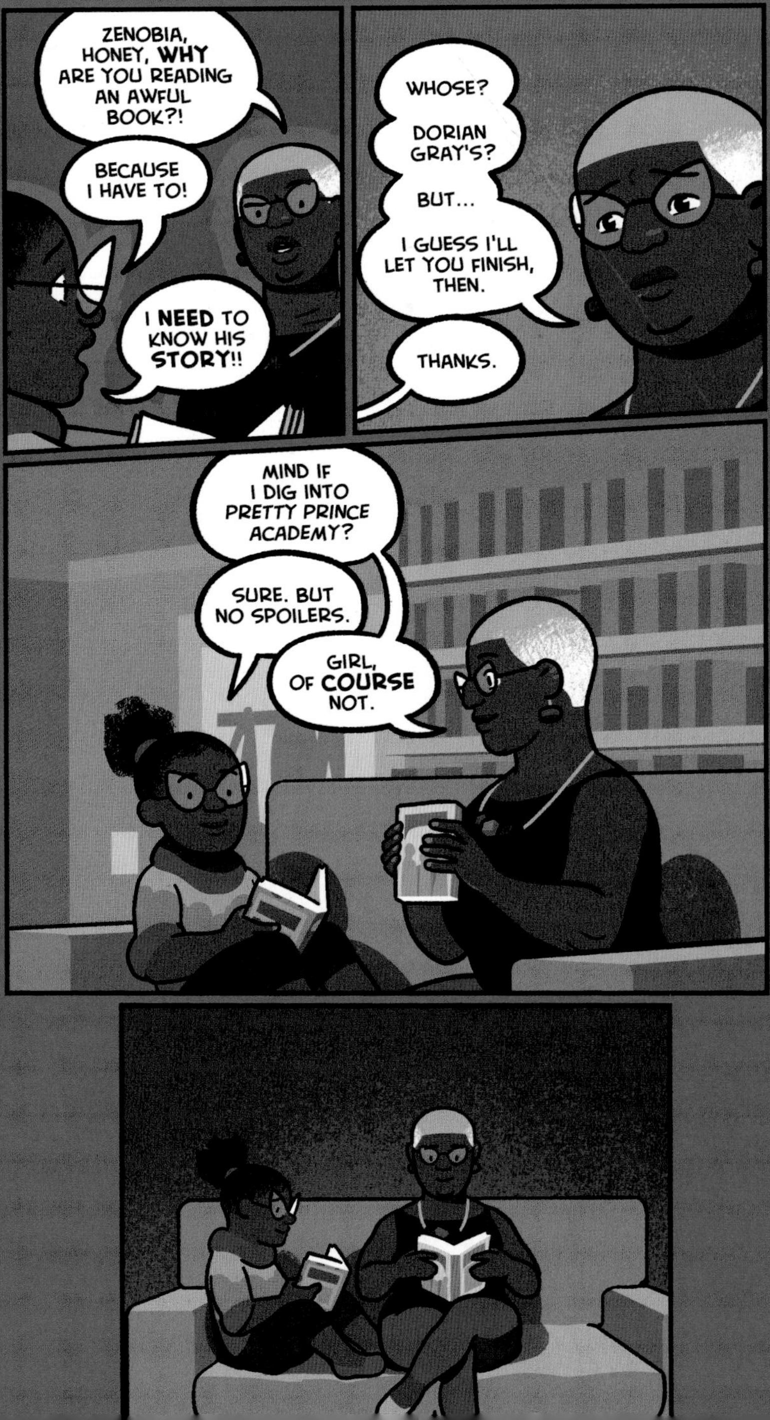
ZENOBIA, HONEY, WHY ARE YOU READING AN AWFUL BOOK?!
BECAUSE I HAVE TO!
I NEED TO KNOW HIS STORY!!
WHOSE?
DORIAN GRAY'S?
BUT...
I GUESS I'LL LET YOU FINISH, THEN.
THANKS.
MIND IF I DIG INTO PRETTY PRINCE ACADEMY?
SURE. BUT NO SPOILERS.
GIRL, OF COURSE NOT.

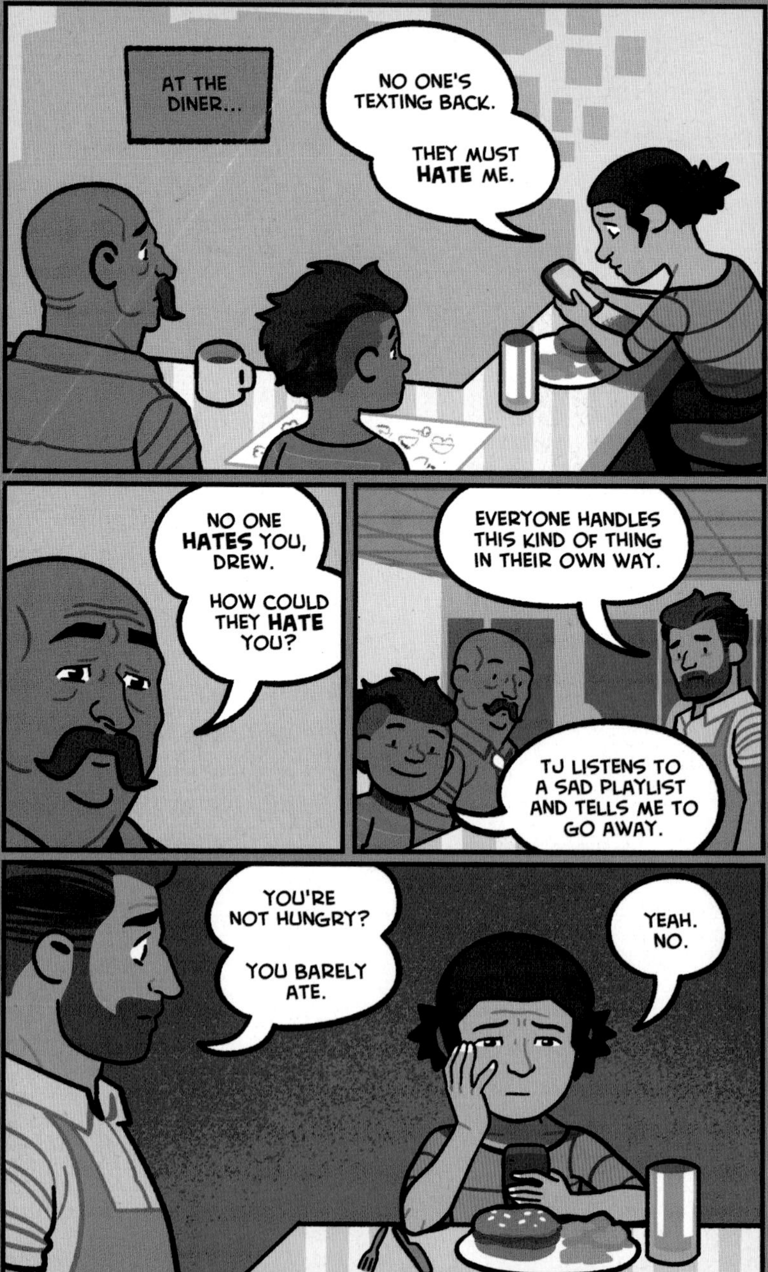
AT THE DINER...
NO ONE'S TEXTING BACK.
THEY MUST **HATE** ME.
NO ONE **HATES** YOU, DREW.
HOW COULD THEY **HATE** YOU?
EVERYONE HANDLES THIS KIND OF THING IN THEIR OWN WAY.
TJ LISTENS TO A SAD PLAYLIST AND TELLS ME TO GO AWAY.
YOU'RE NOT HUNGRY?
YOU BARELY ATE.
YEAH. NO.

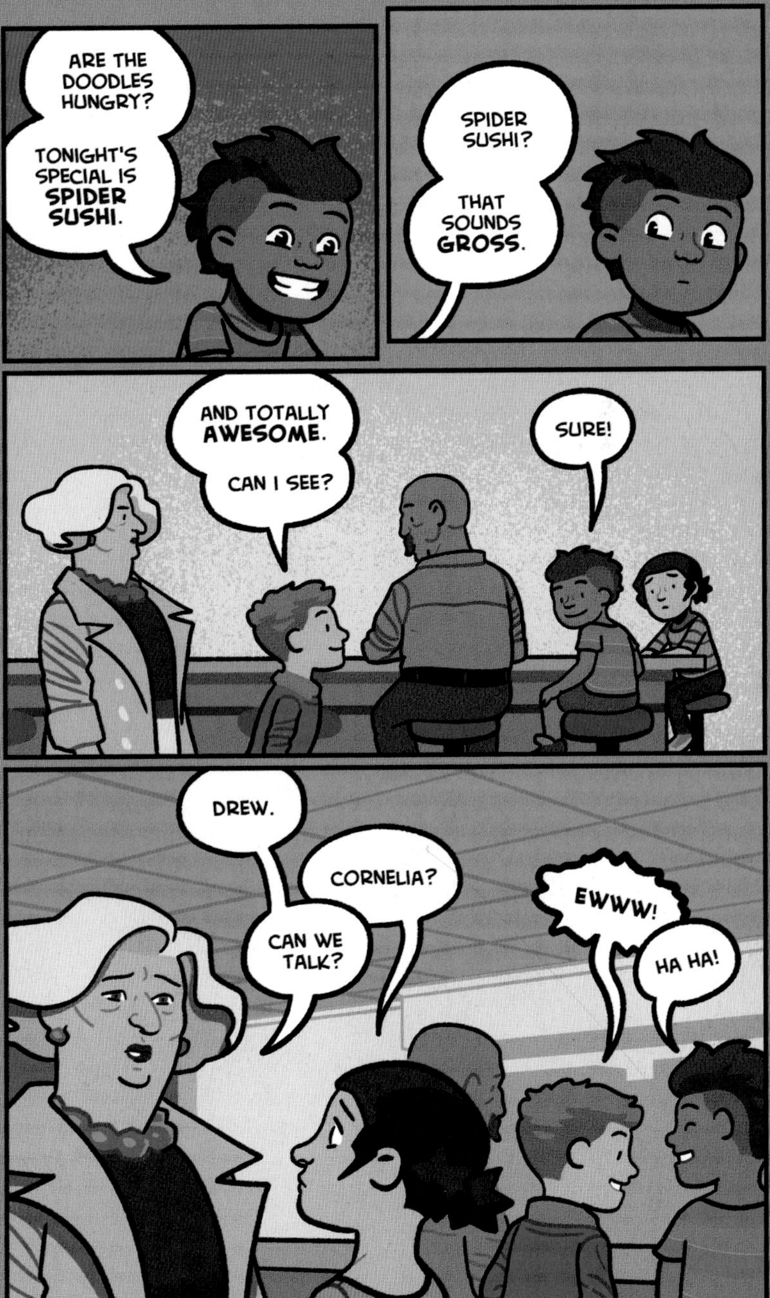
ARE THE DOODLES HUNGRY?
TONIGHT'S SPECIAL IS SPIDER SUSHI.
SPIDER SUSHI?
THAT SOUNDS GROSS.
AND TOTALLY AWESOME.
CAN I SEE?
SURE!
DREW.
CAN WE TALK?
CORNELIA?
EWWW!
HA HA!

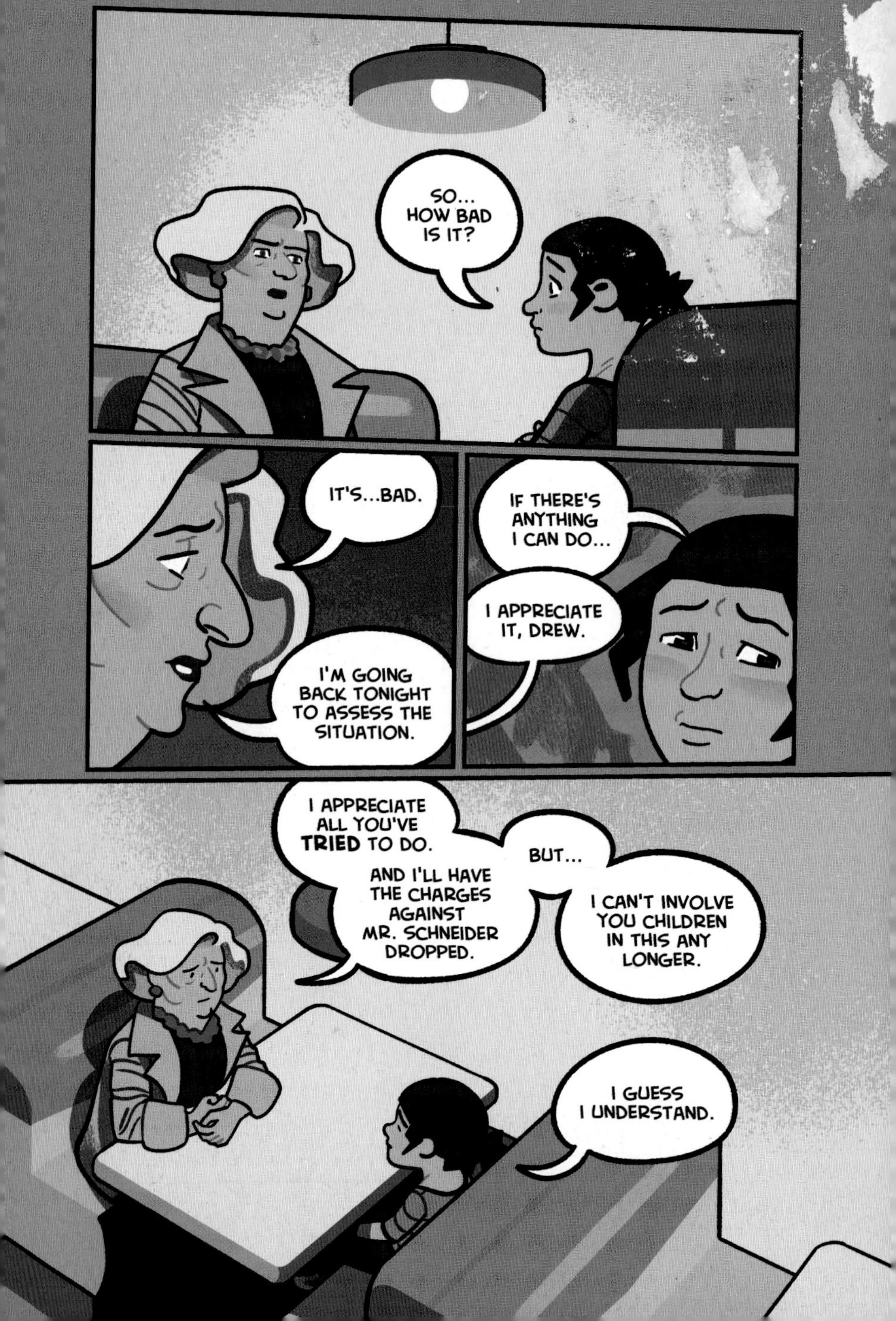
SO... HOW BAD IS IT?
IT'S...BAD.
I'M GOING BACK TONIGHT TO ASSESS THE SITUATION.
IF THERE'S ANYTHING I CAN DO...
I APPRECIATE IT, DREW.
I APPRECIATE ALL YOU'VE **TRIED** TO DO.
BUT...
I CAN'T INVOLVE YOU CHILDREN IN THIS ANY LONGER.
AND I'LL HAVE THE CHARGES AGAINST MR. SCHNEIDER DROPPED.
I GUESS I UNDERSTAND.

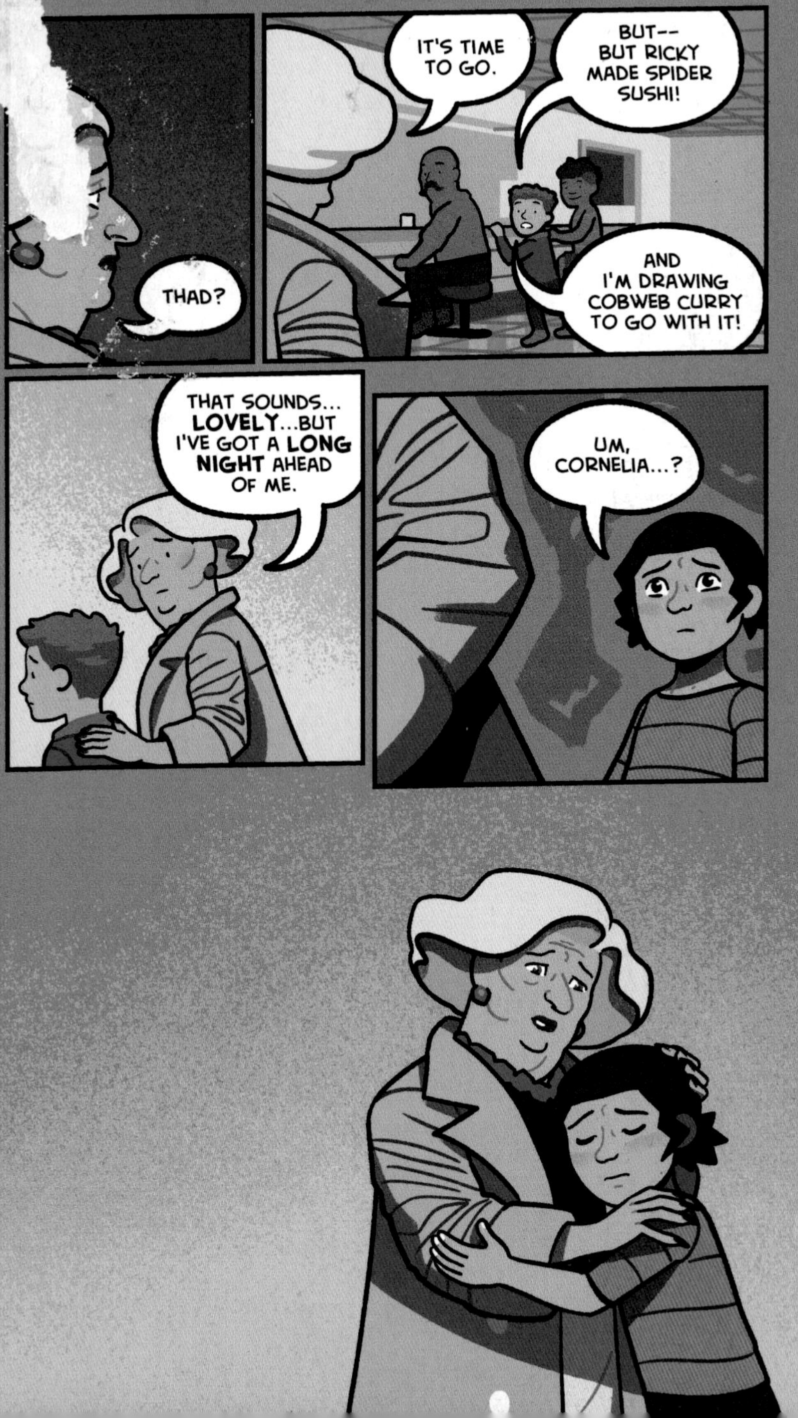
THAD?
IT'S TIME TO GO.
BUT-- BUT RICKY MADE SPIDER SUSHI!
AND I'M DRAWING COBWEB CURRY TO GO WITH IT!
THAT SOUNDS... **LOVELY**...BUT I'VE GOT A **LONG NIGHT** AHEAD OF ME.
UM, CORNELIA...?

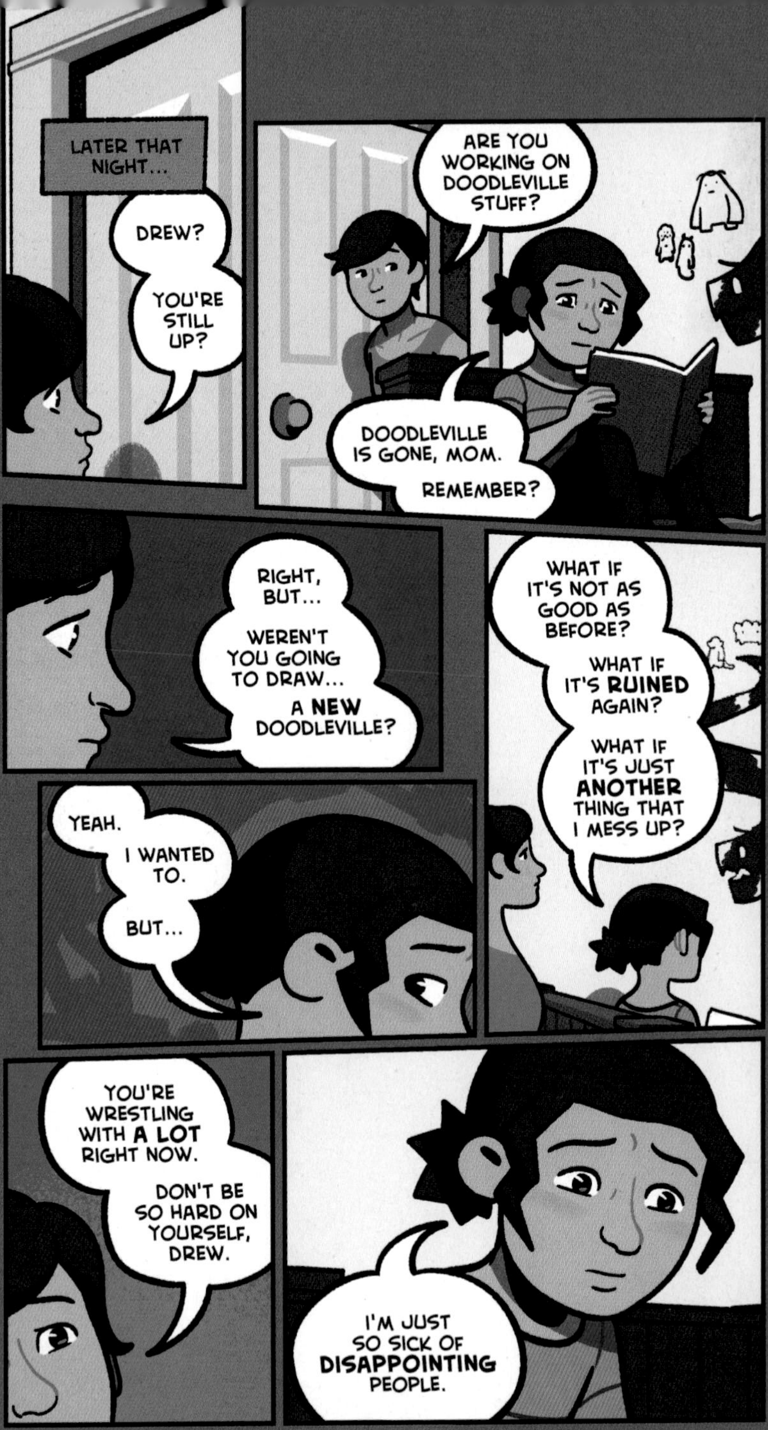
LATER THAT NIGHT...
DREW?
YOU'RE STILL UP?
ARE YOU WORKING ON DOODLEVILLE STUFF?
DOODLEVILLE IS GONE, MOM.
REMEMBER?
RIGHT, BUT...
WEREN'T YOU GOING TO DRAW...
A **NEW** DOODLEVILLE?
YEAH.
I WANTED TO.
BUT...
WHAT IF IT'S NOT AS GOOD AS BEFORE?
WHAT IF IT'S **RUINED** AGAIN?
WHAT IF IT'S JUST **ANOTHER** THING THAT I MESS UP?
YOU'RE WRESTLING WITH **A LOT** RIGHT NOW.
DON'T BE SO HARD ON YOURSELF, DREW.
I'M JUST SO SICK OF **DISAPPOINTING** PEOPLE.

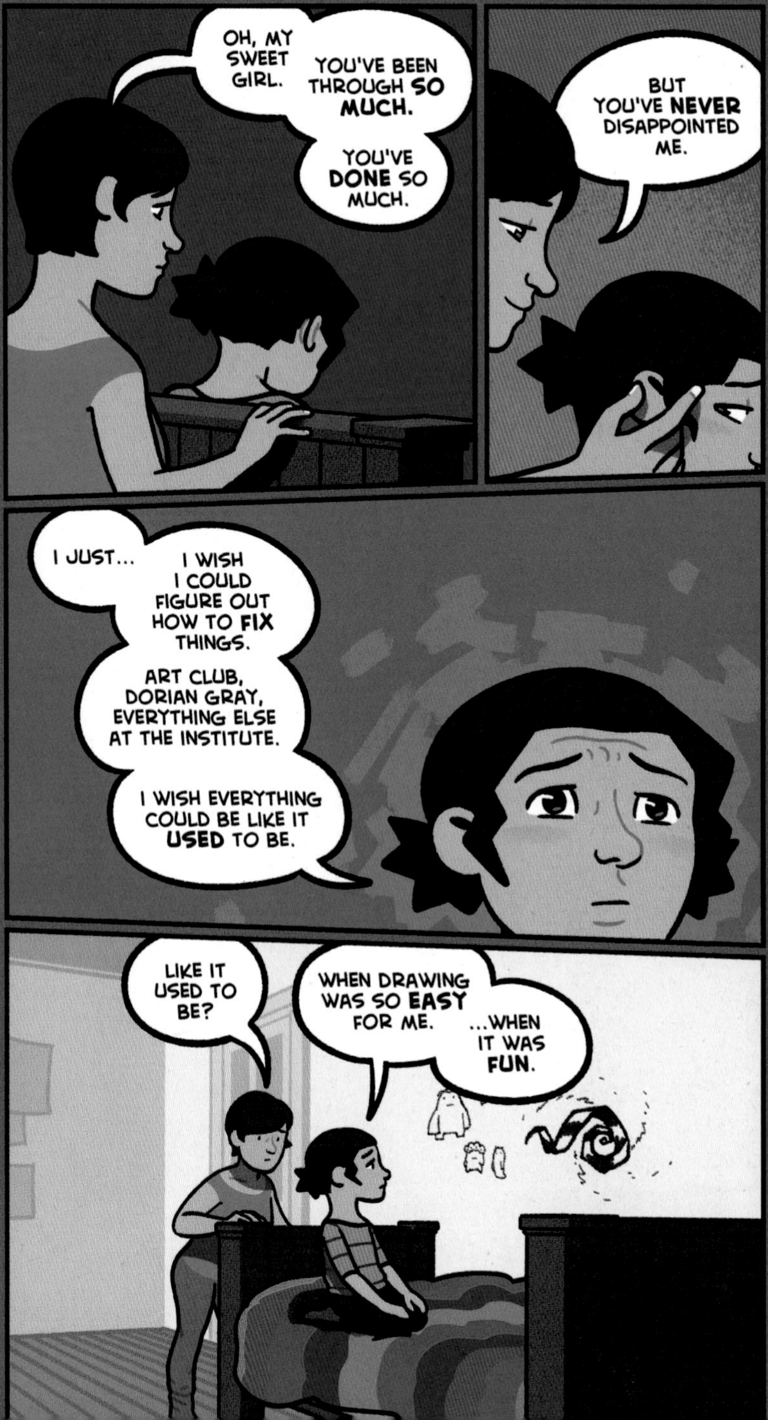
OH, MY SWEET GIRL.
YOU'VE BEEN THROUGH SO MUCH.
YOU'VE DONE SO MUCH.
BUT YOU'VE NEVER DISAPPOINTED ME.
I JUST...
I WISH I COULD FIGURE OUT HOW TO FIX THINGS.
ART CLUB, DORIAN GRAY, EVERYTHING ELSE AT THE INSTITUTE.
I WISH EVERYTHING COULD BE LIKE IT USED TO BE.
LIKE IT USED TO BE?
WHEN DRAWING WAS SO EASY FOR ME.
...WHEN IT WAS FUN.

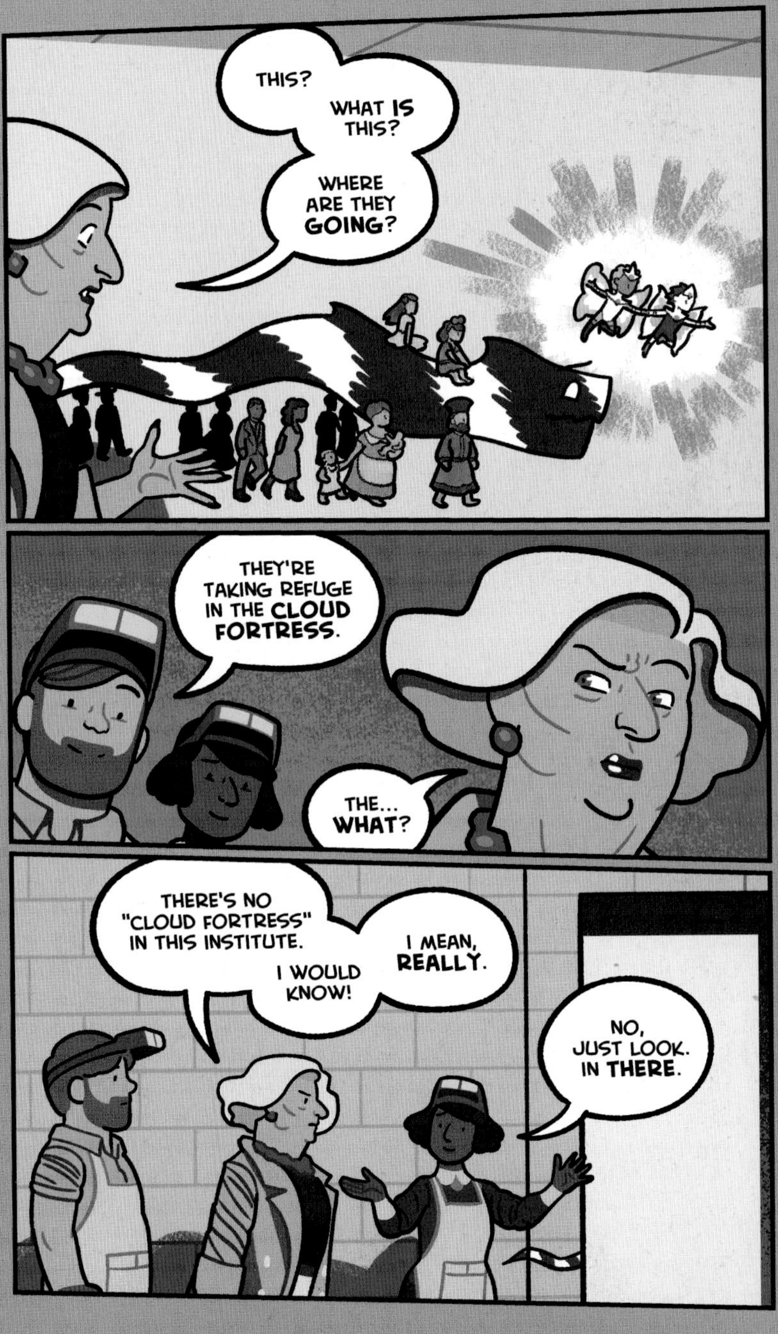
THIS?
WHAT IS THIS?
WHERE ARE THEY GOING?
THEY'RE TAKING REFUGE IN THE CLOUD FORTRESS.
THE... WHAT?
THERE'S NO "CLOUD FORTRESS" IN THIS INSTITUTE.
I WOULD KNOW!
I MEAN, REALLY.
NO, JUST LOOK. IN THERE.

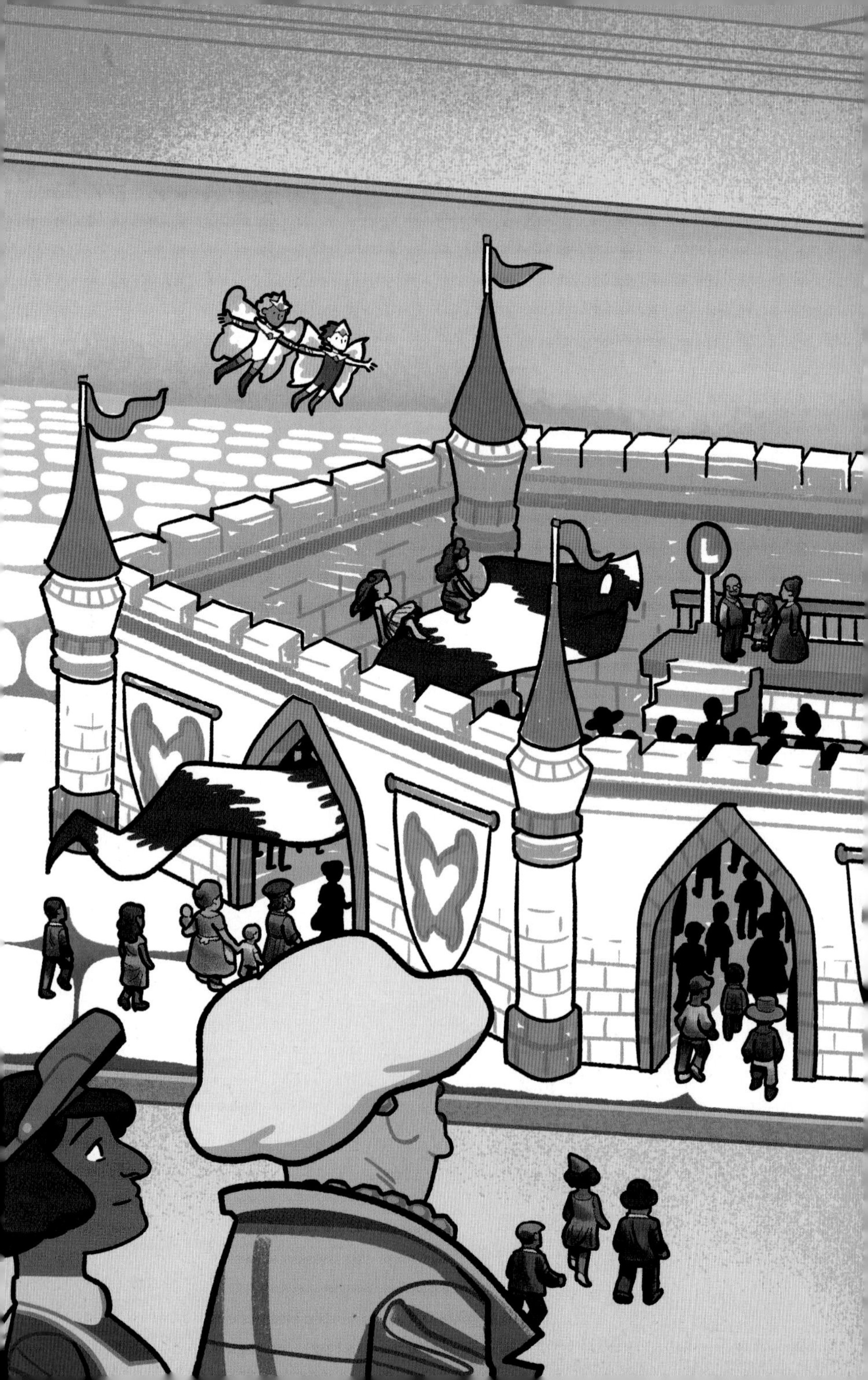
L

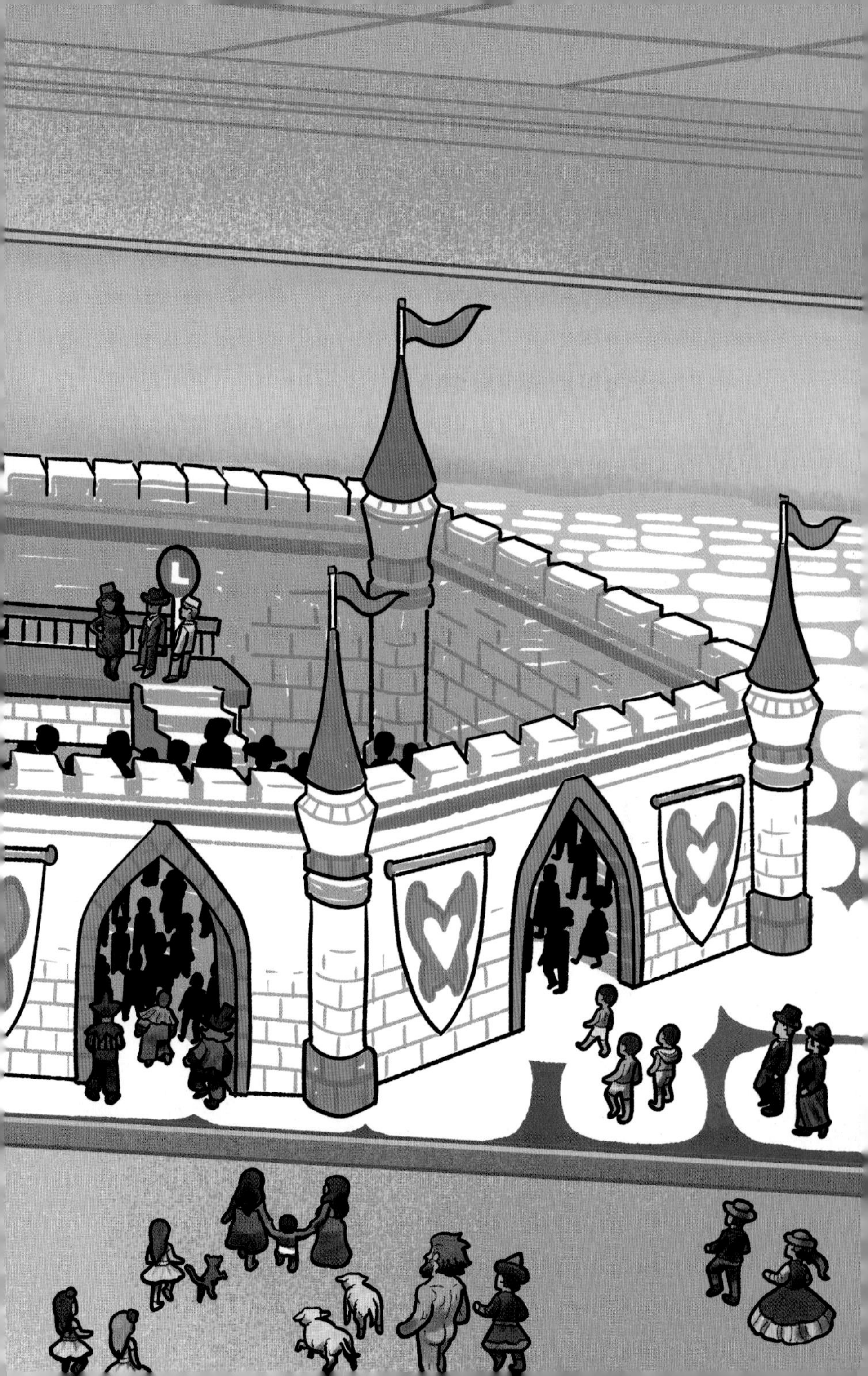
L

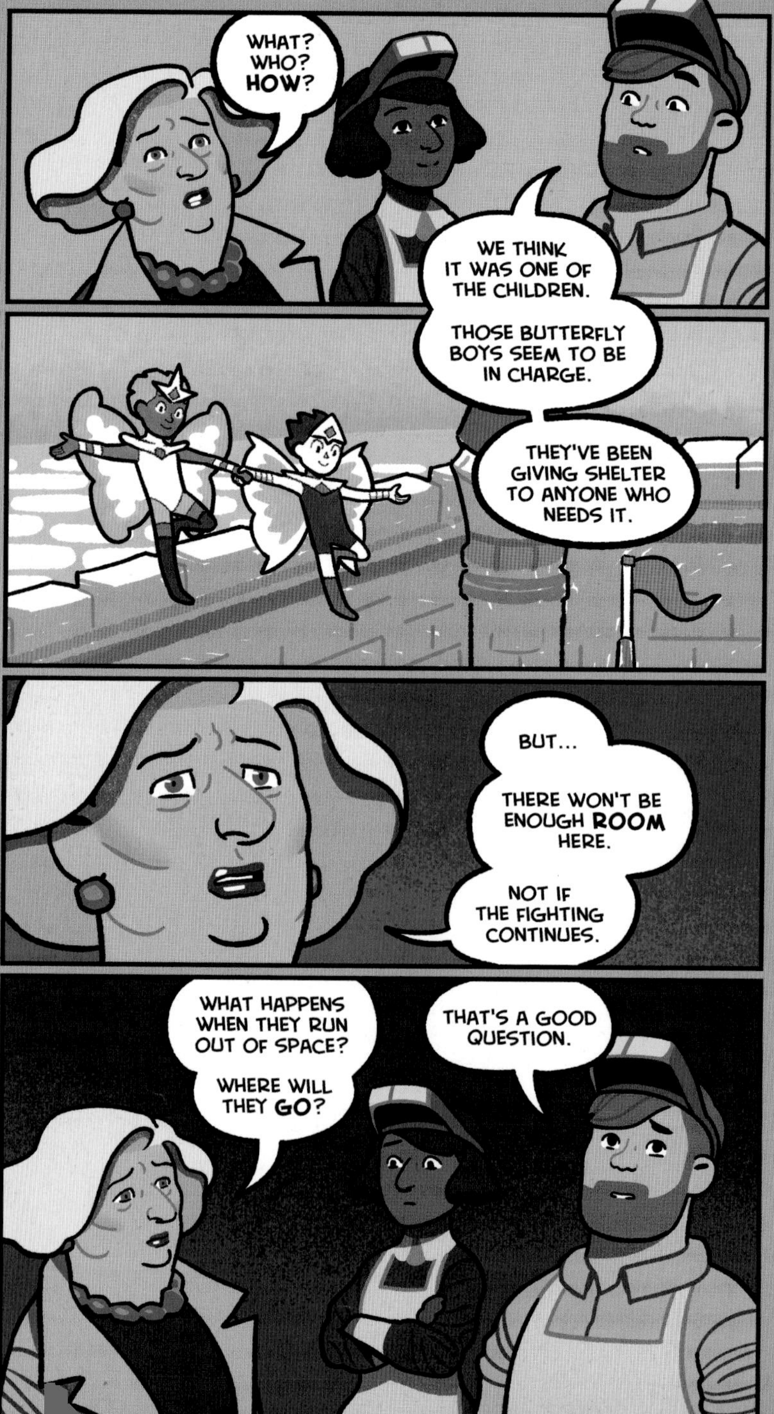
WHAT? WHO? **HOW?**
WE THINK IT WAS ONE OF THE CHILDREN.
THOSE BUTTERFLY BOYS SEEM TO BE IN CHARGE.
THEY'VE BEEN GIVING SHELTER TO ANYONE WHO NEEDS IT.
BUT...
THERE WON'T BE ENOUGH **ROOM** HERE.
NOT IF THE FIGHTING CONTINUES.
WHAT HAPPENS WHEN THEY RUN OUT OF SPACE?
WHERE WILL THEY **GO**?
THAT'S A GOOD QUESTION.

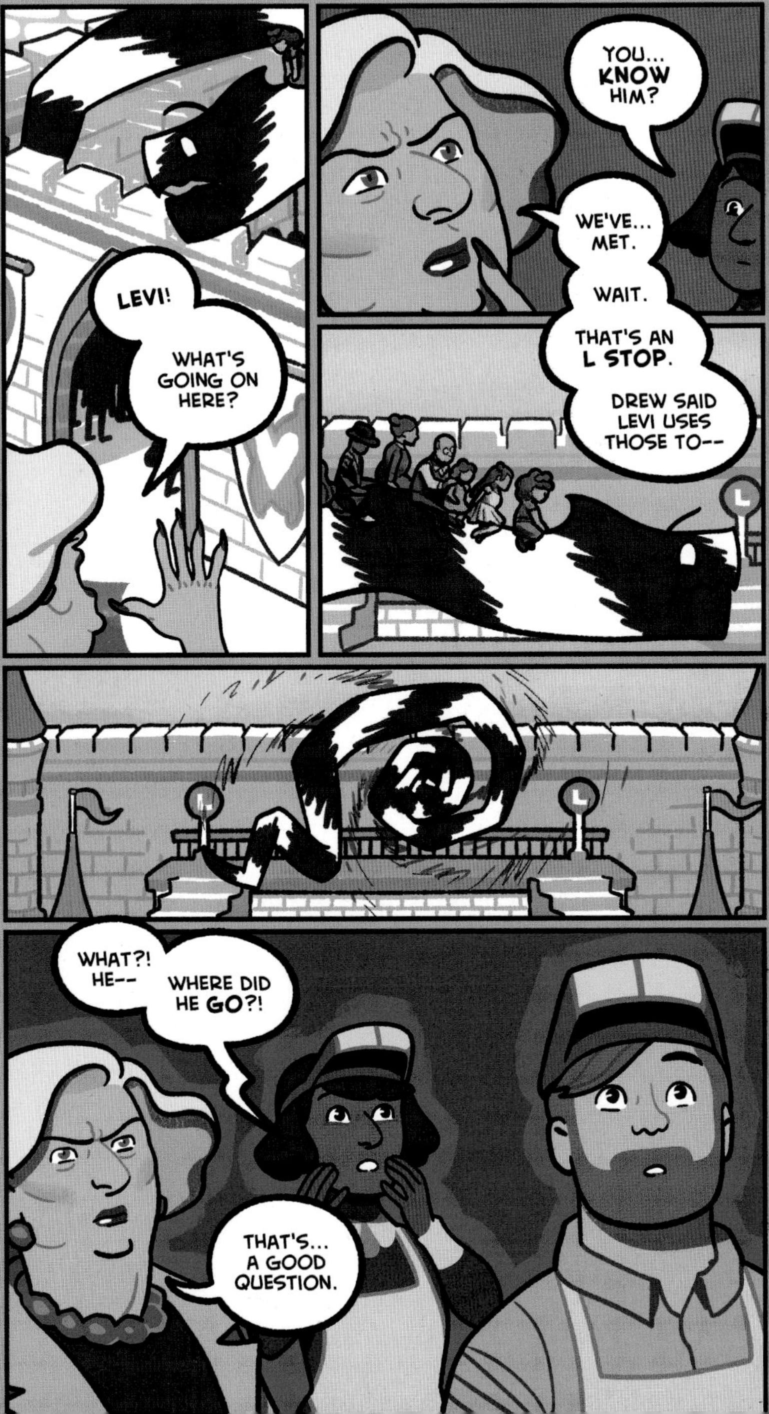
LEVI!
WHAT'S GOING ON HERE?
YOU... KNOW HIM?
WE'VE... MET.
WAIT.
THAT'S AN L STOP.
DREW SAID LEVI USES THOSE TO--
L
L
L
WHAT?! HE--
WHERE DID HE GO?!
THAT'S... A GOOD QUESTION.

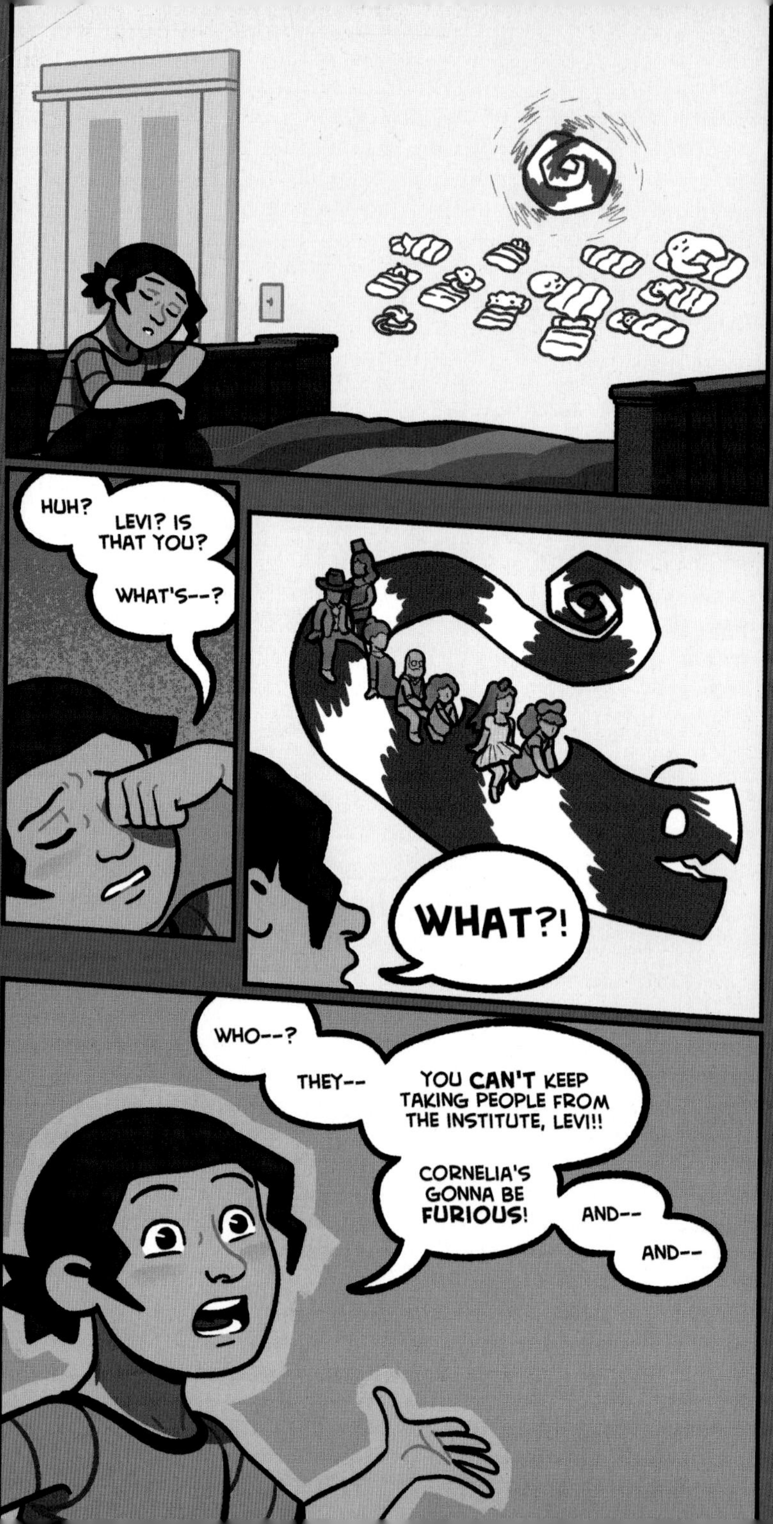
HUH?
LEVI? IS THAT YOU?
WHAT'S--?
WHAT?!
WHO--?
THEY--
YOU **CAN'T** KEEP TAKING PEOPLE FROM THE INSTITUTE, LEVI!!
CORNELIA'S GONNA BE **FURIOUS**!
AND--
AND--

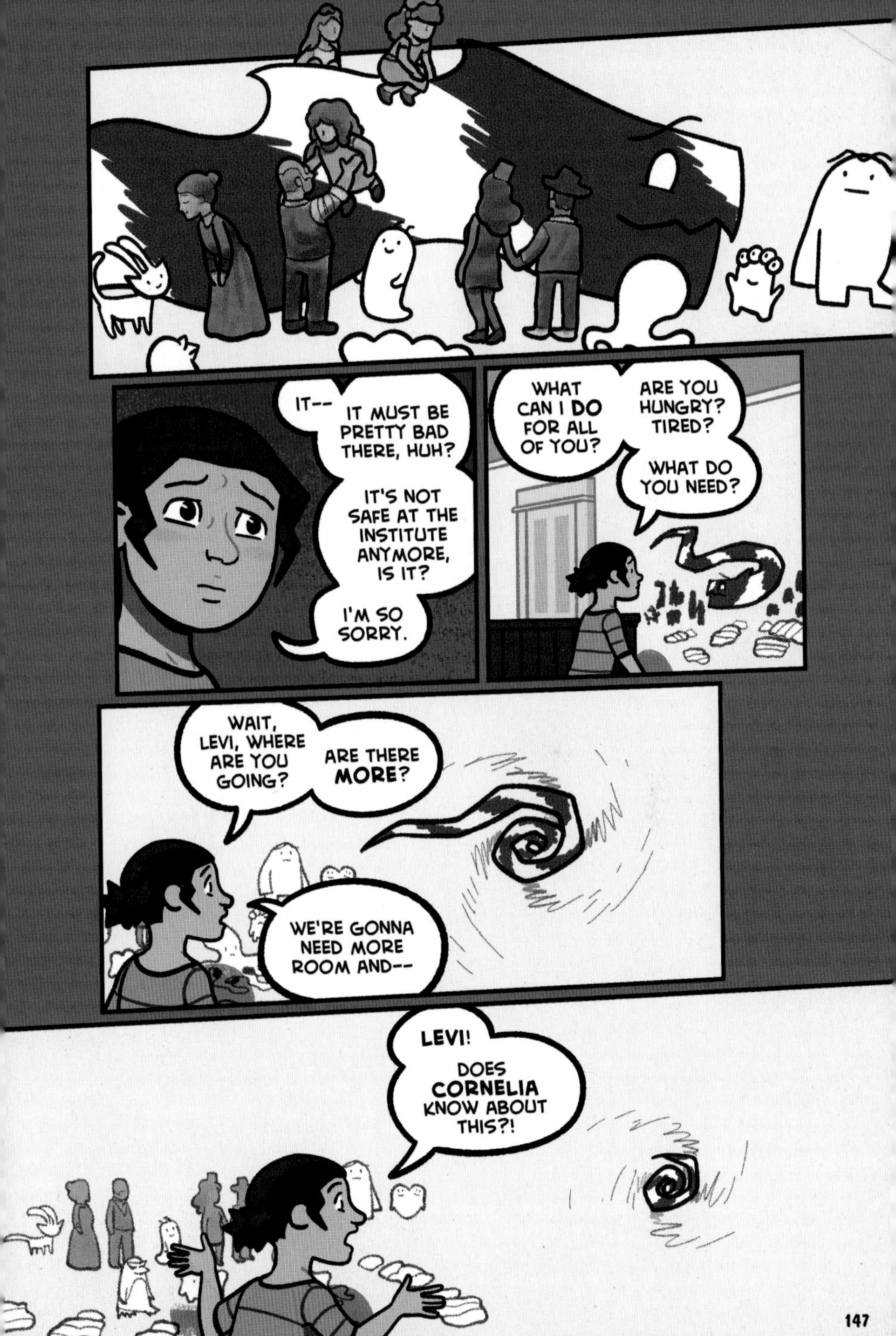
IT--
IT MUST BE PRETTY BAD THERE, HUH?
IT'S NOT SAFE AT THE INSTITUTE ANYMORE, IS IT?
I'M SO SORRY.
WHAT CAN I **DO** FOR ALL OF YOU?
ARE YOU HUNGRY? TIRED?
WHAT DO YOU NEED?
WAIT, LEVI, WHERE ARE YOU GOING?
ARE THERE **MORE**?
WE'RE GONNA NEED MORE ROOM AND--
LEVI!
DOES **CORNELIA** KNOW ABOUT THIS?!

CHAPTER 5: THE ART INSTITUTE EXODUS

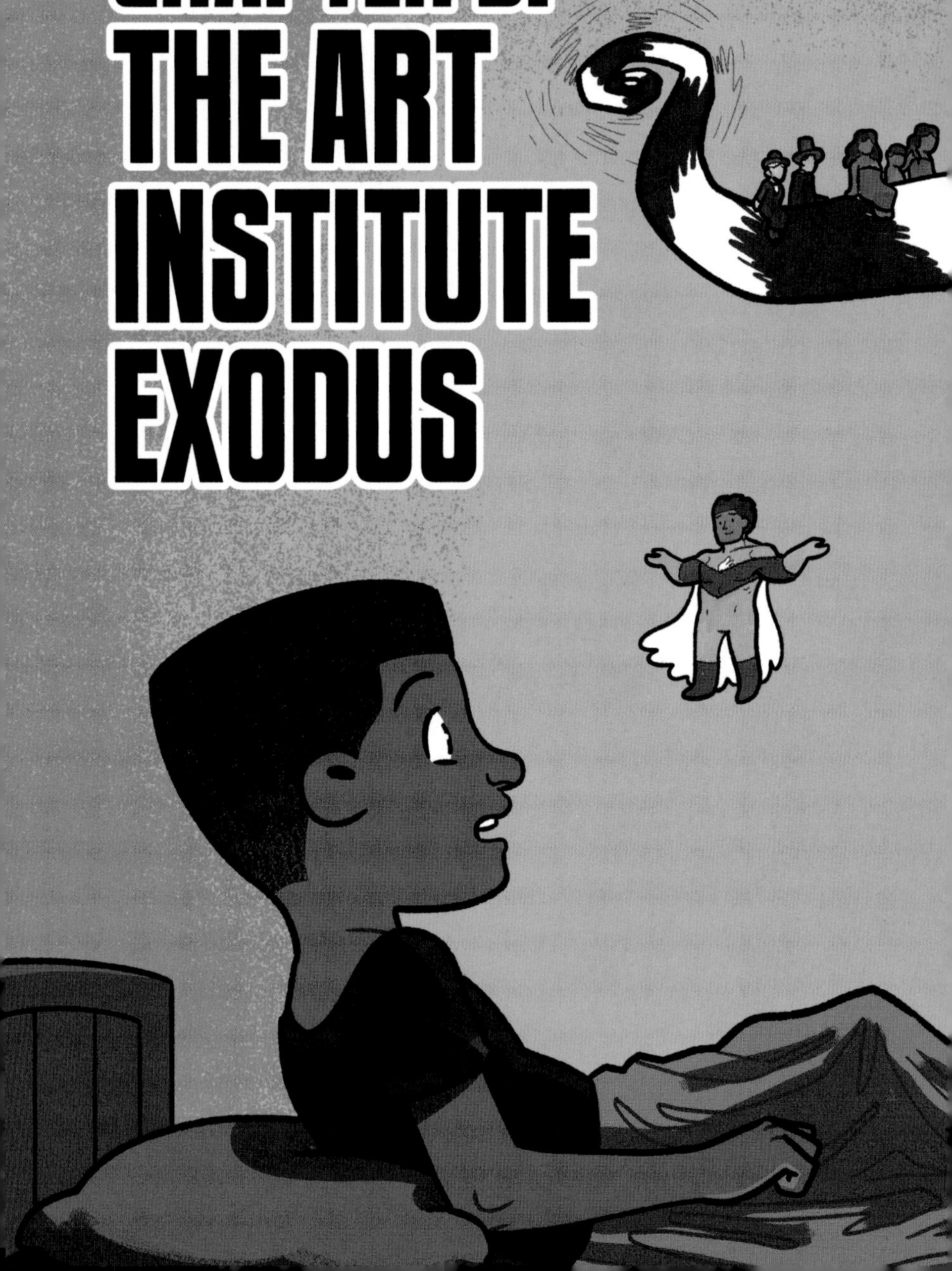

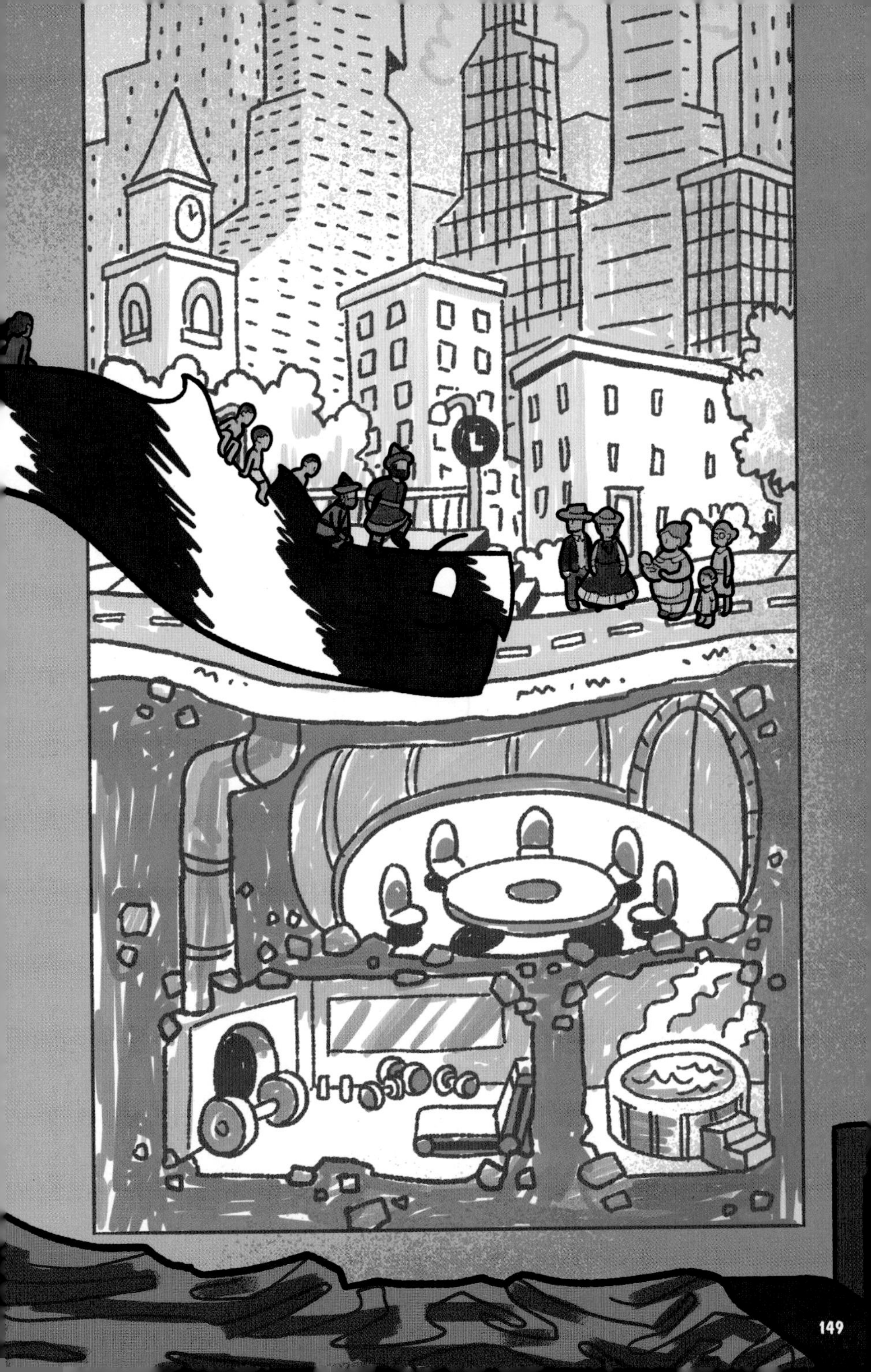
L

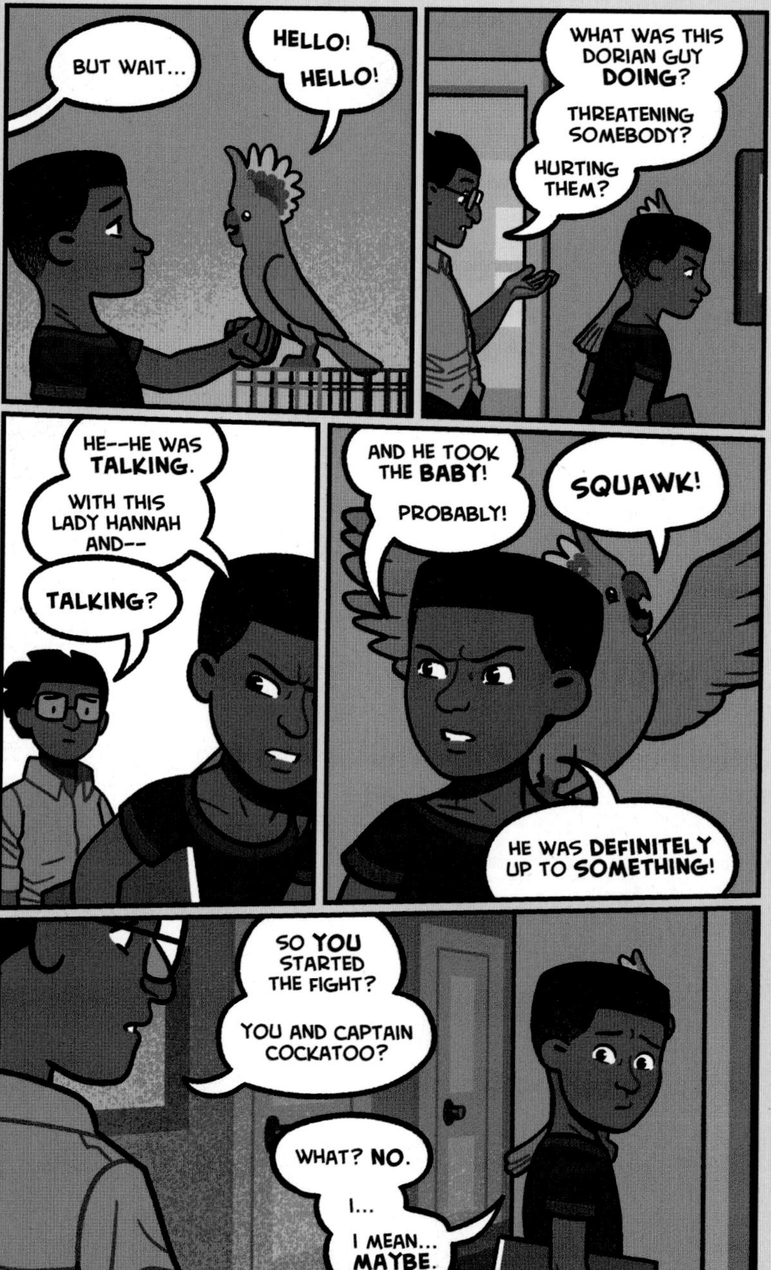
BUT WAIT...
HELLO! HELLO!
WHAT WAS THIS DORIAN GUY DOING?
THREATENING SOMEBODY?
HURTING THEM?
HE--HE WAS TALKING.
WITH THIS LADY HANNAH AND--
TALKING?
AND HE TOOK THE BABY!
PROBABLY!
SQUAWK!
HE WAS DEFINITELY UP TO SOMETHING!
SO YOU STARTED THE FIGHT?
YOU AND CAPTAIN COCKATOO?
WHAT? NO.
I...
I MEAN... MAYBE.

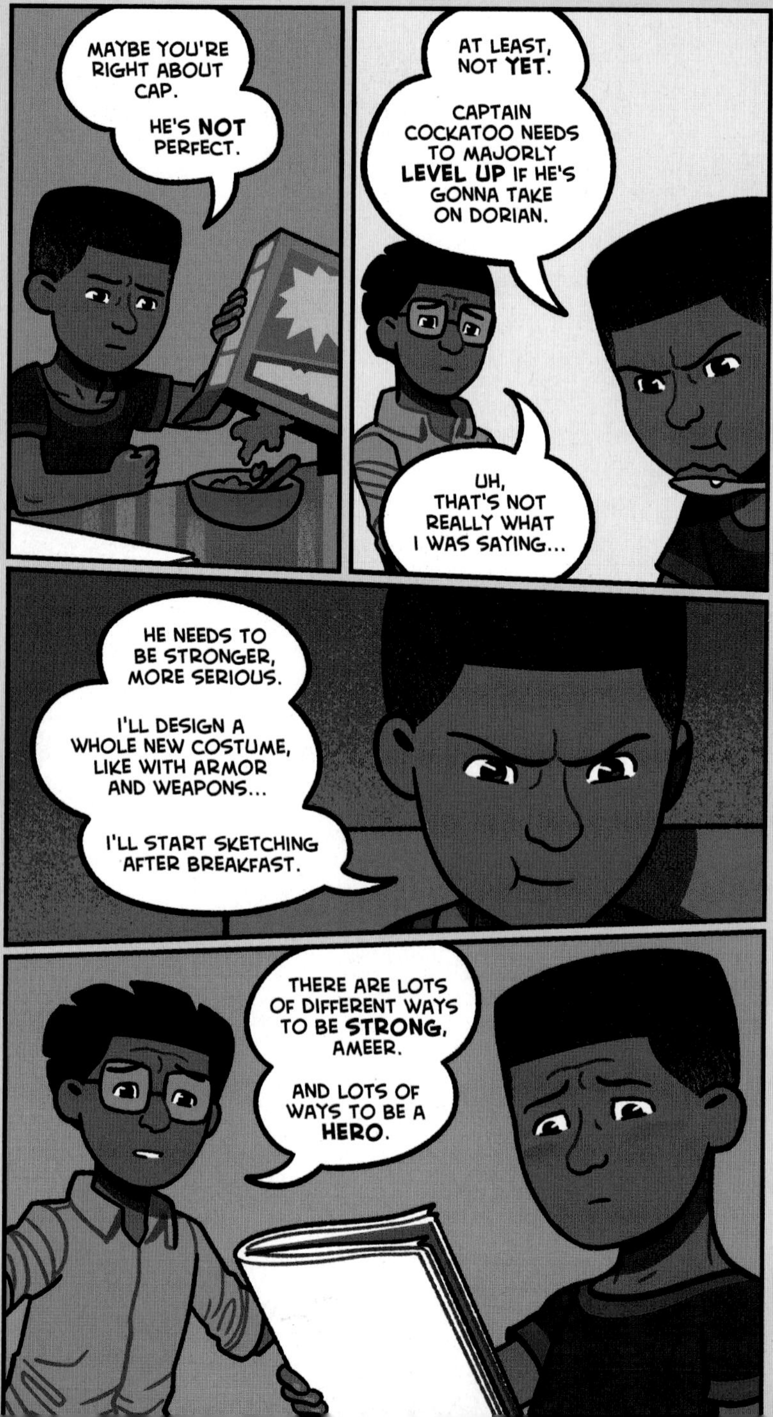
MAYBE YOU'RE RIGHT ABOUT CAP.
HE'S **NOT** PERFECT.
AT LEAST, NOT **YET**.
CAPTAIN COCKATOO NEEDS TO MAJORLY **LEVEL UP** IF HE'S GONNA TAKE ON DORIAN.
UH, THAT'S NOT REALLY WHAT I WAS SAYING...
HE NEEDS TO BE STRONGER, MORE SERIOUS.
I'LL DESIGN A WHOLE NEW COSTUME, LIKE WITH ARMOR AND WEAPONS...
I'LL START SKETCHING AFTER BREAKFAST.
THERE ARE LOTS OF DIFFERENT WAYS TO BE **STRONG**, AMEER.
AND LOTS OF WAYS TO BE A **HERO**.

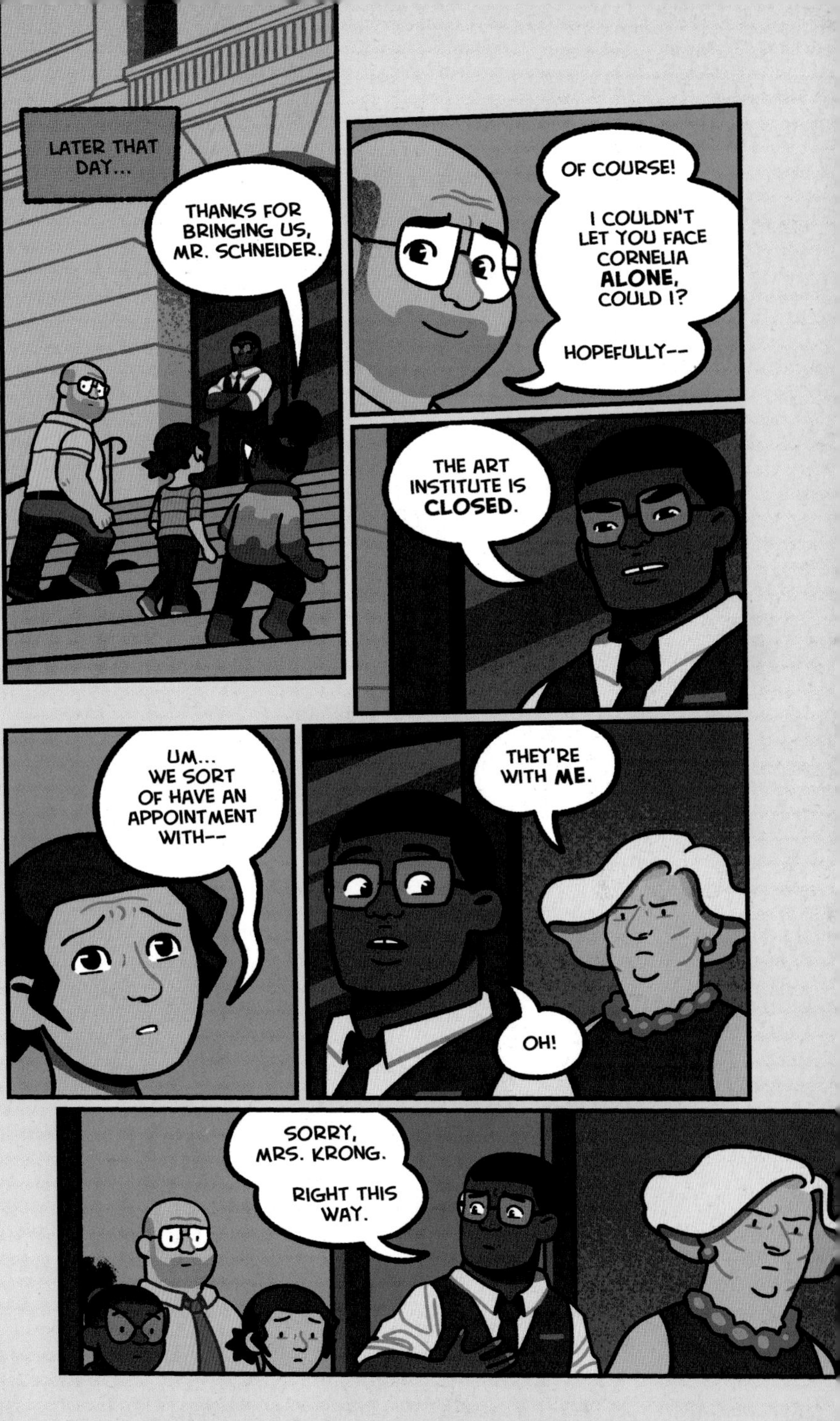
LATER THAT DAY...
THANKS FOR BRINGING US, MR. SCHNEIDER.
OF COURSE!
I COULDN'T LET YOU FACE CORNELIA ALONE, COULD I?
HOPEFULLY--
THE ART INSTITUTE IS CLOSED.
UM... WE SORT OF HAVE AN APPOINTMENT WITH--
THEY'RE WITH ME.
OH!
SORRY, MRS. KRONG.
RIGHT THIS WAY.

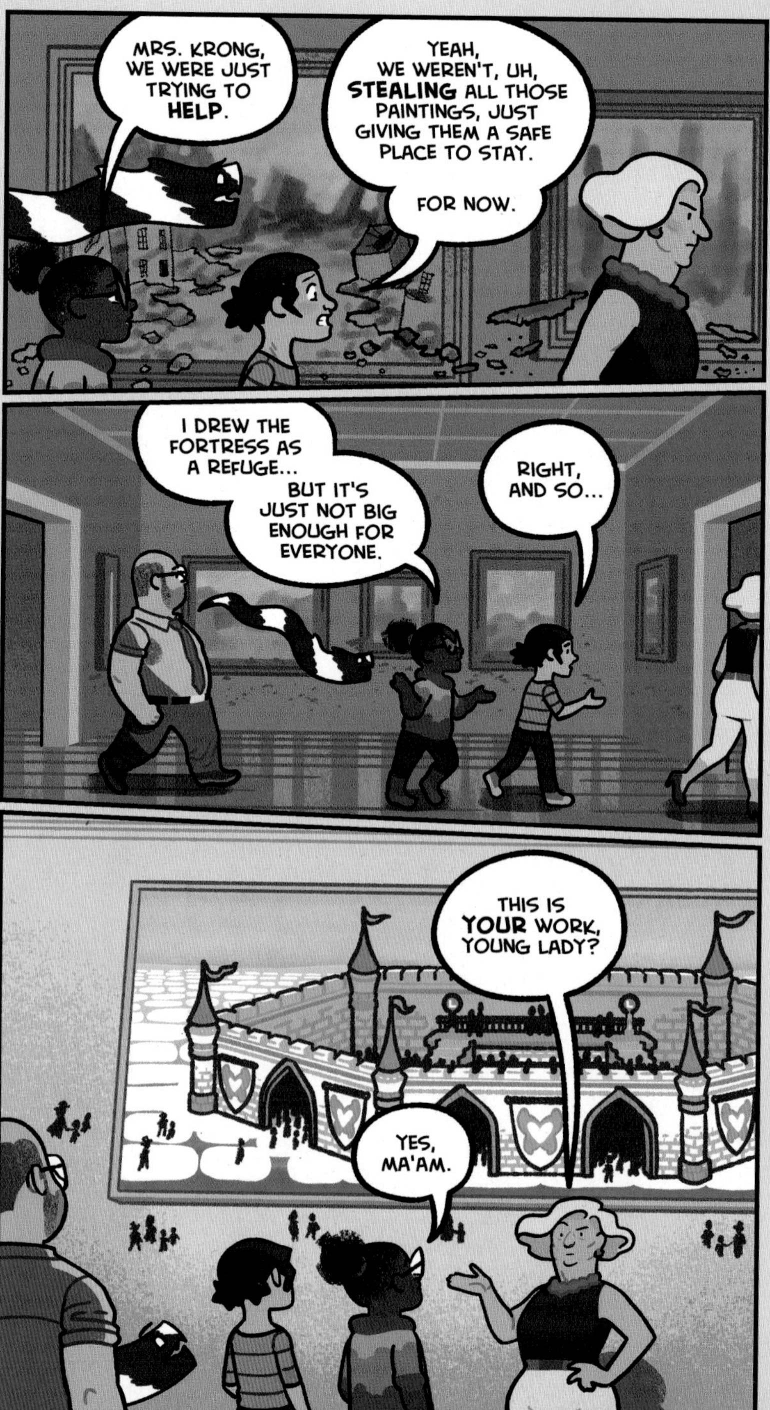
MRS. KRONG, WE WERE JUST TRYING TO **HELP**.
YEAH, WE WEREN'T, UH, **STEALING** ALL THOSE PAINTINGS, JUST GIVING THEM A SAFE PLACE TO STAY.
FOR NOW.
I DREW THE FORTRESS AS A REFUGE...
BUT IT'S JUST NOT BIG ENOUGH FOR EVERYONE.
RIGHT, AND SO...
THIS IS **YOUR** WORK, YOUNG LADY?
YES, MA'AM.

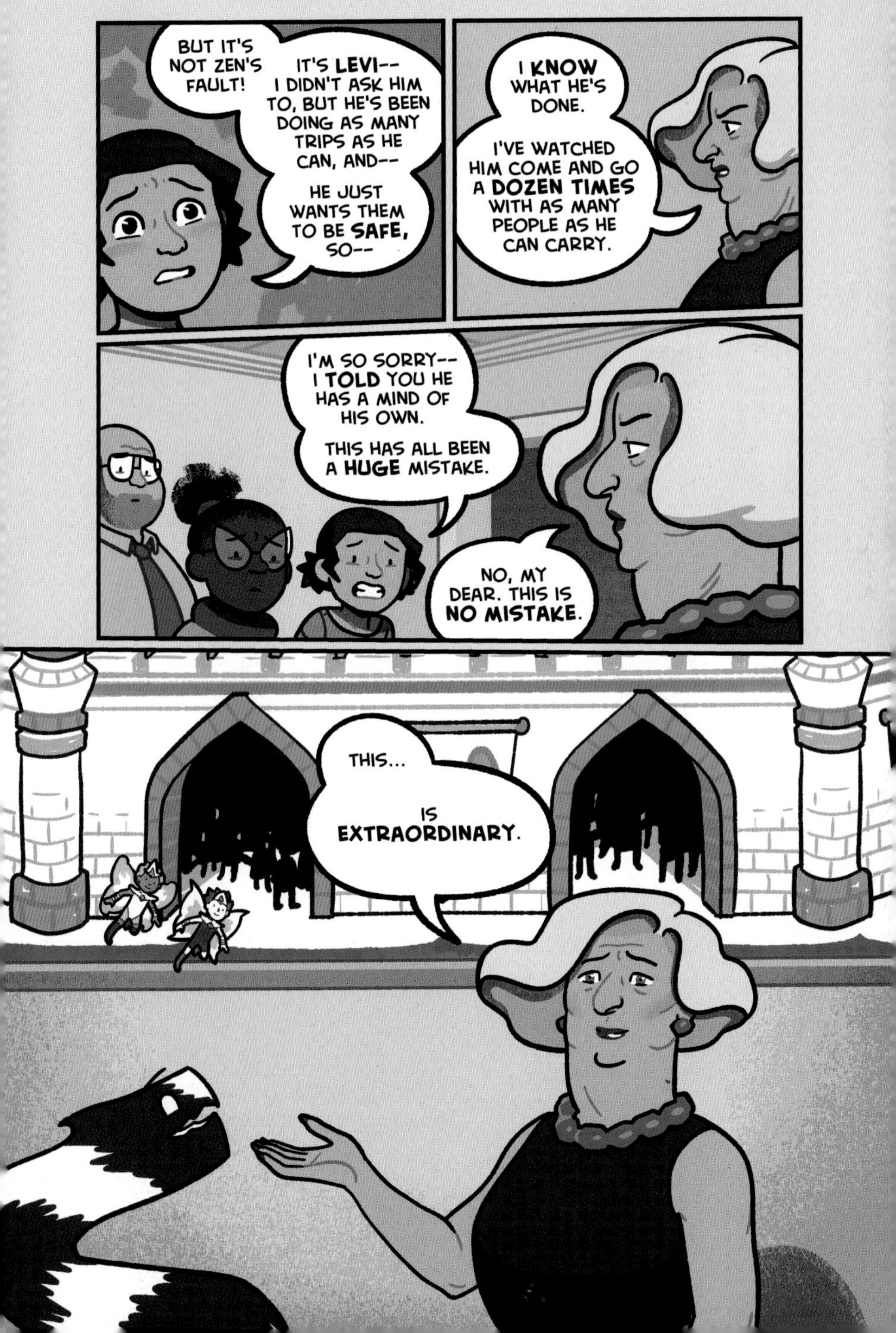
BUT IT'S NOT ZEN'S FAULT!
IT'S LEVI-- I DIDN'T ASK HIM TO, BUT HE'S BEEN DOING AS MANY TRIPS AS HE CAN, AND--
HE JUST WANTS THEM TO BE SAFE, SO--
I KNOW WHAT HE'S DONE.
I'VE WATCHED HIM COME AND GO A DOZEN TIMES WITH AS MANY PEOPLE AS HE CAN CARRY.
I'M SO SORRY-- I TOLD YOU HE HAS A MIND OF HIS OWN.
THIS HAS ALL BEEN A HUGE MISTAKE.
NO, MY DEAR. THIS IS NO MISTAKE.
THIS...
IS EXTRAORDINARY.

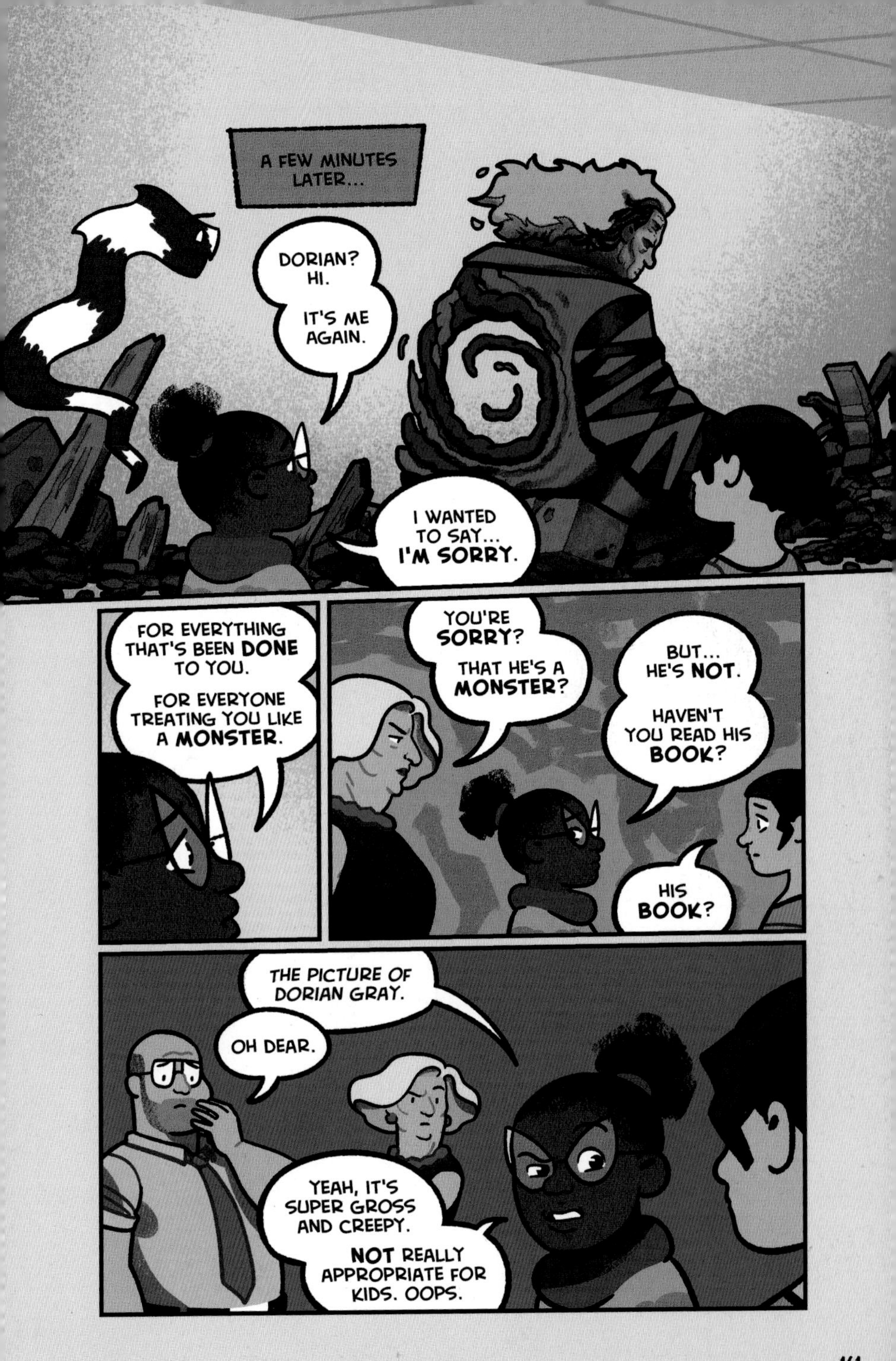
A FEW MINUTES LATER...
DORIAN? HI.
IT'S ME AGAIN.
I WANTED TO SAY... I'M SORRY.
FOR EVERYTHING THAT'S BEEN DONE TO YOU.
FOR EVERYONE TREATING YOU LIKE A MONSTER.
YOU'RE SORRY?
THAT HE'S A MONSTER?
BUT... HE'S NOT.
HAVEN'T YOU READ HIS BOOK?
HIS BOOK?
THE PICTURE OF DORIAN GRAY.
OH DEAR.
YEAH, IT'S SUPER GROSS AND CREEPY.
NOT REALLY APPROPRIATE FOR KIDS. OOPS.

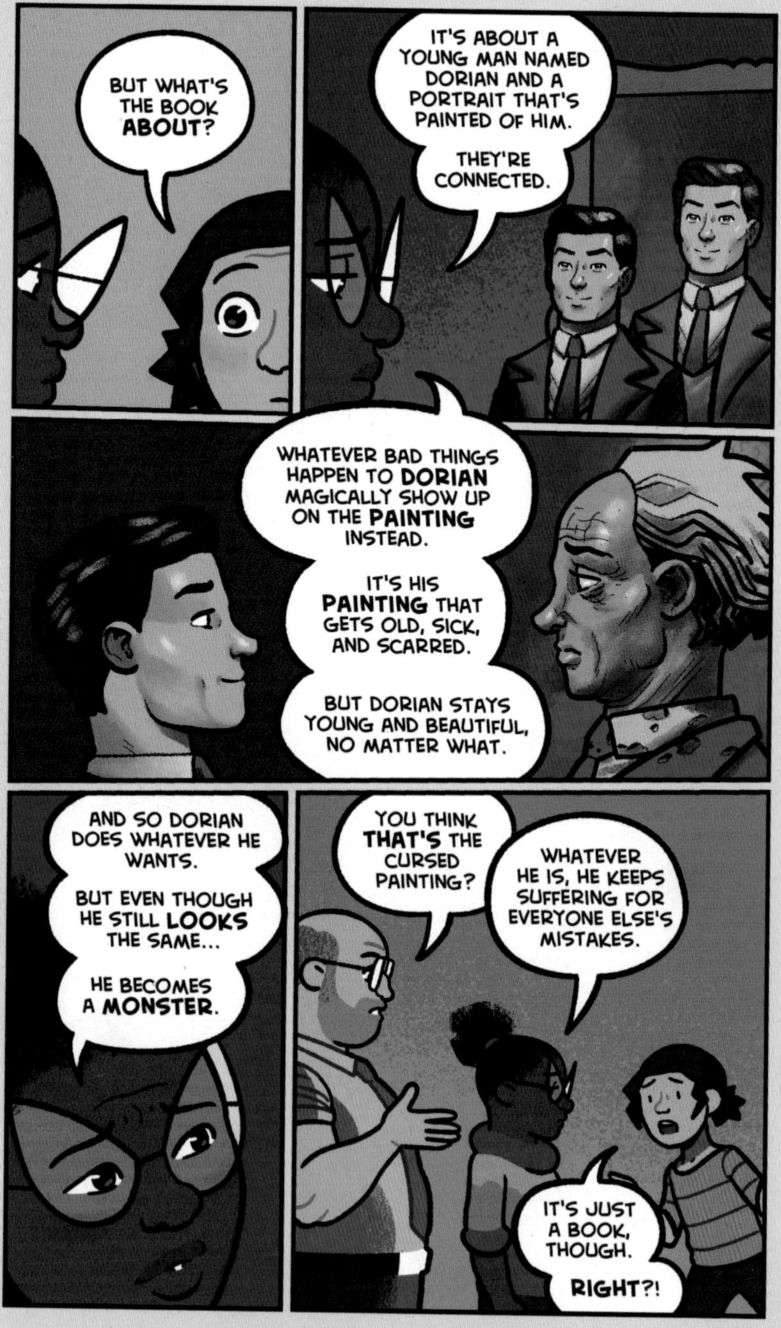
BUT WHAT'S THE BOOK **ABOUT**?
IT'S ABOUT A YOUNG MAN NAMED DORIAN AND A PORTRAIT THAT'S PAINTED OF HIM.
THEY'RE CONNECTED.
WHATEVER BAD THINGS HAPPEN TO **DORIAN** MAGICALLY SHOW UP ON THE **PAINTING** INSTEAD.
IT'S HIS **PAINTING** THAT GETS OLD, SICK, AND SCARRED.
BUT DORIAN STAYS YOUNG AND BEAUTIFUL, NO MATTER WHAT.
AND SO DORIAN DOES WHATEVER HE WANTS.
BUT EVEN THOUGH HE STILL **LOOKS** THE SAME...
HE BECOMES A **MONSTER**.
YOU THINK **THAT'S** THE CURSED PAINTING?
WHATEVER HE IS, HE KEEPS SUFFERING FOR EVERYONE ELSE'S MISTAKES.
IT'S JUST A BOOK, THOUGH.
RIGHT?!

169

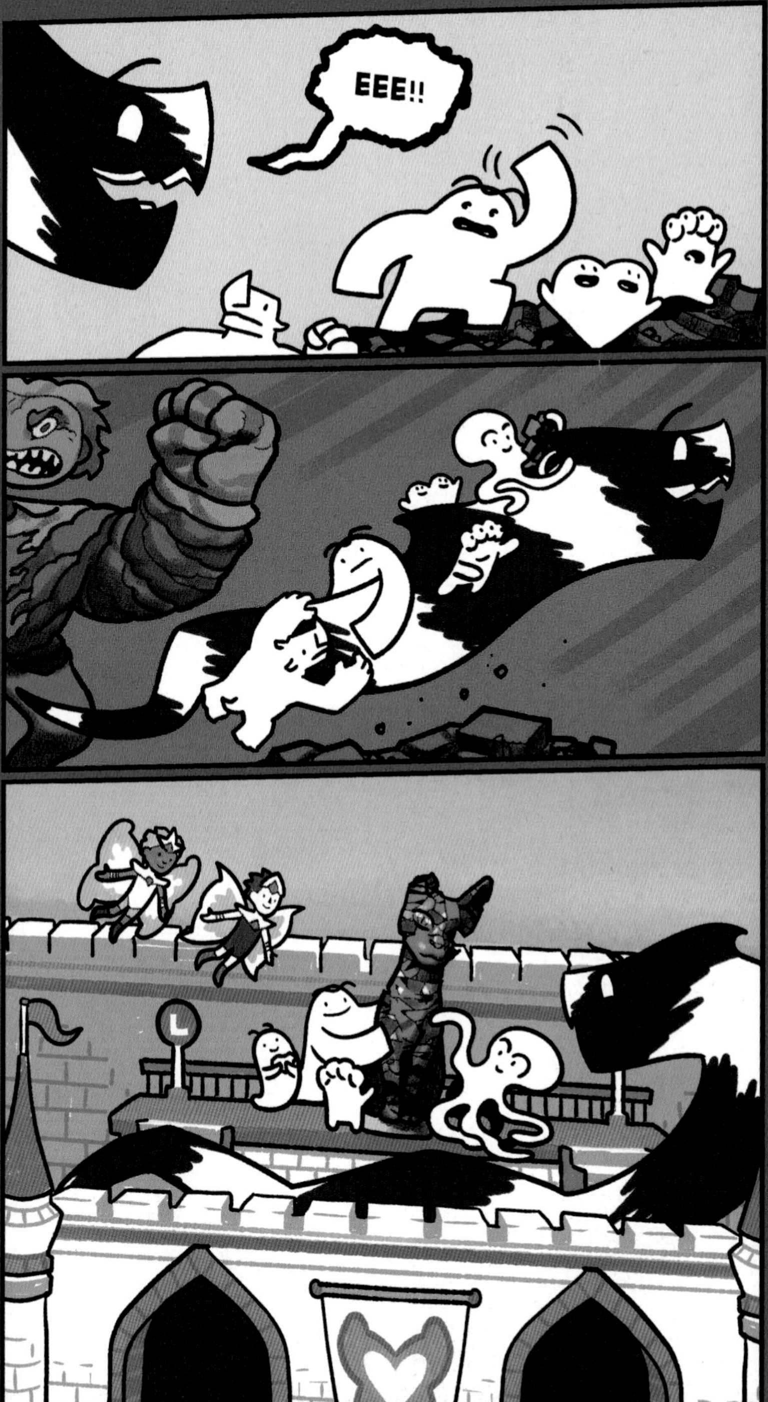
EEE!!

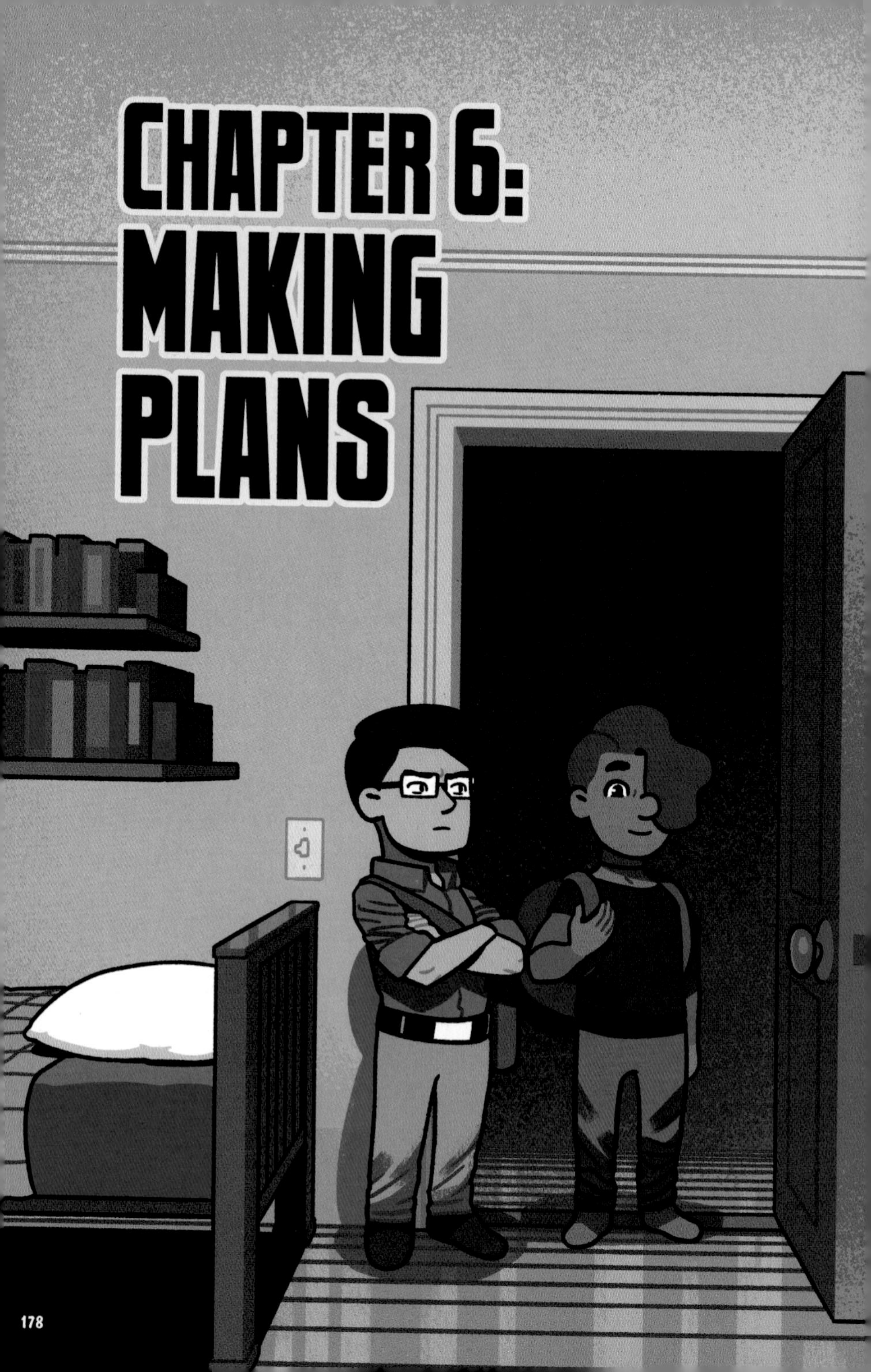
CHAPTER 6:
MAKING PLANS

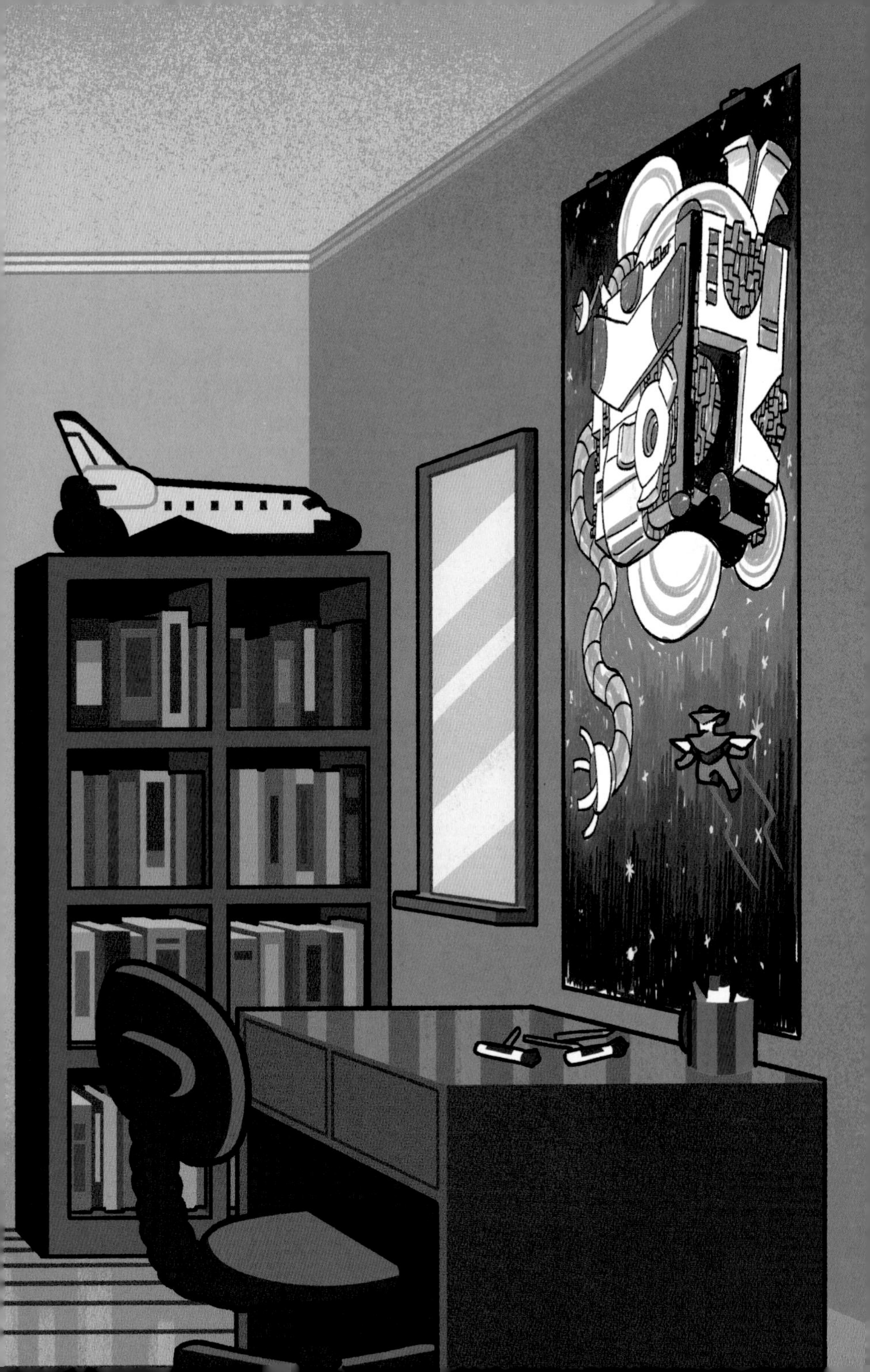

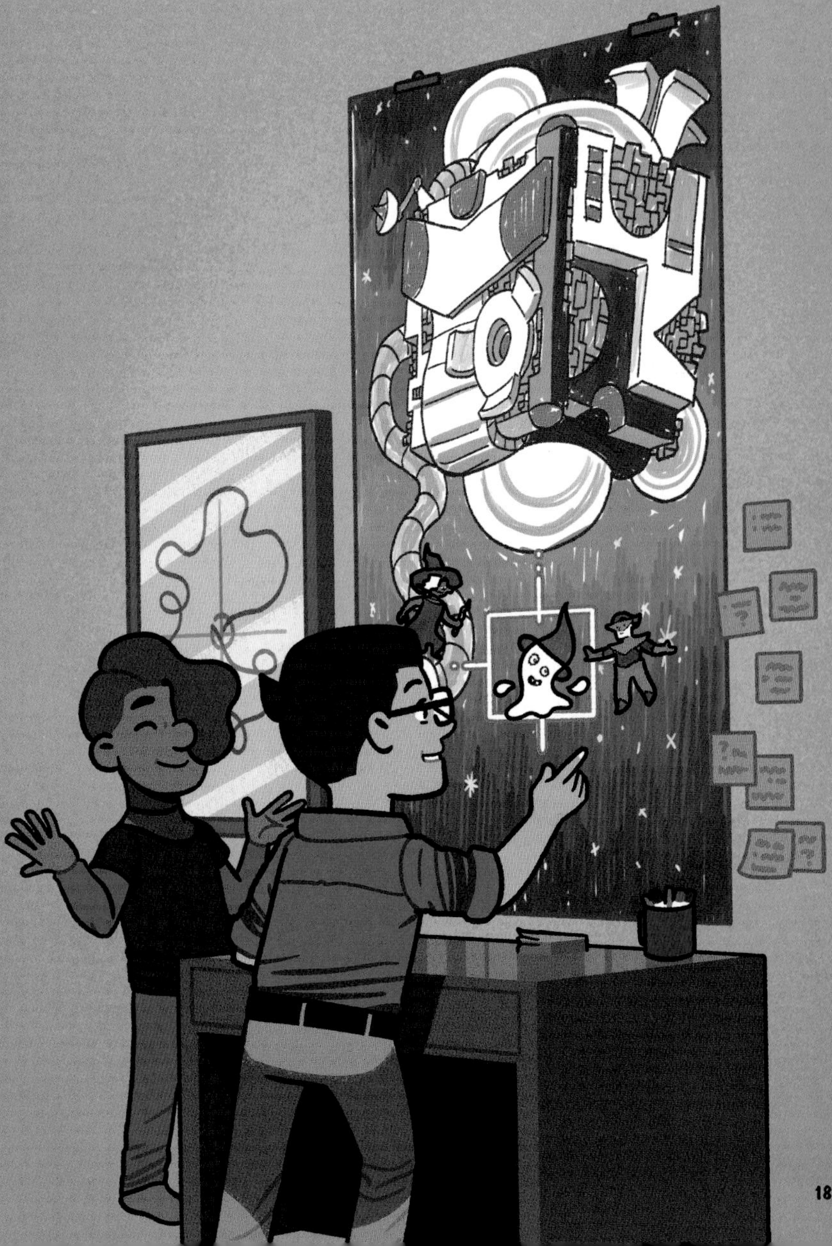

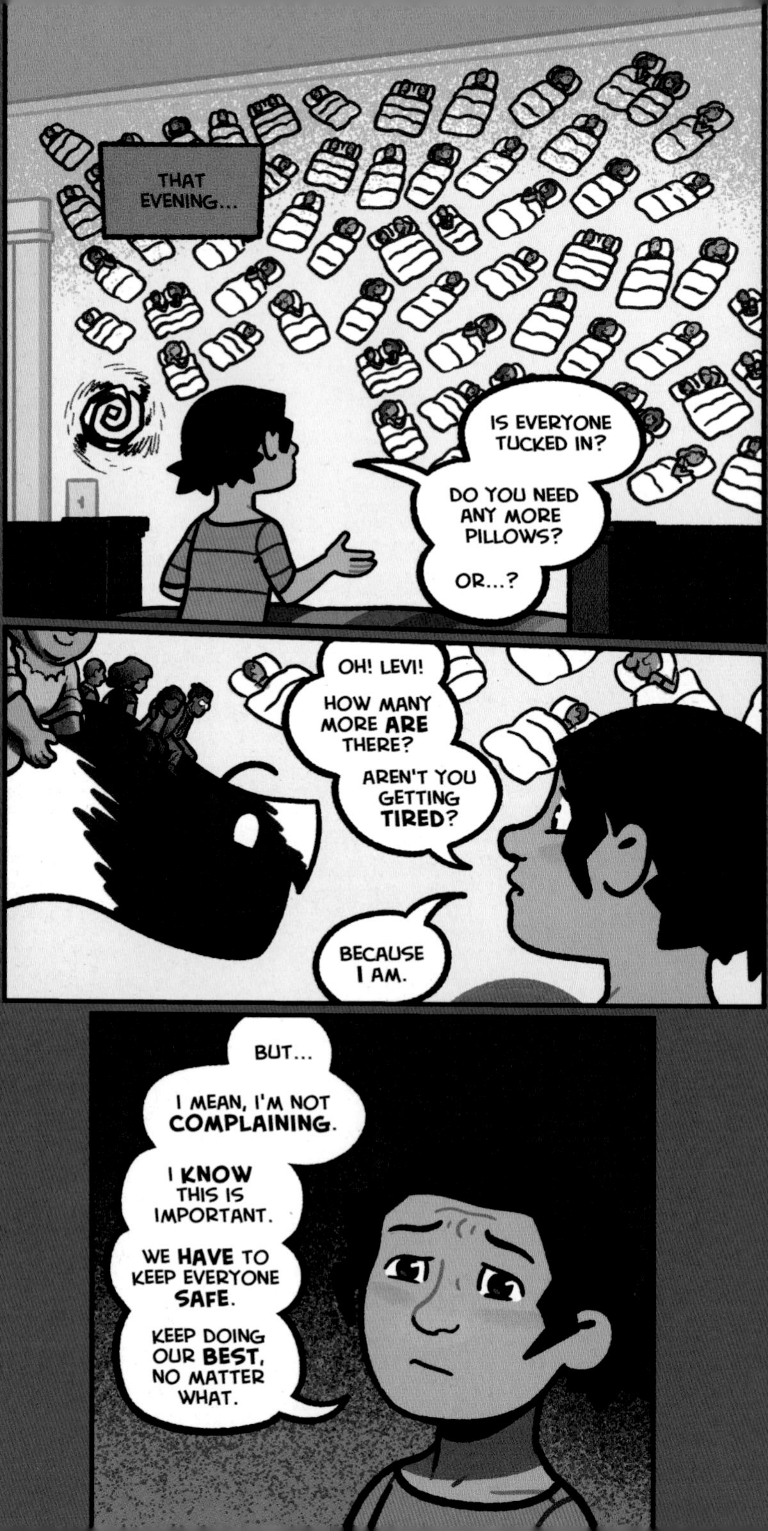
THAT EVENING...
IS EVERYONE TUCKED IN?
DO YOU NEED ANY MORE PILLOWS?
OR...?
OH! LEVI!
HOW MANY MORE **ARE** THERE?
AREN'T YOU GETTING **TIRED**?
BECAUSE I AM.
BUT...
I MEAN, I'M NOT **COMPLAINING**.
I **KNOW** THIS IS IMPORTANT.
WE **HAVE** TO KEEP EVERYONE **SAFE**.
KEEP DOING OUR **BEST**, NO MATTER WHAT.

185

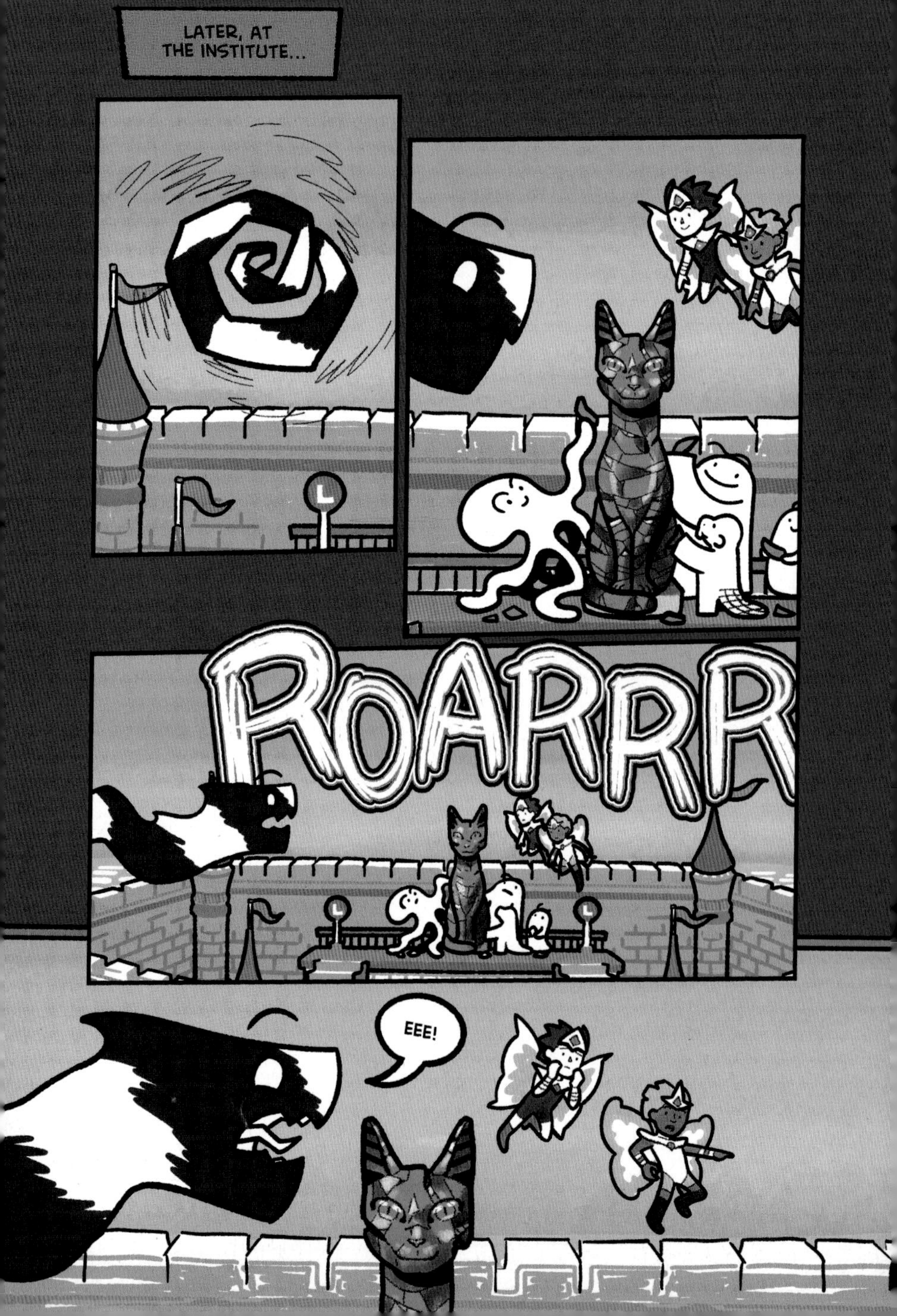
LATER, AT THE INSTITUTE...
ROARRR
EEE!

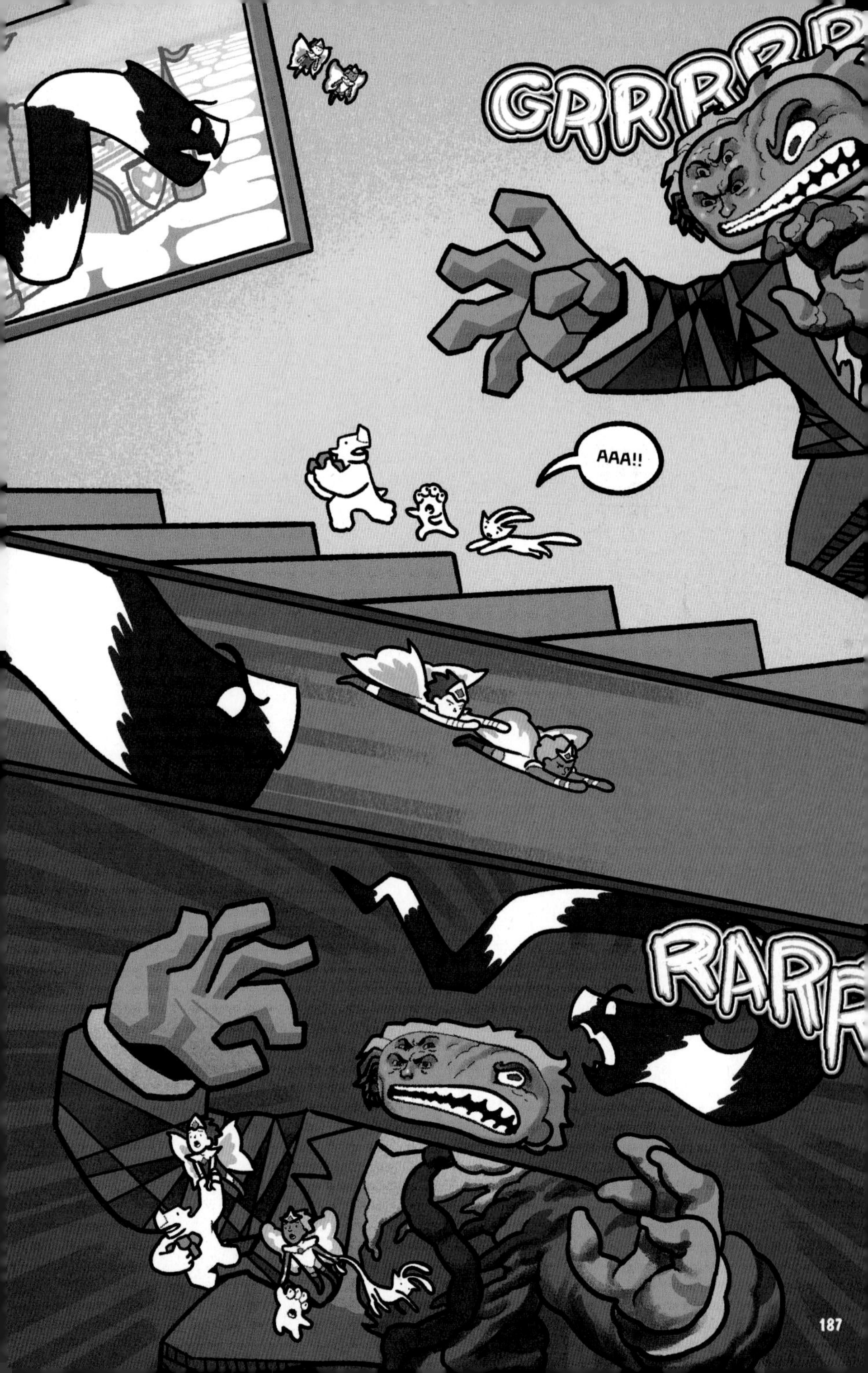
GRRRR
AAA!!
RARR

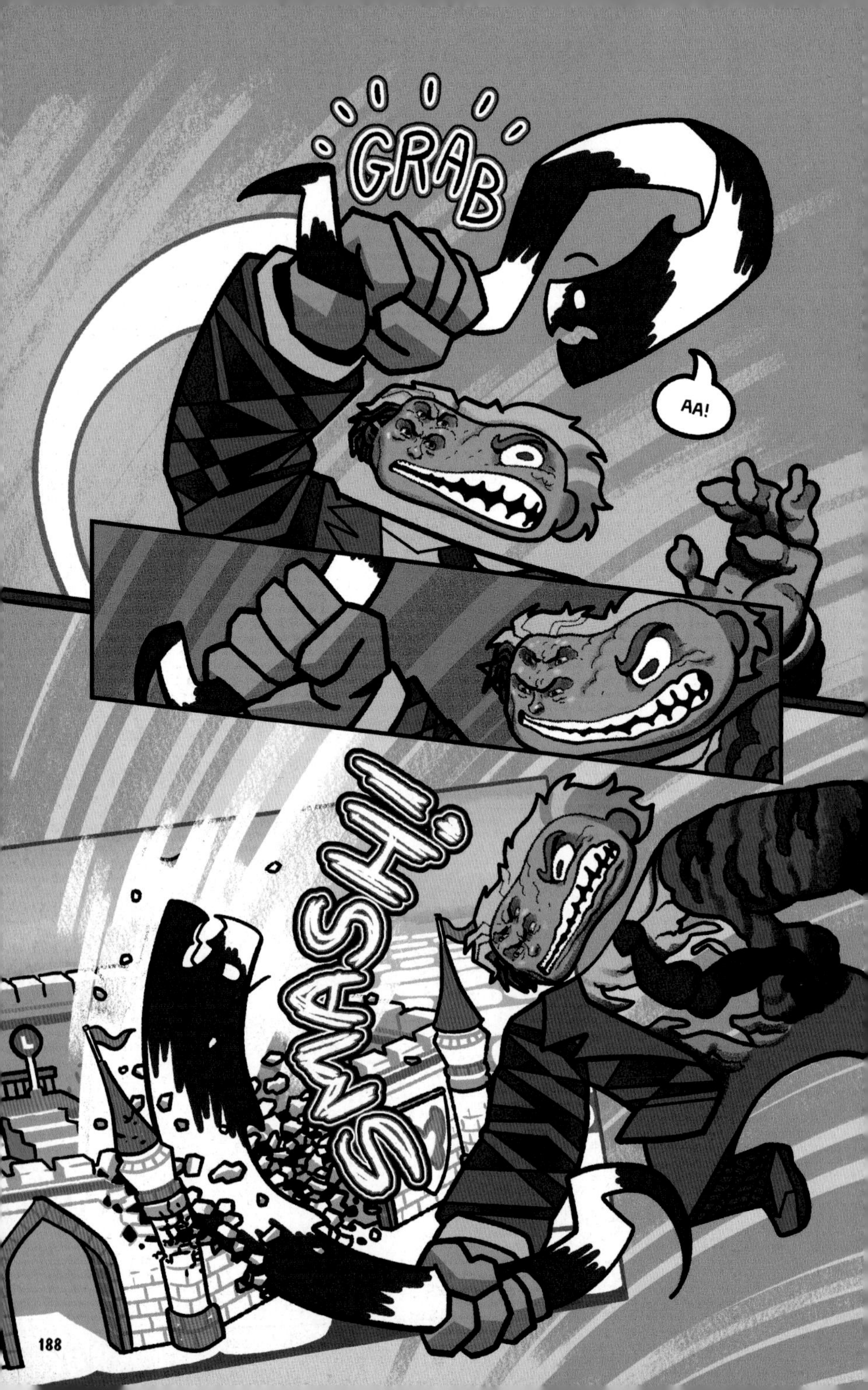
GRAB
AA!
SMASH!!

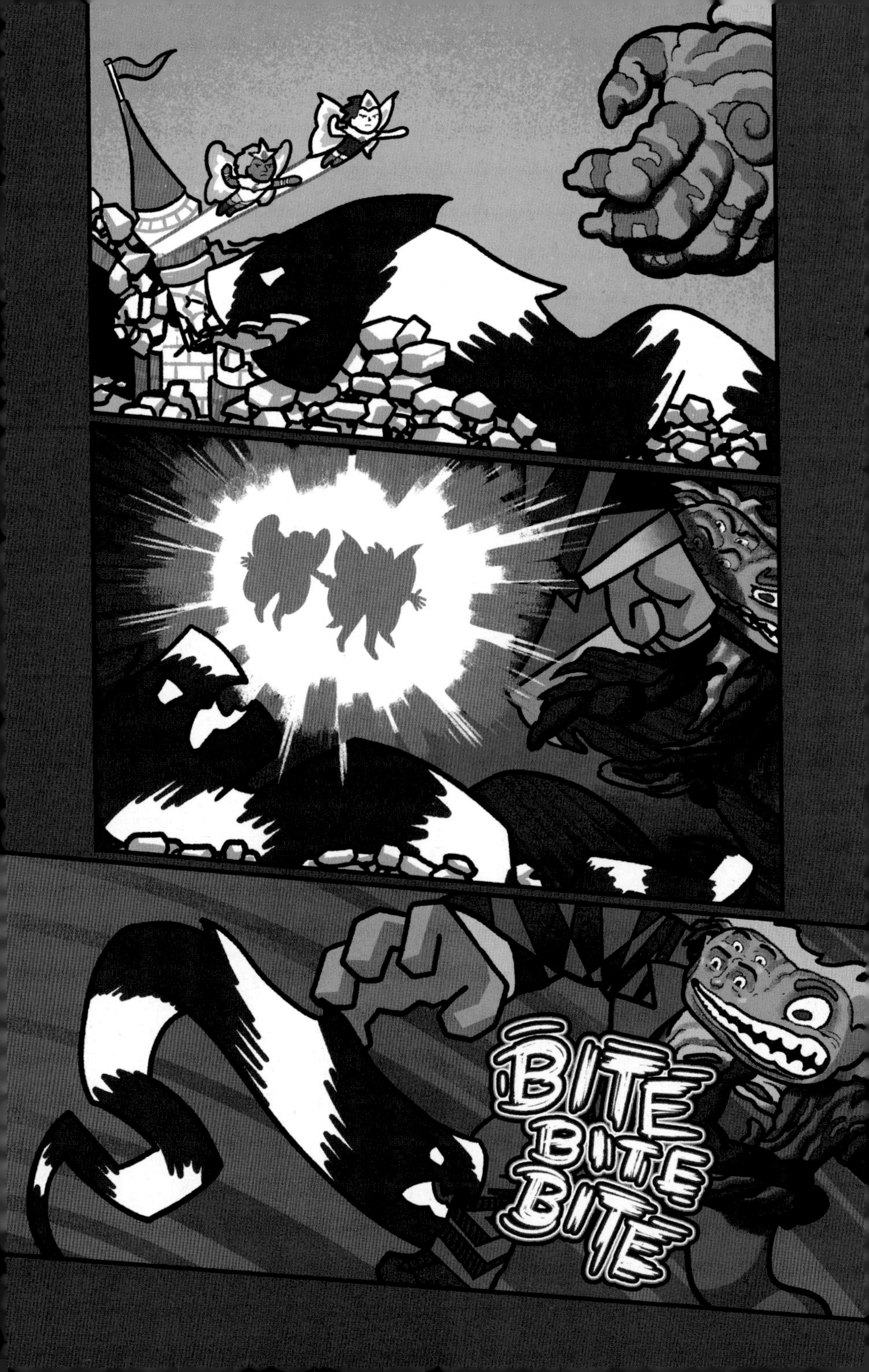
BITE BITE BITE

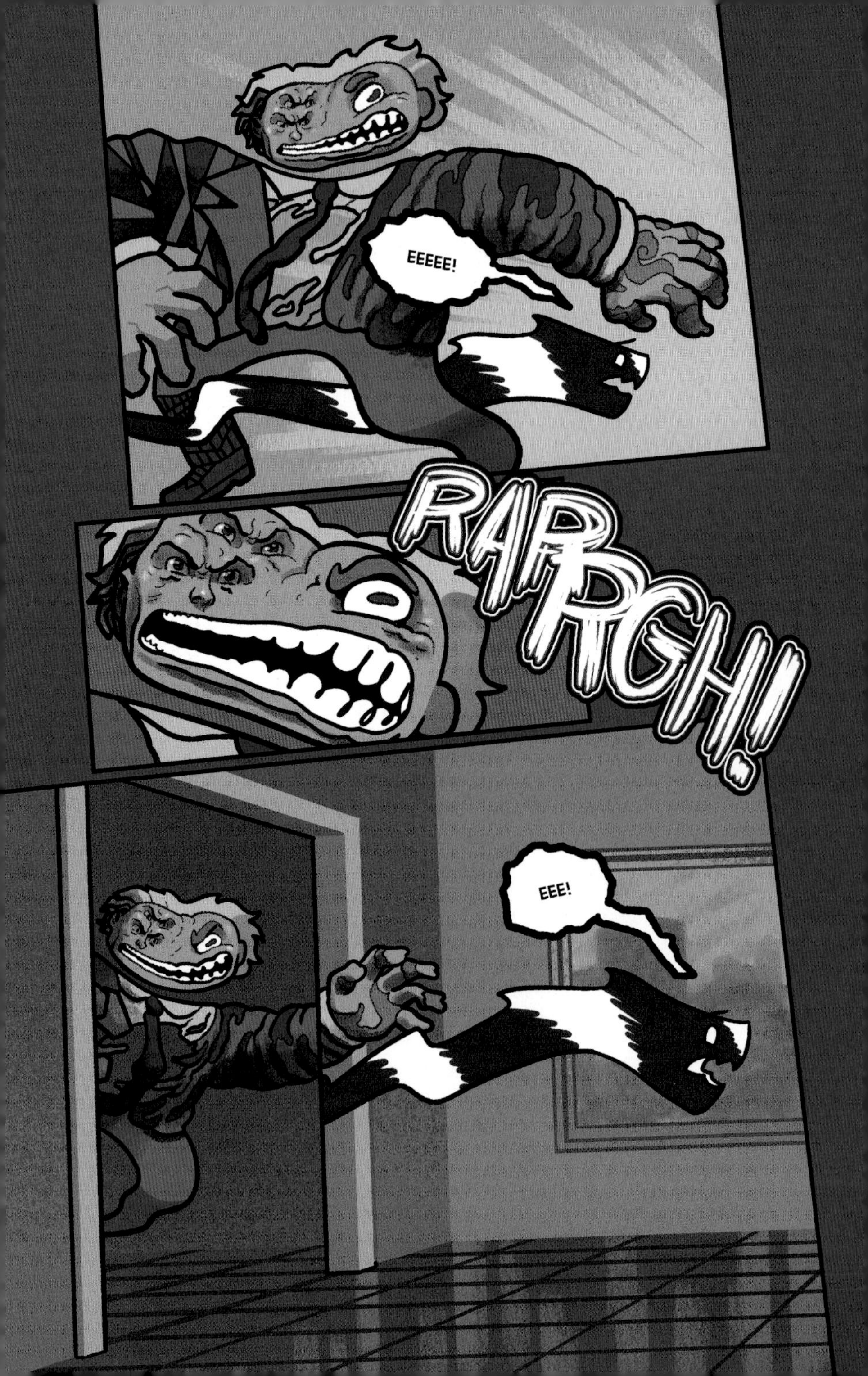
EEEEE!
RARRGH!!
EEE!

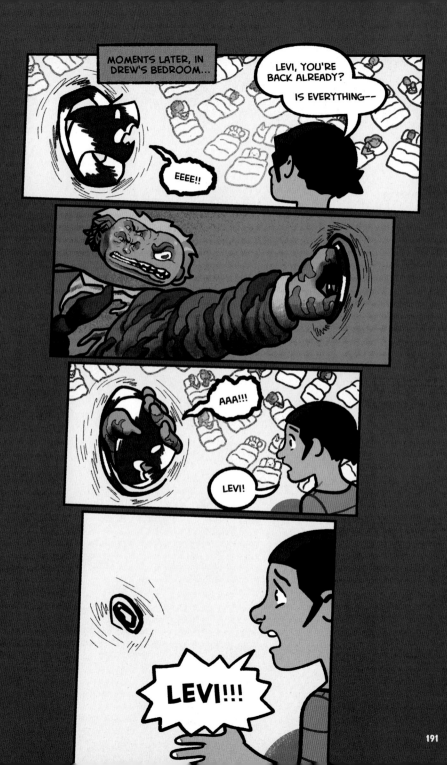

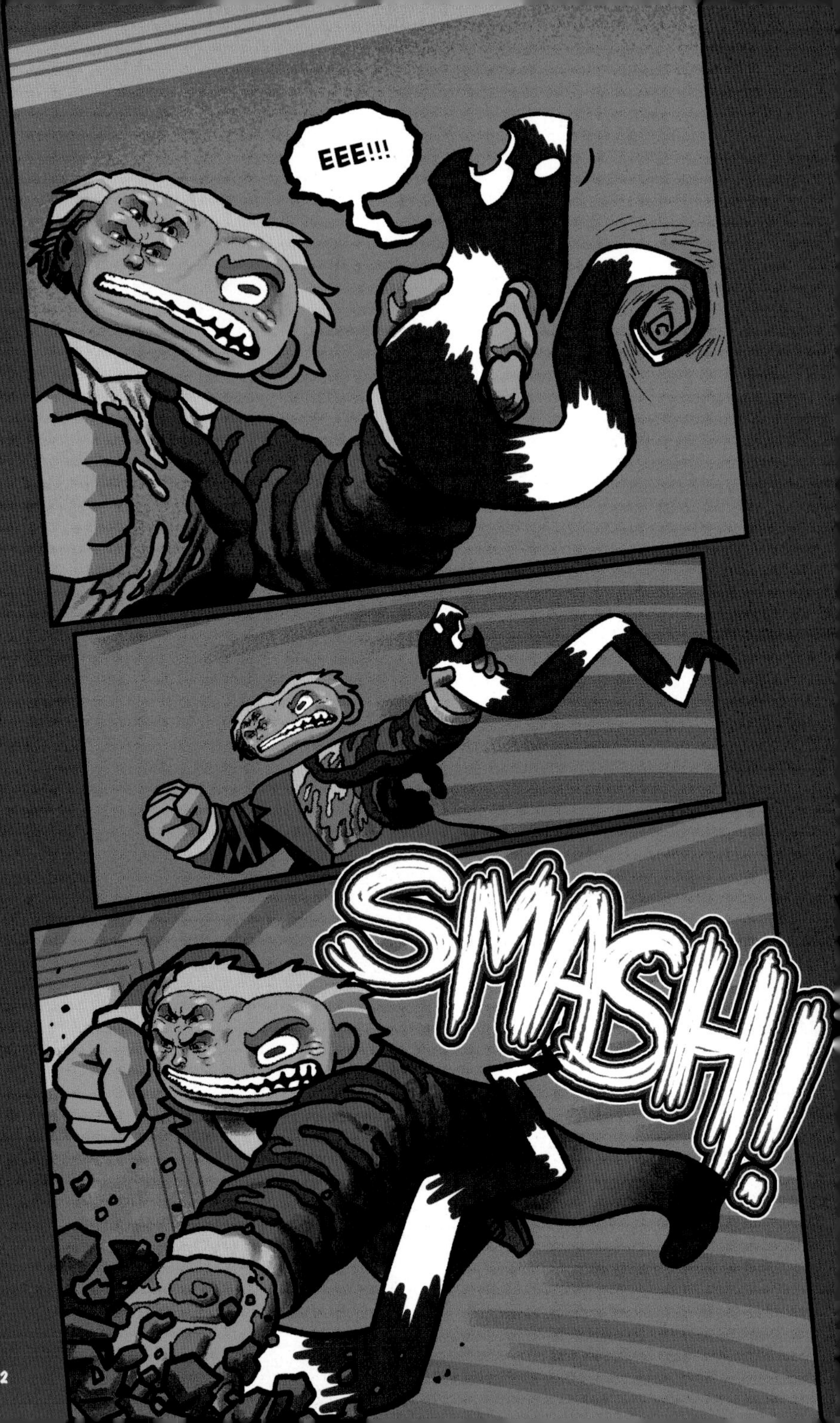
EEE!!!
SMASH!!

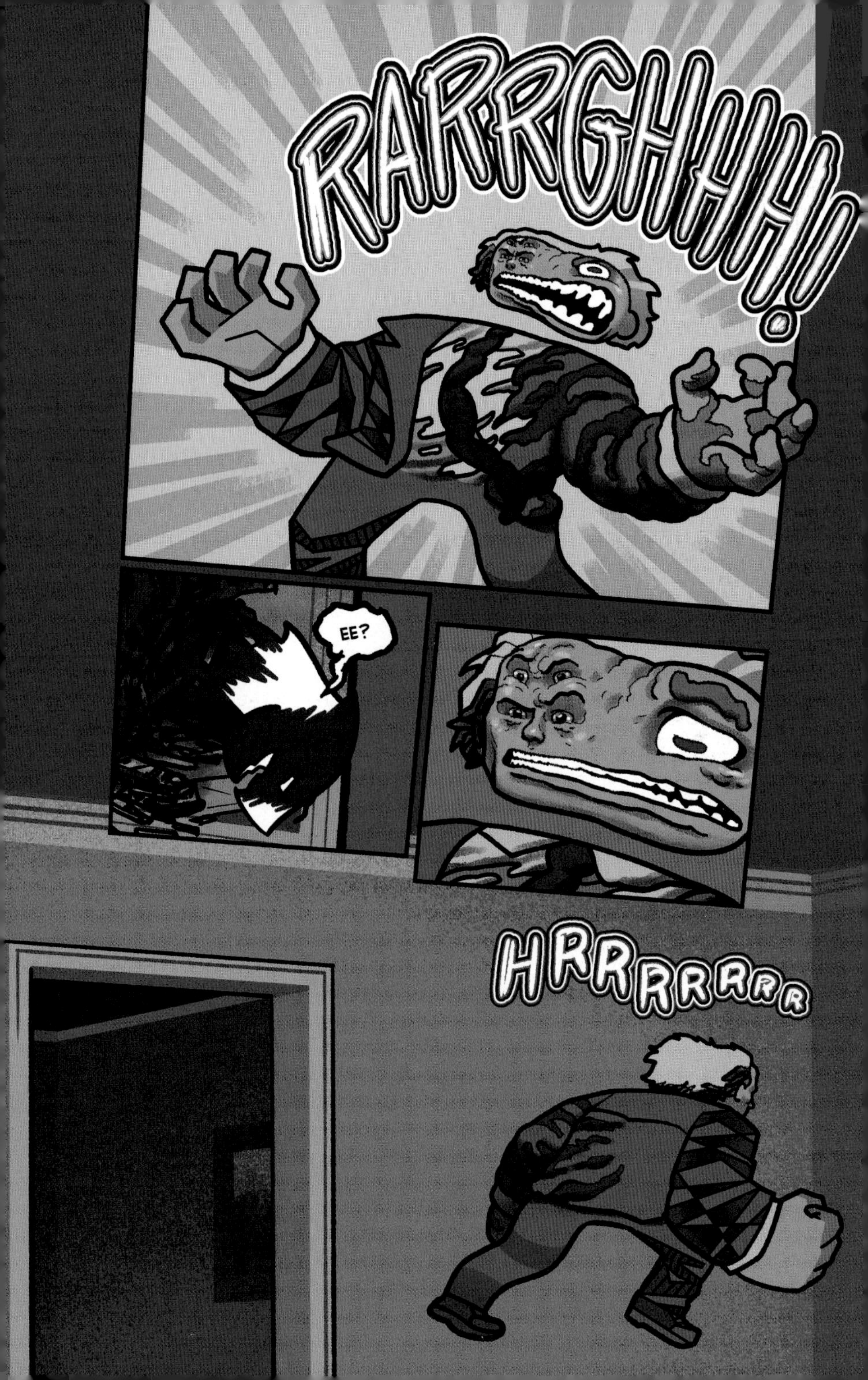
RARRGHHH!
EE?
HRRRRRRR

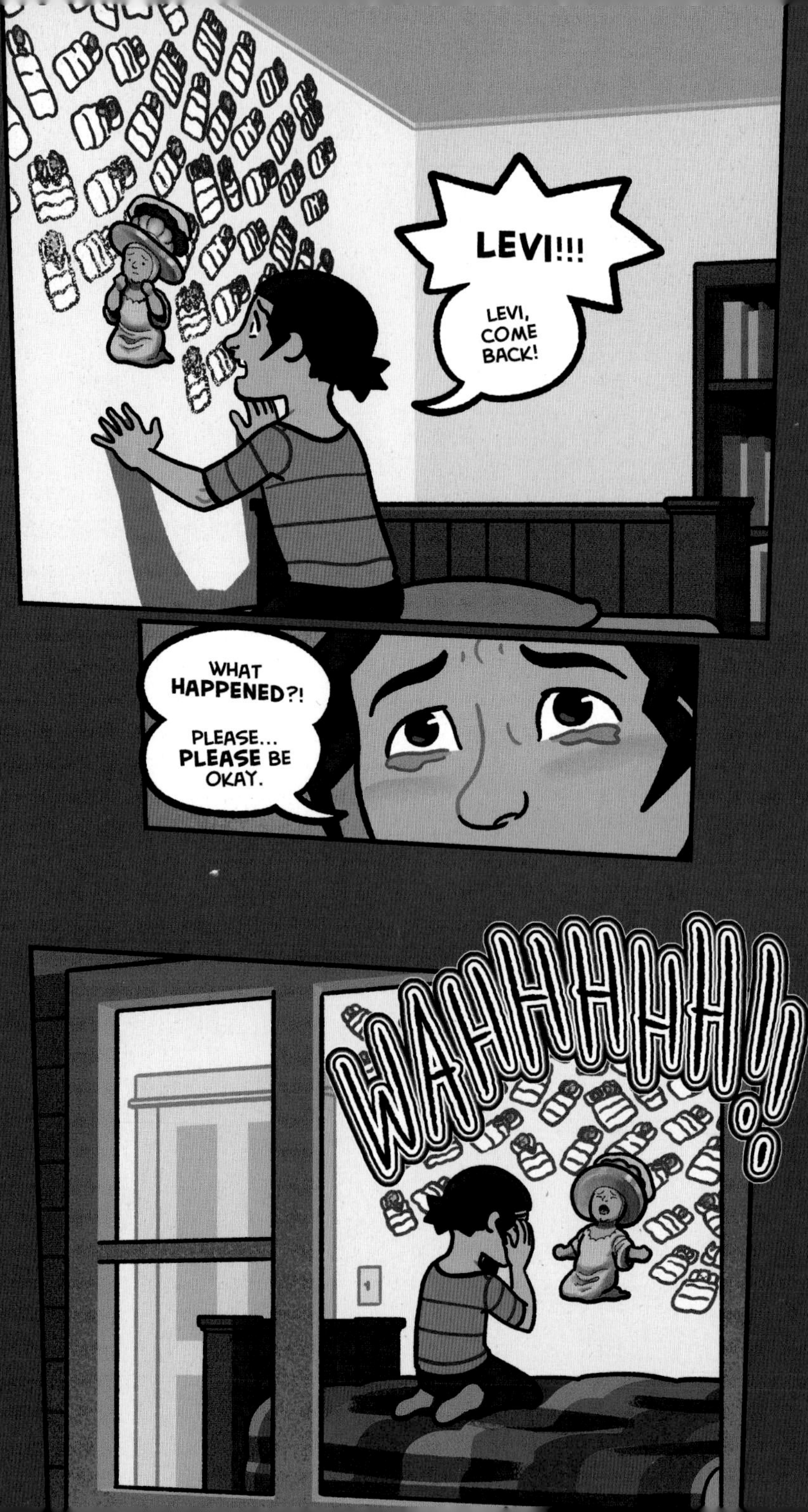
LEVI!!!
LEVI, COME BACK!
WHAT HAPPENED?!
PLEASE... PLEASE BE OKAY.
WAHHHHHH!!

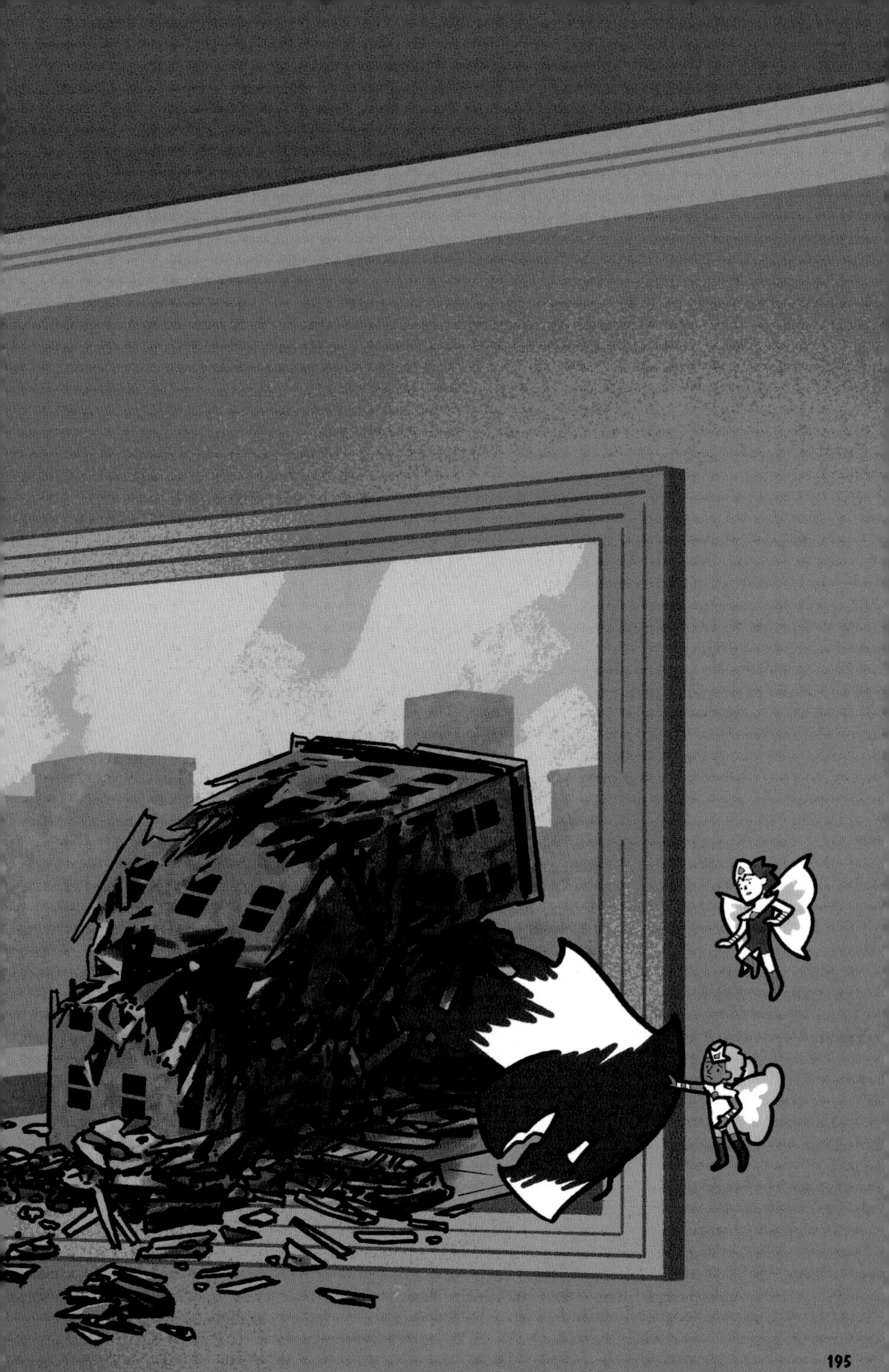

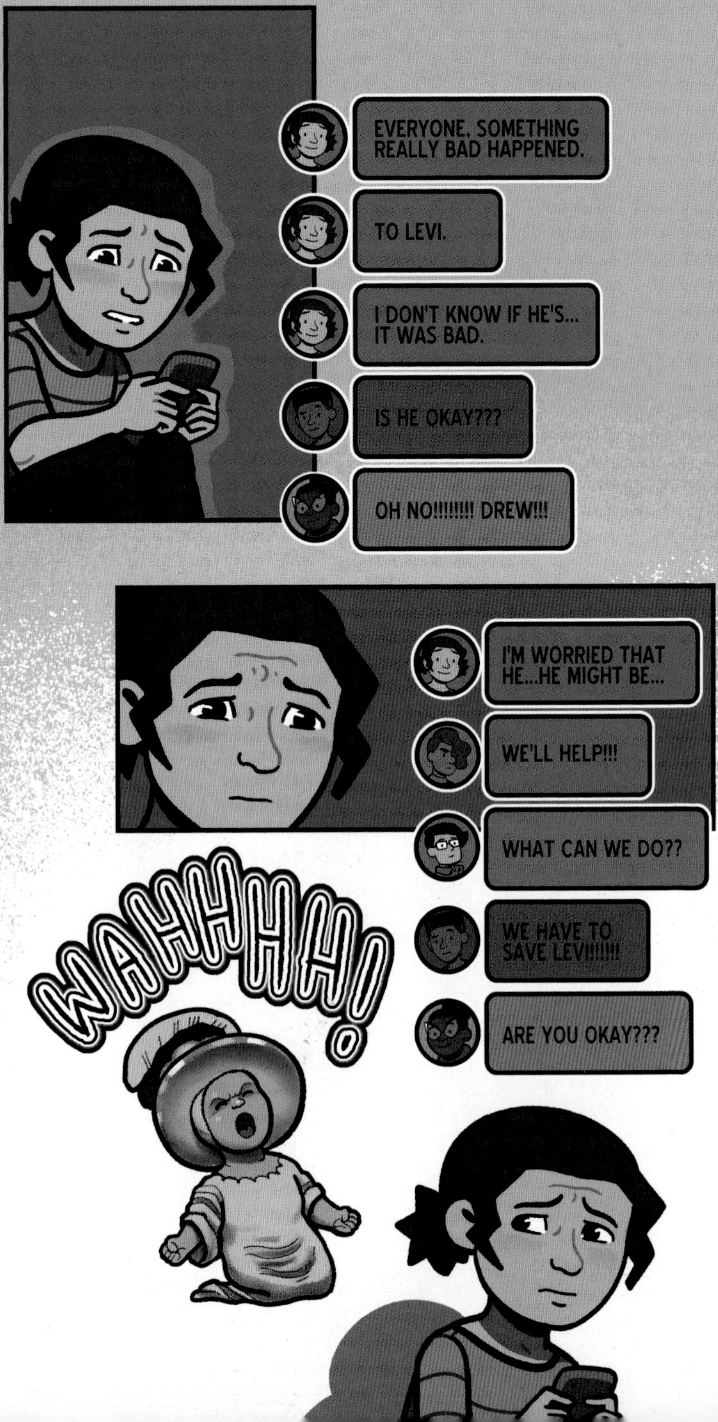
EVERYONE, SOMETHING REALLY BAD HAPPENED.
TO LEVI.
I DON'T KNOW IF HE'S... IT WAS BAD.
IS HE OKAY???
OH NO!!!!!!!! DREW!!!
I'M WORRIED THAT HE...HE MIGHT BE...
WE'LL HELP!!!
WHAT CAN WE DO??
WE HAVE TO SAVE LEVI!!!!!!
ARE YOU OKAY???
WAHHHA!

CHAPTER 7: REUNITED

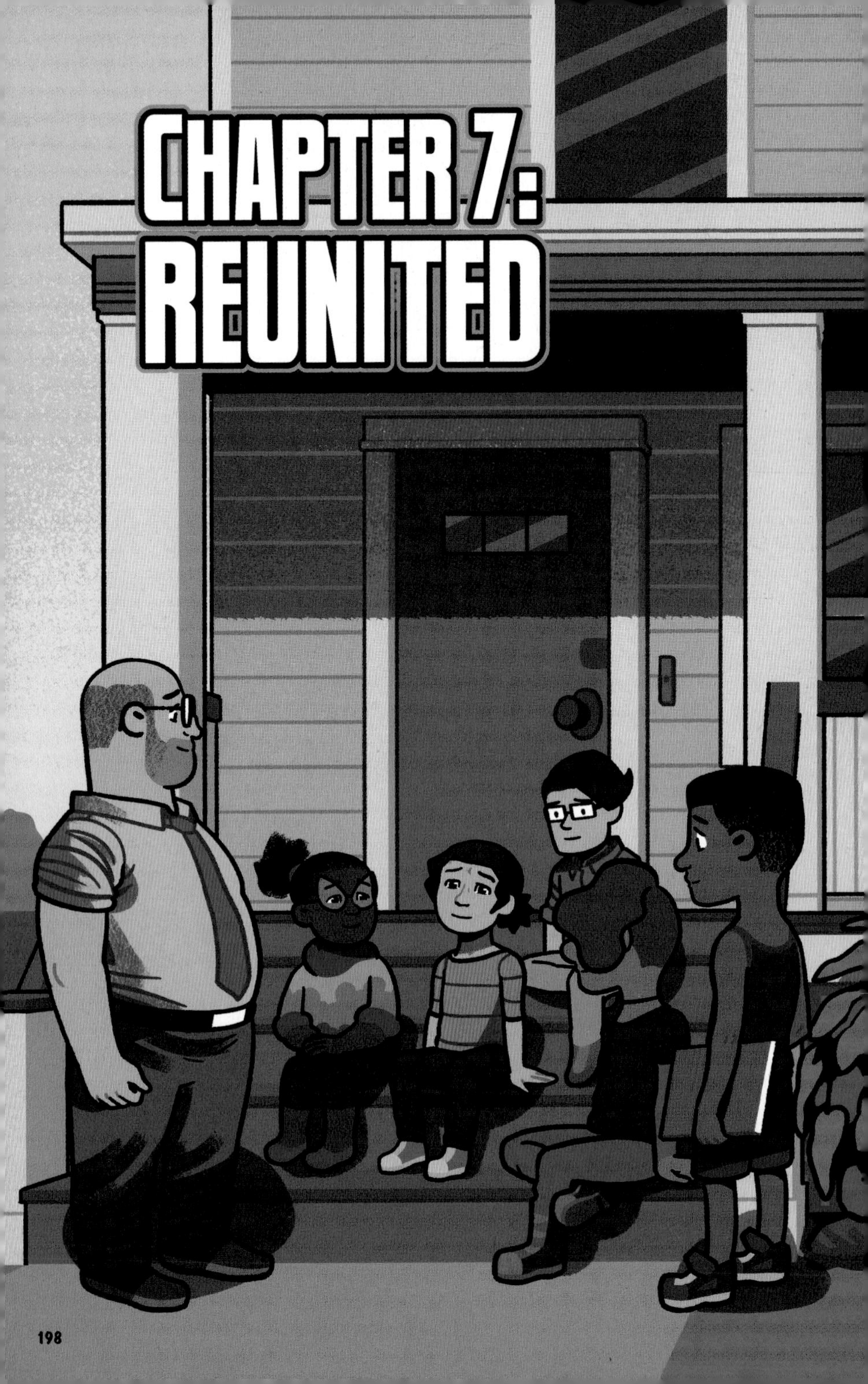

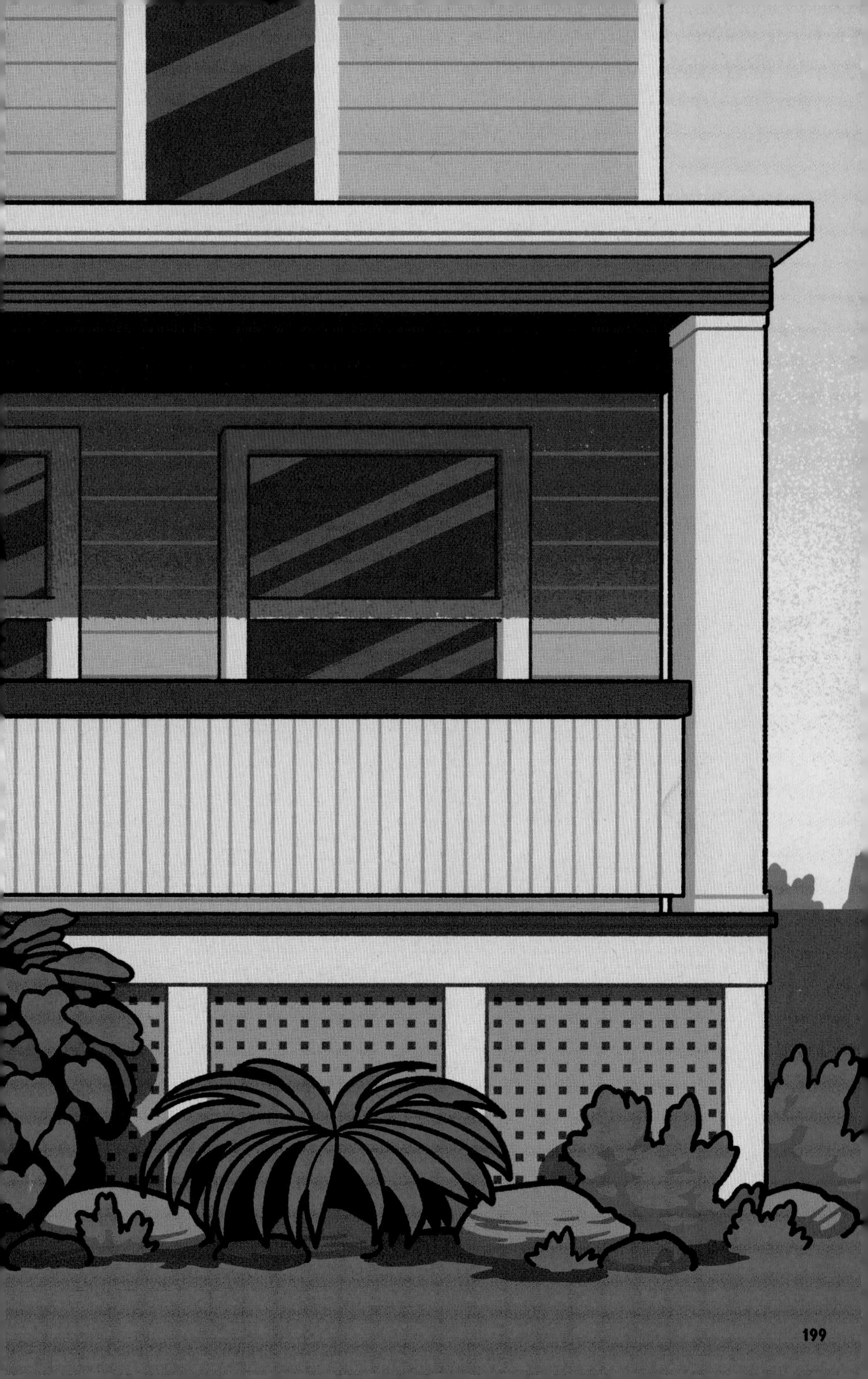

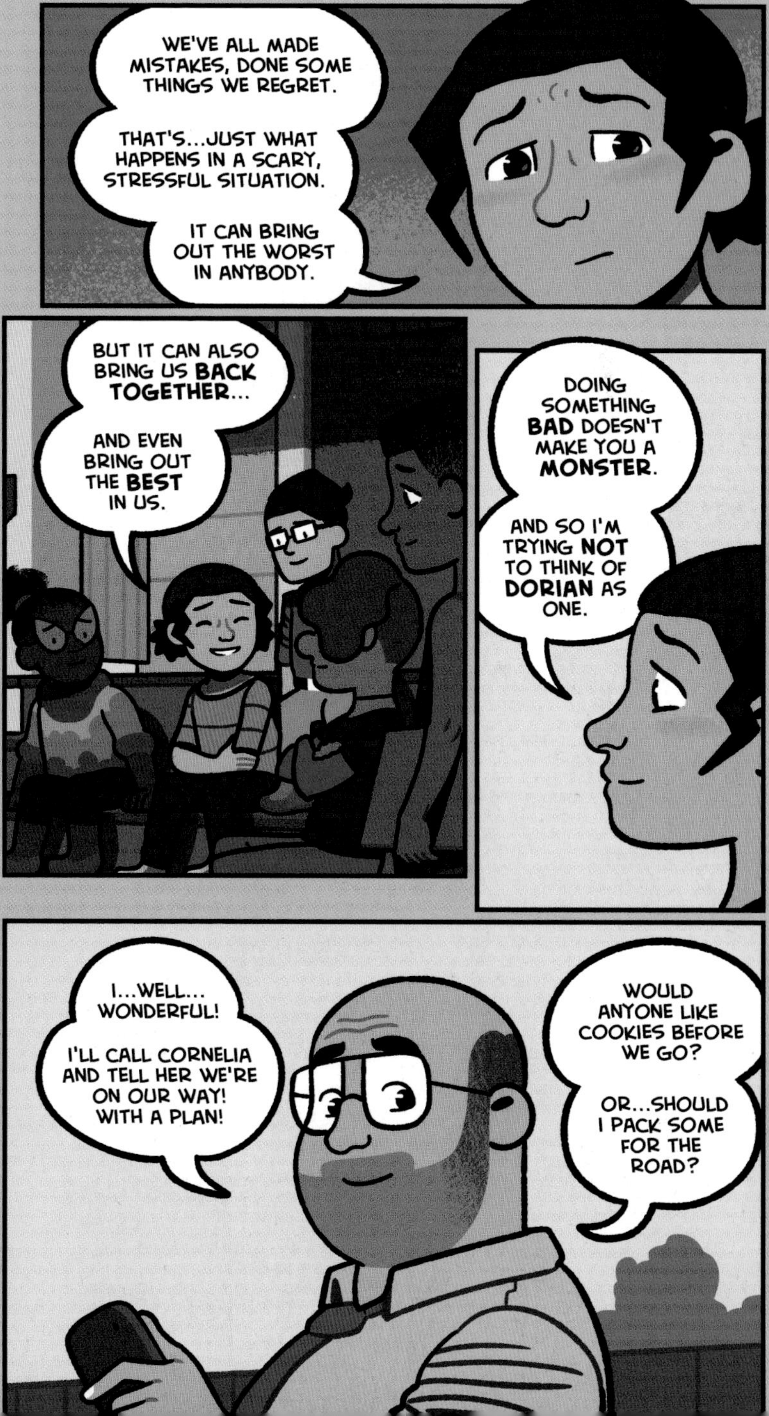
WE'VE ALL MADE MISTAKES, DONE SOME THINGS WE REGRET.
THAT'S...JUST WHAT HAPPENS IN A SCARY, STRESSFUL SITUATION.
IT CAN BRING OUT THE WORST IN ANYBODY.
BUT IT CAN ALSO BRING US **BACK TOGETHER**...
AND EVEN BRING OUT THE **BEST** IN US.
DOING SOMETHING **BAD** DOESN'T MAKE YOU A **MONSTER**.
AND SO I'M TRYING **NOT** TO THINK OF **DORIAN** AS ONE.
I...WELL... WONDERFUL!
I'LL CALL CORNELIA AND TELL HER WE'RE ON OUR WAY! WITH A PLAN!
WOULD ANYONE LIKE COOKIES BEFORE WE GO?
OR...SHOULD I PACK SOME FOR THE ROAD?

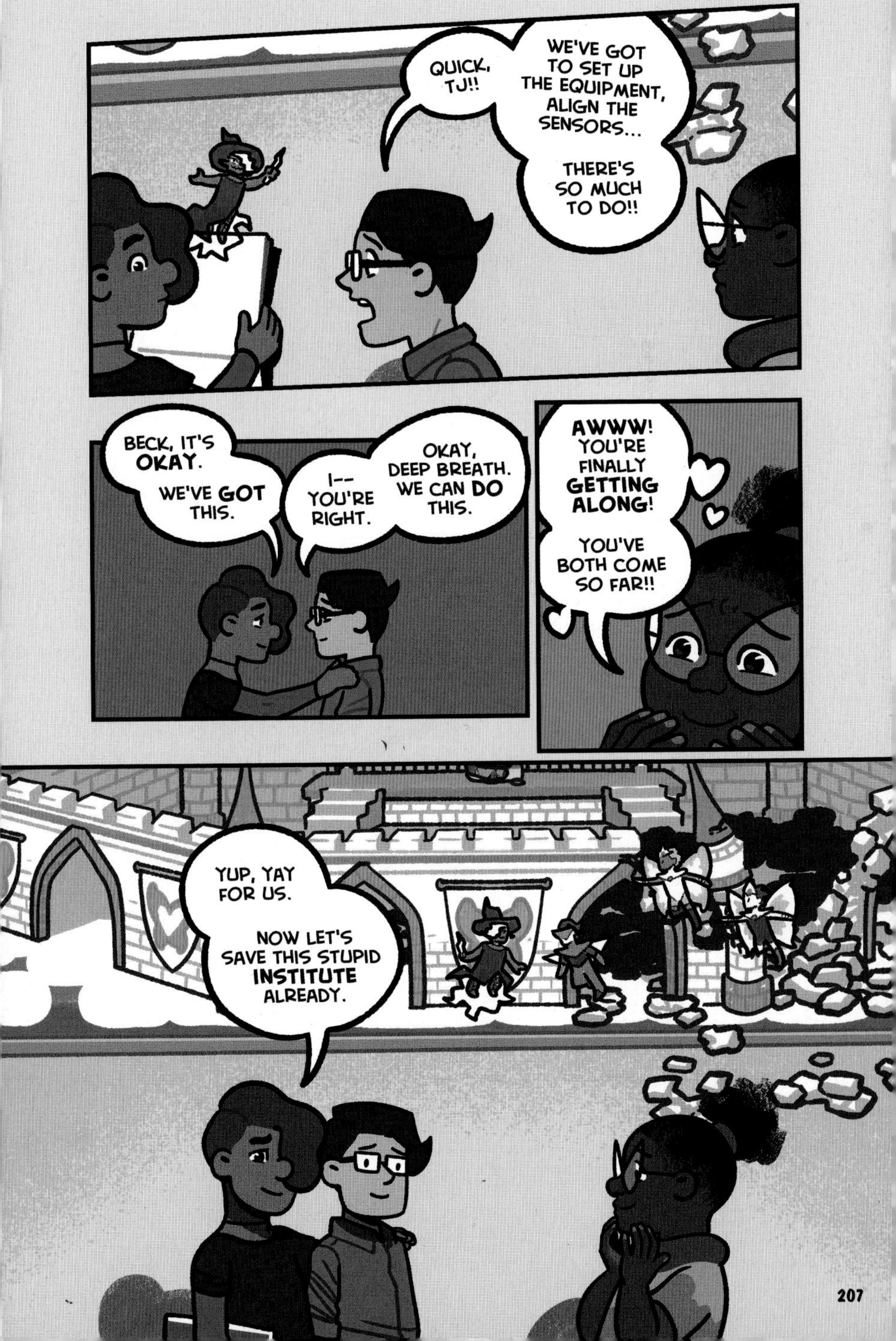
QUICK, TJ!!
WE'VE GOT TO SET UP THE EQUIPMENT, ALIGN THE SENSORS...
THERE'S SO MUCH TO DO!!
BECK, IT'S OKAY.
WE'VE GOT THIS.
I-- YOU'RE RIGHT.
OKAY, DEEP BREATH. WE CAN DO THIS.
AWWW! YOU'RE FINALLY GETTING ALONG!
YOU'VE BOTH COME SO FAR!!
YUP, YAY FOR US.
NOW LET'S SAVE THIS STUPID INSTITUTE ALREADY.

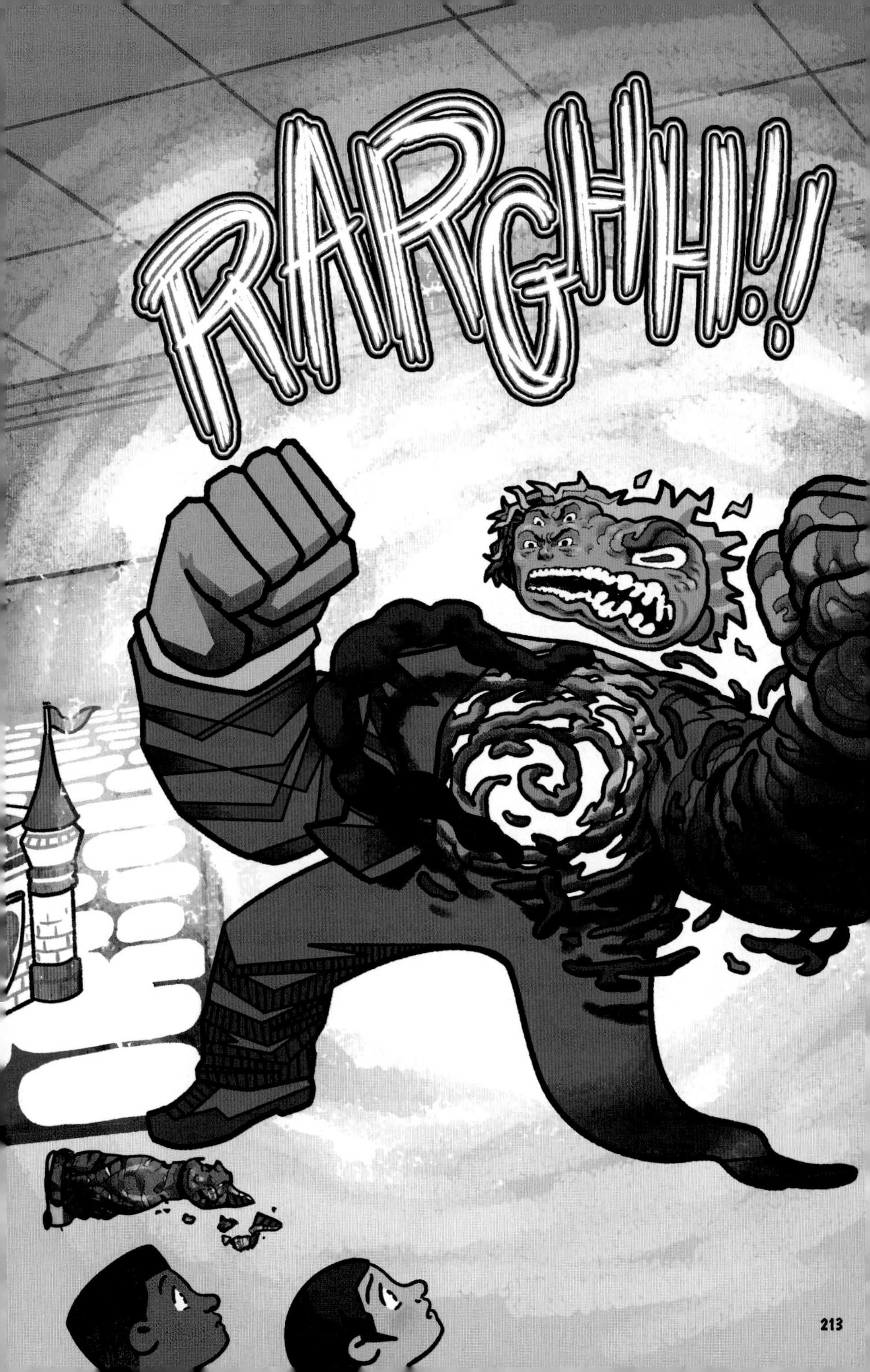
RARGHH!!

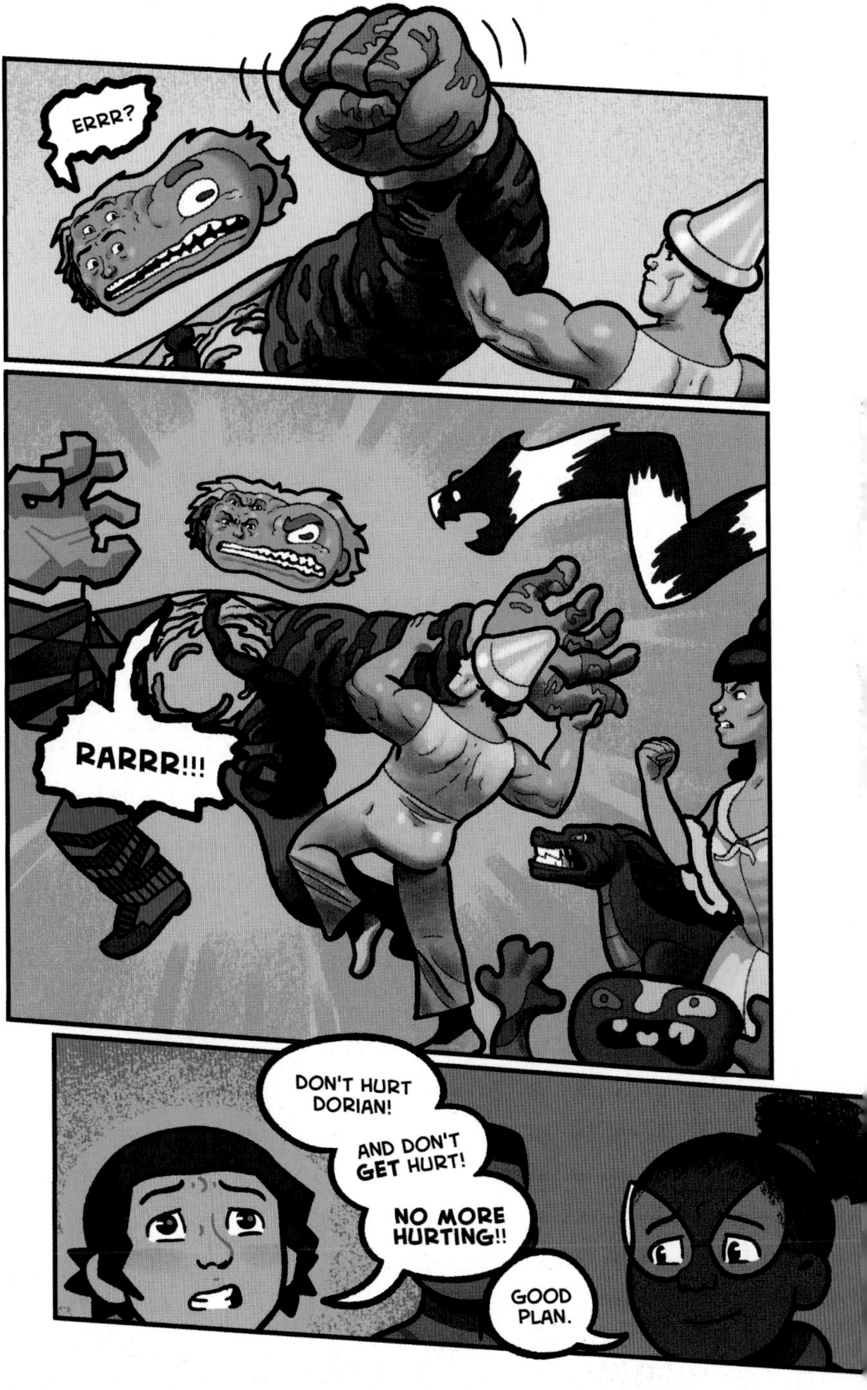
ERRR?
RARRR!!!
DON'T HURT DORIAN!
AND DON'T GET HURT!
NO MORE HURTING!!
GOOD PLAN.

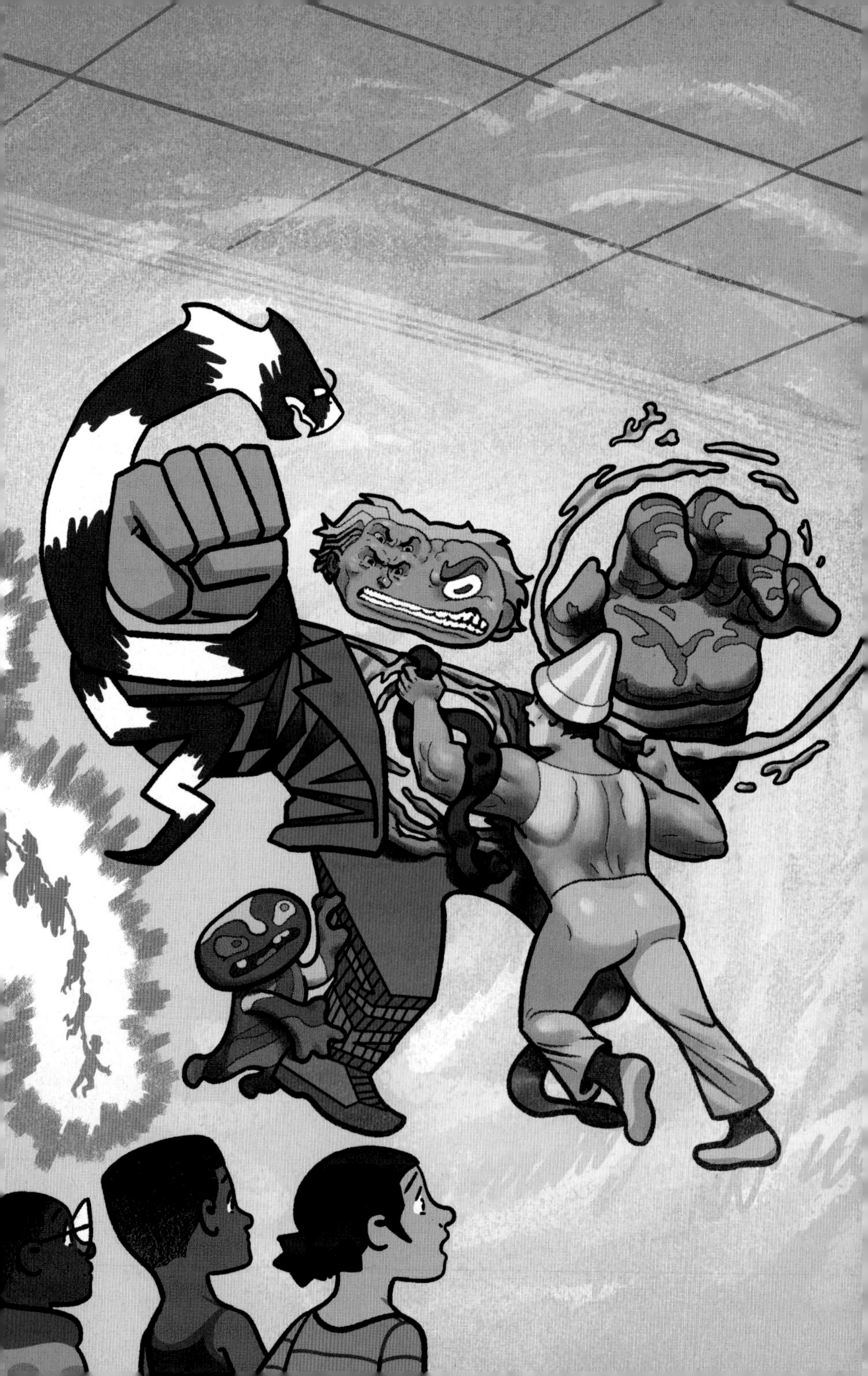

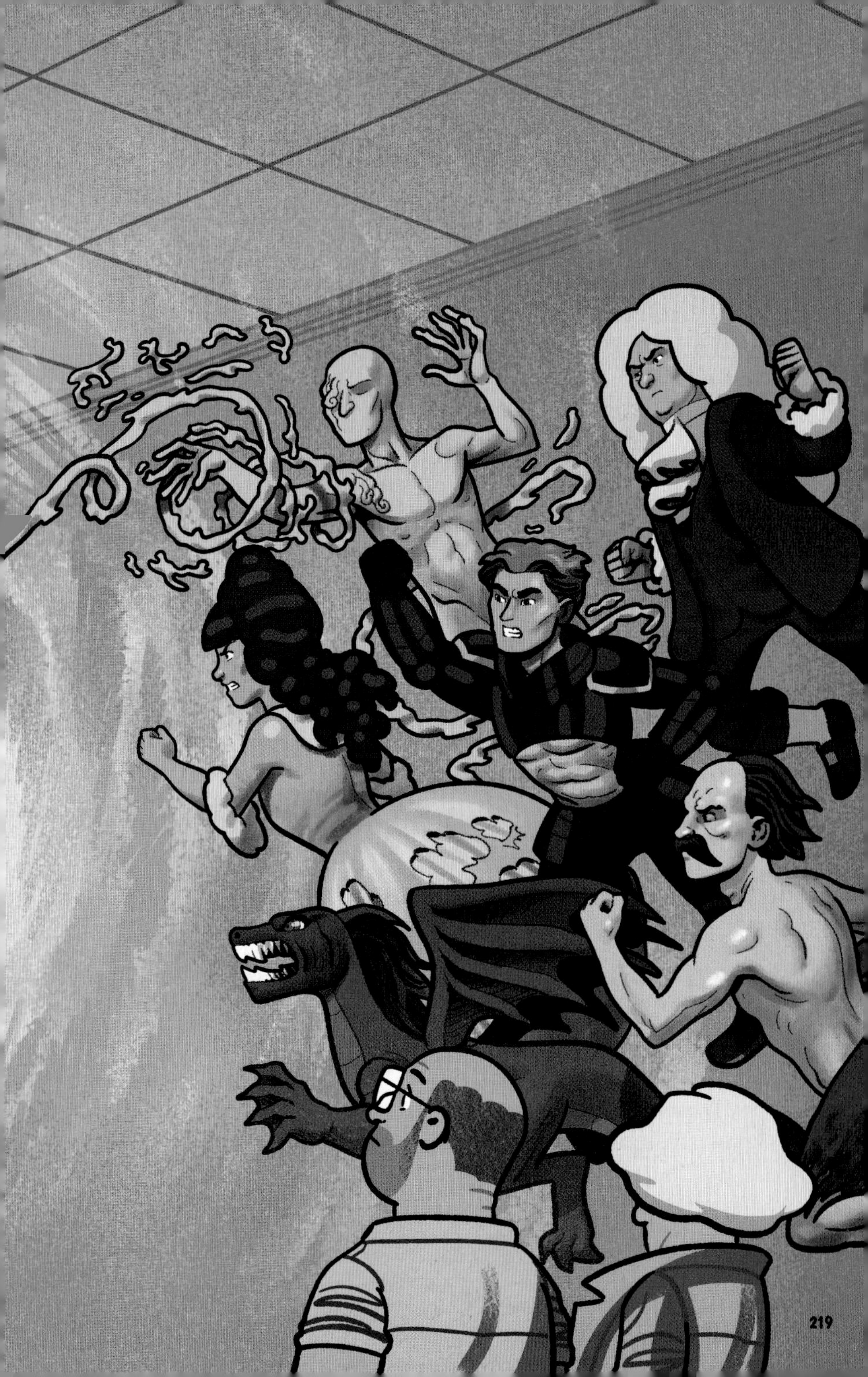

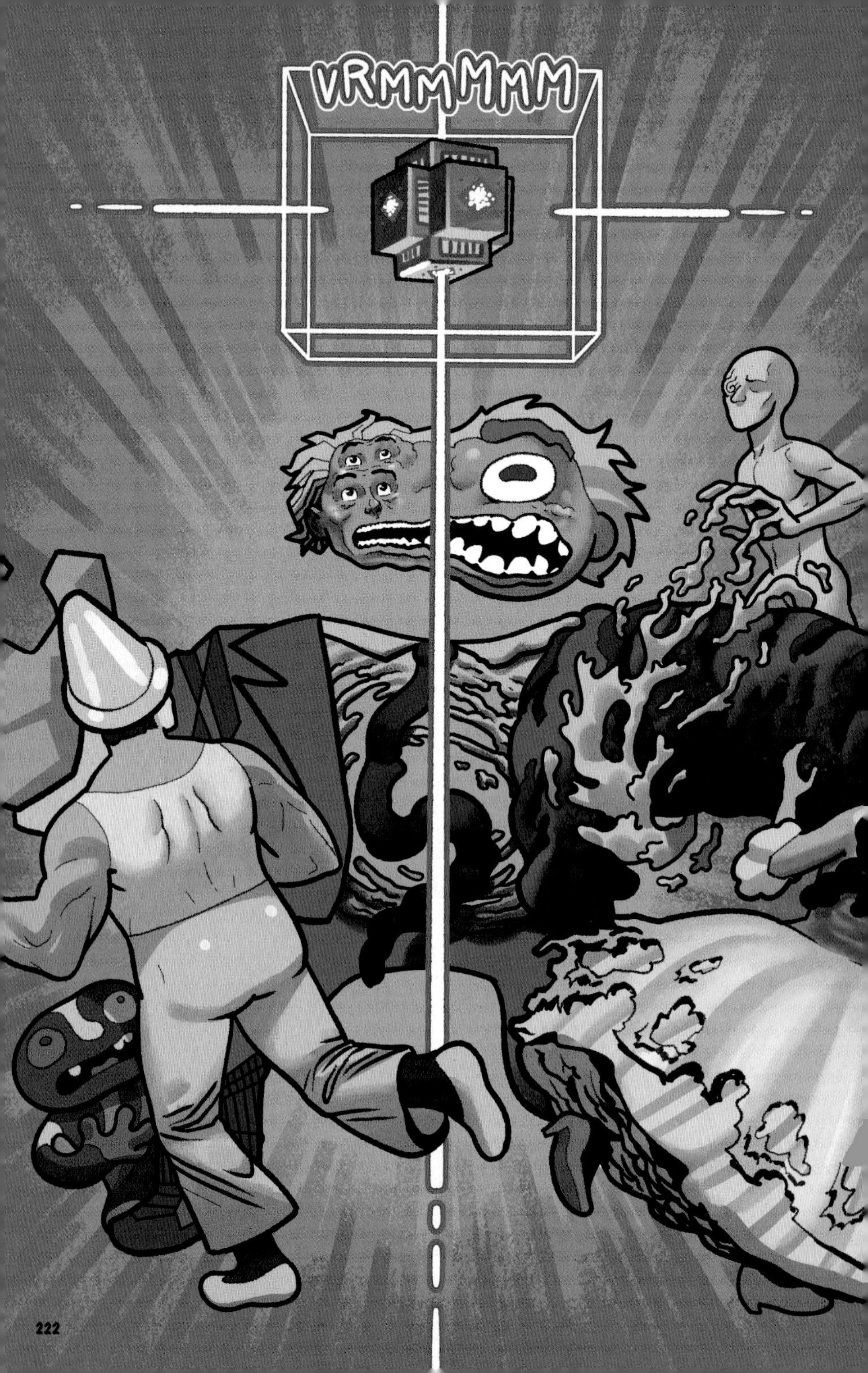
VRMMMMMM

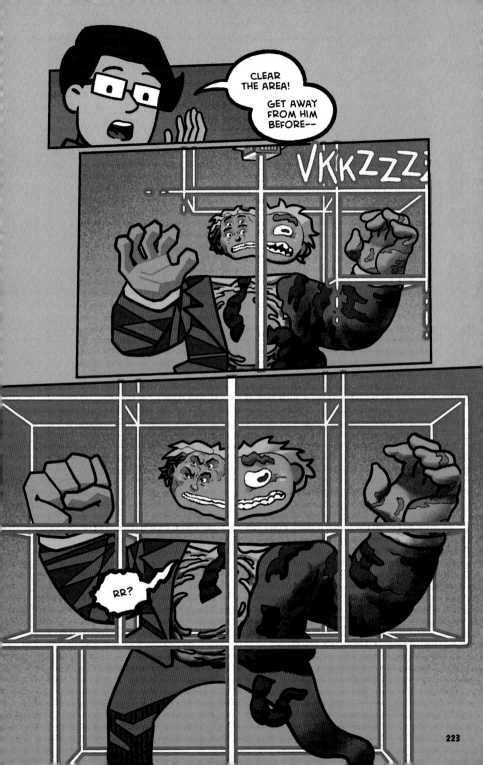

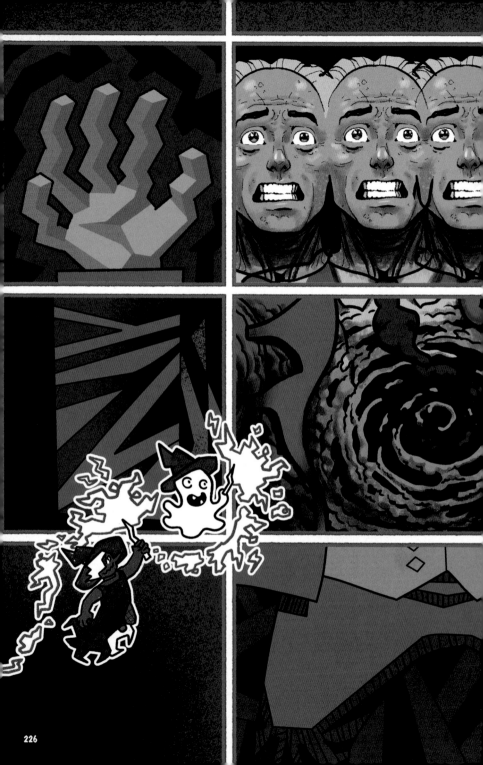

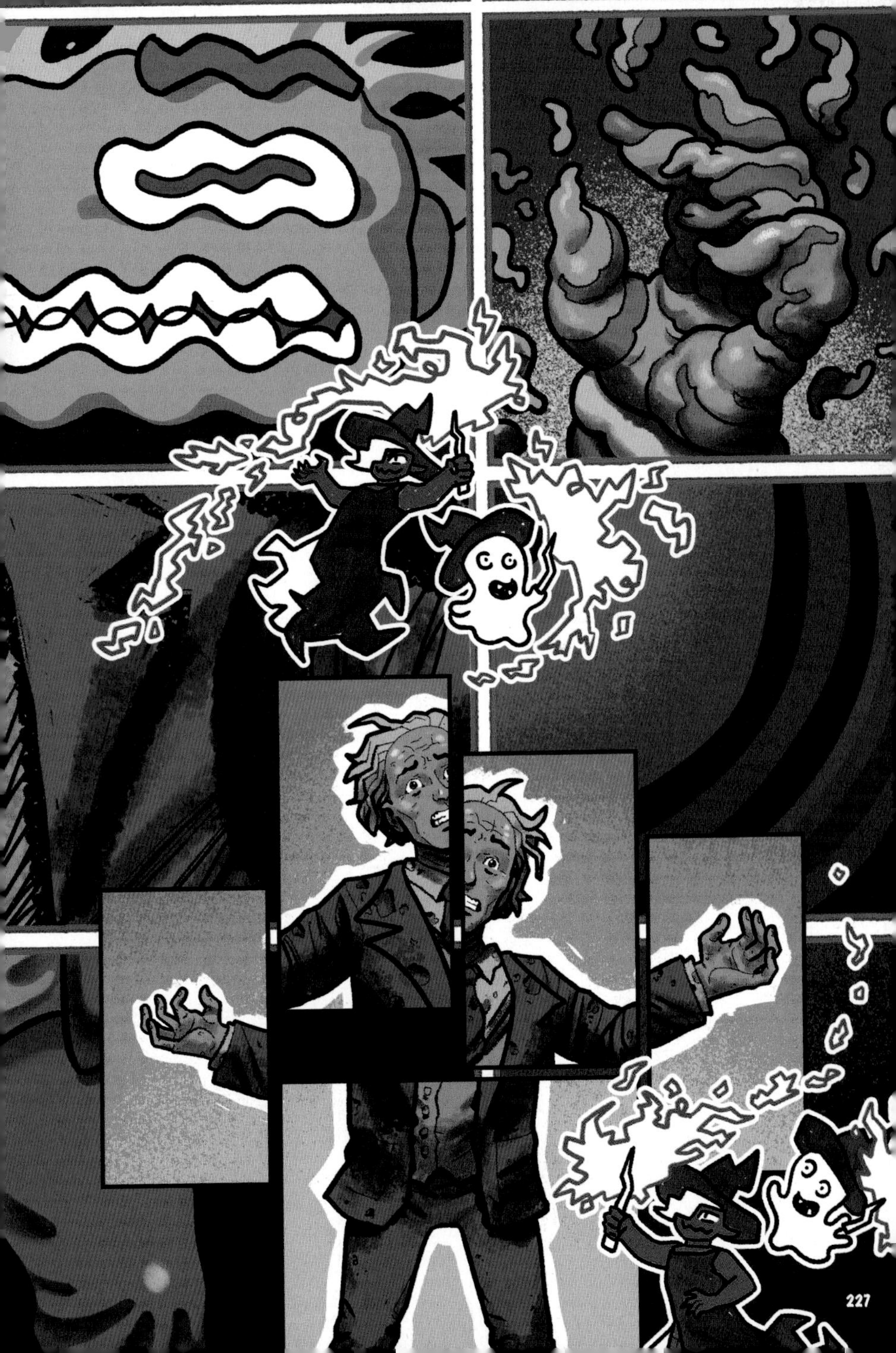

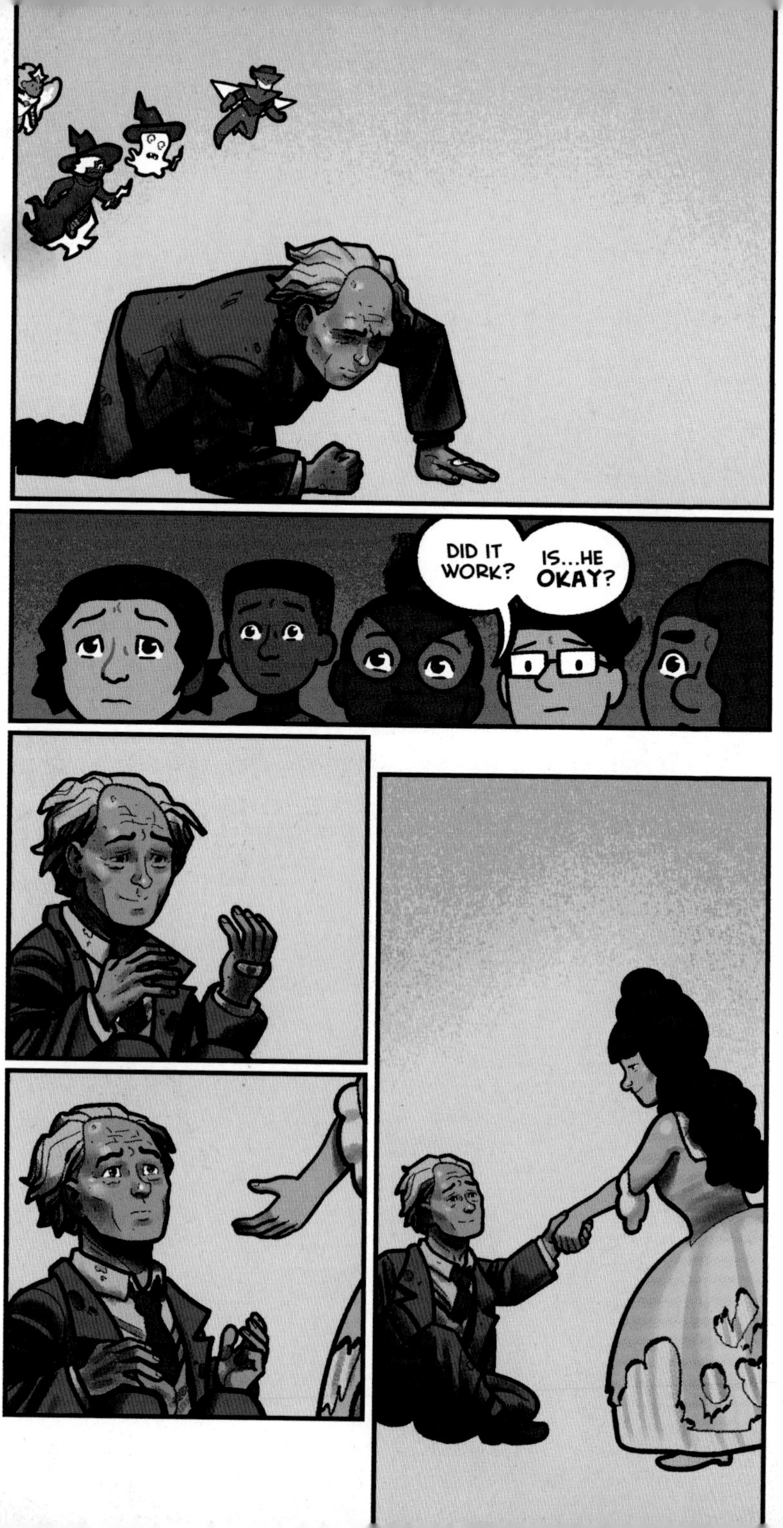
DID IT WORK?
IS...HE OKAY?

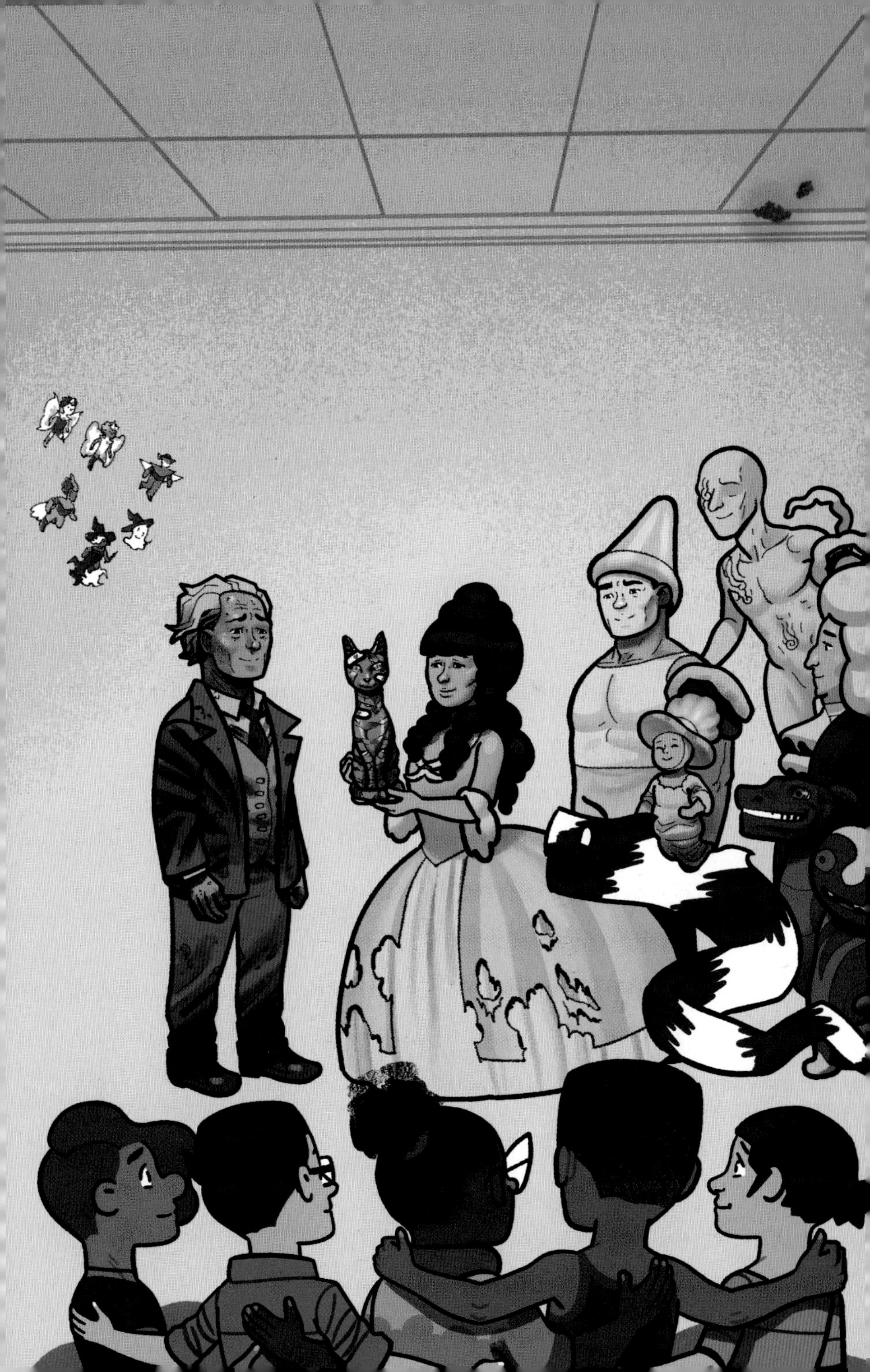

CHAPTER 8: GETTING STARTED

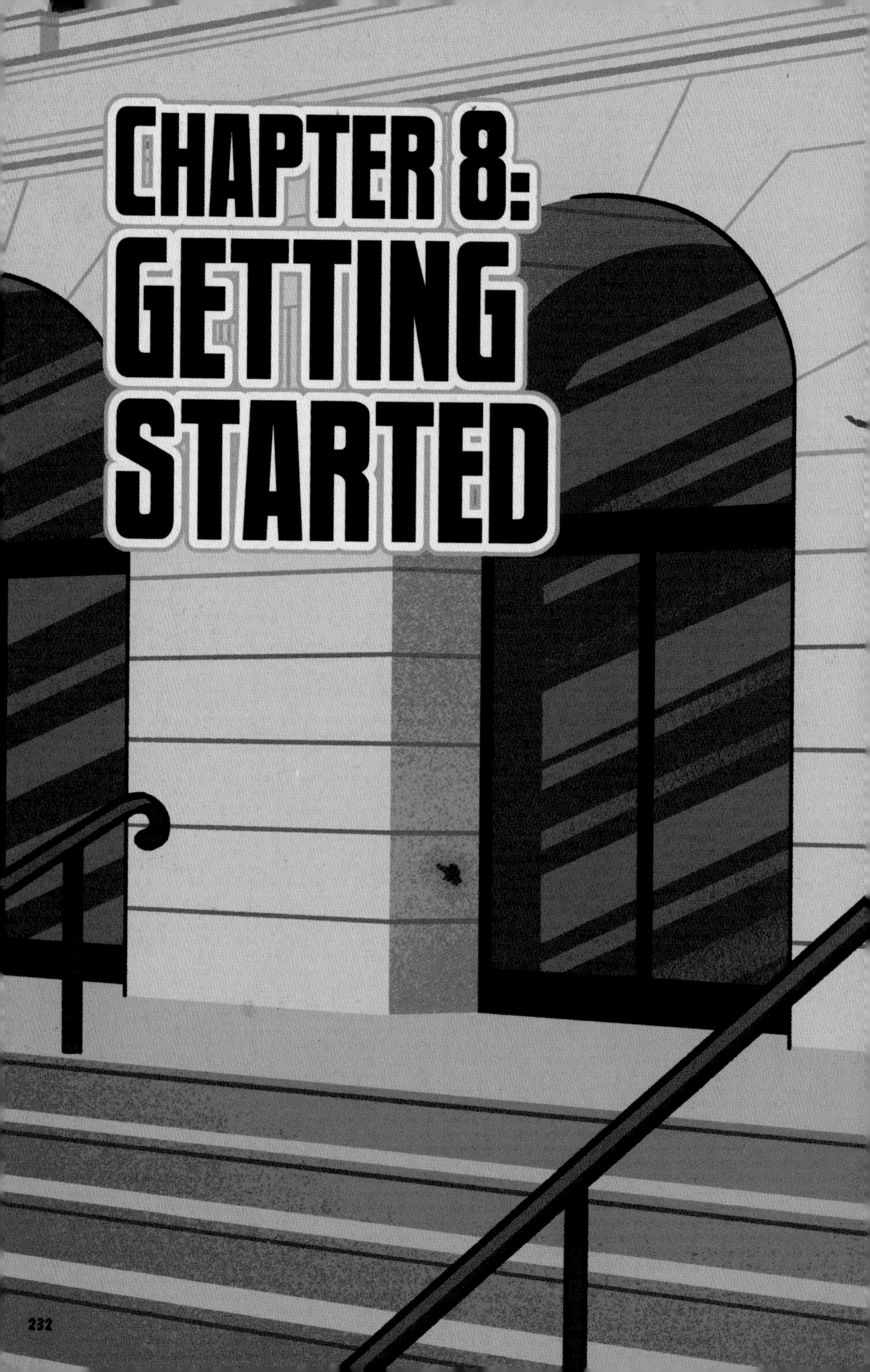

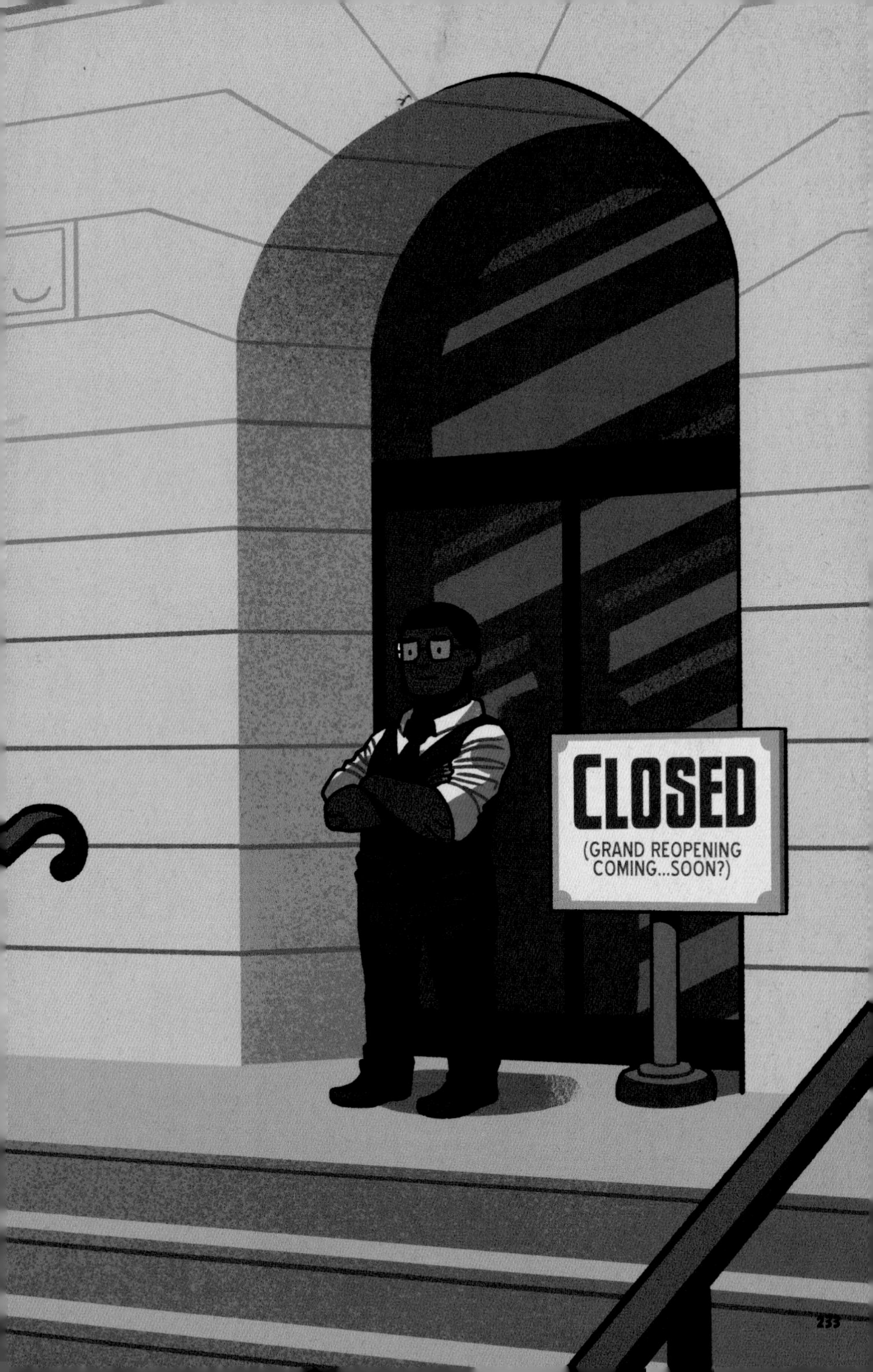
CLOSED
(GRAND REOPENING
COMING...SOON?)

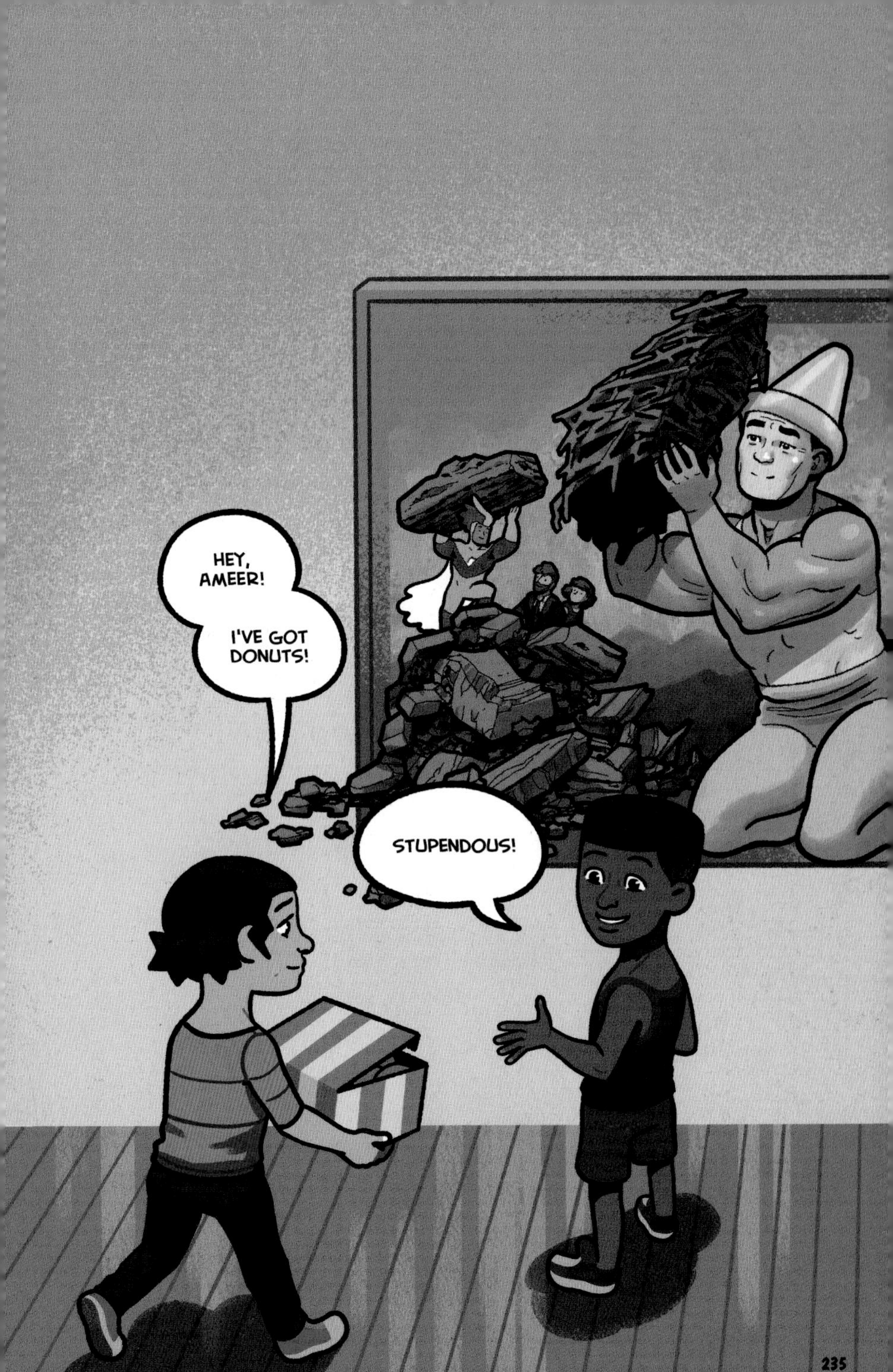
HEY, AMEER!
I'VE GOT DONUTS!
STUPENDOUS!

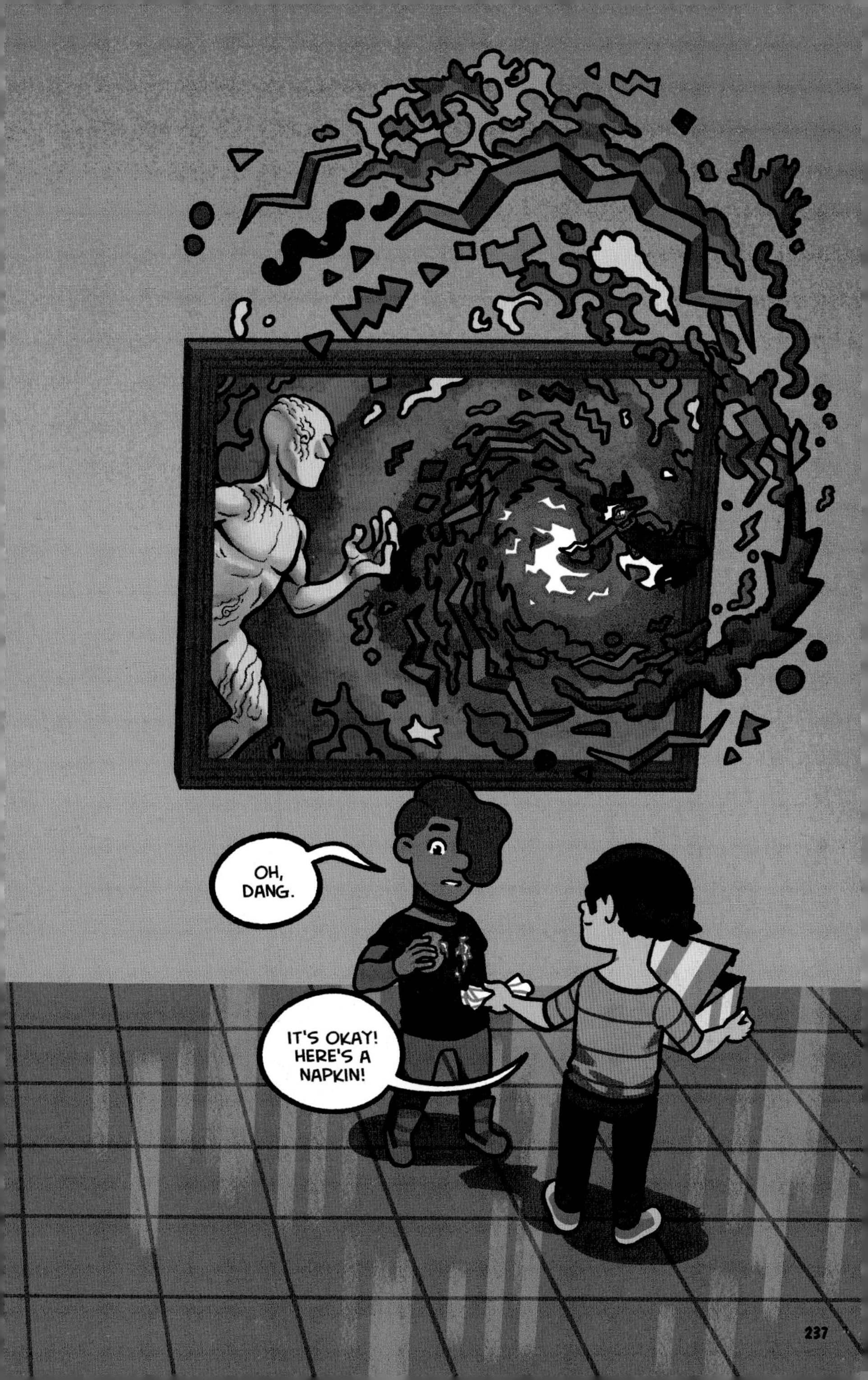
OH, DANG.
IT'S OKAY! HERE'S A NAPKIN!

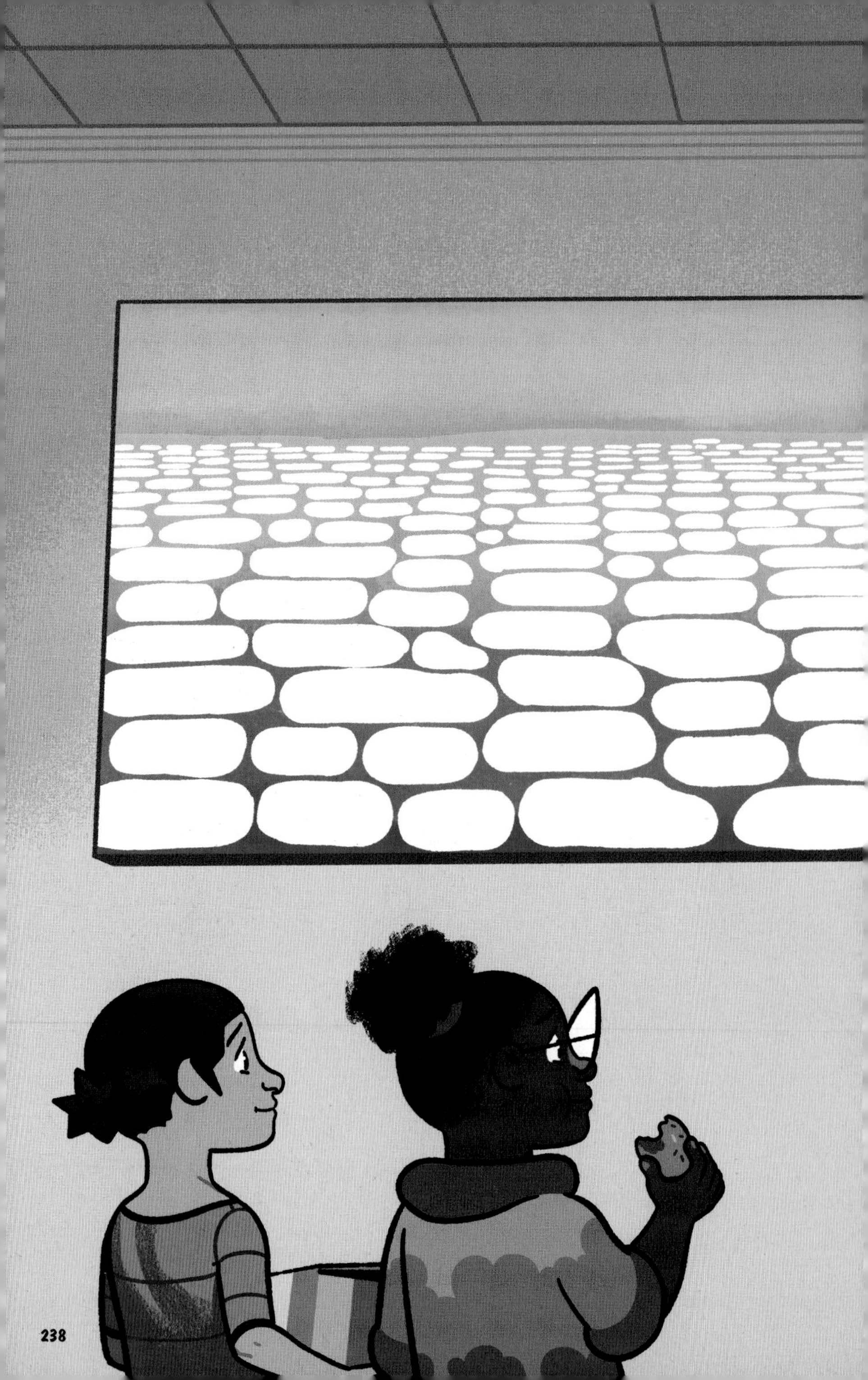

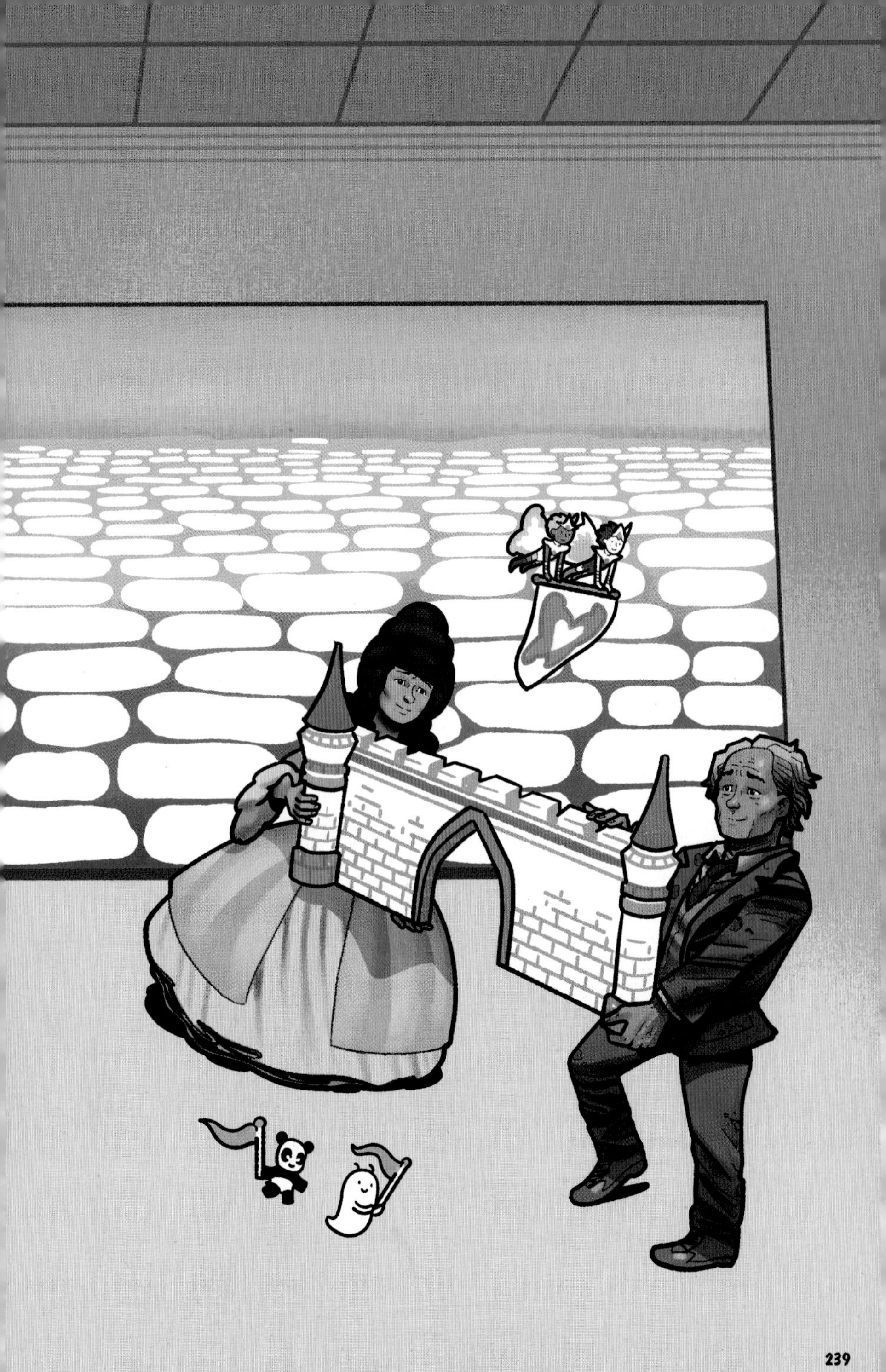

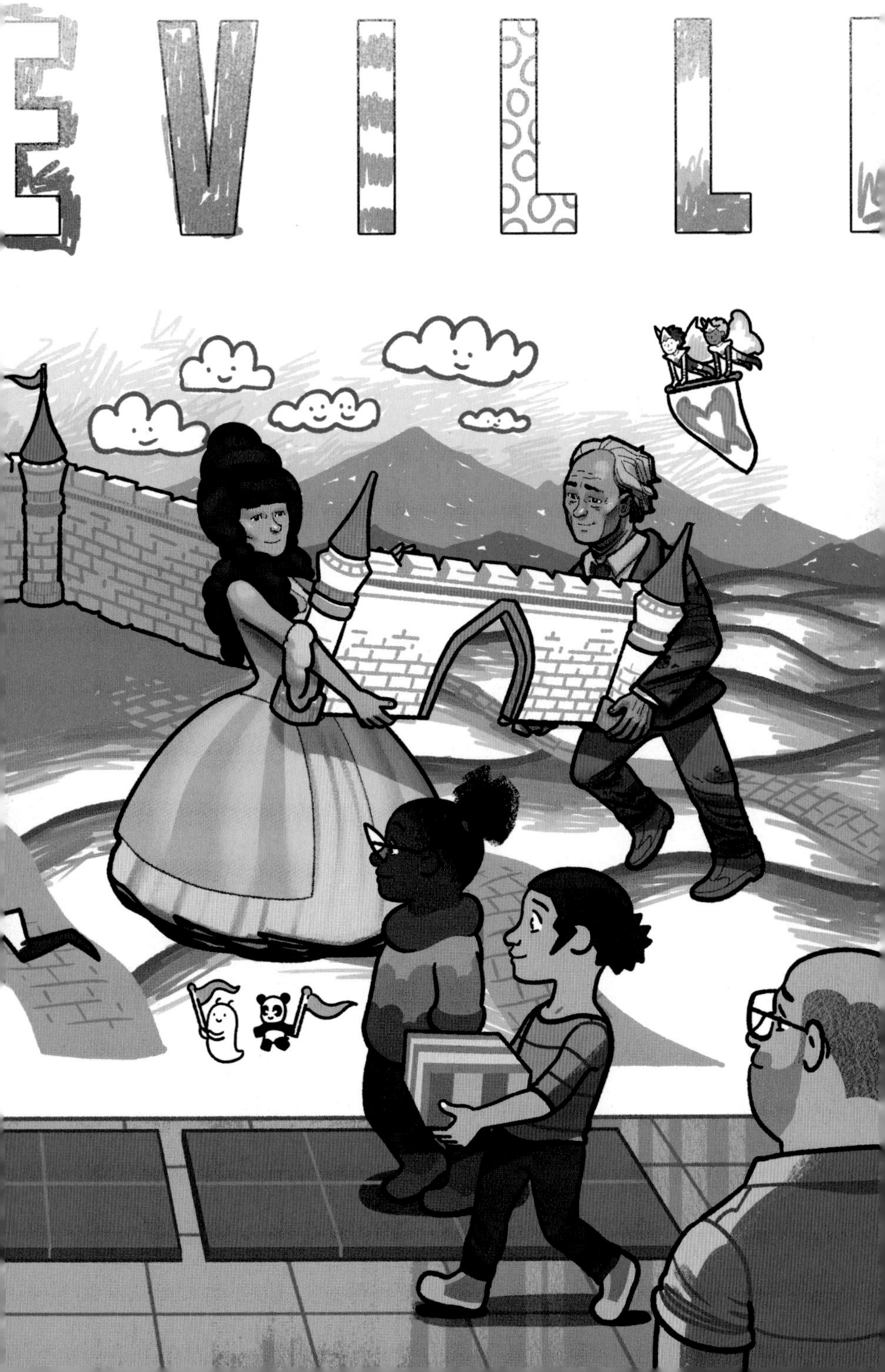
EVILL

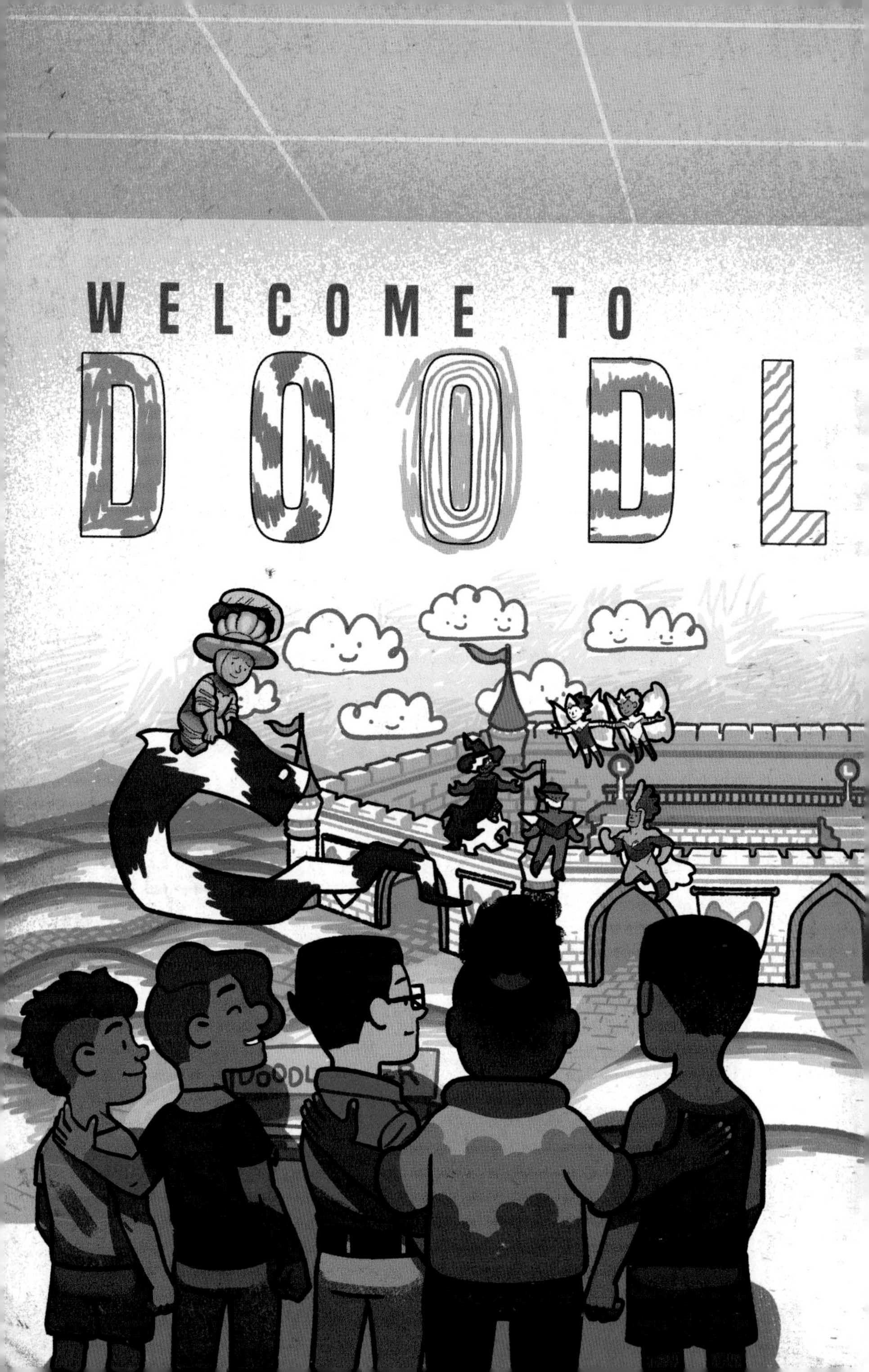
WELCOME TO
DOODL

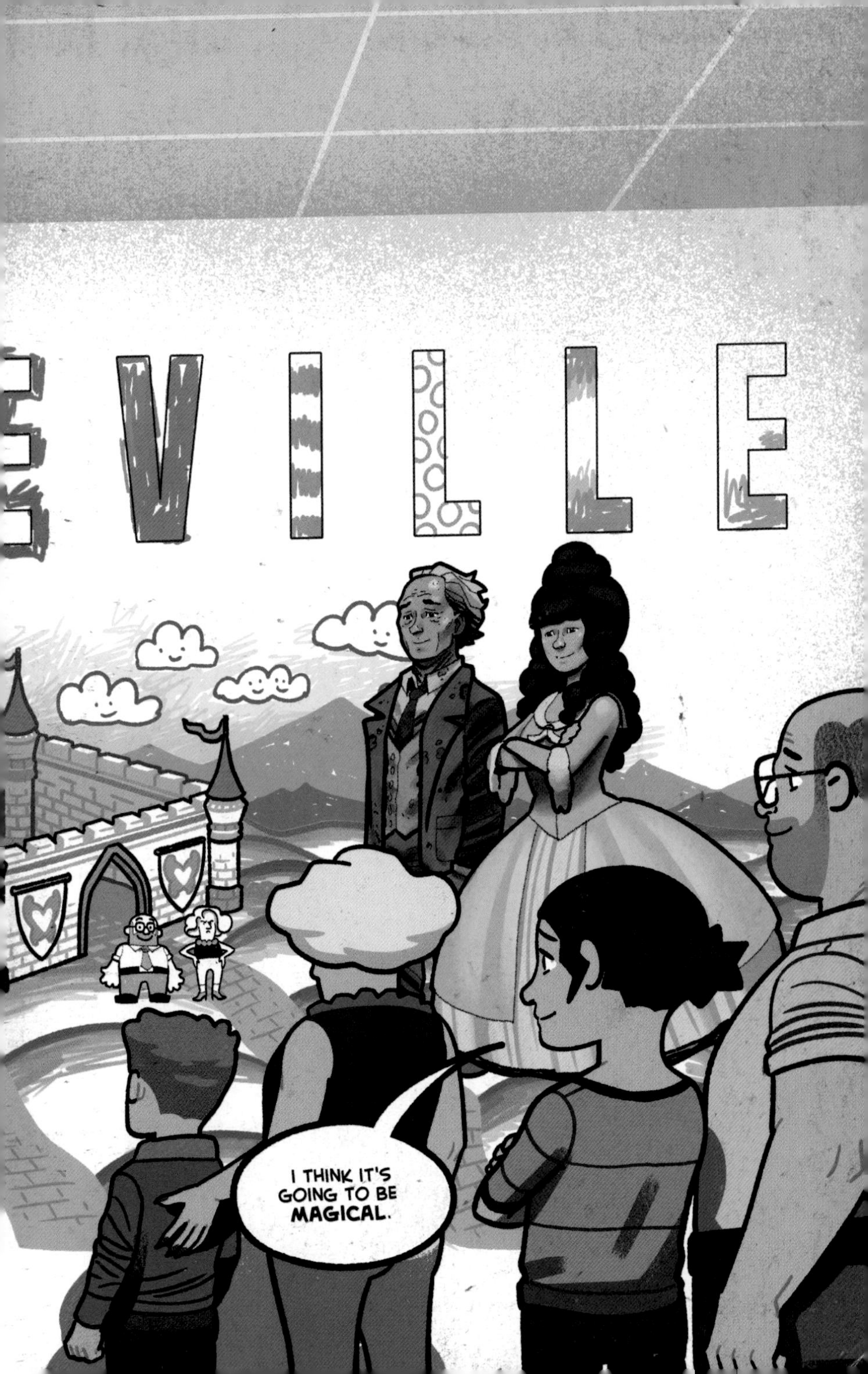
VILLE
I THINK IT'S GOING TO BE MAGICAL.

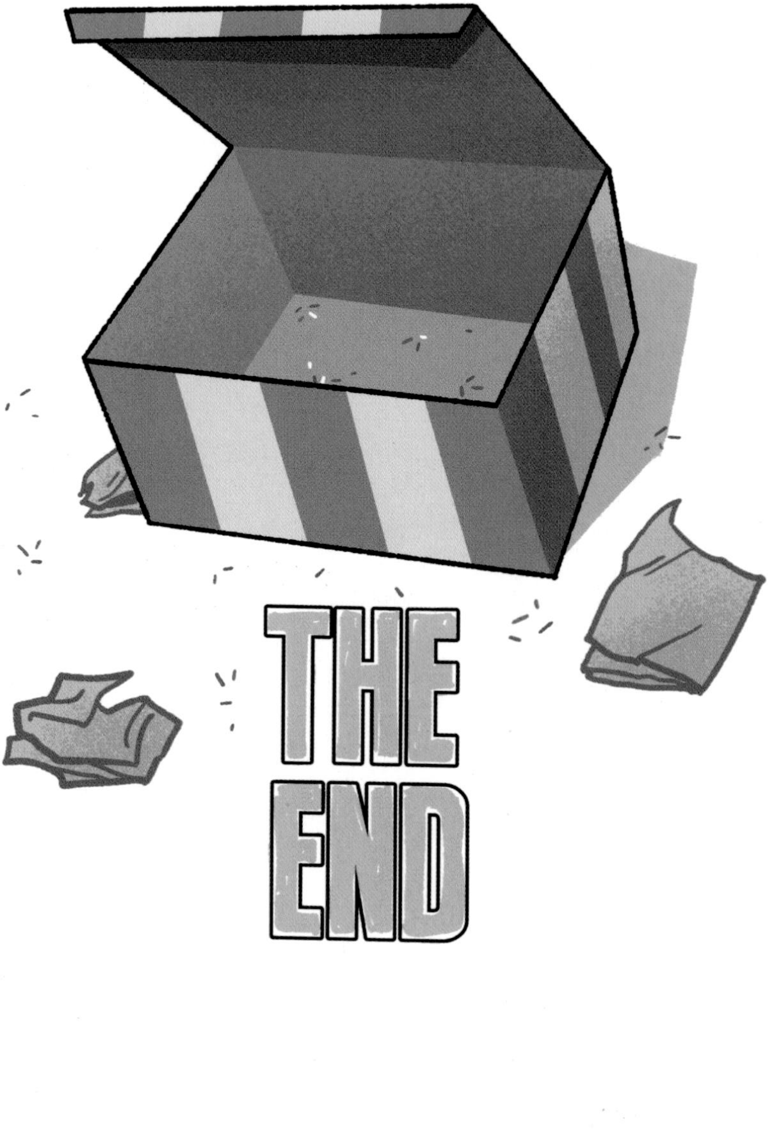
THE END